To Maureen

D1528126

Also by the Author

Safely Buried

–

Acknowledgments

I owe a debt of gratitude to several persons who provided information or services that helped me write this book.

Charlotte Sellers, a former small-town newspaper editor like me and now a volunteer at the Jackson County Genealogical Society in Brownstown, Indiana, gave me advice on conducting genealogical research.

David Gohn, a prosecuting attorney in Bloomington, Indiana, answered my questions on procedural matters in criminal cases.

My wife, Maureen, once again served as first reader, critic, and artist. Her pastel painting adorns the cover of this book.

Our son, Jesse, an editor at *The New York Times,* designed the front cover of this book and helped edit the manuscript.

Our daughter, Abigail, proofread the final manuscript. She is a freelance writer who has published many articles in women's magazines. This year she also wrote her first book, a nonfiction work that will be published by an imprint of HarperCollins in 2017.

The More You Stir It

CHAPTER 1

STRANGE FRUIT

"Hey, why don't *you* write stories like this one, Phil?" the Presbyterian minister shouted at me. Shaking his fist fire-and-brimstone style, he read out loud a sentence from the latest exposé in *Mothermucker,* an alternative newspaper that some kids at the high school were publishing: "The Walmart store in Campbellsville was built on land that was stolen from the widow of a black man who was lynched by the Ku Klux Klan in the summer of 1936." He flipped the *Mothermucker* on my desk and said, "Now *that's* what I call hard-hitting journalism."

"Are you working up your next sermon, Bob?" I asked him.

The Reverend Mr. Robert Harnish, who preferred to be called Pastor Bob, shook his head in dismay. "Damn it, Phil, try to be responsive once in a while. We're talking investigative reporting here, not Sunday sermons."

I tilted forward in my chair and stared at the article I was trying to edit on my computer screen. I was used to Pastor Bob's pop-in visits to my office at *The Campbellsville Gleaner,* where I had the grandiose title of editor-in-chief. He had a lot of opinions to share with me. I liked to tell him he should have been a newspaperman instead of a preacher.

"Man, you're rude today," he said with mock outrage. "Stop working. I subscribe to your paper. You ought to be paying attention to me. What kind of drivel are you hacking out now? Maybe you should get a job on the *Mothermucker* and do some real reporting."

"Yeah, maybe I should."

"Don't get testy now."

I yawned and stretched and reached for the *Mothermucker.* Its front-page story was written by Kelly Marcott. "Tell me, Bob," I said, "did you put your protégé up to writing this?"

His body went rigid, like a huge mime frozen in shock. "Phil, Phil, Phil, you know me better than that," he said. "Kelly's not my protégé, but he could be yours. I think you should get to know him. He needs a professional newsman for a mentor. You'd like him. Then again, maybe you wouldn't—he's a lot like you."

I took that as a compliment disguised as an insult rather than vice versa.

The Reverend Mr. Robert Harnish—to use the *Gleaner's* style for referring to ministers of all stripes—offered to set up a meeting for me with Kelly.

"Let me think about it," I replied. I promptly thought about it for five or six seconds and stopped thinking.

No matter how much alike the Rev thought Kelly Marcott and I were, I was not eager to meet him. I took him for an obnoxious kid who'd be more interested in showing me how brilliant he was than in listening to anything that I might have to say.

I began flipping through the third issue of *Mothermucker.* It was more like a magazine than a newspaper. It was comprised of eight sheets of paper, printed by computer on both sides and stapled down the left. It looked as if it had been designed by someone who had just discovered what you could do with desktop-publishing software. Half a dozen different typefaces swam on every page. Small words overprinted big ones. Headlines tilted at weird angles or bled off the page. The cover featured a full-page photo of Klansmen in front of a burning cross, with the title "Very Strange Fruit Once Grew on Courthouse Tree" flaming across their robes. Most of the articles seemed harmless: movie and music reviews, a survey of local bands, a diatribe against the city's anti-cruising campaign, a demand to dump the school's entire athletic program and use the money to improve the arts curriculum.

But the article about the Klan was not harmless. It named twenty-eight men who had belonged to the Klan in the 1920s and '30s. The list included some of the most prominent names in Meridian County. Hundreds of descendants might be surprised to learn that their fathers or grandfathers had belonged to the Klan—if the allegations were true.

"Did you see this?" I asked Bob. "It says at least two of the Klansmen are 'allegedly' still alive. Real smooth, huh? I think he means 'reportedly,' don't you? It says Cletus Johnson lives in Evansville and Charles C. Ford is in a nursing home here in Campbellsville."

Bob nodded. "Uh-huh. Charlie belongs to my church. I hope nobody tells him that the truth about his lurid past has finally caught up with him. He might have a heart attack. I wonder if he still has his Klan regalia. Maybe he wears it to bed on cold winter nights."

I said, "Listen to this. The article says, 'Any and all members of the Klan that are still alive should be arrested and tried for murder.' How old are these guys? If the lynching was in 1936, that was"—I did the math—"seventy-six years ago. They must be in their nineties or over a hundred."

"That's right. You'll want to get a picture of the cops pushing Charlie out of the nursing home in his wheelchair."

"Then it says, 'Myrtle Peterson, wife of one of the Klansmen, bought the dead man's property at a sheriff's sale because his widow could not pay the taxes on it.' Is that true? Where did your friend Kelly get his information?"

"I don't know. Maybe he made it up."

"I wonder how he got those names."

The Rev's glibness began to fade. "That's something you can ask Kelly. But he probably won't want to reveal his sources anymore than you would."

I said, "He might change his mind when he gets hit with a few lawsuits for libel and defamation of character."

Bob's narrow ski-jump nose got even thinner as he inhaled. Then he exhaled and said, "You could explain that to Kelly. He needs to know the possible consequences of his actions, though I don't think anything will come of what he's written in the *Mothermucker*. What good would it do anybody to sue him? He's just a kid. He doesn't own anything." Bob looked like a sly bunny as he grinned. "Now, if the *Gleaner* were to reprint Kelly's article, that would be a different story. Ed would get sued for every cent he's got. You'd get sued too."

On that note, my boss, Edward J. Wylie, owner and publisher of the *Gleaner,* marched into my office. "Who's gonna sue us?" he demanded.

Bob said, "Good morning, Ed," but went on talking to me: "Of course, the truth is an absolute defense against libel."

I leaned back and stared at the faintly buzzing lights on the ceiling. One of the four fluorescent tubes had burned out, and the others had blackish ends and were beginning to flicker. "Somehow I don't think we are dealing with absolute truth here," I said. "It sounds more like a blast of unprovable allegations—a blast from the past." I handed Ed the copy of *Mothermucker* that Bob had given me.

"What's this?" he asked as if ready to toss it.

"Read the lead story," Bob said. "Some of your ancestors might be mentioned in it."

My boss's eyes skimmed the helter-skelter columns. "What is this crap?" he said. His rimless glasses rode low on his nose, and the fringe of white hair above his ears made him look more like Friar Tuck than ever. He was getting heavier, which worried him, and he couldn't wait to leave for his winter home in Fort Myers, where he could shed some pounds on the golf course. He glared at Bob and said, "You're not suggesting we put this garbage in the *Gleaner,* are you?"

"It's nice how you never have to repeat anything here," Bob replied. He pointed toward the front office. "Did you ever notice those spots on the walls, Ed? Those are ear marks. Whenever you're talking to somebody, some staffer has an ear glued to the wall."

Ed was reading the Klan article. "With slanders like these, whoever wrote this stuff is going to get himself tarred and feathered."

Bob goaded him: "What if it's true? Maybe the writer is just exercising his freedom of speech."

"Bullshit."

"Hey, Ed," Bob shot back, "what would you rather read, a juicy story about a lynch mob or 'Mr. and Mrs. Jed Beanblossom motored to Salem on Sunday'?" This was a knock on the items that our country correspondents sent in every week.

Ed dropped the *Mothermucker* on my desk. "File it in the trash," he said.

Bob rolled his shoulders and twisted his neck. "Well, I'm sorry, guys. I'd like to continue this scintillating discussion, but I've gotta get going."

"Don't let us keep you," said Ed.

As the front door closed behind my favorite minister, Ed repeated his standard jab: "He's definitely not one of those half-assed part-time preachers. He's a complete ass if there ever was one."

Whatever he was, Pastor Bob had managed to get inside my head. All morning I wondered if I should look into a lynching that had occurred seventy-six years ago. It was like a mosquito bite that wouldn't stop itching.

CHAPTER 2

SLOPPY REPORTING

I WENT to our so-called employees' lounge for a cup of coffee. Then I picked up Kelly Marcott's article again. It described how Abner Richards, a married man whose age was unknown, had been dragged out of the old county jail and hanged from a tree on the courthouse lawn:

"The white-robed cowards of the Klan kicked him and raised their hoods to spit on him as they dragged him from the jail to the courthouse a block away in the dead of night. Mr. Richards never once pleaded for his life, but all the way up the street he struggled against the thick ropes that bound his hands and feet and gagged his mouth. The strength and dignity he showed in those last minutes of his life shamed his masked killers."

Come on, Kelly. There was no way he could have pleaded for his life with thick ropes gagging him.

Across the street, April sunlight flickered through the oaks and sycamores around the courthouse. Tree shadows dappled the tall windows and yellow bricks. I wondered if Abner Richards had been lynched on one of those trees. The article said he had been charged with breaking into the home of a schoolteacher, a white woman who lived alone on the edge of town, not far from the Richards farm. After his arrest, the sheriff had added a charge of attempted rape.

According to the *Mothermucker,* "Mr. Richards denied all the charges. He had never been in trouble with the law before. The charges were totally made up by people who did not want blacks living in Campbellsville, and later one of them grabbed his land."

The writing set my teeth on edge. The article contained nothing to support its assertions—no evidence from the public record, no quote from someone who was involved in the case. In effect, Kelly Marcott himself was making the claims. As a piece of reporting, the article was a mess. In fact, it was so bad, accusing so many people so recklessly, that I thought no one would take it seriously. So why should I? Forget the whole thing, I told myself.

But instead of taking my own advice, I took a couple rolls of microfilm out of the vault. Most back issues of the *Gleaner* were not on the computer, and I wanted to see what we had on the lynching that Kelly Marcott had dredged up.

Our antiquated microfilm reader squeaked and rattled as I cranked my way through the blur of pages to June 1936. Then I slowed down and began skimming the front-page headlines, which back in those days were seldom bigger than 18-point type in two thin columns. It didn't take me long to find the headline I was looking for:

Colored Man Hung
Behind Courthouse

The story was only six inches long, and few names were provided. The county sheriff, whose living quarters at that time were on the second floor of the jail building, was out of town visiting his wife's parents in Elkhart, and the only deputy on

duty that night was "quickly subdued by the hooded execution-
ers," which the paper described as a "righteous band of vigilantes
who were unwilling to wait for the law to run its course"—not
much different from Kelly Marcott's writing style. The body
was discovered before dawn the next morning by a milkman on
his rounds. "The corpse of Abner Richards, a tall and muscular colored man, was found dangling from a branch of a large
tree behind the Meridian County Courthouse. Mr. Kantner,
an employee of the Shumacher Dairy Company, said it was a
terrible sight to behold, as the victim's eyes had rolled up into
his head and the man had befouled himself." The old *Gleaner*
loved lurid details. The story went on to say that Mr. Kantner
had reported his "grim find" to a Campbellsville city policeman shortly before dawn, which made me wonder what the
police were doing while the lynching was taking place. The rest
of the article explained why Abner Richards had been in jail.

A few days later the paper ran a followup of sorts. The sheriff, now back from northern Indiana, told the newspaper that no
witnesses to the "illegal execution" had been found. The people
who lived in the houses behind the courthouse must have slept
through the entire event. The Klan had apparently taken great
pains not to disturb their slumber, or perhaps the paper had
it right: "No cross was burned at the scene, a fact which may
cast doubt on the general suspicion that the lynching was the
work of the Knights of the Ku Klux Klan, although it is equally
possible that the vigilantes chose not to burn a cross, the bright
light of which could have awakened nearby residents."

I searched the fuzzy gray-white microfilm for more news
about the lynching, but I couldn't find anything but a very
short obituary. Like Abner Richards himself, the story had died
a remarkably quiet death.

I tapped my teeth with my thumbnail and stared out
the window at the stately symbol of justice across the street.

I wondered where Kelly Marcott had obtained his information, especially the names of the alleged Klansmen. His article also had some convincing details in it—where did those come from? Only an eyewitness could have told him that some of the masked killers had raised their hoods to spit at the victim before they strung him up. The boy couldn't have made up a detail like that, could he? Why not? Call it creative journalism. Fictional details juicing up general facts. News as entertainment, just like the news on TV.

No, I said to myself, he didn't make it up. He must have come up with an eyewitness. His biggest mistake was not identifying the source of his information.

I gazed at the courthouse. I knew the Klan used to be strong in Meridian County. In 1936 this was a dangerous place to be a black man. Someone had told me there used to be a sign along the state highway at the southern entrance to the county: "If You Aint White You Better Not Be Here After Sundown."

I began toying with the idea of doing a feature on Kelly Marcott. After all, how many high school kids were old-fashioned muckrakers? But I couldn't write about Kelly's *Mothermucker* without getting into the lynching of Abner Richards. Kelly had accused a lot of people of murder, and the allegations were unsubstantiated. Why would I want to get tangled up in that?

But what if the accusations were true? If any of the men who had participated in the lynching of Abner Richards were still alive, didn't they deserve to be punished for their crime no matter how old they were now? At first it seemed crazy to be thinking about putting a couple of doddering old men on trial for a crime that had been committed seventy-five or seventy-six years ago. Would it be possible to prove they had been among the lynchers? Would it even be possible to prove they had been in the Klan? Then, in a flash of brilliance, it occurred to me that there may have been a trial for the vigilantes back in the 1930s. I could not assume that Kelly Marcott's article had all the facts. Before taking this thing any further, I'd have to do more research.

But I didn't feel like it.

You're getting lazy, Larrison. Do your job.

It was a light news day. I cleared my desk by 3:00. On most days I would have gone home and then come back after supper to deal with that night's meetings and other late news. I also had to help lay out the front page and write the heads for it. But today, instead of going home, I went back to the microfilm reader.

I spent the next two hours cranking my arm off on the ancient machine. I did a careful search of every issue of the *Gleaner* from June 1936 to the Japanese attack on Pearl Harbor in December 1941. I checked every page to make sure I didn't miss anything pertaining to the death of Abner Richards. I found nothing.

I went back over every issue to verify that no pages were missing. They were all there.

It blew my mind that during those five and a half years following the murder of Abner Richards there was not a single reference to the lynching, no report of any arrests or any trial in Meridian County or anywhere else.

My head began to hurt. I leaned back and rubbed my eyes. I saw bright silver flashes. Was I getting a migraine, or were the retinas detaching? God, I was turning into a hypochondriac.

I pushed myself up. My pants peeled off the wooden swivel chair. I went to the restroom, then prepared to refill my bladder with another cup of coffee. Back in my office, I looked up the name Marcott in the phone book. There were several Marcotts, so I called the Reverend Mr. Bob Harnish's office for help. His wife, who doubled as the church's office manager, put me through. When Bob picked up, I heard a soprano screaming at the top of her lungs. I recognized the only opera I had ever seen.

"Hi, Bob," I shouted over *Madama Butterfly*. "Can you tell me how to get in touch with Kelly Marcott?"

The Reverend turned off the music and said, "So you're going to talk to him. Good. I'm glad."

"Do you know his parents?"

"No. They live in Los Angeles. Kelly's staying here with his grandfather, Chester Marcott. You know Chester, don't you?"

"No."

"You should. He's a newsmaker—or at least he was. He's the guy who sold Walmart the land it needed to put a store in Campbellsville, but that was before you rode into town."

"Yes, Walmart got here before I did."

"Not me. That's how I know the land Chester sold Walmart used to be a farm that belonged to Abner Richards."

"Really?"

His laugh nearly ripped my eardrum in half. "Hell yes!" he roared. "Nearly every merchant in Campbellsville had a heart attack when Chester sold that ground to Walmart. They tried their damnedest to keep Walmart out. Chester inherited the property from his wife, Marcia. She *never* would have let Walmart have it. She was the widow of John Barry. They owned Campbellsville Hardware, and they fought like fiends to keep Walmart out of this burg. I bet they both rolled over in their graves when Chester sold that farm to the evil empire."

"I never heard of Campbellsville Hardware."

"It went out of business years ago. John Barry got killed in a car wreck, and Marcia sold the store. That was before she married Chester."

"How did Marcia get to own the Abner Richards farm?"

"You're gonna love this," the Reverend said. "Marcia was the daughter of Waldo and Myrtle Peterson. Waldo's name appears in the *Mothermucker* I gave you. He's one of the guys who helped stretch Abner's neck—allegedly, of course. A few years later Myrtle bought Abner's farm at a sheriff's sale when his widow failed to pay the property tax on it. Myrtle bought it for a song, I was told."

"Something smells rotten," I said.

"Kelly thinks so too, and he's trying to do something about it. Not that there's much he can do."

"Why is he here?" I asked. "Why isn't he with his parents?"

"They're divorced. Kelly told me his mom made him come here. She thought he was running with the wrong crowd in LA. She thinks Meridian County will be a better place for him."

"Let's hope she's right," I said.

After we hung up, I leaned back in my chair and stretched. A tingle of excitement coiled through my belly. I had a hunch I had just learned the source of Kelly's information about the KKK. I thought about giving Chester Marcott a call to see what he might have to say about his grandson's story, but I had a lot of personal business to take care of today. It was Wednesday, one of my two days off, along with Saturday; however, neither day was a real day off. I spent most of my time at the *Gleaner*. I wasn't a workaholic, but I did try to keep busy. I liked working on a small paper. It gave my life some purpose. It kept me off Prozac.

CHAPTER 3

THE TRUTH MUST COME OUT

NEXT morning I asked my boss what he knew about Chester Marcott.

Ed said, "Chester owns a farm in Salt Lick Township. He also has a cabin at the Lake of the Woods Club. It was one of the first things built there when they made the lake back in the 1950s. Chester's father built it as a fishin' shack. His name was Chester too, but everybody called him Buster. He was a charter member of the Lake of the Woods Club. He had a Buick and Chevy dealership, but his first love was raising Black Angus cattle. I think Chester still does some farming, but he's getting up in years now."

I tried to get Chester on the phone. There was no answer at his house in Salt Lick Township, and no listing for his place at the lake. So I asked Ed how to find Chester's "fishin' shack," and at 3:30 I drove out to the lake. I was fishing for a story, and I hoped Kelly Marcott would be there.

The Lake of the Woods Club was on the southern edge of Campbellsville next to the Meridian-Washington State Forest. A sign at the entrance read, "Private—Members and Guests Only." The lake, which covered about 200 acres, was surrounded by some of the finest homes in Meridian County.

Chester's place was not one of them, but it wasn't a shack either. It was a small redwood ranch home on South Drive. It stood midway between a Tudor-style mansion and a modern architectural creation that looked like a prairie house designed by Frank Lloyd Wright. I wondered if Wright actually had built it, but if so, why had I never heard about it? Because I moved in the wrong circles. One thing that Chester's house had going for it was a wide grassy backyard that sloped down to the lake. The two neighboring houses were so big that they had hardly any yards at all.

A woman in a straw sunbonnet was planting flowers in the front yard. She was down on her hands and knees, working in a narrow shadow across the front of the house. Several trays of bedding plants and a big bag of peat moss stood in the sun behind her. I pulled off the blacktopped road into a gravelly area and parked between a pair of pickup trucks.

"Howdy do," the woman called as I climbed out of my car. She pulled herself up as I crossed the lawn. She was older than she had looked from behind, maybe sixty or so, but she was slim and energetic. Her sharp, ruddy face showed a few wrinkles that changed into laugh lines when she smiled.

"Mrs. Marcott?" I said.

"No, she's dead. Dicey Cockerham's the name. I'm a friend of Chester's."

"Oh. Nice to meet you, Dicey."

"Same back at ya."

I stuck out my hand and introduced myself. She rubbed her palm on her jeans, then squeezed my hand in a grip that was unexpectedly strong. "It's so nice today, I decided to set some flowers out," she said. "This place could use a little color, don't ya think?"

"It wouldn't hurt," I agreed, though the dandelion-studded lawn looked colorful enough to me. She was planting impatiens, forget-me-nots, and some little white flowers I didn't recognize. "Red, white, and blue," I said. "Very patriotic."

She laughed. "I didn't think of that when I bought them. I *should* have though. My brain don't work too good anymore. That's what happens when you get past seventy."

"You're putting me on," I said. "You look like you're in your fifties."

"Pshaw, you're not trying to hit on me, are you? Because if you are, you might get more than you can handle. What can I do for you?"

"I'm looking for Chester Marcott," I said.

Through an open window a man yelled, "Whadaya want with 'im?"

I couldn't see the owner of the gruff voice. "Are you Mr. Marcott?" I shouted toward the window.

"That's me." This time the voice came from the front door, about ten feet to the left of the window.

Dicey said, "You woke him up. That's why he sounds like a big grump."

"Oh, I'm sorry," I lied.

"Don't worry about it. He sleeps too much anyway. I worry that one of these days I won't be *able* to wake him up."

An old spring-operated screen door squeaked open, and Chester emerged. "Go ahead," he said, "keep flappin' yer tongue." He paused on his small concrete porch, which was only one step up from the ground. From the sound of his voice and from what Dicey had told me, I expected to see a crotchety old cuss on his last legs. He did sound crotchety, but he was thin and not-bad-looking, with short gray hair and a nice tan. "Don't pay attention to her," he said. "She's got my headstone picked out already, but I ain't ready to meet my maker yet."

I wondered if he used Cialis. I pictured him and Dicey in a pair of clawfoot bathtubs overlooking the lake.

I started to introduce myself again, but he cut me off: "I know who you are. I heard you tell Dicey when you two were flirtin' out here."

"That's right," Dicey said. "You're lucky you woke up when you did."

Chester jabbed a finger at me. "If you're here on account of what Kelly wrote at school, I hope you ain't plannin' to put it in the paper. It's made a big enough stink already."

"Has it?" I said. "I just heard about it yesterday. Reverend Harnish mentioned it."

"That knucklehead." He fluttered his lips in contempt. "How he ever got to be a 'Reverend' I'll never know." He started toward me. "The phone's been ringin' off the wall. That's why I'm here—to get away from the phone. The boy's stirred up a hornets' nest. People are mad, an' they have a damn good right to be."

A bright yellow VW Beetle came speeding to a stop on the road, and a young man with scraggly blond hair jumped out. "Thanks, Glorie," he said and slammed the door. Then he headed straight for the house as if the three of us weren't there. The girl turned the car around and tooted the horn as she drove away.

"Where's your bike at?" Chester called to the boy.

The boy took a couple more steps before stopping to answer the question. "It got wrecked. Some moron drove over it while I was in school."

Dicey said, "Oh no, Kelly. "Do you know who done it?"

With an extremely put-upon expression, he took a deep breath and said, "Some stupid jock, most likely."

Chester grunted and said, "If I had to guess, I'd say it was somebody who didn't like it that you said somebody in his fam'ly used to be in the Ku Klux Klan." When Kelly started toward the house again, Chester turned to Dicey: "See. He don't want to hear it. He's just lucky he wasn't on the bike when it got run over."

Without turning around, Kelly yelled, "Sorry to disappoint you."

Dicey said, "Kelly, you shouldn't talk like that to your grandfather."

Kelly swung open the screen door so hard it banged against the wall.

Chester said, "I've had all I can take. I'm about ready to put 'im on a plane and send him back to his mother. The only thing that stops me is that's just what he'd like me to do."

Dicey said, "No it's not, Chester. Kelly likes it here." She looked at me and said, "Kelly stays here at the lake overnight sometimes."

"That's gonna stop," Chester said.

I took a chance and said, "Mr. Marcott, would you mind if I went in and talked to Kelly?"

"Yeah, I would mind," he snapped. "I don't want you puttin' any of that crap he wrote about in your paper too."

"I wouldn't publish anything that was libelous or defamatory."

"Them's big words. Forget it. Next thing you know, somebody's gonna come drivin' by in the middle a the night and unload a shotgun at my place. I don't need that."

In my sympathetic-hypocrite voice, I said, "I know you don't. Frankly, what interests me most is Kelly's investigative reporting. Not many kids his age are into that. He's a pretty good writer too. I'm thinking of doing a feature on him. By the way, how old is he? What grade is he in?"

Dicey said, "He just turned seventeen. He's a junior in high school."

I thought he looked older than seventeen. I wondered if he flunked a year or two somewhere along the line. No, not possible. He's smart. He can write.

Chester said, "Just drop the whole thing. There's been enough damage done. I don't want nothin' in the paper."

The screen door swung open again, and Kelly marched out. "It's not up to you. If I want to talk to him, I will." Like his grandfather, he had been listening from inside the house. Evidently eavesdropping ran in the family.

Chester shouted, "You will do as I say, or—"

"Or what?"

"—or I will put you and that mouth of yours on a plane with a one-way ticket to California. You can drive your mom and dad crazy instead of me."

Kelly sneered. "Don't we we still have freedom of the press in this country, Mr. Larrison?"

I wondered how he knew my name. Maybe someone had pointed me out to him one day when I was at the high school. I took what he said as a rhetorical question and did not answer it.

He said, "In case you're interested, everything I wrote is true."

"I should hope so," I said. "You wouldn't publish anything that was false, would you?"

"No. Would you?"

His words were snippy, haughty, disdainful. I expected him to ask me what I thought of his article, and when he didn't, I began to feel impressed. He wasn't looking for my approval. No doubt he thought he had produced a masterpiece. He was a lot more sure of himself than I was when I was seventeen. He came across as a precocious, full-of-himself, smart-ass kid. He looked like a surfer just in from the Golden West. His deep-set blue eyes were probing and distrustful. There was an almost feminine sensuousness in his thick, pouty lips. He wore a plain gray T-shirt, faded black jeans, and orange running shoes. The orange shoes seemed like a ridiculous mistake until it occurred to me that he probably didn't want them to match the shirt and jeans. It would have been too conventional. "So what do you want to talk to me about?" he asked.

"You heard what I said to your grandfather, didn't you?"

"You want to talk to me about my interest in investigative reporting. Wow, that'll turn your readers on. What about the lynching of Abner Richards?"

"That's enough!" Chester said. "You can go now, Mr. Larrison."

"Whoa, wait a minute!" Kelly said.

"You keep your trap shut, Chester said. "You caused enough trouble already."

"Can you believe this?" Kelly said to me. "The Klan murders a man because he's black, but I'm the one causing trouble. I'm supposed to keep my mouth shut. Just like all the 'good people' around here have kept theirs shut for the past three-quarters of a century. No thanks."

Dicey sighed. "Here we go again. Chester, Kelly, come on now. It's too nice a day to fight." She waved a hand at the blue sky over the lake.

"See, that's what I mean," Kelly barked. "It's more important to 'have a nice day' than face up to the truth." His grandfather started to say something, but Kelly spoke over him: "It's like all those people who kept their mouths shut when Hitler was wiping out the Jews. Well, nobody's gonna shut me up. There's no statute of limitations on murder. The truth must come out!"

"It was long ago," Chester said. "You have no idea what it was like back then."

"Like hell I don't!"

"I won't have you talkin' like that to me, boy."

"I'll talk anyway I want to."

"Don't sass me, boy. Don't sass me."

"Chester, calm down," Dicey said. "Your face is red as a beet."

I chimed in with a cliche: "Chester, Kelly just wants to do the right thing."

I thought he was going to spit in my face. "I want you offa my property!"

Kelly said, "And I want to talk to him."

"Get in the house!"

"No."

"Do what I say!"

Kelly gave me a see-what-I-have-to-put-up-with kind of look. "He treats me like I'm five years old."

"Your mother sent you here to keep you outta trouble. I will do whatever it takes to—"

"What are you gonna do, tie me up?"

Chester began shaking. "Don't sass me. Get in the house. You're not goin' out again till you learn to show respect."

With that, Kelly took off running toward the road. The private blacktopped road surrounded the lake like a horseshoe that began at one end of the dam and ended at the other.

"You get back here," Chester shouted. "You better do what I tell ya, or you're goin' home to your mother."

Without turning around, Kelly raised a hand and gave Chester the finger.

Chester shook his head and gazed at Dicey. "See what I mean? He's got no respect. If I'd ever done that to my father, he woulda beat the livin' daylights outta me."

Dicey hurried to Chester and put an arm around his shoulders.

Chester went on ranting: "What's he doin' here anyway? I never shoulda let 'im come."

"You were just trying to help, Chester."

"A lotta good it's done."

Dicey patted him on the back. "You're doin' a good thing, Chester. You're a good man."

"Bullcrap." He broke away from her and plodded toward the house.

Dicey gave me a forlorn look. "I'm sorry, Phil."

"It's not your fault," I said.

"I'm worried about Chester," she whispered. "I'm gonna put the garden tools in the shed. Then I'll say goodbye to him and go home."

"Don't you live here?"

She acted shocked. "No, Chester and me ain't livin' in sin."

"Oh," I said. "I shot off my mouth before my brains were loaded."

"No offense intended, none taken."

"Where *do* you live, Dicey?"

"In Salt Lick Township, just up the road a bit from Chester's farm. That's his old home place. It's mighty purty out there, not all built up like this is. But the lake here is nice, ain't it?"

"It sure is," I agreed.

CHAPTER 4

BEGGING THE QUESTION

I WAS halfway back to town when I saw Kelly walking along the highway ahead of me. For a second I wondered how he had gotten there so fast. Then I realized he must have cut through the property across from Chester's house, whereas I'd had to drive in the opposite direction to get back to the entrance to the club. He was trying to hitch a ride, and I pulled onto the shoulder in front of him.

"Hop in," I said as he approached my window.

He ran around the car and got in. "Thanks," he said.

A slow-moving fertilizer truck was bearing down on us from behind, so I peeled out as soon as Kelly slammed the door. My car, a two-year-old light-blue Honda Accord coupe, had better pickup than my little Civic used to.

The weather wasn't hot, but Kelly had already worked up a sweat. His Nikes were muddy now. Terrific. He'd get mud all over the floor.

"Where to?" I asked him.

"You can drop me off on the courthouse square if you're goin' that way."

"That's where I'm going."

"Cool," he said.

His profile had a bright silver edge that disappeared as we passed some trees. I wondered if I had seen his aura. Not that I believed in that stuff. He seemed tense and stiff.

"So," he said, "you gonna do a feature on *Mothermucker* and me?"

I knew Ed wouldn't want me to publish the nearly obscene title in the paper, but I didn't have to worry about that yet. "I'm thinking about it," I said.

"If you don't want to, I know a couple of guys at the radio stations who might be interested in doing it."

That was the wrong thing to say. He couldn't play me off against the disembodied voices on the radio. "How long have you been here?" I asked, giving the question a second meaning, which was that he probably hadn't been around long enough to know that the radio guys hardly ever developed an original story. Most of them were lifted nearly verbatim from the *Gleaner*.

"A few months," he replied.

"Did you start school at the beginning of the spring semester?"

He edited my question: "the beginning of the trimester."

Thank you." He was rude. I felt like putting him in his place, but all I said was, "How do you like it here?"

"It could be worse," he said.

"Hasn't anyone told you this is God's country?" I cracked.

He looked at me as though I must be crazy. "Afraid not. How long have *you* been here—your whole life?"

"Not quite. Around eleven years." I glanced over at him. "Why? Are you going to write a feature story about me?"

"Maybe I should. You scratch my back, I scratch yours. That's how the game is played, isn't it?"

"I wouldn't know."

He gave me a snarky grin.

Traffic slowed to a crawl as we reached the middle of town. It was rush hour, and we began inching along from light to light. I asked Kelly if he had made any friends in school.

He tossed his hands. "Some."

I asked if he knew who had wrecked his bike. He shook his head. "It could have been any one of fifty or sixty goons—uh, I mean student-athletes."

I had to raise my opinion of him. He seemed more like a college student than a high school kid. I had read somewhere that kids grew up faster in California than they did here in the heartland. Damn it, *heartland* had wormed its way into my vocabulary.

"Your grandfather blamed your bike's getting wrecked on your article about the Klan. Do you think he's right?"

"Certainly. Don't you?"

I shrugged. "I don't know. I wouldn't jump to that conclusion."

"Ffffuck, that's no jump. It's the most likely explanation."

"You have any personal enemies?"

"Yeah, every nitwit in the school."

"Well then *that* might be 'the most likely explanation.' "

He gaped in disbelief. "You think the article's a piece of shit, don't you?"

"No, it was interesting." That sounded like damning with faint praise, so I added, "It made a strong statement and was well organized, but—"

"Here comes the big but."

If *big but* was meant to be a pun, I liked it. "But one thing disappointed me," I said. "You didn't back up your assertions. You identified several persons as members of the lynching party, but you didn't say where you got your information."

He said, "They weren't assertions. They were facts."

I felt as if I were still an adjunct instructor teaching Journalism 101. "You begged the question," I said, and just in case he didn't know the meaning of that term, I explained it: "You *assumed* as true what you needed to *show* was true. If you report that someone committed a crime, you should support your allegation somehow, for example, by identifying the source of your information." It sounded so basic, I almost wished I had kept my mouth shut, but I babbled on: "You don't want to come across as if you yourself are accusing somebody of a crime, unless you want to get sued for libel or—"

"I might get sued," he shot back, "but I won't get convicted of libel as long as what I said was true."

He was right, of course, but I completed the thought he had interrupted: "—or for defamation of character. And even if what you said *is* true, you can't expect readers to take your word for it. You have to support what you said with facts." I stopped for a red light and turned to face him. "By the way, where *did* you get your information?"

"That's confidential."

"Okay, but you could have said something like 'according to a source who asked not to be identified.' You need to do something to show that you yourself are not the source of the allegation. Otherwise, how do your readers know you just didn't make it all up? See what I mean?"

"I know what you mean," he said, "but Grampaw never asked not to be identified, so it would have been a lie to say he did. I don't lie to my readers."

"So your grandfather *was* your source," I said.

"No, he was not."

I wasn't expecting that. "Then who was?" I asked.

"My dad, sort of."

"What's that supposed to mean?"

He held back a few seconds, then said, "One day Mom and Dad were watching an old black-and-white movie on TV. It was about the Klan, and it was set in Indiana. I started watching it too, and Dad said there were some old photos of the Klan up in the attic at Grampaw's house back in Indiana. He said they were photos of members of the Meridian County klavern of the Ku Klux Klan, and their names were on the photos."

"Now you're talking," I said. "That's evidence."

"And my dad said they lynched a man—a black guy— behind the courthouse in 1936. But I didn't think I should quote my own father in the article. It would've sounded rinky-dink."

"How did your father learn about the lynching?"

"He said his grandfather told him—my great-grandfather."

"Kelly, was your great-grandfather in any of those photos?"

"I asked my dad that, and he said no."

"What about your grandfather—was *he* in the photos?"

"I asked him that too, and again he said no. He said Grampaw was too little. He was born in 1931. He only would've been five years old in 1936, when Abner Richards was lynched."

He should have said *would've been only five years old,* but I didn't correct his misplaced adverb.

I turned left on US 50, which was Main St., and when we were five or six blocks from the courthouse, Kelly said, "This is good. I'll get out here."

I pulled over to the curb. "I thought you wanted to go to the courthouse square."

"This is okay. Thanks for the ride, Phil."

"You're welcome."

He got out and slammed the door. In the rearview mirror I watched him run back the way we had just come. He disappeared into an alley. I thought about following him to see where he was going, but I didn't want him to spot me. I wanted him to trust me. Besides, he was probably just heading for a friend's house.

I was glad to hear that Chester could not have been involved in the lynching of Abner Richards, but at the same time I wondered if Kelly would have told me if either his great-grandfather or Chester had been. I wanted to think he would have confided in me. After all, we were on a first-name basis now. We were friends.

I was also worried about Kelly. What if some of those Klansmen were still around, and what if they didn't like being called lynchers and murderers in a rag called *Mothermucker?* Maybe there'd be another lynching on the courthouse square.

CHAPTER 5

A PLEA FOR HELP

WHEN I got to the office the next morning, I found a message from Kelly in my voice mail: "Mr. Larrison, I've been suspended from school. The principal told me I'll probably be expelled—for defamation, like you said. He wants to talk to the superintendent of schools first though. So much for freedom of speech. I guess the Bill of Rights doesn't apply to Campbellsville High School. I just want you to know everything I told you is true. I had proof too. I had actual photographs of the lynching, with the names of the Klan on them, but Grampaw must've found them, because they're not where I put them. I was planning to publish the photos in the next issue of *Mothermucker*. The Klansmen are wearing their robes and hoods in the photos, but their names are all on the back." There was a brief delay, then: "Well, I guess that's it. Thanks for the ride yesterday." He hung up.

The message sounded like a plea for help. Kelly had left it just ten minutes ago.

I phoned Chester's house again. There was no answer, but I remembered his complaining about the phone ringing off the wall. He might be letting it ring. I tilted back in my chair and folded my hands on my head. I wished Kelly had been more careful with the photos. His article in *Mothermucker* identified the alleged lynchers. He should have done a better job of protecting the evidence he had found. Now he was screwed.

I needed a cup of coffee, my third of the day already, so I went to the cubbyhole that Ed called a lounge and dropped a quarter in the jar. The only other person in the front office was the new receptionist, an attractive young woman named Nickie, who wore too much perfume. In the back of the building, the press crew was getting ready to run off a special tabloid section for Farm Safety Week. Warning buzzers and whirrs and thuds kept sounding as the pressmen jogged the rollers and attached the plates. I closed a couple of doors between me and them to lower the decibel level and carried my cup of caffeine back to my office.

Ed showed up a few minutes later. With a long yawn he said, "Good morninguhhhhhhhhnnn." He sat in one of the two wooden chairs in front of my desk and asked, "What have we got today, Philip?" For some reason or no reason he had started calling me Philip. Without waiting for an answer, he said, "Let's go to Mackey's. I'll buy you a cup of coffee."

I said, "I have one," and raised my mug to prove it.

"Come on, we have to keep Mackey's in business."

We crossed the street and cut through the green space around the courthouse. It was a nice day, and a bright orange sun rose above the square clock tower as we walked. I told Ed about my visit with Chester and Kelly.

"Do you think the kid's telling the truth?" Ed said.

I flipped my hands. "I don't know. Yesterday I did, but his credibility took a hit when he told me his proof of who lynched the black man had disappeared. He thinks his grandfather took it."

"Don't print those names. Without proof, there's no story."

"Yes, Ed, don't worry. . . . But I think he's telling the truth. I'm willing to give him the benefit of the doubt. We'll see what happens."

"Chester's right. The kid ought to go back to la-la land."

"Maybe he's on his way there right now. I called Chester's house this morning, but no one answered. Maybe he's driving Kelly to the airport right now."

"Yeah. Chester might want to get him out of the state before the lawsuits start flying." His loud laugh made a squirrel run up a tree.

It was midmorning, and Mackey's Grill was mostly empty. We sat in our usual booth in the back, next to the kitchen door and the jukebox. A new waitress—they came and went—took our order. This one's name was Beth Ann. She looked as if she should still be in school, and she seemed disappointed when all we ordered was coffee.

Russell Garriot, the county extension agent, who had been sitting by himself at the counter, came over to join us. He wrote a weekly column on farming for the *Gleaner*. It was mostly a summary of news releases from Purdue.

After the usual chitchat, I asked him if he knew where Chester Marcott's farm was.

In a smooth south-Hoosier drawl, he said, "Yes, it's up near Zummie." He pronounced Zumma as the locals did. "Do you know where that is?" he asked me.

"Yes."

He went on as if I had said no: "You take State Road 135 up toward Brown County. Where 135 makes a sharp right, there's a county road that goes left. That's Zummie Road. Go over the steep hill, and when you get to Zummie, hang a right. Go out past the old school and keep going till you come to the next county road—it's CR 1150N, as I recall. Make a left there, and Chester's farm is a mile or so straight ahead. Look for an old brick farmhouse standing pretty far back off on your right. Chester's got a nice little spread there, pretty as a picture. There's a stone fence all around it like you see down in Kentucky. The Hoosier National Forest borders on the back of the farm."

"Thanks, Russell."

"That's all right, Phil."

I finished my coffee while Ed and Russell discussed commodity prices. Then I escaped.

Back at the paper I found the Reverend Mr. Bob Harnish giving a sermon in the front office. Despite being a loyal Democrat and a supporter of President Obama, he was railing against Ben Bernanke, Chairman of the Federal Reserve Board, and Timothy Geithner, Secretary of the Treasury. He called them "a pair of fascists in bed with the big Wall Street bankers." Presently his congregation consisted of one person, Nickie. He glanced over his shoulder as I entered the building, but he didn't stop talking. I gave him a quick, "G'morning, Bob," and hurried to my office. He went on ranting for half a minute, then came after me.

"I guess you heard what happened to Kelly," he said. His tall, somewhat overweight frame filled the doorway.

I acted busy, surveyed my desk, turned on the computer. "He's been suspended," I replied. "He left a message on my phone this morning."

"Right. He called me too. What happened to due process, not to mention freedom of speech?" He paused a few seconds before rattling on: "You ought to write an editorial, Phil. The school should be *teaching* the Bill of Rights, not subverting it."

"Why don't you write a letter to the editor?" I suggested.

"You're the writer."

"You're the preacher."

"I don't have time. I've got two funerals today. They're dropping like flies—which reminds me. . . ." He looked at his watch. "I'd better go. I just wanted to tell you about Kelly, in case you didn't know."

"Thanks."

He pointed a finger at me. "Write that editorial."

I watched him walk out to his car, which was covered with paw prints of cats. He and his wife liked cats and hummingbirds. She was an artist. Most of the paintings in their house were of hummingbirds.

Before getting into my daily grind, I called Chester's house again. This time he answered on the first ring, which took me by surprise. I stumbled over my words: "Uh, Ches—Mr. Marcott, this is Phil Larrison. Uh, I had a call from Kelly this morning. I'm returning his call."

"Is that a fact." It wasn't a question.

I said, "He left a message on my phone."

"Well, try somewhere else. He didn't call you from here." The sticky smack of saliva punctuated each word. "I've not seen 'im since yesterday, when you was out there at the lake."

"Do you know where he is?"

"I do not."

"When do you think he'll be home?"

"Your guess is as good as mine. They kicked him outta school."

"I know. His message said he'd been suspended."

"Soon as he shows up again, I'm sendin' him back to his mother. I've had enough of his crap."

"The school year's almost over," I said. "Kelly needs to finish the term."

"Tell that to the principal," Chester said. "You want to know sumpin'? That story he wrote about the Klan, ya know? Well, three members of the school board—three out of five—are related to the men he said lynched that black feller. You don't expect them to let Kelly go back to school, do ya?"

I said, "Chester, if what Kelly wrote is true, and if he can produce evidence that the people he named were in the Klan and lynched a man, I don't think there's any way he can be kicked out of school. I don't think they have the right to suspend him, if all he did was tell the truth. But he'll need proof to back it up." I let that sink in. I was hoping he would realize he should give the photos back to Kelly.

Chester's tone softened, and his English improved slightly: "Look. Mr. Larrison, I know you're tryin' to help the boy, but I don't want him causin' no more trouble. He's done enough damage already. It seems to me like the best thing he can do now is go back to his mom." As an afterthought he added, "And his dad." He exhaled in my ear. "I'm tired of fightin' with 'im. He got outta line again last evenin'. I didn't even know he went to school today till Jimmy Dobbs called me up and said he'd jist had a talk with 'im and booted him out."

Jimmy Dobbs was the principal of Campbellsville High School.

"What did he do last night?" I asked.

Chester let his breath out slowly, then said, "Me an' Dicey was fishin' down at the pond, and she had to go back to the house to use the facilities. She went in by the pantry door and heard a lotta noise upstairs. She went up an' caught Kelly in my bedroom, goin' through the chest a drawers. I didn't even know he was in the house. I never seen 'im come home. I don't know how he got there. His girlfriend musta dropped him off on the road. Dicey said she told him he shouldn't be goin' through my stuff, but he kept right on pullin' drawers out and goin' through my clothes. Dicey left him there and come runnin' down to the pond, and we went back up to the house together, but by then he was gone. He never come back last night, nor this mornin' neither."

"He shouldn't have gone through your things," I said.

"That's just one thing he shouldn't of done."

"The only positive spin I can put on it, Chester, is that it shows how important whatever he was looking for is to him."

"That don't give him the right to go through my clothes."

"Chester, he told me he had proof that his article about the Klan is true, but he said you took the proof away from him." I could have said Kelly had accused *him* of going through *his* personal things, but I didn't want to rile him anymore than he already was.

"Them old pictures belong to me," Chester said. "The boy took 'em out of a chest up in the attic. He never asked for my permission. I never gave him permission to take 'em and make the names public. I'm thinkin' of puttin' a match to 'em. That'll be the end of it."

"I know how you feel," I said. "Kelly told me they were photos of the Ku Klux Klan and they had the names of the Klansmen on them. I think he felt it was his duty to reveal that they had lynched a man."

The volcano erupted: "He had no business puttin' them names out an' diggin' up somethin' that happened over seventy years ago."

"I know how you feel," I said. "He should have asked your permission, but you mustn't destroy those photos, Chester. If they somehow prove who killed Abner Richards, they're very important."

His words tripped over one another: "Don't-tell-me-what-I-must-and-must-not-do-who-do-you-think-you-are?"

I expected him to hang up. Quickly I said, "I'm sorry, Chester. I shouldn't have said that. And Kelly shouldn't have opened the chest without your permission."

"He *broke* it open. It was locked."

"He shouldn't have done that."

"You're damn right!"

I took a different tack: "Chester, I've been told that Kelly's mother sent him here for his own good, because he was in a bad crowd in Los Angeles. Does Kelly help you take care of your farm?"

He took another huff and puff, then admitted, "He helps some."

"I bet it's good for him."

"If it is, it don't show."

"How big a farm do you have?"

He was silent again, then: "Tell me somethin', young feller—how is it any of your business how big my farm is?"

"I was just thinking how Kelly could be a real help to you."

"I jist told ya—he's some help. But it's not like I farm thousands of acres. It's more like a hobby now. I grow a little corn and soybeans, some wheat and alfalfa, jist enough to keep my hand in."

It sounded as though Chester had a pretty good life—a house at the Lake of the Woods Club and a small farm to enjoy. "Would you mind if I come out to see your farm sometime?" I asked.

"You interested in farmin', are ya?"

"I'd better be interested in it if I work for a paper called the *Gleaner,* don't you think? How about if I come out there tomorrow morning?" Tomorrow was Saturday, but the only thing I had to do was my laundry.

"What for?" he demanded.

"I'd just like to see your farm. I understand it's got a stone fence around it. I didn't know there were stone fences around here. It might make a nice picture for the paper."

He thought about it, then said, "If that's all you want, I reckon it'd be all right. You know how to get here?"

"Yes, I believe I do."

"I'll be here."

End of conversation. He was gone. I sat listening to laughs and chatter in the front office. I tried to push Chester and Kelly out of my mind so I could get my work done. I woke up my computer and began editing an article about a three-car crash on I-65, but the words blurred as my thoughts went back to Kelly. Maybe I should write a short piece about him for tomorrow's paper. The lead took shape in my mind: "A student at Campbellsville High School has been suspended for publishing an article that names 28 men who allegedly belonged to the Ku Klux Klan in the 1930s and who may have participated in a 1936 lynching on the grounds of the Meridian County Courthouse."

Too long. Too wordy. Boil it down. I ought to talk to Kelly again before putting something in the paper. Maybe I could get Chester to show me the photos. I ought to see Kelly's "proof" about the lynching.

I watched my fingers slide back and forth along the edge of my desk. They seemed to move without my willing them to. It was as if they belonged to someone else.

CHAPTER 6

OLD BUDDIES

B RIGHT sunlight poured through the windows. Only the
gray grime that covered them softened the glare. The windows were open a few inches, and I lay in bed listening to the
birds in the trees.

After a few minutes of this, I got up and fixed my usual
breakfast: coffee, orange juice, toast, and cereal. I was trying to
cut down on sugar, so I had shredded wheat instead of Cocoa
Puffs. Then I showered and shaved, put on the new shirt that
my mother had sent me and a clean pair of jeans, and headed
for Chester's farm. It was only 7:15, but that wouldn't bother an
early riser like Chester. Besides, it would take me half an hour
to get there. I decided to let the *Gleaner* pay for the gas, so I
drove the few blocks to the office, parked on the empty square,
and took a company car.

Zooming toward Zumma, I was surprised to feel a tingle of
excitement in my belly again. I had Kelly and the *Mothermucker*
to thank for that. What a story he had grabbed by the tail. A
black man gets lynched behind the courthouse, a cold case if
there ever was one. Seventy-six years later, half a dozen old gee-
zers get rounded up and sent to prison. Life sentences wouldn't
be fair. Retired Klansmen over ninety years old wouldn't have

enough years left to make such punishment meaningful. Maybe they'd get the electric chair. The story would get national attention. International. The whole world would be talking about Campbellsville, Indiana. Kelly and I would get tarred and feathered and run out of town on a rail—that is, if we didn't get lynched. . . .

Cool it, Larrison, you won't get lynched. In all likelihood nothing will happen. If Chester destroys Kelly's evidence, the whole thing goes up in smoke. *That's* what will happen. The proof of the crime may already be ashes in the wind. This whole thing is a waste of time. What was I doing out here in the stampede of night-shift workers on their way home from work?

My mood had taken a 180-degree turn. I was half tempted to do another one-eighty and turn the car around and go home, but I told myself it was just a bipolar moment. I turned on the radio to take my mind off it but immediately turned it off before some idiotic song would get stuck in my head for the rest of the day. Then I yawned so hard it hurt my ear. The sun was in the side-view mirror. I pushed the button to tilt the mirror and eliminate the glare.

I wished I had thought to bring a cup of coffee and a couple of doughnuts with me.

Several miles west of Campbellsville I took SR 135 north. Long, tubular clouds hung low in the sky like a fleet of alien spaceships. I wound through gently rolling farmland until I got to the spot where 135 made a sharp right. A small wooden sign saying Zumma Road was nailed to a tree. I turned left onto a county road that climbed a steep, forest-covered knob with an abandoned fire tower on top. The road followed the narrow ridge a short distance before making a steep descent on the other side of the hill.

The unincorporated burg had seen better days. It was comprised of a few dozen old houses, a few faded trailers, and a few ranch homes. A weatherbeaten general store that was still open for business stood next to a small post office that had been shut down. Two old churches, one Baptist and one Lutheran, stood at opposite ends of the single street through town. The former schoolhouse had recently been remodeled, reroofed, and renamed the Salt Lick Township Community Center. I had covered the dedication ceremony, and after the speechifying was over, I'd had a slice of strawberry-rhubarb pie and a plate of persimmon pudding.

I had no trouble finding Chester's farm. The stone fence that surrounded the farm made it easy. It was more like a wall than a fence, but because it marked the boundaries of the farm, it was considered a fence. I figured someone must have dug an awful lot of stones out of the ground to build such a long fence. It looked like a job for slaves. Indiana had never been a slave state, but I knew that slavery had existed here when it was a territory. Maybe slaves had cleared the land before Indiana joined the union.

A long gravel lane lined with pear trees in full bloom led straight to the house, which faced the county road. We were having a wet spring, and the field on my right was mostly brown mud with corn stubble sticking out, while the field on my left was a thick green crop of hay or something. The house, a three-story structure with two dormer windows in the attic, was made of dark-red bricks that seemed out of keeping with the stone fence. The way the porch roof jutted out from the house reminded me of a sombrero pulled down over the face of a snoozing man. It was an old house, but I suspected it was not the first one to be built here. The original house had probably burned down or been destroyed by a tornado. This house had an impregnable bunker-like appearance, as if it had been built to withstand anything Mother Nature could throw at it.

A faded green pickup, one of the trucks I had seen at the Lake of the Woods Club, stood in front of the house. I parked next to it and climbed out. A dog began barking behind the house, and half a dozen crows took off flapping and cawing from the trees on the front lawn.

I went up three steps to the porch and knocked on the door, which had a pane of glass covered by a curtain in the upper half. No one answered. A pair of fishing rods lay across the arms of two wooden rocking chairs. I waited a few more seconds, then walked around the right side of the house.

The dog, a black Lab, was standing with its front paws against the fence in a large pen with a concrete floor. He growled softly at me. A weatherbeaten barn stood about a hundred feet away at the bottom of a gradual slope. Its sliding door was wide open. There was no livestock in sight, no mucky barnyard.

"Anybody home?" I shouted, which made the dog growl louder. I figured Chester couldn't hear me, so I walked down to the barn. Inside were several pieces of farm machinery, but not Chester.

I returned to the house, this time to the back door, which was on a small porch with a single lawn chair, the steel bouncy kind. The chair faced the knobs of the Hoosier National Forest a quarter mile away. The door was open a crack. "Hello in there," I called. When nobody answered, I tried again: "Chester. It's Phil Larrison." Still no answer. I figured he was in the bathroom.

I gave the door a push. It moved about two inches and stopped. A full-sized freezer was blocking the door. The opening wasn't wide enough for me to squeeze through, so I put my shoulder to the door and pushed. The freezer wouldn't budge.

The window in the upper half of the door was covered by a shade, but through the edges I saw cans and boxes lying on the floor. A set of empty metal shelves leaned against the freezer.

I walked around the other side of the house. A white propane-gas tank stood midway between the house and the hayfield.

Back on the front porch, I knocked on the door again, but no one came. There were four windows, two on each side of the door. They were covered with drapes, but through a narrow slit in one pair of drapes I saw a lamp and a chair lying on the floor. I yelled, "Chester! Kelly! Anybody home?"

No response.

What to do, what to do? The two rooms I had seen were a wreck. What difference would one more piece of broken glass make?

I grabbed one of the fishing rods and was about to use the handle to smash the window when some rarely used common-sensical part of my brain clicked on and, instead of breaking into the house, I tried the doorknob.

The door opened with a creak. I put the fishing rod back against the wall and went inside. "Anybody here?" I yelled.

The living room was a disaster zone. Every piece of furniture was overturned or pulled apart. A TV set lay against the side of a stairway in front of the door. A big buck's head with several antlers missing stared at me from inside the fireplace. Lamps, throw rugs, chairs, desk drawers, magazines, framed pictures—all were strewn around the room. Gaping holes in the walls revealed the ooze of old plaster between narrow boards. An ebonite phone lay on the floor.

Where was Chester? His truck was out front—but how did I know it was his? Maybe it belonged to whoever had torn up the house. Maybe the demolisher was still here somewhere. I thought I felt eyes on my back. I turned around, but no one was there.

I stepped through the debris. Nearly every step I took crunched on broken glass. The only other sound came from an inch-long fly buzzing back and forth between the living room and a parlor on the other side of the stairs.

A wide archway led from the living room to the dining room, which was another disaster area. A curved-glass china cabinet lay face down, its curios and dishes scattered around it. A long cherry table lay flat on the floor with its legs sticking up like a dead bug's. One of the matching chairs dangled from the top of a massive sideboard, whose drawers had been emptied and then tossed around the room. The sideboard itself was still standing, though it had been pulled a couple feet away from the wall, which now had a ragged hole in it. A corner curio cabinet lay in ruins.

I couldn't help wondering if Kelly had made it out here yesterday and ransacked the house searching for the photos that his grandfather had taken from him. Was he that angry? Two paintings that looked like the work of nineteenth-century Indiana impressionists were impaled on chair legs. A fireplace poker coated with plaster dust hung out of a wall. An ornate brass birdcage stood next to the upside-down table. With its tiny door hanging open, it looked like the shocked survivor of an earthquake.

I crunched my way to the kitchen. It was nearly impassable. I saw no point in trying to pick my way through the wreckage of cupboards and appliances. The refrigerator, with its motor humming, lay on its side with its door open and half its contents soaking in a puddle of water on the floor. The kitchen was a miniature dump of smashed furniture, emptied-out drawers, broken jars, spilled milk, cereal boxes, cans of soup, tea bags, celery stalks, pots and pans, knives and forks. . . . It looked as if someone had gone berserk and smashed and scattered everything in the room. The room smelled of pickles, coffee, garbage, you name it.

Mixed in with the mess was an incongruous shoe sticking out from under a tall wooden cabinet that lay face down on the debris in front of the gas stove. Ceiling-high cupboards hung above the stove, and built-in cabinets with old Formica countertops stood on each side of it. At first all I saw was the shoe, but after I clambered through the smashed dishes, broken chairs, scattered silverware, and smelly garbage, I saw half an inch or so of a white sock in the shoe. The rest of the sock and the man who was wearing it was under the cabinet.

Was it Chester? Who else could it be?

"Chester," I said, "is that you under there?"

There was no reply.

I was at the bottom end of the cabinet. I put my hands under it, bent my knees, and tried to lift it. I nearly busted my gut, but the cabinet did not budge.

I heard my heart thumping. A bead of sweat trickled down my chest. I looked around for something to use as a lever. I found a large cast-iron pot, which I thought would make a good fulcrum.

I decided it would be wise to raise the cabinet from one side or the other, rather than from the top end or the base. I thought there would be less weight to raise that way, but I wasn't sure. One thing I was sure of was that I didn't want to lift it at the bottom end because that would cause the top end to bear down on the poor guy's head.

I cleared a space next to the middle of one side of the cabinet. I turned the pot upside down and set it on the floor alongside the cabinet. Now all I needed was a solid tree branch about six feet long and a couple inches in diameter—or better yet, a steel rod. I went back to the dining room for the poker that was hanging out of the wall.

My idea was to place the poker over the side of the pot and under the cabinet and then push down on the poker to raise the cabinet so I could pull the man out somehow. Unfortunately the poker wasn't long enough and I wasn't strong enough to move the cabinet the slightest bit.

"Who's here?" a woman shouted from the living room.

It took me a few seconds to place Dicey's voice. I had been making so much noise, I hadn't heard her enter the house. Sweating, I let go of the poker and called, "Dicey, it's me, Phil Larrison." As I stood up, Dicey stepped into the kitchen with a double-barreled shotgun in her hands.

"Whadaya doin' in here?" Dicey asked as if she didn't remember me. She was sweating too, and her short white hair stuck out like wet feathers on a bird.

I straightened up and flexed my back. "I came to talk to Chester," I said, "but I'm afraid I'm too late."

She hiccuped, and the shotgun jerked. Her finger twitched in front of the two triggers. "Too late for what?" she asked, eying me suspiciously

I said, "I think Chester's under this cabinet. He's either dead or unconscious. I was trying to pull him out in case he's still alive. You can see a shoe and sock here where I am."

Her gun hit the stove as she stumbled forward to see for herself. When she reached a spot where she could see the shoe, her lips began trembling. "That looks like Chester's shoe. How'd he get under the pie safe?"

So that's what it was, a pie safe. "I guess someone knocked him down and pulled it down on top of him," I said.

Still clutching the shotgun, she worked her way past the sink and the dishwasher, both of which stood against the back wall of the house. The refrigerator had been there too, before it was toppled. The door on the dishwasher was hanging open, with the top of it touching the floor like a ramp. Someone must have stepped on it or jumped on it while it was hanging open.

"I'd like to get my hands on whoever done this to Chester," Dicey said. She knelt down next to the shoe, and a low moan came out of her throat. She tried to pull Chester out, without success. She straightened up and wiped the sweat off her forehead. "We have to get the pie safe offa him. He might still be alive. You lift. I'll pull."

"I tried to raise it," I said. "I used a fireplace poker as a lever, but it wasn't long enough."

"Then use something else!"

"How about your gun? That might work." She didn't seem to like the idea, so I said, "Okay, don't let me use it. We'll call the police and wait for them to free Chester."

She gave me a miserable look and said, "Here, take the gun. I'm sorry I've not been trusting you. I'm outta my head seein' Chester like this. He was my sweet honey."

As I had done with the poker, I placed the shotgun barrels over the edge of the upside-down pot and underneath the side of the pie safe. Then I pushed down on the gunstock, using the barrels as a lever. The extra length of the shotgun lifted the pie safe just enough for Dicey to pull Chester out from under it, first by a leg, then by an arm.

Chester was clearly dead. He stared at the ceiling with his mouth open. Black-and-purple blotches stained his forehead and nose. A smear of blood stained one side of his face. The blotches on his scalp seemed darker than ever.

"Poor Chester, he didn't deserve this," Dicey said. "Should I close his eyes?"

"I wouldn't," I said. "Let the police see him as he is." Immediately I rethought my advice. "Oh heck, Dicey, if you want to close them, go ahead. Who am I to tell you what to do?"

She knelt down and kissed Chester on an eyebrow. She gently closed his eyes. With little sobs and murmurs she held his face between her hands. Her lips moved in silent prayer.

CHAPTER 7

THE LEGEND

I TRIED to call the Sheriff's Department on my ancient BlackBerry, but out here in the sticks I couldn't get a signal. I needed a new phone big time. I'd probably have to buy one myself since Ed didn't want to upgrade our freebies.

"We can call from my house," Dicey said, "but I hate to leave Chester alone like that."

"He won't mind," I said. "Let's go. I'll drive."

"No, I don't want to leave my truck here. I'll drive it home. You follow me."

Dicey carried the shotgun out to the truck, a black Dodge Ram. "I don't usually bring a gun in with me when I come to see Chester, but when I seen the front door was open and heard you makin' a racket in there, I thought I might need one."

"I'm glad you didn't shoot first and ask questions later."

"You're lucky I didn't." She climbed inside the truck and hung the gun on a rack in the rear window. The truck was polka-dotted with bird droppings, and the company car I was using had collected some too.

Dicey lived in a cottage about a quarter mile away. The small, poor-looking house had a sharply peaked roof, and the sides were covered with ripply whitewashed tarpaper. It stood on a low rise against the long view of farm fields to the south. I thought there couldn't be more than two rooms inside. A pretty yard compensated for the plain appearance of the place. Two redbud trees were in full bloom, and a pair of dogwoods were just getting started. Clusters of daffodils spread down the rise to the road.

"The flowers look sad," Dicey said. Beaten down by recent rain, the daffodils hung their heads as if mourning for Chester.

Dicey seemed frailer as she climbed out of the truck and led the way to the cottage. Her hand shook as she opened the front door, which was unlocked.

Inside, the place was surprisingly cozy. Gingham curtains hung on the windows. An oval braided rug covered most of the floor in the living room. A potbelly stove stood in a corner, with an old cameo-back love seat and a bentwood rocker facing it. The phone was on the wall next to a doorway that led to a small kitchen.

I called the county jail in Campbellsville—I knew the number by heart. The sheriff wasn't there, so I gave my report to Jesse Holsapple, who was now a regular full-time deputy.

"We'll get a car out there right away," he said. "Stay at the scene, but don't touch anything."

"It's too late for that," I said. "His neighbor showed up, and we already moved the body. It was under a tall cabinet. We thought he might still be alive."

"Then don't touch anything else."

"It's too late for that too."

"Way to go," he said in disgust.

After I hung up, Dicey said, "I could use a cup of coffee. What about you?"

"I sure could," I said, "but not right now. We'd better get back to Chester's place." I was thinking I probably should have stayed with the body and let Dicey go home and call the police. It was stupid for both of us to go. But I had wanted to make the call. Why? Did I want credit for finding the body? I thought I had outgrown that sort of thing.

Back in the truck, Dicey lamented, "Chester would still be alive if Kelly hadn't come here. Why'd his mother have to send him here? She shouldn't have asked Chester to take care of him."

"Do you think Kelly killed Chester?" I asked.

"I ain't sayin' that." Her stomach growled like a rusty spring. She patted her belly and said, "Pardon me. No, what I meant was I think whoever killed Chester did it because of what Kelly wrote about that lynching. Nobody ever tried to harm Chester before, so it looks to me like that article of his is what got Chester killed."

She was breathing faster. I hoped she wasn't about to have a heart attack. One dead body at a time, please.

She ran on: "And I'll tell you somethin' else. This don't make Kelly look good. A coupla days ago I caught him searchin' Chester's bedroom. Chester and me was fishin' down at his pond, an' while we was there, I had to use the bathroom, so I went up to the house. When I got there, I heard somebody makin' a racket upstairs. I went up real quiet like and caught Kelly goin' through the chest-a-drawers in Chester's room. I said, 'What are you doin' there, Kelly?' He said he was lookin' for some old photos he had found. He told me he had been keepin' them in his room, but his grampaw must've taken them. I told him he shouldn't be goin' through Chester's things. I tried to get him to go back to the pond with me, but he wouldn't go, so I went back by myself and told Chester what he was up to. Chester dropped his fishin' rod and hurried back to the house as fast as he could. I went with him, but by the time we got there, Kelly was gone."

When Kelly had been in my car two days earlier, he talked as if he had seen the evidence he needed to prove who killed Abner Richards. "When did this happen?" I asked Dicey. "Was it the same day I met you and Chester at the lake—Thursday afternoon?"

Dicey clutched her knees as if to keep her hands from shaking. She looked all worn out. "Yes, I think so," she said. "My memory ain't as good as it used to be, but that's when it was, the last time I was at million-dollar lake. Chester needed to settle down and relax after what Kelly put him through. His nerves were shot, so I said let's get somethin' to eat at my house and then we'll go an' do some fishin'. Chester loved to fish."

I said, "So you and Chester got back to the house, but Kelly was gone. Did he come back later that night?"

"I don't know. I didn't stay there overnight. What do you take me for?" She laughed, then added, "Chester an' me are friends—I should say we *were* friends—and that's all we were, nothin' more." She smiled ever so slightly. Had I blinked, I would have missed it. "Sadie, Chester's dog—now that I think of it, I ought to check on her and make sure she's got some food and water. Anyway, Sadie was barkin' at somethin' in the woods. Chester said it must be Kelly. He said Kelly must be watchin' the house and waitin' for a chance to search it again. 'But he'll never find what he's after,' Chester said—his exact words."

"Why? Did Chester destroy the photos?"

"I don't know. He never told me."

"Where did Chester stay at night, out here on the farm or his house at the lake?"

"The farm mostly. He loved the farm. He didn't have much to do with his neighbors at the lake."

She started the truck and drove the short distance to Chester's house.

"We probably should wait out here till the police come," I said.

Dicey ignored this and climbed out of the car. I followed her up the steps to the porch. She opened the door cautiously, as if someone might be hiding behind it. Then she went straight up to the second floor.

Instead of going with her, I plodded through the wreckage in the living room and dining room again. It was a weird compulsive thing—I wanted to make sure Chester was still there. Sure enough, he hadn't gone anywhere. He was right where we had left him. The only difference was his face looked grayer, but it may have been a trick of the light.

The floor creaked overhead. I went back to the front room and up the stairs. I found Dicey in one of the bedrooms.

"This is Kelly's room, what's left of it," she said.

Only two of the second-floor rooms had been totally trashed. In Kelly's room, a gutted mattress with a screwdriver stuck in it lay half on the floor, half up against a window. The box spring, its bottom cover cut in strips, stood propped against a dresser. Nearly every spindle in a Jenny Lind bed had been snapped like a toothpick. An old iMac computer that looked like a space helmet with a shattered window stared at me from the floor. Every drawer in the room had been dumped. Books and magazines lay everywhere, with pages spread open like butterfly wings.

Someone was looking for something, and it wasn't Kelly, I said to myself. He wouldn't have wrecked his own things, and Chester wouldn't have hidden it in Kelly's room, not when there were a thousand other places he could have put it.

The only other room that had been turned upside down was an old-fashioned sewing room with a wire mannequin. As we picked through the debris, we heard a siren in the distance. We stuck our heads in the other rooms and went up to the attic.

As the siren drew closer, we hurried down to the front porch and waited for the police.

Sheriff Carl Eggemann arrived in a cloud of gray dust that drifted slowly past his brown-and-tan cruiser. He killed the siren and flashers and talked to someone on his radio before climbing out of the car. Right behind him was an SUV driven by Slim Jim Simpson, the county's crime-scene investigator. He nodded at me and walked over to the front porch and waited for the sheriff.

Baseball season was underway, so the sheriff was wearing a Cincinnati Reds cap. He touched the brim by way of tipping it to Dicey. "Morning, Miss Cockerham," he said. "How're you doing today?"

"Not good, Carl."

"Chester was a friend of yours?"

"A good friend."

I wasn't surprised that Carl knew Dicey. He was an old-fashioned politician who seemed to know everybody in Meridian County. Tall and thin, always polite and affable, he was a decorated veteran of the Vietnam War and was now serving his second term as sheriff after holding several other local offices. He was the Democrats' biggest vote getter in the county.

A third police car came up the lane trailing a plume of dust. Deputy Eli Bobb, paunchy and round-faced, pulled himself out of the cruiser, then reached back inside for a roll of police tape.

"I'll need to talk to both of you," Carl told Dicey and me, "but first I'd like to take a look around inside." He and Slim Jim went into the house.

Eli began taping the front porch, and when Dicey started up the steps, he barred her way by stretching the tape in front of her. "Sorry, ma'am," he said.

Dicey said, "I'd like to see Chester again."

"You'll have to wait till the sheriff says it's okay."

Miffed, Dicey said, "Are we allowed to sit on the porch? That's where we was before you boys got here."

"I guess it'd be okay," Eli said.

We sat on the glider. I rocked it back and forth with my feet.

"I'm goin' to miss my old fishin' buddy," Dicey said. "I'd come over early sometimes, and we'd catch a mess of bluegill and fry them up for breakfast."

"That sounds good," Eli said as if unaware he had irritated her.

"Things won't be the same without Chester," she added.

The glider squeaked as we rocked. Dicey went on talking, as much to herself as to me. Every now and then she wiped her eyes on her sleeve.

About fifteen minutes later the sheriff reappeared. The first thing he did was ask me how I happened to be there today. He half stood, half sat against the porch railing as I explained how I had met Chester at the Lake of the Woods Club when I went to talk to his grandson about his article on Abner Richards. I asked Carl if he had seen Kelly's story. He said no, so I summarized it for him and explained that Kelly had published it in his underground newspaper, *Mothermucker.*

"Don't forget about the photos," Dicey said.

Carl, who had been staring straight down at the floor while I spoke, looked at me over the top of his glasses and said, "Photos?"

"You tell him, Dicey," I said. "All I know is what you told me."

Deputy Bobb appeared on the other side of the screen door and listened.

The sheriff took out a small pad and took notes as Dicey spoke. She described how she had found me trying to uncover

Chester's body in the kitchen, how she had caught Kelly searching Chester's room Thursday evening, and how Kelly had disappeared again when she went to get Chester. She concluded, "I think it was the story Kelly wrote about people that used to belong to the Ku Klux Klan that got Chester killed. I think somebody was lookin' for them photos."

Carl said, "This boy Kelly—who are his parents?"

"Chester's son, Dale, is Kelly's father," she replied, "but it was Kelly's mother that sent him here to stay with Chester. Chester said she was tryin' to keep the boy out of trouble. So what happens? He's here a few months and he gets himself in a real mess."

"Where do the parents live?" Carl asked.

"Los Angeles. They're divorced."

"What did you mean by saying Kelly 'disappeared again' when you went to get Chester?"

Dicey told how Kelly and Chester had gotten into an argument at the lake Thursday afternoon and how he ran off and made Chester mad.

"Dicey," the sheriff said, "did Chester and his grandson get in another fight yesterday?"

"I don't know. I didn't talk to Chester yesterday. I spent the day with my sister Mary Beth in Pekin. She's doin' poorly. I went to help her."

"Do you know where Kelly is now?" Carl asked.

"No. Chester's truck is still here." She pointed to the old pickup. "So Kelly's not taken it. He could be at his girlfriend's house."

"What's her name?"

"Glorie, G-L-O-R-I-E. I don't know her last name." She stopped, then had a thought: "The only other place he might be, far as I know, is out in the woods. When Kelly moved here, he kept to himself a lot. Chester told me he fixed up a treehouse that his dad built out near the Wilderness Area when he was a boy. Kelly even slept in it some nights. He's only been here since the beginning of the year."

"Can you tell me where the treehouse is?"

"Chester showed me once. We followed a trail that starts outside the wall on the west side of the farm."

Carl looked at his deputy, who was still lurking in the doorway. "How are you at finding treehouses, Eli?"

The deputy replied, "Not too good in the wilderness." He pushed the screen door open and joined us on the porch. "Sheriff," he said, "do you mind if I put my two cents' worth in?"

"Go right ahead, Eli."

"Okay. When you see how the house is all torn up, you have to wonder why somebody who was just lookin' for some old pictures would hack holes in the walls like that."

"Good point," Carl said.

Eli went on: "I'm wonderin' if it mighta been done by somebody lookin' for Chester's treasure."

I said, "What treasure?"

"You don't know?" Eli laughed. "You're out of touch, Phil." He hooked his thumbs in his belt, swaggered to the end of the porch, and spat on the grass. "Everybody in these parts thinks Chester had a fortune in cash money hid all over the house. Ain't that right, Sheriff?"

"That's poppycock," Dicey said.

"Why would he hide a fortune in the house?" I asked Eli.

"They say it's because he didn't trust banks," he said. "Everybody thinks he made a bundle offa that land he sold Walmart. Rumors started goin' around that he had the money stashed all over the house."

"That's a lot of bull," Dicey said. "Chester was no fool. He wouldn't hide his money in the house. What if the house caught fire and burned down? We have to worry about fires out here, you know. The nearest volunteer fire station is ten minutes away, and till the firemen would get here, it would be another fifteen minutes at least, and besides, half those boys couldn't put out a fire in a trash can."

Sheriff Eggemann looked at his deputy. "You don't believe that old story, do you, Eli?"

Dicey said, "It's a bunch of cockamamie nonsense."

"No, sir," Eli replied. "I've always thought it was just a legend, but some folks might believe it. And times are hard right now. Maybe somebody decided to come pokin' around here, and Chester got in their way and got himself killed."

Carl flipped his notepad shut and pushed himself off the railing. "Well, at least now we have more than one suspect," he said. "Anybody who ever heard that tale about Chester's so-called treasure is a 'person of interest,' as we say nowadays. We've got a lot of work to do, Eli."

"I don't know, Sheriff," the deputy said. "It sounds to me like the kid is the main suspect. He mighta heard them rumors and went searchin' for his granddad's money at the same time he was tryin' to find them pictures."

"No," I said, siding with Carl, "there are plenty of other suspects. Kelly listed the names of twenty-eight men who he said belonged to the Ku Klux Klan in the 1930s. He called them murderers. Some of them are still alive, and the ones who are dead probably have relatives in the area. Maybe some of them read Kelly's story and didn't like it. Maybe they blamed Chester for giving Kelly the information about the Klan. Then there are the photos. Maybe someone ransacked the house trying to find them so they could be destroyed."

"The house got ransacked all right," Eli said, "but I don't see no sign of a break-in."

"The front door was unlocked when I got here," I said. "Maybe Chester knew the killer—or killers. Maybe he let them in. Maybe some Ku Kluxers came out here to get those photos one way or the other."

"Okay, Phil," Carl said, "how about you let me have a copy of that article the boy wrote. We'll look into it." He turned to Dicey. "Do you know if there's a recent picture of Chester's grandson in the house?"

"There was one on the refrigerator." Her chin trembled ever so slightly as she went on: "I hate to say this, but Kelly's been in trouble with the law before. In California. He was arrested for selling marijuana. Chester told me so."

"Do you know how much they found on him?" Carl asked.

"No, I don't. Chester didn't say."

Carl said, "Possession of marijuana is treated as a misdemeanor in California. He's lucky he wasn't caught with it here."

Eli nodded in agreement. He looked like a fish as he slid his tongue from side to side between his upper lip and teeth.

Carl said, "Is there anything else I should know?"

Dicey shook her head.

Carl's face panned from hers to mine. "Phil?"

"I don't think so, Sheriff."

I could have told him that Chester had threatened to send Kelly back to Los Angeles, but Dicey's remarks had put enough suspicion on Kelly.

CHAPTER 8

CRIME SCENE

I GOT my camera out of the car and grabbed a few shots of the house from out front. Dicey was worried about Chester's dog, which had been barking all morning. I trailed along with her to check on it. When Sadie saw her, she began yelping and whining. "You poor thing," Dicey said, "you're out of water. I'll go get you some."

Dicey opened the pen carefully to keep Sadie from getting out, but as soon as she stepped inside, the dog was all over her. "Down, Sadie! Down!" she scolded, and the big Lab obeyed, more or less. Dicey refilled the water bowl with a hose that was attached to an outside faucet on the house. The dog's food was in the pantry, but Deputy Bobb said Dicey could not re-enter the house until Deputy Simpson had completed his investigation.

The county coroner, Travis Baker, arrived as we were standing out front. "I would have been here sooner, but I had a funeral," he said. Travis was a part-time officeholder and a full-time undertaker. He also owned the Dairy Queen.

Sheriff Eggemann took Travis inside, then came back out and told Deputy Bobb to get on the radio and call for an ambulance. "If you can't raise the hospital," he said, "drive up to the top of Zumma Hill where the old fire tower is and call from there. And Dicey, we're going to need a set of your fingerprints, please."

"Why?" Dicey asked. "Do you think I killed Chester?"

Slim Jim appeared in the doorway and said, "No, ma'am. We just need to eliminate any of your prints we might find in the house." To me he said, "We won't need yours, Phil. We've got them on file from the Garth case."

The Garth case was a double murder I had gotten tangled up in two years earlier.

The dog began barking again, and suddenly Dicey shouted, "Kelly! Where've you been?"

Kelly stood at the corner of the house and stared at us with a puzzled look on his face. "What's going on?" he asked.

Eli, who had just settled into his cruiser, slowly climbed out and gazed at Kelly over the roof.

Kelly resembled a rabbit that was ready to bolt. His jeans were ragged, his orange Nikes covered with mud, his T-shirt torn, sweaty, and drooping. Matted hair lay on his shoulders, and a beard of golden stubble gave him a touch of maturity.

"It's your granddad, Kelly," Dicey said. "He's—"

Eli cut her off: "You're Kelly Marcott?" His burly frame swept against the side of the cruiser like a giant brush in a carwash.

Kelly glared at Dicey. "What about Grampaw?"

"Whoa," Jim said, "you can't come in here."

"Why not? I live here."

Dicey said, "Your grampaw's dead, Kelly. He's been murdered."

"Huh? What are you talking about? What happened?" He started toward the porch, but Sheriff Eggemann stepped in front of him.

"I'm sorry, son," Carl said. "You can't go in till Deputy Simpson is finished with his investigation."

Kelly yelled in Carl's face, "What happened to my gram-paw?" He tried to go around Carl, but Carl grabbed his arm. Kelly was startled. I thought he might take a poke at Carl.

Eli said, "Want me to cuff him, Sheriff?"

Carl turned to Kelly. "Do we need to do that, son?"

"I'm not your son," Kelly shot back. "Let go of my arm." He looked as if he wanted to sink his teeth into the sheriff.

I said, "Kelly, the police aren't finished inside. Let them do their work."

"What the shit!" he said. "What happened? Who murdered Grampaw? I want to see him."

The sheriff said, "You can see him later. Let's sit down here on the porch now. I'd like to talk to you."

"About what?"

Carl let go of Kelly's arm and raised the yellow police tape over their heads. Sweat ran off his face. He was too old for this kind of thing. Jim disappeared in the shadows of the living room.

Kelly plopped down on the glider so hard a cloud of dust enveloped him. "I want to know who killed my grampaw," he shouted to no one in particular.

"That's what we mean to find out," Carl said. "Maybe you can help us."

"How am I supposed to help?" Kelly snapped. "I just heard about it."

"How long have you been living here?" Carl asked.

"Since the beginning of the year."

"That's long enough for you to know what was going on in his life. Was your grandfather having any trouble with anyone as far as you know?"

"If he was, he never told me," Kelly said.

"What about you?" Carl said.

"What *about* me?"

"Were you getting along with your grandfather?"

"What the freak is this? You think I killed Grampaw?"

"I didn't say that, son."

Kelly scoffed at him. "It's what you think though, right?"

"Your attitude is not helping you, son."

"So you do think I killed him. You think I murdered my own grandfather. You're an idiot."

Carl said, "I understand you wrote something that upset your grandfather. Is that true?"

"Is what true—that you *understand* I wrote something? Yeah, I guess that's true."

"He's a real smartass," Eli said, looking up at us through the porch railing.

Unperturbed, Carl said, "You know what I mean, son. Answer the question, please."

Kelly's re-hot face looked like a firecracker that was about to explode. He blurted out, "Grampaw didn't like what I wrote about a black man who got lynched by the Ku Klux Klan in 1936. He said it would just stir things up. But it's about time somebody stirred things up. The Klan's gotten away with murder long enough. It's time the truth came out. And now they probably did it again. I bet you any money it was the Klan that killed Grampaw. That's who you ought to be investigating, the fucken Ku Klux Klan."

"Kelly!" Dicey said. "Don't talk like that."

Carl said, "Where were you last night, son?" He glanced at his watch. "Uh-oh, I just remembered I was supposed to go shopping with my wife in Louisville today. She's going to have my hide."

No one except Deputy Bobb laughed.

Kelly answered Carl's question: "I was with a friend."

"What's your friend's name?"

"What's the difference?"

Dicey said, "Kelly, tell the sheriff what he wants to know."

"Why? So he can accuse somebody else of murder?"

"I haven't accused you of murder," Carl said.

Dicey said, "Your grampaw was worried about you last night. You shouldn't've ran away like you did."

"Yeah, well—" What promised to be another smart remark was recast out of respect for the dead: "I'm sorry about that."

"You should be," Dicey said. "Chester loved you very much."

Kelly pounded both fists on the seat cushions. "What's that supposed to mean, that you don't think I loved *him?*" Diamondlike tears formed in the corners of his eyes. He struggled to hold them back. "I want to see Grampaw! I want to say goodbye to him." His lips curled in a sneer that showed straight white teeth. "But these morons think I killed him. They want to know if I have a freaken alibi. I don't believe this. They think I killed Grampaw!" Suddenly he pushed forward and lunged off the glider as if catapulted by a spring. He broke through the sheriff's outstretched arm and raced inside. Eli ran up the porch steps in hot pursuit but held up to let Carl go inside first. Dicey and I were right behind them.

As Kelly fled through the wreckage in the living room, he shouted, "I guess I did all this too, huh?"

When Kelly reached the kitchen, the startled coroner said, "Hey, don't come in here."

By the time I got there, Kelly was kneeling on the floor next to Chester. He was trapped now. The sheriff was behind the pulled-out stove near Kelly, and Eli filled the doorway. The coroner just stared. Jim Simpson wasn't there. I figured he had gone upstairs to see what the rest of the house looked like.

"I'm sorry, Grampaw," Kelly was saying. "I'm sorry." Finally the tears came. They streamed out of his eyes and dripped onto Chester's shirt.

The sheriff let him grieve over his grandfather for a minute or so. Then he said, "This is a crime scene, son. We've got work to do here."

When Kelly didn't budge, Dicey said, "Kelly, come with me." She squeezed past the sheriff and put her hands on Kelly's shoulders. "Come on now, let's go."

I could see Eli didn't like how Carl was handling the situation. It made me wonder if Eli was thinking about running for sheriff in the next election, which would be in 2014, two years from now. Carl was in his second term, so he couldn't run for sheriff again. If he wanted to stay in politics, he'd have to find another office. He had already been county clerk, county auditor, and county treasurer. What was left? County recorder. County surveyor. Maybe he'd take his political career to the next level and run for the General Assembly.

Back on the porch, surrounded by four adults, Kelly slumped on the glider. A light wind rustled the trees, and two buzzards circled over the farm.

Dicey asked Kelly if he wanted to call his parents in California to tell them about Chester's death. He did not answer. Next, Dicey said he could stay at her house if he wanted to. "You can't stay here by yourself," she added. "It's too depressing. And I could use some company. It's scary knowing there's a killer on the loose in the neighborhood."

"Aren't you afraid I might kill you too, Dicey?"

"Don't say things like that," Dicey said.

Kelly looked up at Carl. "Are you gonna put me in jail?"

"I wasn't planning on it. I'd just like to ask you some questions."

"Such as?"

"Such as what were you apologizing for a few minutes ago when you said you were sorry to your grampaw."

Kelly exploded: "You think I was saying I was sorry for murdering him? Do you think I'm that stupid? I was saying I'm sorry for getting him killed by the Ku Klux Klan. That's what I was apologizing for. In 1936 the local klavern of the Klan lynched a black man named Abner Richards. I found photos in Grampaw's attic that were taken at the scene of the lynching behind the courthouse in Campbellsville. The Klansmen's names are on the back of the photos. I published the names in my newspaper. It's called *Mothermucker, the Mother of All Muckrakers.*"

Dicey said, "Oh, Kelly, that might be what got your grandfather killed."

"You think I don't know that?" he said on the verge of tears. "Some of the Klansmen that I named—or maybe some of their descendants—showed up here and tried to make Grampaw give them the photos, and when he wouldn't do it, they killed him and tore the house apart trying to find them. I just hope they *didn't* find them."

"Why do you say that?" Eli asked.

"So *I* can find them. Grampaw got mad at me for publishing the names. He took them out of my room while I was in school. The photos prove who did the lynching in 1936."

Eli said, "If the Klan came calling here, I'm surprised they didn't burn a cross."

"Like I said," Kelly retorted, "maybe it was some of their descendants. Any of the lynchers who are still alive must be very old now. But it could have been other members of the family who killed Grampaw because of the photos."

"How many people knew about those photographs?" Carl asked.

Kelly said, "We delivered sixty copies to bigwigs around town, and we left 300 copies around the high school so students and staff could pick one up and leave a voluntary donation."

"Did your article about the lynching mention the photos?"

"Yes, of course. I had to let readers know how I came up with the names of the Klan who killed Mr. Richards."

Carl said, "I'm surprised you didn't publish the photos too while you were at it."

"I didn't have enough money to print all the extra pages it would've taken, and I wanted to get this issue out. I was planning to run the photos in a special issue next week."

I said, "What about the photo on the front page of *Mothermucker?*"

"I got that off the Internet," Kelly said. "I wanted a graphic for the front page, but I didn't want to run display type over the photo of Abner Richards. I thought it would be disrespectful."

I felt like telling Kelly he had done the right thing. When you've got a big story, you shouldn't sit on it. You should get it out before somebody else finds out about it and scoops you. But I probably would have sat on this one myself. I would have had it lawyered. And I would have tried to talk to any persons in the photos who were still alive. Instead I said, "Don't kick yourself, Kelly. You broke the news. It would have been nice to have the photos with the story, but now you have time to give the people in the pictures a chance to comment."

"They don't deserve a chance to comment," he said.

Carl said, "I'd like to have a list of the people you delivered copies to."

"I won't do that," Kelly said. "You don't have the right to know what papers people might be reading. That's private." He stopped and thought about something. His temples pulsed slightly. "I did too much talking already," he said." I told everybody who helps me put out *Mothermucker* that I had old photographs I was gonna publish in the next issue. I should have kept that to myself, and I should have realized some creeps would come after the photos to keep them from being published. I should've kept my stupid mouth shut. It's my fault Grampaw's dead, okay? I'll take the blame for it. I got him killed."

He seemed edgy. I thought he was going to bolt again, but instead he leaned forward, propped his elbows on his knees, and rubbed his eyes. His stringy hair hung down like a dirty mop, and the back of his neck sported a huge mosquito bite.

The sheriff stood up to stretch his legs.

From the screen door came the crime-scene investigator's voice: "Can I get those fingerprints now, Sheriff?"

"Sure, Slim. You want to do it inside or out here?"

"Out there'll be fine."

Carl told Kelly that he'd like to have a set of his prints too. "It's not that I think you're guilty, son, but your prints are probably all over this house, and we need to be able to tell which prints are yours and which ones belong to somebody else."

"Do what you gotta do," Kelly said.

Slim Jim used the small table to fingerprint Kelly and Dicey. Inkless fingerprinting he called it. When he was finished, Dicey asked Kelly if he'd had anything to eat.

"I'm okay," he said.

"You must be hungry," she said. "Come on, we'll go to my house. I'll fix you some lunch."

"Mind if I tag along?" I said.

"Of course not. Any other takers?"

"No thanks, Dicey," Carl said. "We're going to be busy here for a while."

Dicey got into her truck, and Kelly rode with me. He smelled like dusty sweat. As we drove out the lane, I tried to get him to tell me where he had spent the past two nights.

Kelly said, "Like I told the cops—with a friend."

"Your girlfriend, Glorie?"

"It's none of your business."

"Why? What's the problem?"

"I don't want to get anybody in trouble, that's all." When I didn't ask a follow-up, he seemed to think better of acting hostile. "Okay," he said, "I came back to see if I could get Grampaw to give me the photos back. I was hoping he had cooled off. He had threatened to send me back to LA, and I didn't want to go. And now I want to go back even less. There are things I have to do here."

Dicey made us baloney and Swiss-cheese sandwiches. While Kelly was wolfing his down, Dicey said, "You should call your mother and father, Kelly. They need to know what happened."

He went on eating.

I went back to Chester's house to talk to the sheriff some more. I wanted some quotes for my story. Since the *Gleaner* did not publish on Sundays, the story would not appear in the paper till Monday. I decided to put a few paragraphs on our website today. Edward didn't like giving the news away free, but he didn't like getting beat by the radio stations either.

CHAPTER 9

WHAT GOOD WOULD IT DO?

I SPENT half the day Sunday writing up Chester's murder. Unless nuclear war broke out between the United States and North Korea, the *Gleaner* would lead with my story tomorrow. I included Deputy Bobb's idea that the killing may have stemmed from a burglary, with some thief trying to find the fortune that was rumored to be hidden in Chester's house.

I also reported the other possible motive that was on the table: "It has been suggested that the murder may be related to several old photographs of members of the Ku Klux Klan. The *Gleaner* has learned that these photos, which Marcott reportedly had in his possession at the time of his death, may reveal the identities of several Meridian County men who allegedly took part in the lynching of a black man in 1936."

I was still working on the story when Travis Baker, now in his role as undertaker, walked into my office and stood waiting for me to stop typing. I didn't want to stop, but I figured he had something to tell me about Chester's murder. "Hi, Travis," I said. "What's up?"

He laid a filled-out obituary form on my desk. Chester's name was on the first line. I hadn't even thought about an obit yet. I should have, but I hadn't. "Thank you, Travis," I said. "How did you come up with this so fast?"

"I had it on file," he said. "Chester and his wife—his second wife, Marcia—they gave me the information when they preplanned their funerals years ago."

"Excellent."

"There's not much there," he said in his slow, funereal voice, "but that's all Chester wanted to say about himself." He hesitated before asking, "Do you think you can get the obituary in tomorrow's paper?"

"Yes, of course."

"Because the funeral is on Wednesday. . . . I would have brought it in yesterday, but I had trouble reaching Chester's next of kin to make the arrangements. I had to track down his son, Dale. I couldn't get ahold of him until this morning. He lives in California."

"Don't worry about it. The obit wouldn't have run till Monday, even if you had brought it in yesterday."

"I realize that, but you could have put it online."

"That's right. I'll get it up today."

"I've not given it to the radio stations yet. I'll wait till tomorrow."

It was touching to see he didn't want to make us mad. We had him well-trained. "Thank you," I said. "We won't get scooped." I laughed, but I wasn't joking.

"You're welcome," Travis said.

"Have you done an autopsy on Chester's body yet?" I asked.

He shook his head. "I don't do autopsies. A pathologist at the hospital will do it."

"Really? I didn't know that. After all these years."

"We learn something new every day, don't we?"

"I guess so. When do you think you'll get the official cause of death?"

"Sometime tomorrow. Would you like me to give you a call?"

"Yes. I'd appreciate it."

He nodded, after which he said, "Well, I'd better be on my way."

"Thanks again, Travis."

As soon as he left, I picked up the form he had dropped off. I decided I might as well write the obit myself so I wouldn't have to edit someone else's work. As I always told prospective reporters, the great thing about working on a small paper is that you get to write a lot of different kinds of stuff.

Chester Marcott

Chester Marcott, Jr., 80, of Meridian County, died late Friday night, April 13, on the family farm near Zumma.

Born Oct. 11, 1931, he was a son of the late Chester "Buster" Marcott and his wife, the former Elizabeth Caudill. He was a farmer all his life.

In 1951 he married the former Elma Bonebrite, who preceded him in death. In 1986 he married the former Marcia Peterson Barry, who also preceded him in death.

Survivors include his son, Dale, Los Angeles, Calif.; his daughter-in-law, Angela, also of Los Angeles; and one grandson, Kelly, who was living with him in Meridian County at the time of his death. A brother, Gordon, died in infancy.

Visitation will be from 9 to 10 a.m. Wednesday, April 18, at the Baker & Frederickson Funeral Home in Campbellsville.

Burial will follow at Riverside Cemetery, with the Rev. Mr. Robert Harnish officiating.

No flowers are requested. Memorial donations should be given to the United Way of Meridian County.

Next, to work the kinks out of my legs, I took a stroll to the coffee machine. I still wanted to write a sidebar for my story about Chester's murder, and so I made up a headline for it while I blew on my superheated brew:

Victim's Grandson Suspended
From School for Klan Article

I summarized the main points that Kelly had made in his *Mothermucker* article, but I left out the names of the alleged Klansmen. I did include the fact that Kelly had said he told a number of persons that his grandfather possessed photos of the lynching. I also revealed that Kelly had said he intended to publish the photos in "an underground newspaper that he distributed at Campbellsville High School." The sidebar concluded with Kelly's theory that Chester had been killed by one or more persons who were searching for the photos and who wanted to prevent them from being made public.

I gave myself the rest of the afternoon off to wash my car. Then, for supper, I made myself a tomato-and-lettuce sandwich with mayonnaise on two thick slices of Italian bread. At 5:45 I set two alarm clocks for 8:15, just in case the batteries in one of them died. Then I found an old movie to watch on TV and let it put me to sleep. When the alarms went off, I went back to work to help get the paper out.

• • •

AN autopsy was performed Monday morning, and, true to his word, Travis called in the news. The autopsy revealed that

Chester had died of massive brain injuries caused by several blows to the head with a heavy unidentified object.

Later that day I called Jimmy Dobbs, principal of Campbellsville High School. I asked him why Kelly had been suspended from school.

He said, "You're not going to put that in the paper, are you, Phil?"

I said, "We're talking First Amendment rights, aren't we, Jimmy?"

"Jeez. The kid threatened to bring the damn ACLU down on my head, but I guess he went to you instead. If you've got a few minutes, why don't you come on over here. There's a few things I'd like to tell you about, as long as you don't put it in the paper."

Ignoring his last ten words, I said, "I'll be right over."

Campbellsville High School was a long L-shaped structure on the north side of town. Rising above the one-story class-rooms was a new gymnasium that seated 9,700 people, nearly a quarter of the county's population. Next to the campus was an upscale subdivision with homes starting at $490,000—big bucks for Meridian County. My ex-wife lived in one that cost more than $750,000.

The school day was nearly over. Yellow buses were lined up outside, and the office area was a noisy beehive. Boys in drooping jeans and girls in shorts milled around the hall outside the glass walls. A pretty girl with wavy black hair smiled at me when I happened to look her way. For a second I wished I was back in high school, though when I had been there, I couldn't wait to get out.

Jimmy Dobbs seemed heavier every time I saw him. His puffy face was getting jowly, and whenever he lowered his chin, his neck looked like a stack of tires—the Michelin man. I couldn't understand how he had become a school principal. His spelling was terrible, and his grammar was worse. But he was regarded as a good disciplinarian, and he was trying to get the school board to impose a dress code.

"Would you shut the door, please, Phil," he said as I approached his oversized desk. I went back to close the door, and he put his elbows on the desk and began scratching his bushy brown eyebrows. Then he put his hands behind his neck, flopped back in his high swivel chair, and pretended to laugh. "Jeez, I hope you're not planning to put that Ku Klux Klan garbage in the paper. I tore up every copy of that crummy rag I found laying around somewhere. I shoulda banned it when it first come out. Kelly said it was an alternative to the 'airheaded mindlessness' of our school paper." Jimmy twitched his bulbous nose and snorted. The snort turned into a gleeful chuckle as he added, "By the way, he don't think much of your paper, Phil. He calls it the Wipe."

I took this as an insult from Principal Dobbs rather than Kelly. "That don't bother me none," I replied in my best South Hoosier redneck. "I would've been disappointed in him if he'd said anything else." Then I got us back on track: "Do you think banning his paper would have stopped him from publishing it?"

"No, I guess not, but we mighta been able to eliminate the problem a whole lot sooner." He sat with his arms akimbo, as if his underarms were sweating, and he put one foot up on an open desk drawer. "That kid's been nothin' but trouble ever since he got here. His mother sent him to us from California after he got in trouble out there. For a time I thought we could just outlast him and he'd go back where he come from. But it looks like he's gonna stay." He shook his head in despair. "He's a junior. He has a whole 'nother year to go. I was hopin' he'd go back to California at the end of this term and stay there."

"What kind of trouble was he in out there?" I asked, just in case it was something I didn't already know about.

"I don't think I can say. Privacy, y'know. Aw, what the hey. Possession of drugs—marijuana. All they did was fine him a hundred bucks. His parents paid it. The penalty here's a lot stiffer now. If you're caught with just one single joint, you can get up to a year in jail and a $5,000 fine."

"Yes, it's a bit high."

"It's what we need."

"Do you have any idea if Kelly's been smoking pot since he's been here?"

Jimmy pressed his lips together and squinted, scrunching up the skin at the outside corners of his eyes as if thinking hard. His voice became slow and grudging. "I can't say that he has, but I wouldn't be surprised. We been keepin' an eye on him."

I caught myself starting to nod, as if agreeing with him.

The disciplinarian went on: "At first I thought we were going to have a real problem on our hands. When the first issue of that thing he calls a newspaper come out, the *Motherfucker*— excuse me, the *Mothermucker*—when it first come out, he had a story in it explaining why it should be legal to grow hemp. I gotta hand it to him though. It showed some thought. He went into all the commercial and medical uses for hemp—but you probably seen it yourself."

"No, I've seen only one issue of the *Mothermucker,* the latest one."

"That ain't enough." He rocked forward and in the same motion spun to his right. From the side, he looked dangerously overweight for a man his age, around forty, only eight or nine years older than I was. He sounded half out of breath as he leaned over to open a low horizontal file drawer and reached for the folder at the farther end. "You're in for a treat, Phil," he gloated. "Here's a complete set of *Mothermuckers* for you." He spun back around and tossed the folder onto his desk. "You only seen the latest edition of that rag. There's two others he put out before that one."

The folder contained three copies of every issue. Jimmy flipped through them and passed copies of the first two issues to me.

"You'll see what I'm talkin' about when you read them," he went on. "It's one thing after another. He wants every teacher in the English department to be fired. He says none of them except Miss Carmichael could write their way out of a paper bag. We can't fire 'em. Most a them's got tenure. He says the food in the cafeteria tastes like it was piped in from the sewage plant. The kid is constantly in attack mode. Nothing we do around here is right. He even goes after the athletic department. He says we lured Andy Leatherman here from Bedford-North Lawrence by getting his father a job at Toyota. Jeez, Phil, it's a Japanese plant. I don't have any influence in Tokyo. How could I get the man a job at Toyota? And he says we fired Bobbie Corvino as basketball coach under pressure from Dick Feller because Dick's son Terry wasn't gettin' enough playin' time, and so Dick got himself appointed to the school board to get rid of Bobbie. Jeez almighty, I tell ya, it goes on and on." He slumped in his chair, fagged out, arms dangling.

"I've heard that Bobbie Corvino story too," I said. "Is it true?"

Lowering his voice a few decibels, he said, "Hell no. We went 6-and-15 in Bobbie's last season. *That's* why his contract wasn't renewed."

"But the next season you won the sectional with sophomores that Bobbie helped develop since they were in middle school. He turned the program around."

"He deserves some of the credit, not all of it."

"Some people say he was the best coach Campbellsville ever had."

"Are you one of them?" he asked me.

"He was the best as long as I've been here."

He folded his arms on his chest and sneered. "Everybody's entitled to their opinion."

I glanced down at the two issues of the *Mothermucker* on my lap. Their front pages, which looked like amateurish imitations of *Wired* covers, were even more jumbled than the issue I had seen, but I had to admit they looked alive.

Jimmy ran on: "He says we should scrap the whole athletic department and use the funds to offer more courses in the arts. Wouldn't that go over big in a basketball-crazy town like this?" His upper lip curled inward in a mirthless laugh, which revealed a row of shiny white teeth that seemed too small for his broad face. "As you can imagine," he said, "Kelly Marcott's not winning any popularity contests with our student-athletes."

"How about your student-students?"

He pursed his lips and frowned at me. "He has his fans, I'll give him that. The girls are crazy about him—some of them anyway. They think he's the coolest thing since ice cream. Personally, I don't know what they see in him. Well, yes I do. He looks like a rock star. They think he's this long-haired California dude with a guitar in one hand and a surfboard in the other." He leaned forward and lowered his voice to a whisper. "Half the girls in school would probably lay down for him."

I said, "Maybe that's why your student-athletes don't like him."

"Could be. But I know they hate his guts for saying the basketball program is corrupt and we should be made to forfeit every game we won last season."

I tried not to laugh. The more I heard about Kelly, the more I liked him. "How long will he be suspended?" I asked.

Jimmy drew himself up. "Off the record, okay? He's been suspended for one week, but I'm thinking he oughta be expelled."

"You'd expel him a month before the end of the school year?"

"It's his fault, Phil. He brought it on himself."

"Didn't you just say everyone's entitled to have an opinion?"

"Freedom of speech is one thing. Responsibility is another. Kelly Marcott is irresponsible." Jimmy was getting into his stride: "Take what he wrote about that lynching. It's slanderous. Those are good people he condemned. The Klan is long gone from around here, but he's went back in the past and blackened the names of people who never had nothin' to do with the Klan. I'm referring to the children and grandchildren of the men he alleged were in the Klan. Except he didn't say 'alleged.' He probably don't know the meaning of the word. He came right out and called them murderers. He's even been threatening to publish some photographs he claims will back up his story. He told me he has old photos that tell who was in the Klan. He said their names are on the photos. But even if he does have photos and names, so what? They were taken— when? Back in the 1930s. What good would it do to publish them now? All it would do is hurt a lot of good people who had nothin' to do with the lynching." Jimmy looked overheated, and now his arms began flailing. "But what the hell does he care about this community? He blows in here from southern California and starts rippin' us apart. I tell ya, Phil, that kid's a menace. The sooner he's outta here, the better. That's off the record, remember."

I waited for the rhetorical dust to settle. I did not argue with him. All I did was ask if there was anything else he could tell me about Kelly Marcott.

He said, "I think I told you enough."

I thanked him for his time and left.

CHAPTER 10

THE EULOGY

CHESTER'S funeral took place Wednesday morning at the Baker & Frederickson Funeral Home in Campbellsville. The casket was not open, and sprays of flowers were arranged in a crescent around it. When I arrived, about fifteen persons, including Kelly's parents, were in the viewing room.

Kelly was standing between his parents in a short receiving line to the left of the casket. He was wearing a dark-blue pin-striped suit, which seemed incongruous with his long, straggly hair. Angela Marcott looked a lot like her son. She had the same high-boned features, though hers were less sharp, giving her a strong yet feminine look. Her blonde hair was nearly the same shade as Kelly's, but it was much shorter, with waves of cornsilk brushing past her ears. In her light-pink lip gloss, a faint glow of rouge on her cheeks, and a touch of greenish-blue eye shadow, she reminded me of a country singer. She wore a straight black dress and a thin silver necklace. The simple dress made her face even more striking. I couldn't take my eyes off her.

Every couple minutes she sniffled into a crumpled tissue. Whenever someone expressed sympathy, she leaned forward, taking the person's hand or nodding sadly as they exchanged a few words. Although Chester was her ex-husband's father, not hers, she seemed to be doing most of the mourning. Dale Marcott was in and out of the line and all over the room, talking or laughing with old acquaintances, ducking outside for a cigarette, or huddling with one of the undertakers in a side room. He was an inch or so taller than I was, which made him about 6-1 or 6-2, and he was in better shape—he didn't have to suck in his gut to avoid looking heavy. His thick brown hair had a windblown look that was glued in place, and when he wasn't talking to someone, his lips were always half parted in a kind of half smile.

About ten minutes before the prayer service was to begin, the Reverend Mr. Robert Harnish arrived. After speaking to Cletus Frederickson, who was co-owner of the funeral home, and to Angela, Dale, and Kelly, he spotted me in the last row of folding chairs and sat down beside me. I asked him if Chester had been a member of his church, and he said, "Chester didn't belong to a church. Kelly got his mom to ask me to say a few words here and at the cemetery." He nudged me with his shoulder and whispered in my ear, "Poor Chester's probably roasting in hell right now."

I said, "With your influence, you ought to be able to get him out."

"Don't count on it." This was followed by another whisper: "Imagine having to spend eternity in hell because of the sins of one short lifetime. It don't hardly seem fair now, do it?"

"Is that what you're going to say in your funeral oration?"

He snickered softly. "No. Chester's getting generic eulogy number two." He poked me with his elbow. "Stick around. You might enjoy it." Then his broad-shouldered, black-suited, Roman-collared figure rose above me like a parody of the grim reaper, and he wandered off as if in search of a victim, smiling at people and shaking hands along the way.

I worried about Bob. He had moved here a few years before I had, and I was concerned that someone in his church would hear him cussing and get him fired.

His eulogy was less generic than advertised. Right off the bat he gave it a personal touch by saying that even though he had not known Chester a long time, he had gotten to know him fairly well during the past few months. "We met thanks to Chester's grandson, Kelly," he said, staring directly at him. "Kelly loved his grandfather, and Chester was devoted to him."

Kelly's head dipped, and his mother put an arm around his shoulder.

"And," Pastor Bob continued, "yesterday I had a good talk with Dale. He told me how Chester had tried his damnedest to make him do the right thing when he was growing up. I also spoke with Chester's daughter-in-law, Angela, who grew up in Martinsville, not too far from here. You know, when your in-laws love you, you must be doing something right, and Angela loved Chester. She told me he treated her like his own daughter."

A new tissue went to Angela's eyes.

A lengthy Biblical passage came next—the generic part of the talk, no doubt—and then the conclusion: "The essence of being a Christian is to love God and to love your neighbor as yourself. By that standard, I believe Chester was a good Christian—even if he wasn't a Presbyterian." That line got a laugh. "He cared deeply about his friends and family. Just ask his next-door neighbor, Dicey Cockerham. She and Chester were longtime fishing buddies. She's told me that Chester went out of his way to help people. 'Chester wouldn't want me to tell you this,' she said, 'but I think other people should know what a good man he was.' That's what she said."

Dicey was sitting in the second row. She was wearing a gray dress with a lacy collar that looked like a doily.

The Rev continued: "Dicey knew Chester as a generous, caring person who believed charity should be practiced quietly. He was always willing to help people who were down on their luck, and he would not take a thing in return. That is true Christian charity. And so now, as we bid farewell to Chester, we ask God to bless him for his virtuous acts, to forgive him for his sins, and to grant him eternal rest and peace."

A chorus of "Amens" broke out. Pastor Bob consoled Kelly's parents again, and Travis assembled the pallbearers. As I drifted toward the door with the other mourners, I heard several of them compliment Bob on his talk.

Someone had stuck a small black flag on the hood of my car. I joined the funeral procession to the cemetery. It was a breezy day with a low, flat sky that was the color of Dicey's dress.

At Chester's grave the trees filled with rushes of wind, fell silent, and filled again. Angela Marcott sat next to Kelly under the tent. The wind blew their hair. I began to wonder if the tent would blow away. The chair next to Kelly was empty, but after a few minutes Dale Marcott came and sat on it. Flowers from the funeral home had already been placed on a green outdoor carpet around the rectangular hole under Chester's coffin. When everyone had gathered around the tent, Reverend Bob began speaking again. Whenever the wind swooshed through the trees, it was impossible to hear him.

I was standing about ten feet behind the Marcott family, with several people between us. I watched the wind blow Angela's hair. I was ready to look away the instant her head might start to turn in my direction. Bits and pieces of the "Twenty-Third Psalm" reached my ears.

Through the far end of the tent I saw a big car, a beat-up, once-maroon Pontiac, crawling past the gravestones. It stopped on the narrow driveway about thirty yards away, and the man at the wheel, a husky black guy, sat watching for a few minutes and then drove off. I wondered if he might be one of the people Chester had helped. Maybe he wanted to pay his last respects but felt uncomfortable about joining us. Trailing blue smoke, the car rambled away slowly, as though searching for another funeral.

Bob finished praying, and the mourners took turns placing single flowers on Chester's casket. People stood around talking under the trees. I watched Kelly and his parents walk toward the limousine in which they had arrived. Except for the fact that Angela and Dale did not speak to each other, they looked like a regular family. I followed them between the marble stones and caught up with them next to a small mausoleum.

"Hi, Kelly," I said. "I'm really sorry about your grandfather."

"Thanks," he said.

He didn't do the honors, so I introduced myself to his parents, first Dale, then Angela.

"Nice to meet you," Angela said.

I had warmed to her so much already that the distance in her voice came as a stark disappointment. Dale shook hands firmly, with the grin on his face. I began to think it wasn't a grin. It was just the way he looked.

"When did you get in to town?" I asked them.

After an uneasy pause, Angela said, "A couple days ago." She began moving toward the limo again.

"I went and got them in Grampaw's truck," Kelly told me. "That's all I've been doin' the past few days, driving back and forth to the airport in Indianapolis."

His mother said, "You had to do everything, Kelly." Cars were starting up. "We'd better get going."

"Right," I said lamely. "Good talking to you." The ever-present grin on Dale Marcott's face made me think he was laughing at me, as if he thought I had put a move on his ex-wife, which maybe I had. I felt like kicking myself for talking to them.

I headed for my car. I thought about hanging out at the cemetery for a while to see if the black guy would return. But what would I say to him if he did? . . . How are you connected to Chester Marcott? . . . Did he give you a handout? . . . Did you kill him and tear up the house looking for his fortune? . . .

Come on, Larrison. What's gotten into you? You're thinking like a racist.

I slammed the car in gear and drove back to the paper.

CHAPTER 11

LAST WILL AND TESTAMENT

THE grin on Dale Marcott's face must have changed to a scowl during the reading of his father's will. Chester had left nearly everything to Angela, whom he also named executrix of his estate. He left Dicey his so-called fishing shack at the Lake of the Woods Club and some valuable antiques, among them a Tiffany lamp and an ornate rolltop desk, both of which had belonged to Chester's mother. Unfortunately the lamp had been smashed when Chester was murdered. He also left Dicey a shotgun and two fishing rods. A notation in the will read, "The shotgun is to help you protect yourself when I ain't around to look after you. You can get rid of that old rusty one you got." The will had been prepared by his lawyer, Clyde Goen, and witnessed by a county commissioner and a veterinarian.

"That remark about leavin' me one of his shotguns is supposed to be funny," Dicey told me between bites of a pork-tenderloin sandwich at Mackey's the day after the funeral. "Like he says, I already got a shotgun. It was pointin' at you the other day. Chester was always tryin' to make me mad by sayin' a woman needs a man to look after her. I'd say to him the only thing I need a man for is to take the trash out and set it by the side of the road once a week. I quit burnin' it years ago because I was afraid of startin' a forest fire." Tears welled in her eyes. "I can't believe Chester left me his place at the lake."

She had come to see me shortly after the reading of the will at the lawyer's office. I wasn't expecting her. "Chester's done a crazy thing," she blurted out as she entered my office. "He cut Dale out of his will. He left most everything to his daughter-in-law, Angela."

I wondered why she was telling me this. Had we become good buddies without my realizing it? Then I decided she just wanted someone to talk to. She probably didn't want to go home and think about Chester.

I said, "I wonder what he had against his son."

Dicey sat down and faced me across my desk. "This ain't good," she said, wagging her head. I'm afraid there's gonna be trouble. I don't know what got into Chester. He never told me he was leavin' me his fishin' shack. He knew better than to tell me. He knew I wouldn't've let him."

"What kind of trouble are you expecting, Dicey?"

She pursed her lips, then said, "You know they're divorced, don't you?"

"Yes."

"Well then, you can imagine. Dale is not exactly thrilled that his ex-wife gets nearly everything."

"Do you think Dale will contest the will?"

Her lips tightened again. "I don't know what he'll do. He threw a fit when he heard what Chester done. He started cussin', and then he accused Angela of weaseling her way into Chester's good graces. He said that's why she sent Kelly to stay with him. Angela said, 'No, I sent him here to get him as far away from you as I could.' When she said that, Dale's eyes turned as black as two lumps of coal. He looked as mean as a tick. It was down-right scary."

The funeral had blown my normal routine, and I didn't feel like working. I stood up and took the day's press releases out of my tray and dumped them on our new reporter, Madison, who had graduated from Franklin College with a degree in journalism last year. Madison appeared to be less than totally frazzled today, so I figured she could handle a little more work. Then I asked Dicey if she'd like to get some lunch.

As usual, Mackey's was full at lunchtime. We sat in the side room where the Exchange Club met for breakfast once a week. The original booths were in this part of the restaurant. They were roomier than the new fiberglass booths in the main section, but the old vinyl seats were crisscrossed with duct tape. I ordered a meatball sandwich. It was taking a chance. Dicey ordered a pork tenderloin.

We talked about the weather till our food arrived. Then I asked Dicey if Chester had left Angela any money. Not that it was any of my business.

Dicey was busy chewing. She chewed faster, then gulped down the food and said, "She got most all of Chester's money and most of his property—everything except what he left me."

She dabbed her lips with a napkin and proceeded to tell me about the things Chester had bequeathed to her. With the clean side of the napkin she wiped her teary eyes.

I took another bite out of my sandwich. I hated to admit it, but Mackey's had good food. The cockroaches must have thought so too, because at least once a week I spotted one of them scurrying along the green baseboards that were thick with paint and painted wires. "Was Chester rich?" I asked.

Dicey leaned forward and whispered, "You know what, I never actually thought of him as rich." She stared past me toward the plate-glass windows and the traffic on Main Street.

"Oh, I knew he owned some farmland, and I thought he must be pretty well-off, especially after his second wife, Marcia, died, but I never thought of him as bein' rich. He never acted like he had a lot of money. He was always just himself." She sipped her iced tea through a straw. "But Mr. Goen the lawyer said Chester's estate is worth well over $2 million. Mostly it's in the land he owned. Good farmland is sellin' for around $7,000 an acre these days, and Chester had 200 acres, plus or minus. And besides that he had the house at the lake."

"Right. That must be worth a little bit of money too."

"I imagine."

"Was he land poor, Dicey?"

"I used to think so. He'd complain about his property taxes and say he might have to sell the farm if they kept goin' up. But as far as I know, he never sold an acre of ground."

"Hmm. So now Angela owns the farm. Why do you think he left it to her instead of Dale?"

She held her hands over her plate and rubbed her fingertips together to get the crumbs off. "I didn't know Chester till we got to be neighbors some twelve years ago. That's when I moved just up the road from him, but it was years before we became friends. So I don't know what happened between him and Dale." She put her elbows on the table and began rubbing her eyes. "But from some of the things Chester told me from time to time, I know Dale was a lot of trouble when he was growin' up. Chester said Dale drove his mom crazy—that was Chester's first wife, Elma—and it was even worse for Marcia because by the time she came along Dale was a lot older. She just couldn't handle him, especially after her accident."

"What happened?"

"She got bit by a snake. Chester told me a copperhead got her while she was hangin' out wash. After that snake bit her, she was never the same, Chester said. She was nervous and sickly.

She had the shakes a lot, and she'd cry for hours on end. Chester thought the snake's poison must have affected her nerves. He said it got to the point where she was almost helpless." Dicey's eyes narrowed as she said, "Believe you me, I watch where I walk when I go outside, and I keep the grass mowed nice and short around my house."

In the booth behind Dicey, a big heavy guy in Oshkosh coveralls half turned around and said, "If you want to keep snakes away, lay yourself a thick hose around the edge of your yard. That'll do it."

"Poppycock," she said to him.

"Try it. You'll see."

She scooted toward me and lowered her voice: "I don't think Chester would've disinherited Dale for somethin' he done as a boy. My guess is it was because of what he done to Angela."

She left the thought hanging till I asked what Dale had done, and then she frowned again. This time several creases appeared in her otherwise wrinkle-free brow. It made me wonder if she owed her fairly smooth face to cosmetic surgery, though until now she hadn't struck me as a woman who would get a facelift. "I don't know what all happened between them," she finally said, "but some years back Chester told me Dale had cheated on her almost from the day they got married. Chester had no truck with infidelity. He disapproved of divorce too, but he did not hold it against Angela for divorcin' his son. It was all Dale's fault. Dale abused her, Chester told me. He felt sorry for Angela. He said she was a good wife and mother. He told me so more than once. He knew she was havin' problems with Kelly. She had to work, and she couldn't keep an eye on him all the time, so he got in with the wrong crowd. Chester was glad when she asked him if she could send Kelly to stay with him."

She went on talking about Chester and Kelly—the things Chester had done for the boy, how much Chester loved him, and Chester's determination to do a better job with him than he had with Dale. By the end of our lunch I knew more about the Marcotts than any other family in Meridian County.

On our way back to the *Gleaner* I said, "What about Angela? You said Dale was abusive. Do you think she's safe, since Dale got cut out of the will?"

Dicey's dress fluttered in the breeze, and for a moment she had the brisk, bright-eyed look of a young woman. "Let's just say, if it was me, I'd think about puttin' some extra locks on the doors."

"Do you think she'll sell the farm?" I asked.

"Maybe . . . eventually. At the lawyer's she said she wants to move into Chester's house with Kelly and start fixin' the place up. The two of them've been stayin' at a motel the past few nights."

There was one other thing on my mind, but I kept it to myself. Dicey had said that Chester's lawyer put the value of his estate at more than $2 million. I figured that must include the money Chester had received for the land he sold Walmart—land that once belonged to Abner Richards. It was prime commercial real estate, a big piece of land on the main drag. At $7,000 an acre, his 200-acre farm was worth $1.4 million. It was easy to see how his estate could be worth more than $2 million, counting the house at the lake and the money from Walmart.

I walked Dicey back to her truck and saw her off. Then I did something I had been meaning to do for several days: I took the latest *Mothermucker* out of my desk and went over the names of the Klansmen. Next, I asked our society editor, Eunice Gormley, the county's gossip-in-chief, to look at the list of names and tell me if any of the men were still alive.

"Sure, give it here," she said. I pointed out the names, and she tilted her head back to read them through her bifocals. "I don't recognize all of them," she said, "but I know Glen Okovic and Henry Barker are still with us. And Joe Betz and Aloysius Green—that must be Allie Green. And a few months ago I had some news in my Campbellsville items about Charlie Ford and old Mr. Sayers—Wendell Sayers. Both of them are in nursing homes, last I heard. Of course, there might be others that are still alive or moved away."

"That gives me something to start with," I said. "Thanks, Eunice."

"You're welcome. I hope you're not going to say they were in the Ku Klux Klan."

"I won't say that unless I know for sure."

"I wouldn't touch it with a ten-foot pole," she said. "You'll make a ton of people mad."

A ton was 2,000 pounds, so I estimated that if Eunice was right, I'd make about ten people mad. Not bad, I thought—the *Gleaner* could afford to lose ten subscriptions. But the number could go a whole lot higher if the six Klansmen had a lot of relatives.

Step two in my investigation was the telephone book. All six names that Eunice had given me were listed.

There was no answer at Glen Okovic's place. At Henry Barker's, a woman who said she was Mrs. Barker told me he was taking a nap and she didn't want to wake him. There were three nursing homes in Campbellsville, and I located Charlie Ford and Wendell Sayers in the first two I called. I decided to drop in on them right away, before they kicked the bucket.

Charlie's son, an old man himself, happened to be visiting when I showed up at the Campbellsville Convalescent Home. He told me his father had recently had a stroke. He tried to make him sit up straight, but Charlie kept leaning sideways, staring at the TV with his mouth open.

Old Mr. Sayers was in the Twin Lakes Health Center. He lived in the assisted-living section and looked perfectly fine;

however, when I tried to talk to him, he got up and strolled over to the nurses' station, where he started moving things around on a desk. An aide in a red shirt guided him back to his chair. "He's trying to help us," she said. "We let him help, unless he has company."

That was enough investigating for one day. I spent the rest of the afternoon in my office. Later, on my way home, I picked up a pizza at Papa John's and ate it while I watched the so-called news on TV. It was like watching News for Dummies. To help us dummies understand the news, just about every other story contained a clip from a movie or sitcom. I caught myself leaning sideways, staring at it with my mouth open.

CHAPTER 12

THE POSSE

IT was a year and a half since the first time I had played detective, and the tingling in my belly was back. It was a blend of excitement, vainglory, and fear—fear because I had nearly gotten myself killed more than once, yet here I was, playing the game again. The urge was irresistible, so the next day, after lunch, I drove out to Chester's farm.

As I crossed the ridge above Zumma, I saw a long column of smoke unwinding in the distance. My first thought was that Chester's house was on fire. I raced down the hill, slowed as I went through the sleepy town, wondered how it got the name Zumma, and then stepped on the gas again. The smoke grew thicker as I approached the farm, and it wasn't until I reached the stone fences that I saw the smoke was coming from beyond the house and off to the right. The fire itself was out of sight.

I parked in front of the porch and walked around the side of the house to get a better look at the fire. Sadie began barking like crazy in her pen. The blaze looked dangerous. Fat orange flames engulfed a heap of smashed furniture and other debris. The smoke was so black it resembled an oil-well fire. Through the clouds of smoke the sun was a faint white disk that appeared and disappeared.

Kelly came out the back door lugging a big box of trash. He staggered down the steps toward me and the fire. "Hey, Phil, what are you doin' here?" he asked, half out of breath. "You come to help me clean out the house?"

"I thought it was on fire," I replied, tagging along with him.

He hiked his load a few inches higher. "Naa," he said. "Everything's under control." His gray T-shirt was soaked with sweat.

"You want some help with that?"

"No thanks. I got it."

"You need a wheelbarrow . . . or a truck."

"I'm okay."

I followed him down the path toward the pond. It was a good-sized triangular pond that covered at least an acre. Feeding it was a small creek that came from the west side of the farm. The creek had been dammed up to form the pond. I had not realized how high the dam was. On top of it were two Adirondack chairs and an old bathtub, which, as I could tell from the fishing tackle scattered on the ground around it, was used for holding the catch of the day.

I let Kelly struggle on toward the fire by himself while I sat myself down on one of the chairs to admire the view. It was a pretty spot. The way the ground rose toward the house reminded me of a famous painting of a girl lying in a field and looking up a hill at a house, but I couldn't think of the name of the artist or the name of the painting. I told myself one or the other would come to me. I watched some buzzards soaring over the farm and hoped they wouldn't bombard me. After a minute or two, frogs began croaking.

I shifted my chair to watch Kelly. He lugged his load toward the fire, stopped several feet short of the flames, and dropped the box on the ground. He shook the kinks out of his arms and then began tossing pieces of broken furniture into the flames.

When he finished, he walked away from the blaze and pulled his T-shirt up to wipe his face. When he saw that I was still on the dam, he gave me a wave, and I waved back.

Suddenly he froze with his arm in the air. Then he whirled around and took off running through the smoke toward the woods beyond the back of the farm. I turned to see what had spooked him. A police cruiser had just arrived at the house. Its lights were flashing, but its siren was off. Now, however, it made two loud whoops and started down the hill. The siren began screaming. Angela Marcott came out the back door of the house, stopped to see what was going on, and ran after the car.

Kelly had a long way to go to the woods. There was no way he could outrun the car, and there was no place to hide. Much of the farm was last year's stubble. Stupid kid, always running, I said to myself.

Or maybe he wasn't so stupid.

The cruiser bounced buoyantly through a field of daisies as it picked up speed. At the bottom of the hill, the ground leveled out in front of the dam, and when the car got there, four fantails of water sprayed out from behind as it plowed into the seepage area in front of the dam. The spray became muddy, and in a few seconds the wheels were buried in standing water.

The siren went on screaming until someone switched it off. I recognized the voice of Deputy Jesse Holsapple yelling, "Dammit! Dammit! Dammit to hell!"

Kelly stopped running and turned around. He shaded his eyes with his hand, then took off again.

The car doors swung open, and Sheriff Eggemann and his deputy stepped out into the muck. They weren't happy when they saw me grinning at them from the top of the dam. The sheriff raised a bullhorn to his mouth and aimed it at Kelly. "Attention, Kelly Marcott," he said slowly and firmly. "This is

Meridian County Sheriff Carl Eggemann. I have a warrant for your arrest for the murder of Chester Marcott. I am ordering you to surrender."

Kelly kept glancing over his shoulder.

Holsapple extricated himself from the far side of the cruiser and marched through the marshy water until he reached higher ground on the face of the dam below me. He glared at me again and then sat on the ground to empty water out of his boots. With some difficulty he got the boots back on and started running after Kelly, sort of. Jesse was more than a little chubby, and he couldn't run very fast.

The sheriff kept repeating his order through the bullhorn until Kelly's mother came running diagonally down across the dam. She was wearing a UCLA sweatshirt, and her hair was wet. "Are you out of your mind?" she yelled at Carl. "Kelly didn't kill his grandfather. What's the matter with you?" Carl glanced up at her, then resumed ordering Kelly to surrender.

Kelly kept running.

Loping after him, Holsapple pulled his pistol out of its holster and fired two shots in the air.

Angela screamed.

Kelly began zigzagging.

Carl lowered the bullhorn and unhooked a walkie-talkie from his belt. I hurried down the dam to hear what he'd say.

"No more shooting, Jesse," Carl said over the walkie-talkie. "Understood?"

Holsapple's voice crackled, "Understood, Sheriff."

Carl said. "I'm going to call the jail and get more men out here. We'll catch him. You keep after him, but no more shooting."

Carl got back in the car to radio the jail. I figured the radio worked because the Sheriff's Department had an antenna on top of the old fire tower on Zumma Hill. I heard the sheriff talking to a dispatcher named Deborah, pronounced De*bor*ah. First he told her to send out any deputies and special deputies who were available. "We'll be searching deep woods," he said. "Tell the boys in the posse to bring their horses, pronto." He also said she should call the State Police Post in Versailles, pronounced Ver*sales,* to see if they could send a K-9 unit over here. "And," he added reluctantly, "we need a wrecker to pull a cruiser out of the mud."

Angela was still staring at Kelly's shrinking figure. I climbed back up the forty-five-degree slope to join her.

"What are *you* doing here?" she demanded. "Did you come with the police?"

"No. I came to see you."

"What for?"

"I want to talk to you about Chester."

"I've got nothing to say to you."

"Why? What did I do?"

"Hah, as if you don't know."

The sheriff waded through the watery ground and climbed the dam. By the time he reached us, he was panting hard. "What the devil brings you out here today, Phil?"

"Working, Sheriff. Just like you."

"Working, huh?" His chest rose and fell. "If I see a picture of that cruiser in the paper, don't you ever even think of talking to me again."

"Carl, it never occurred to me to take a picture of that car. But now that you mention it. . . ."

"I'm warning you, Phil."

"Come on, Carl. What happened to your sense of humor?"

Angela took one step toward the sheriff and said, "Why are you chasing my son?"

Carl said, "A warrant's been issued for his arrest, ma'am."

"That's ridiculous! Kelly didn't kill Chester."

"The evidence suggests otherwise."

"What evidence?"

Carl held back a few seconds, then said, "We found the murder weapon, ma'am. Your son's fingerprints are on it."

"What murder weapon?"

Carl hesitated as if deciding whether to release the information. "A baseball bat," he finally said. "It was found in the kitchen."

Angela gaped in disbelief. Then she stammered, "You, you think Kelly hit Chester with a baseball bat? That, that's insane! Kelly couldn't do that. And why would he leave the bat in the house if he used it to kill Chester? You think he's stupid? Don't you think he would've got rid of it?"

Calmly Carl said, "I'm sorry, ma'am, but people don't always do the rational thing, especially when they're under stress."

Angela snapped at me: "You think Kelly killed him too, don't you? I saw what you put in the paper. Anybody reading it would think Kelly killed him."

I said, *"I* don't think Kelly killed him."

"Then why did you say he was kicked out of school?"

"I said he was suspended."

"You made it sound like he *must* have had something to do with it. You said Chester took away certain photos that Kelly found—photos of the Ku Klux Klan. For God's sake, you made it sound like Kelly killed him to get those pictures back!"

"You're twisting what I wrote."

"Like fun I am."

Her choice of words surprised me. I would have expected *like hell,* not *like fun.* "I think the story was fair to Kelly," I said. "It even gave his theory of the murder."

"Yes. He thinks the Ku Klux Klan did it because of that story he wrote." She got after the sheriff again: "That's who you should arrest, the Ku Klux Klan, not my son." She clutched the back of her neck with both hands. "This is nuts. God, it's a nightmare. How can this be happening?" She squeezed her face between her forearms till the sides of her elbows touched.

The fire made a loud pop, and the rifle-like sound made her jump. Her arms fell to her sides, and some of the toughness in her face went away. "I need to put the fire out," she said. "If it gets windy. . . ."

"That's a good idea, ma'am," Carl said.

She grimaced as if she didn't need him to agree with her. To no one in particular she said, "Where I live we worry about wildfires."

"I thought you lived in Los Angeles," I said. "You don't get wildfires in the city, do you?"

"We could where I live, in Eagle Rock. Kelly and I have an apartment at the foot of the Verdugo Hills. The hills are covered with dry weeds. The whole thing could go up in flames, houses and all."

"That's no good."

"Tell me about it."

Carl said, "Where do you think your son's going now, Mrs. Marcott?"

"I don't go by 'Mrs. Marcott' anymore. We're divorced."

"Sorry, ma'am. Do you know where Kelly might be going?"

"I don't have the slightest idea."

The three of us watched Kelly roll over the stone fence in the distance. He took one last look at Holsapple, who was only a third of the way from the bogged-down cruiser to the fence. Then he ran toward the woods, which seemed to swallow him.

"If I'm not mistaken," Carl said, "that's the Hoosier National Forest out there. Off to the west is the Charles C. Deam Wilderness Area. I hope your boy doesn't get lost in there, ma'am."

Angela walked away in a huff.

I followed her toward the fire. About ten feet from the blaze, she bent down and picked up the end of a garden hose. She loosened the nozzle and began spraying the flames. When I caught up with her, I saw that the hose was actually a series of connected hoses that came down from the house.

"That's a lot of hoses," I said.

"No kidding."

The wind shifted, and the smoke was in our faces. We tried to sidestep the swirling cloud, which seemed to pursue us.

"Do you think you'll stay here?" I asked. "I understand Chester left you his farm."

"How do you know that?"

"Dicey Cockerham told me. Do you know Dicey—Chester's friend?"

"We met at the funeral."

"She lives just up the road from here."

"Yes." She went on circling the fire and dousing the flames.

I said, "Dicey told me Chester left her his cabin at the Lake of the Woods Club. It's a house really, not a cabin."

"I know. I've been there in the past. It was nice of him to leave it to her."

"It sure was," I said. "What do you plan to do with the farm?"

The question seemed to irritate her. She moved away without answering. The fire hissed whenever the water hit it. Finally she said, "I don't know what I'll do. I haven't had time to think about it." She appeared to think about it for the next three seconds, then said, "Maybe Kelly and I will stay here. He could finish high school—that is, if they don't put him in prison, which it looks like they mean to do."

I thought she was going to cry, but she held back the tears and continued hosing the charred rubble. The smoke followed us as we circled the blackened area in the field. I got to wondering . . . if Kelly's seventeen, how old is his mother? I did the math. She looked like she was still in her twenties, but that would mean Kelly had been born when she was no more than twelve. If she'd had Kelly when she was sixteen, she'd now be thirty-three, about a year older than I was. If she had waited till she was eighteen, she'd be thirty-five. . . .

I picked up a rake that was lying on the ground and helped separate the chunks of smoking wood. "You must have been close to Chester for him to leave you most of his property," I said.

She shook her head. "Not really. We hardly ever saw each other after Dale and I moved to California. That was over ten years ago. Then we broke up. But Chester kept in touch. I have to admit, he made more of an effort than I did. He always sent Kelly something special for his birthday and at Christmas . . . a nice watch . . . a ruby ring that belonged to his father—Chester's father I mean . . . an old gold coin now and then." Her voice quavered. "Poor Chester. He liked being a grandfather. I think he wished Dale and I had stayed here instead of moving to LA. The move was Dale's idea." The sheriff approached while she was speaking, and her voice grew louder: "Chester was thrilled when I called up last Christmas and asked him if it was okay if Kelly came and stayed with him for a while. I knew it would be. Chester loved Kelly. And Kelly loved him." She teared up again and said, "Kelly never would have hurt him."

Carl said, "Last time I was here, there was some talk of a treehouse your son has out in the woods. You wouldn't happen to know where it is, would you?"

"No I would not," she said.

"Did your boy ever say anything about it to you?"

"No."

He fell silent. He was obviously unconvinced. "All right," he said. "If there's anything else you'd like to tell me, give me a call, would you, please."

"I have nothing else to tell you."

Carl nodded once, then headed toward the house.

When he was out of earshot, Angela said, "I think I'll go after Kelly too. I need to make sure nothing happens to him."

"I wouldn't do that if I were you," I said. "You could get lost in the woods, and you don't want to interfere in a police investigation."

"I don't plan to 'interfere,' but I've got to do something."

"What you can do is get Kelly a lawyer."

Her right hand went to her mouth, but instead of biting her nails, she curled her fingers into the palm of her hand. "You're right. I'll do that," she said.

A police car arrived in a cloud of dust, and two more sirens became audible in the distance. Angela and I followed the sheriff around the front of the pond.

While the sheriff was talking to his men, I sneaked my camera out of my car and grabbed a few shots of the bogged-down cruiser from the top of the dam.

I thought about following Kelly and Holsapple into the forest, but I took the advice I had given Angela and stayed put. Instead of getting lost in the wilderness, I could photograph the posse going after Kelly—if it showed up. The Meridian County Sheriff's Department Posse usually just rode in parades. It would make a good shot if I could get men on horseback galloping toward the knobs. . . .

A few minutes later two long horse trailers came up the lane between the pear trees. My plan changed again. I raced back to the pond and started hoofing it across the field to beat the posse to the forest. I alternated running and walking, and when I looked back and saw the posse coming toward me, I ran as if the riders were chasing me.

I reached the stone fence about two minutes before the posse. I climbed over it and ran several more yards.

The horses came galloping across the field, the riders yelping like cowboys. I clicked off shots as fast as I could with my old Nikon.

I got a great shot of the first horse and rider jumping the fence, with the rest of the posse in the background.

CHAPTER 13

HELLO, I LOVE YOU

By the time I got back to the house, two more police cars had arrived, and Sheriff Eggemann was busy organizing his manhunt. Angela was standing on the porch, biting a fingernail. She stopped biting as I approached.

"Where were you?" she asked me.

I held up my camera. "Out by the woods."

"Oh, I thought you left."

"Not yet." I stopped at the foot of the steps. She looked angry and afraid. "Are you okay?" I said. It was a dumb question, but so what.

"It's a nightmare," she said. "Those horses. The yelling and laughing. It's a game to them. I expect to see them dragging Kelly back here at the end of a rope."

I thought she was about to cry. "I know what you mean," I said.

"It's all my fault. I never should have made Kelly come here. He wouldn't have written about the Ku Klux Klan, and Chester would still be alive."

I climbed the three steps to the porch. "You sound like Kelly," I said. "He blames himself for Chester's death."

"If anyone's to blame, it's me, not Kelly."

Sheriff Eggemann hurried over to the porch and asked Angela for permission for some of his men to drive across the top of the dam and through the field.

"Do I have a choice?" Angela replied.

"I have a warrant for your son's arrest," Carl said, "but if you don't want us to tear up your winter wheat, we'll go around it."

"I didn't even know it was wheat," Angela said. "Go ahead, tear it up if you want to. Just don't hurt my son, please. He's not a killer."

"Thank you, ma'am." Carl tipped his Cincinnati Reds baseball cap and returned to his men.

"Don't worry," I told Angela. "They won't hurt Kelly. Carl will make sure of that."

We watched a convoy of three police cars plow single file through the wheat. The cars contained a total of seven men— the sheriff, four regular deputies, and two special deputies. Adding the five members of the posse who were already in the woods, much of the county police force was now pursuing Kelly. If a crime wave broke out today, the citizenry would have to depend mainly on the Campbellsville Police Department and a few state troopers who were stationed in the county.

When the convoy reached the untilled cornfield, the cars split up and headed in three directions: northwest, north, northeast. Angela stared blankly as the cars diminished in size. She licked her lips, and our eyes happened to meet. She looked away.

"You know what," I said, "I could use a cup of coffee. How about you?" She didn't answer. Several buzzards soared over the farm. There was no way to put a positive spin on that. "Come on, Angela," I said. "I'll make the coffee. I'm real good at it."

Slowly she turned and faced me. She looked weary, hope-less, defeated. I thought she was going to tell me to buzz off and leave her alone, but instead she said, "The coffee maker got smashed, but I have some instant."

We went inside. The living room was nearly empty. The furniture that was totally wrecked had been removed. Only the gutted sofa and a wingback armchair were left. They seemed to stare at the opposite wall as if wondering where the TV was. The dining room was even emptier, but the kitchen was more or less normal.

Angela took a small jar of Folger's out of the refrigerator. "I hope this is okay. It's old, but it's all I have."

"As long as it's still coffee, I'll drink it. But give it to me. I said I'd make it."

"I think I can handle it."

I would have sat at the round pedestal table in the corner, but there were no chairs, so I stood in the archway between the kitchen and dining room and watched her run water into a dented tea kettle. When she turned the stove on, it made a pop-pop-pop sound as the flame appeared. She seemed conscious of my gaze. I made an effort to focus on the back of her head so she wouldn't catch me looking at her figure. When she turned around, our eyes met, and I wondered if she could see electricity shooting out of my ears. I said, "Where do you think Kelly will go if he gets away from the police?"

Her lips tightened inward as she thought. Finally she said, "He'll probably go to his father. Dale told him where he's staying."

"Where's that?"

"In a motel."

"Which one?"

She folded her arms. "Why do you want to know—so you can tell the police where Kelly might be?"

"No. Whatever you tell me will be confidential." When she did not reply, I added, "I'm programmed to ask questions for

the data banks in my head. It's for future reference, that's all."
It sounded like gibberish.

"I'm sorry," she said. "That was rude of me. I'm just worried about what will happen to Kelly if the police catch him."

"Don't worry about that. You can trust Sheriff Eggemann."

"That's not what's worrying me." She hesitated, then opened up: "Kelly's been in trouble with the police before. He was on probation. I had to get special permission for him to leave LA and stay with Chester. It wasn't easy."

"What did he do?"

The kettle started whistling, but she ignored the shrill noise. "Promise you won't put it in the paper?"

"I promise."

"Okay. He sold some pot to a couple friends of his at school. It wasn't much, just a few grams, total. He wasn't trying to make money. He just wanted to get back what it cost him. But the word got around, and he was arrested. It was a first offense, so he didn't have to go to jail, but now he's got a record for selling drugs."

"The sheriff probably knows about it already."

"Damn." She puffed out her cheeks. Her lips fluttered as she let the air out. *"Damn it!"* She turned off the stove and lifted the kettle. It shook in her hand as she poured the water into a mug and a cup. "God, I'm a nervous wreck. You want some milk and sugar? No, there's no milk. We finished it at breakfast."

"That's okay. Black is good, and I never use sugar. I'm sweet enough." She didn't laugh. "Let's sit out front," I said.

It would have been nice to sit on the porch with a hot cup of coffee and look at the scenery, but the police cars and horse trailers that were scattered on the lawn were a constant reminder of what was going on in the woods. It was the Day of the Horse: a line of low gray clouds moving in from the west resembled a battalion of seahorses with curly tails dangling over the knobs.

"Angela," I said, "are you going to be okay out here?"

She shrugged. "We'll see."

"I don't think you should stay here by yourself."

"What do you have in mind?" she asked as if she already knew.

I laughed it off. "Do you have any friends or relatives you could stay with?"

"In Martinsville I do. That's where I grew up."

"I know. Pastor Bob mentioned that in the talk he gave at Chester's funeral."

"That's right. He did."

How'd you meet Dale?"

"At a basketball game in Martinsville. I was a cheerleader. Go Artesians! He came to the game with some friends from down here. At halftime he walked up to me and said, 'Hello, I love you, won't you tell me your name?' I found out later it was a line from a song."

"Good line. He stole it from The Doors."

"He made me laugh. I should have told him to get lost. It would have saved me a lot of grief." She sipped her coffee. Then she let out a little sigh and rested her cup on the arm of her chair, but she continued to hold it. "I should have known better. He was a junior. I was a sophomore. I was only fifteen, young and dumb. I started going with him."

"How'd you manage that? Martinsville must be something like seventy miles from here."

"It's not that far, and there's a good shortcut. You take Indiana Highway 135 into Brown County. Stay on 135 till it makes a sharp left turn at a big old grocery store. Instead of going left, go straight ahead onto a county road that goes to Pike's Peak. When you get to Pike's Peak, you turn left and go to Stone Head, where you pick up 135 again. Go north on 135 till you get to Indiana 46, then go west to Bloomington. Stay on 46 through Bloomington till you get to Indiana 37. Go north on 37 to Martinsville. You'll save several miles if you go that way."

"It's still a long trip."

"Yes, but Dale had a motorcycle and a car. He came to see me four or five times a week. And he phoned me every night."

"What a romantic guy."

"I thought so. I really fell for him. It was the biggest mistake I ever made. There were warning signs. I never should have married him. But I got pregnant in high school."

"Maybe you shouldn't have married him," I said, "but I don't think you should look back either. I don't believe in regrets. We do what we think is best at the time. Look at it this way—if you hadn't fallen for him, you wouldn't have Kelly."

"I know," she said. "That's what I tell myself."

I blurted out, "I had a busted marriage too."

"You did? I'm sorry."

"I was sorry too, for a long time."

"What happened?" she said.

"She found another guy. I wasn't rich and exciting enough."

"Oh. She sounds like a—never mind, I won't say it."

"You don't have to. I said it all five years ago." I raised my mug to my lips and peered at her over the top of it. Her face rose in relief from the green hills and graying sky. I didn't like the sweatshirt she was wearing. Was she trying to hide her figure? You're an idiot, Larrison. Why would she do that? And besides, she'd have to work at it more—she'd have to wear a burkha.

She had beautiful eyes. Her nose tilted upward just the slightest little bit. I had a weird urge to get up and kiss the tip of it. "Maybe you should check into a motel in town," I suggested. "It might be dangerous staying out here in the boondocks by yourself."

"I'll be all right. There's a gun right next to my bed—a big shotgun that belonged to Chester."

"Would you have the nerve to use it?"

"I don't know. But I need to stay here in case Kelly comes back. I want to be here for him. We're in this mess together."

"Okay, but keep that gun handy."

It was almost noon. I set my mug on the floor and stood up. "I'd better get going," I said. "I'd like to stick around till the cops come back, but I need to go to work. My boss will be wondering what happened to me."

"You'd better go then."

"I'll call you later to check on Kelly, okay? Maybe he'll show up after the police leave."

"If they don't shoot him!"

She followed me to the door and watched me get into my car. I looked behind me as I backed away from the porch, and when I turned around to wave goodbye, she was gone. That was a downer.

CHAPTER 14

SOMEONE TO TALK TO

WHEN I got back to the *Gleaner,* Ed grumped, "Where have you been all day? I was beginning to think you quit."

"No, Ed. Where else could I find such a high-paying job."

"Very funny, Philip. Har-har-har."

I told him how the sheriff had tried to arrest Kelly and how he had sent for the posse to track him down him in the forest.

"Did they catch him?" Ed said.

"I don't know, but I got some good shots of the mounted posse jumping a stone fence," I said.

"Find out if they caught him."

"Yes, Boss, I will do that."

He grinned and said, "That should sell a few papers." He started for the door but stopped. "I won't be in tonight. My wife's dragging me to Louisville for a play. She's got tickets to Actors Theatre." He paused, then added, "Maybe I can get out of it."

"Go to the play, Ed," I said. "I'll make sure the press crew doesn't forget to print the paper."

At 4:30 I called the jail to see if the sheriff was back.

He wasn't, so I called again at 5:30.

"Jeez, Phil, I just got in," he crabbed. "Give me a minute to catch my breath."

"Sorry, Carl. I just wanted to ask you what happened today. Did you catch Kelly Marcott?"

"No."

"What happened?"

"He got away. That's what happened."

I felt kind of bad for feeling glad. I was losing my objectivity. My credibility would be the next thing to go.

Carl went on: "We weren't in the Wilderness Area, but we might as well have been. Those woods are thick, and the hills are steep. We need a K-9 unit in this county. I put in for one in my last budget, but the county council, in its wisdom, turned down my request."

"Would you like me to put that in the paper, Carl?"

"I would not like that one iota." He sucked air in noisily, then blew it into the phone. "I'm too old to be climbin' up and down those damn hills."

I laughed at the rare "damn." Then I dragged some information out of him about the hunt for Kelly. It was like pulling teeth.

After hanging up, I went to work on a detailed story about the warrant that had been issued for Kelly's arrest and the hunt in the hills. I described how Kelly had fled into the Hoosier National Forest as soon as he saw the sheriff's car with its flashers on. I had a hard time deciding whether to include the fact that a police cruiser had gotten stuck in the mud below the dam. In the end I decided I had to include it. Carl wouldn't be happy with me, but if I left it out, readers would wonder why the sheriff hadn't gone after Kelly right away in the car.

I thought about calling Angela to ask if Kelly came home after the police had left, but I doubted that he would have shown up that soon. And if he actually had returned, would

Angela tell me? She might be afraid I'd notify the police and put it in the paper. I wasn't sure what I should do. My instinct was to print the news. My first duty was to my readers. On the other hand, if Angela would refuse to talk to me unless I promised it would be off the record, well, I could go along with that.

I phoned her at the only number I had for her—Chester's. There was no answer. Where was she? Just not answering? Was Kelly there? I was tempted to race back to her house, but I had tons of work to do.

I called Judge Maxwell, who had issued the warrant for Kelly. I thought I'd ask him if Kelly would be tried as an adult and see if that opened up any other lines of questioning, but the judge was out of town, so I called the county prosecuting attorney. He told me he had just been given the case and had nothing to say about it at this time.

In addition to my own story, I liked to check everything else that the staff churned out. We had a news editor and a sports editor, and there was Ed too, but I tried to check everything anyway. I was far too anal. Anal people can't be happy. But if a single mistake got past me, I'd be miserable for one, two, or three days, depending on how big the mistake was. And there were always mistakes.

• • •

I WASN'T terribly hungry, so I skipped supper to lose some weight. That gave me the extra time I needed to finish my story and look over the other stuff we had for the front page, as well as a couple of features.

At 9:05 I got my third or fourth cup of coffee and went to the composition room. We made up pages on computers now instead of pasting them up on the slanted tabletops, which were still there from before the time I joined the staff as a reporter. I helped lay out the front page, and I wrote a three-column headline for the story about Kelly:

Grandson Is Charged
With Marcott's Murder

Now all I had to do was hang around and check the late stories coming in. There were no meetings on Friday night, and spring sports wrapped up early. The main thing was to see if anything major had occurred on the national or international scene. The *Gleaner* did not run much news about the world outside Meridian County, just the major stories from AP.

With the pressure off, I went to the front office and stared outside through my reflection. Behind the Courthouse, the tree on which Abner Richards may have died took on an eerie amber sheen from the streetlights. Was it really the same tree? It was a giant, thick oak, so it probably was. In the press room at the back of the building, bells rang and cylinders jogged as the crew attached plates. A spell of loneliness crawled over me. I thought of Angela, alone in her empty farmhouse. I wondered if she felt lonely too. I thought about calling her again. She wouldn't be in bed already, would she? It wasn't even ten o'clock. Or I could take a ride out there and make sure she was okay. Maybe I'd spot a cop staked out somewhere, waiting to nab Kelly if he came home.

I went back to my office and tapped in her number. I felt kind of jumpy, like a little kid calling a girl for the first time.

She picked up on the first ring. "Hello?"

"Angela, it's me—Phil." I always felt guilty when I used bad grammar, but *it's I* was just too awkward."

"Oh. Hi." She sounded disappointed. She probably had been expecting Kelly.

"Have you heard from Kelly yet?"

"No, nothing."

"The police didn't catch him."

"I know. I saw them come back on their horses. I went out to see if they had Kelly with them. They said he got away."

"That's right."

"I don't know if that's good or bad. Now he's a fugitive. He's probably afraid to come home in case the police are waiting for him, but he can't stay out in the woods all night."

"He's got some kind of treehouse," I told her. "Maybe that's where he is."

"A *treehouse?* He never said anything to me about a treehouse. How do you know that?"

"Dicey told me about it. Don't go looking for it. You'll get lost in the woods."

"A treehouse—that's the first piece of good news I've had all day. Maybe he can stay warm." She seemed to relax a little bit. "I've been worried sick about him. I was going to go shopping just to get out of the house, but I thought Kelly might come back while I was gone, so I stayed here." She took a deep breath. "God, I'm going crazy. I jump every time I hear a noise, and this house is full of noises. I wish Kelly would come home and the two of us could go back to LA and act like none of this ever happened. It's making me a nervous wreck."

"Is there any other place you can go for a while?"

"Until today I was planning to go and visit my parents. But I can't now, not with Kelly gone. I never should have sent him here. He was better off in LA."

"Listen," I said, "if you ever need help, give me a call, anytime."

"Are you a psychiatrist? That's what I'm going to need, the way I'm going."

"Maybe you *should* go see your parents. I don't think you should stay in that house by yourself."

"I have to be here in case Kelly comes back."

"Yeah, I understand. But as long as you're by yourself out there, if you ever need someone to talk to, give me a call."

She laughed and said, "I'll keep that in mind." I thought she was going to hang up, but she added, "Thanks, Phil, but you don't have to worry about me. If somebody breaks in, I'll hear him. I'm a light sleeper, and there's a double-barreled shotgun right next to my bed."

CHAPTER 15

THE EXALTED CYCLOPS

I HAD trouble sleeping that night. I kept waking up and worrying. Not just about Angela. My so-called investigation of the Klan was going nowhere. At 2:30 a.m. I dragged myself out of bed and took some Tylenol. That helped me get to sleep. In fact, I slept so well that I didn't wake up again till 9:45.

Damn it, Larrison, you should have set the clock.

I heaved my legs out of bed. My head swam as I got up. I staggered to the bathroom like a drunk. On the plus side, as I studied my nearly 200-pound body in the mirror, I thought I might be a pound or two lighter this morning. My teeth seemed a shade whiter too. Maybe it was the light. Whatever it was, these seeming improvements made me feel slightly better about myself. If I could lose just two pounds a week, in a month I'd be down to 190 again.

For breakfast I had a cup of coffee and a slice of toast, that's all. I didn't feel hungry, so why eat? I phoned Angela to make sure she was all right, but there was no answer.

A copy of the *Mothermucker* lay on my desk. I did not relish the idea of working the list and trying to find the guys who were still alive. They could be anywhere, and they were probably too old and decrepit to have done the kind of damage I had seen at Chester's house. Then too, some other Klansman whose name wasn't on the list—or some relative of his—may have murdered Chester. Not only that, but the killing may not have had any connection to the Klan. Maybe Deputy Bobb was right—maybe the killer was someone who was hunting for the money that Chester had supposedly hidden in his house. Speculation was futile. Maybe I should just forget the whole thing.

But I still had the names of the four men who Eunice Gormley had said were still alive: Joe Betz, Glen Okovic, Henry Barker, and Aloysius Green. I couldn't give up without talking to them. Even if they had nothing to do with Chester's murder, I might get a clue to who did. If nothing else, I might learn if any other old Klansmen were still alive. I might get lucky. One of these old lynchers, fearful that his days were numbered and his soul was headed for hell, might break down and confess to lynching Abner Richards, murdering Chester Marcott, or both crimes.

I looked up the four names on whitepages.com, but I did not phone them. I jotted down their addresses. Better to take them by surprise. I drank another cup of coffee and began to take a bite out of a doughnut, but I stopped myself and put it back in the box. The act of self-denial made me feel stronger. I went to the bathroom again and wet my hair, dried it with a towel, put a dab of gel on it, rubbed it in, and combed it. Then I put on some clothes that didn't need to be ironed.

It was a clear, crisp, sunny day. I got in my car and went looking for Glen Okovic.

I found him on the east side of town. He had a first-floor apartment in a shabby two-story complex behind a strip mall on Main St.

"What can I do you for?" he said in a gravelly voice before I finished introducing myself. He was short, thin, and slightly stooped, with faint wisps of hair combed sideways across a blotchy scalp.

We talked in a dim living room with a few pieces of old, heavy furniture on a threadbare rug. We got off to a chatty start. For some reason he thought I was the sports editor of the paper and asked me what I thought of Cincinnati's chances of winning the pennant this year. That led to a long autobiographical account of his baseball-playing days. He seemed happy to have someone to talk to, and I thought it would be a snap to get him to reminisce about the Klan.

I asked if he had happened to read my article about Chester's murder.

"I did," he said. "It makes you wonder what this world is coming to when a man's not safe in his own home." He glanced around the room as if killers were about to come through the windows.

"Chester's grandson, Kelly, has been charged with the murder," I said. "It's in today's paper, the *Gleaner.*"

"I seen it." A scowl creased the side of his mouth. "So the boy killed his own grandfather?"

"I don't think so, and Kelly denies it."

"That's what you'd expect him to do, ain't it?"

"Kelly thinks Chester was killed by someone who wanted to shut him up."

"I seen that in the paper too."

I was impressed. He still read the paper. I wondered how old he was. If he had participated in the lynching of Abner Richards, I figured he would have had to have been at least eighteen years old at the time, which would make him ninety-three or more today. He looked every bit of it.

"Mr. Okovic," I said, "Chester's grandson wrote an article in a school paper naming a number of men who were in the Klan in the 1930s."

"What's your point?"

"Your name is on that list, sir."

"Is it?" He pushed himself out of the chair. "It's been nice talking to you. Goodbye." He turned his back to me and started toward the front door.

I remained in my overstuffed but uncomfortable chair. "Were you a member of the Klan, Mr. Okovic?"

Without answering, he opened the door and stood with his back against it. His slightly bent posture suggested that of a humble servant.

Still sitting, I said, "How do you feel about Kelly Marcott's saying that someone who was—or is—a member of the Klan killed Chester to keep him quiet about the murder of Abner Richards?"

He tried to clear his throat, then reached for a hand cuspidor setting on a windowsill. He spat into the container and closed the lid. "We're done talkin', Mr. Larrison," he said. "Now you get yer ass outta here."

"Don't you want to respond to Kelly Marcott's accusations?"

There was a flicker of interest in his eyes, as if he were tempted to say something, but he shook his head and said, "I do not." He stared at me and pushed the screen door open. A sunny shimmer that resembled a rainbow dappled the screen.

As I left, I said, "Thank you for your time, Mr. Okovic. If you change your mind and want to—"

"You have a lot of nerve," he said. "I want you to leave." If eyes could kill, I would have been dead.

From Okovic's house I went a few miles north on SR 11 into Bartholomew County and turned right on a road that connected with US 31. I went a few miles north on 31 and found Joe Betz sitting in front of his house. He was barefooted, and a dog was licking his feet. A sea of weeds surrounded the house, which had once been a general store and a filling station. Two old pumps with glass globes on top of them still stood out front.

I followed a short path made of flat creek-bottom stones through the weeds. Mr. Betz did not raise his eyes until I was about six feet away from him. As soon as I introduced myself, he growled, "Get offa my property."

"I'd like to talk to—"

"I got nothin' to say to you." He didn't look like a man who was more than ninety years old. He was stocky and overweight and had a drooping belly. His short white hair reminded me of a worn-down toothbrush.

I said, "I'd just like to ask you a few questions, Mr. Betz. I believe you were in the Ku Klux Klan back in the 1930s, weren't you?"

"What are you, some kind of moron? Don't you understand plain English? I got nothin' to say to you. Get outta here."

The dog was still licking his feet, which as a result were extremely clean. The front door creaked open, and a big blonde in her forties or fifties stepped out of the house. Her breasts bulged in a tight T-shirt, and her thighs oozed out of cut-off jeans. "What's the problem, Pop?" she said as she chewed a wad of gum, or maybe it was a wad of tobacco. She peered at me as if deliberating my fate.

"I'm from the Campbellsville paper," I said. "I'm writing a story about the Ku Klux Klan. I understand your dad used to be a member of the Klan."

The big blonde said, "Oooh, a smartypants." Her gaze slid below my belt as she went on: "You ain't fed Butch yet, have you, Pop? Why don't you tell him to eat this guy's pecker."

Betz leaned forward and spat at my shoes. He missed by an inch and grinned at my displeasure. The beast kept licking his feet.

"That's a fine animal you've got there," I said to the blonde. "What else does it lick?"

I shouldn't have said that. It was unprofessional. I was stooping to their level. But it felt good. A barrage of four-letter words bounced off my back as I walked to my car.

This time I drove to the south side of Campbellsville, where Aloysius Green lived in the Jar-Nel Trailer Park. I wondered what the name stood for—Jarvis and Nell maybe.

When I knocked on the door, a woman inside the neighboring trailer shouted, "They're in Illinois—with the carnival."

Her face was hidden by a venetian blind that covered a small horizontal window. "When will they be back?" I asked the window.

"What do you want?"

"When are they coming back from Illinois?"

"Are you a friend of theirs?"

"Yes."

"You want to leave a message?"

"No thanks."

"You a bill collector?"

On my way to the car, I glanced at the trailer's front window, which curved out over a bed of tulips. Filled with reflections of fluffy white clouds, the grid of small windowpanes resembled a wall of TV screens, each carrying part of a huge image. The woman seemed to hover among the clouds as she watched me leave.

The last name on my list belonged to Henry Barker. He lived in a Tudor-style mansion in what used to be the most exclusive part of Campbellsville. I found him and his wife out front on a spacious, well-kept lawn. He was lounging in the shade on an aluminum chair while a stout, fairly attractive, and much younger woman walked slowly around the lawn, looking at flowers while gabbing on a cell phone. She ended the call as I approached. I introduced myself, and we shook hands.

"It's nice to meet you, Mr. Larrison," she said. "I'm Eve, Henry's wife." She looked about twenty years younger than her husband, but that still would have put her in her seventies.

With some effort, Mr. Barker pushed himself out of his chair. A tall, thin man with a full head of white hair, his movements were rickety, but his voice was firm. "So you're the famous Phil Larrison," he said, shaking hands. "I'm surprised we haven't met before." He had a polished, professional bearing. "It's an honor to meet you. I believe I've read every word you've ever written in the *Gleaner.*" I wondered if I was about to get the sandwich treatment: phony praise, genuine criticism, phony praise. "Let's go inside and talk," he went on. "The bugs are getting bad out here, and we're barely into spring." With a sarcastic laugh he added, "It must be global warming."

"I told you to spray yourself," his wife scolded. "You never listen."

"Did you say something, dear?" He laughed at his own question and led the way into the house.

Either Mrs. Barker was an excellent housekeeper or she had an excellent cleaning woman. Nothing seemed out of place, and I didn't see a speck of dust. A brown leather sofa and two matching armchairs faced one another across a glass-topped cocktail table. I suspected the top of the table was made of glass so it wouldn't hide too much of the oriental rug that the furniture was standing on. A similar grouping lay at the other end of the room, and plush wall-to-wall carpeting lay under everything, including the rugs. When we sat down, I felt as though I should keep my feet in the air.

Mrs. Barker offered me a glass of lemonade, which I accepted.

"Henry?" she asked.

"Yes, I'll have one too, please," he said.

While she went to get our drinks, Barker said, "You've had some very interesting articles in the paper lately, Mr. Larrison. I'm referring to the ones about Chester Marcott, of course."

"Thank you," I said. "As you may already have guessed, that's what I came to talk to you about."

"Ah-hah." He seemed amused, flattered. "I can't say I'm surprised, Mr. Larrison. May I call you Phil?"

For half a second I considered saying no, but of course I said, "Of course."

With extremely careful steps, Mrs. Barker came back carrying two glasses of lemonade. They were only two-thirds full, no doubt to avoid sloshing the lemonade out. She set them on the cocktail table, then put a coaster in front of me and moved one of the glasses onto it. She did the same for her husband. With both hands, his long fingers reached for the glass. Without further ado, his wife left us alone.

Barker raised the glass of lemonade to his lips, again using both hands.

"Have you seen today's paper, Mr. Barker?" I asked.

He nodded as he sipped his lemonade, then said, "Yes, I have."

"Then you know that Chester Marcott's grandson, Kelly, has been charged with his grandfather's murder."

"Yes."

"He says he's innocent."

He chuckled. "What would you expect him to say? He wants to pin the crime on the Ku Klux Klan. But he has no proof, has he, Phil? All I've heard—or rather, all I've *read*—are unfounded allegations."

"The grandson's theory is not unreasonable," I said. "If someone was afraid Chester had evidence that could be used to identify the men who lynched—"

" 'If' . . . 'could be' . . . it's mere speculation." He set his glass on the coaster and sat back with his arms crossed at his waist.

"Mr. Barker," I began.

"Call me Henry, Phil."

"Did you know that Kelly has identified you as being a member of the Klan when Abner Richards was lynched."

He stiffened in surprise. "I was not aware of that," he said. "If that's the case, I believe I'll have to talk to my lawyer about it."

"Kelly also says he's seen photographs of the men he identified."

This time he feigned surprise: "Oh? Really? Then where are they? Have *you* seen them? Do you have them? If so, I wish you would show them to me."

It was warm in the house, and I began to feel hot. I hoped it didn't show. I drank some more lemonade. "Do you deny that you were a member of the Klan?" I asked.

"You haven't answered *my* question, Phil, so why should I answer yours?" He inhaled slowly. The long breath pinched his nostrils together and turned into a yawn, which he tried to stifle by keeping his mouth closed. "Let me put it this way," he went on. "I'm not ashamed of anything I've done. But under the present circumstances, I don't see what I have to gain by answering your question. There's no evidence that the Klan murdered Chester Marcott. And besides, the last I heard, the Klan was a secret society. If I belonged to a secret organization, I would respect its privacy."

"So you don't deny that you were in the Klan?"

"I neither deny nor confirm it. It's none of your business."

"Well," I said, "we'll see how you respond if the photos turn up."

"Another 'if.' I don't believe any such photos *will* turn up. I don't believe they exist. I don't believe they ever existed."

"We differ on that, sir."

"Obviously. But you have no proof of their existence. Just hearsay."

"It's more than hearsay."

"Is it?" One side of his mouth opened in a wry smile. "Then produce the photographs." As if tired all of a sudden, he leaned his head back and looked at me along the sides of his long, straight nose. His hairless nostrils reminded me of a double-barreled shotgun. "You know what I think?" he said. "I think the most likely reason Chester got killed was money. You touched on that possibility in one of your articles. You reported a rumor that money was hidden in the house. Is that what newspapers should do—report rumors? Well, as a matter of fact, there may be some truth in it." He paused for effect. "Did you know that Chester was a coin collector?"

"I've heard something along that line."

"I understand he had a large collection of gold coins. But I haven't seen it with my own eyes, so you can call it hearsay, but I do believe it's true."

"How do you know it's true?"

He stared at the ceiling as if trying to recall. "I don't remember. It was at a meeting, years ago." He thought some more. "It may have been a United Way board meeting. We were tossing around names of people we could tap for large pledges."

I said, "I heard a rumor that he had a fortune in gold hidden in the house."

"I heard it was a coin collection."

Just then Mrs. Barker returned. "Excuse me," she said. "Henry, I'm going to the hairdresser. Then I have some errands to do."

"Take your time, dear."

She smiled at me and said goodbye.

After she left, Barker said, "She's always doing something, running off somewhere."

"She's very nice," I said.

"That she is. I wouldn't have married her otherwise." As an afterthought he said, "She's my third wife. My first wife died.

My second one was no good—I divorced her. Eve is wonderful. I'm blessed."

I tried to catch him off guard: "What was your rank in the Klan? Off the record, were you the imperial wizard or grand dragon or what?"

He chuckled softly. "You're flattering me. No. Those offices are much higher than mine. As long as you promise not to put it in the paper, I'll tell you what my position is."

He pushed himself out of his chair and waited for me to promise, which I did. Then he proudly said, "I am the exalted cyclops, president of the Meridian County klavern of the Ku Klux Klan."

"Thanks for telling me," I said. "I never knew an exalted cyclops before."

"I know it's become popular for newsmen to mock the Klan," he went on. "The Klan is an easy target for the media. But look around the world today. Look at what's going on in Africa—tribal warfare, genocide, terrorism, the most savage forms of violence. Doesn't it prove that the Negro is not the same as the white man? Negroes obviously can't govern themselves. They slaughter one another like animals in the jungle. The Klan seeks to maintain the purity of our race, for white people *are* the superior race. If we dilute our race through interracial marriages and misguided social policies, eventually we will fall into the same kind of savage anarchy we see in Africa and other parts of the world. Our way of life will be destroyed. When more people realize this, the Klan will rise again."

"You know," I said, "some people might say that anyone who thinks he's superior to everyone else is actually inferior."

"I'm disappointed in you, Phil. That rejoinder is beneath you."

As we reached the front door, he laid a surprisingly strong hand on my shoulder and said, "I hope you won't mind if I offer you a word of advice. Don't blame the murder of Chester Marcott on the Ku Klux Klan. You'll upset some very good people and cause nothing but trouble."

"Thanks. I'll consider myself properly threatened."

He acted surprised. "I'm not threatening you, Phil. It's just a word of advice. You can take it or leave it."

"Fair enough," I said. "I'll leave it."

CHAPTER 16

HUNCHES

As I drove back to my apartment, things began to disappear—the lines in the middle of the street, a letter in the middle of a word on a billboard. It was the first sign of a migraine coming on. My migraines were caused by stress. Stress and eyestrain, the doctor said. This one was all stress, courtesy of Henry Barker. Would I wake up in the middle of the night and find a cross burning in the backyard? Would I wake up at all the next morning?

I stiffened my arms on the steering wheel and tried to hold off the migraine. There was no headache yet, so I kept driving. The headache started when I had trouble parking the car along the curb.

By the time I got inside my apartment, my field of vision was shrinking. Short rows of tiny bright connected silver triangles were flashing like strobe lights. I lay on the sofa and closed my eyes. The auras got worse, but the pain began fading. I told myself to stop thinking. . . .

The phone woke me up. At first I didn't know where I was. Then I reached backward behind my head and fumbled with the receiver. "Hello?" My voice sounded scratchy.

"Phil? Is that you?" Angela said.

"Yes." I sat up and glanced at the clock. It was 2:55. I'd been asleep since before noon. The auras were gone, but I didn't feel quite right.

"Are you okay?" Angela asked.

"Yes. . . . It's just a headache. . . . I get migraines." I had trouble forming the words. Was I having a stroke? You're too young to have a stroke, I said to myself. But maybe I wasn't.

"I'm sorry," Angela said. "I'll let you go."

"No, I'm okay now. . . . What can I do for you?"

"Did you take anything for your migraine?"

"Uh-huh. . . . I'm okay. . . . How about you? . . . You okay?" Quit saying okay, I told myself. You sound like a parrot.

"I'm good," Angela said. She hesitated, then added, "I just had a call from Kelly."

"Really? That's great. Where is he?"

"I don't know. He wouldn't tell me. He just wanted to let me know he's all right. And he *swore* to me that he didn't kill Chester. Of course, I knew he hadn't. He was on the phone less than a minute. He said the line might be tapped. He didn't want the call to be traced."

My head felt a tad clearer. "He needs to turn himself in," I said.

"I know. I tried to tell him, but he said, 'So long, Mom,' and hung up."

I wondered if he was with his father. I kept the thought to myself. "Well, at least you heard from him," I said.

"Yes. It's good to know he's all right, but I'm still worried."

"Sure."

"I'm thinking maybe I'll go visit my parents for a day or two. I'd like to get out of this house. It gives me the creeps."

"I don't blame you. Get outta Dodge."

"But then I wouldn't be here for Kelly."

"You need to think of yourself too."

I wondered if Kelly was with his grandparents in Martinsville. I was about to ask Angela if Kelly may have gone there, but it occurred to me that if he was right about her phone being tapped, the Meridian County police would hear me and have him picked up by the cops in Martinsville. But so what? It wasn't my job to help Kelly stay out of jail. Besides, if the cops were listening in, they had already heard Angela mention her parents. They weren't stupid. They'd get the same idea I had. Sheriff Eggemann might be on the phone with the Martinsville police right now.

"Angela," I said, "do you think Kelly went to your parents' house?"

"Hmmm. That never occurred to me. It's an hour away, and he doesn't have a car."

"Maybe a friend took him."

"Oh God, that settles it. I'm going up there. You might be right—maybe that's where he is."

"Or maybe not. I'm just guessing."

"I don't care. I'm going."

"Okay. If you find Kelly, make him turn himself in."

"I'll try."

I thought about offering to go with her, but she had said she wanted to visit with her parents a day or two, which meant I'd have to drive another car in case we didn't find Kelly and she stayed behind. Even so, if I felt sure he was there, I would have gone whether she wanted me to or not. I would have tailed her all the way to Martinsville. But it was an incredible long shot, and I had too many other things to do.

After we hung up, I felt completely at sea. I didn't know what I should do next. It took an effort of will—it seemed like a major decision—to make a cup of coffee. While I waited for the water to boil, I thought about what I had suggested to Angela—that one of Kelly's friends may have driven him to Martinsville.

Maybe his girlfriend, Glorie. Maybe *she* was helping him hide from the police. I was on a roll. I had made another decision: talk to Glorie.

The wife of our sports editor, Steve Carpenter, worked in the office at the high school. Her name was Kim. I called her to ask if she could give me Glorie's last name.

"Sure, Phil. It's Kovacs. Why? Is she in trouble?"

"Not that I know of."

"She's on the tennis team," Kim said. "You want to talk to Steve?"

"It's not necessary. You told me what I need to know."

"Here he comes."

"Okay. Thanks, Kim."

The phone changed hands, and Steve said, "Hey, Phil, what's up?"

"Hi, Steve. I'm sorry to bother you at home."

"That's okay."

"I just needed a name. Kim gave it to me."

"I heard. Glorie Kovacs. She plays number-1 singles. She's pretty good. She's only a junior, so she'll be back next year."

While he was telling me how good she was, I looked up the name Kovacs in the phone book. There was only one listing: Kovacs, T. Preston, 24 Persimmon Trace, Campbellsville. I had no idea where Persimmon Trace was. I asked Steve if he knew.

"Yeah, Shale Creek Golf Course. She's got a tennis match Monday. I thought I might get some pictures. We haven't done much with tennis this year, and the girls are 5-and-0."

"Sounds good to me."

"I thought maybe four or five shots, if we have the space."

"That's your call, Steve."

Steve was a good sportswriter, but he had some problems with grammar. Last week I caught "between he and Crockett" in one of his stories. I had a little talk with him about it. I explained that prepositions take the objective case.

After we hung up, I called the home of T. Preston Kovacs.

A woman answered with a sunny "Hel-lo-o." I introduced myself as Phil Larrison from the *Gleaner* and asked to speak with Glorie. Her voice turned fake grumpy as she said, "I wish you *could* speak with her, but she's not here."

"Oh. Is this Mrs. Kovacs?"

"Yes."

"Do you know when she'll be home, Mrs. Kovacs?"

"Call me Mae. No, I don't know when she'll be home. We were supposed to go shopping together in Bloomington, but it looks like she stood me up. Would you like to leave a message for her, in case she does come home one of these days?" Her voice was bright and lively again, like the music in the background.

"Uh, no. Thanks though." I heard myself speaking in rhyme. "Does she have a cell phone, Mae?"

"No. I'd call her myself if she did. She *did* have a cell, but she got in a little wreck because of it, and her father took it away. What's this about, Phil? Why do you want to talk to her?"

"We're thinking of doing a photo feature on the girls tennis team."

"Oh, that would be nice."

"Well, thanks, Mae. I'm sorry I bothered you."

"No bother, Phil. If you find Glorie, tell her I'm still waiting for her."

I doubted that I would find Glorie, but if I did, I had a hunch I'd find Kelly too.

CHAPTER 17

NUMBER-1 SINGLES

THE tennis match was well under way when I arrived. I joined two dozen or so parents and students on a small set of bleachers alongside the first court, where Glorie was playing. About another dozen fans, mostly mothers, were scattered on lawn chairs behind the five courts, watching the matches through the tall green cyclone fence. Glorie had already won the first set, 6-0. Her serve was too much for the other girl.

30-love . . . 40-love. . . .

Steve Carpenter was on the job, roaming from court to court inside the fence. Right now he was stooping on the orange clay between the number-3 singles and number-1 doubles courts, grabbing shot after shot—thank God we didn't use film anymore.

The Lady Highlanders looked good in their new uniforms: dark-green polo shirts, short blue-and-green tartan skirts, and bright-green tights that flashed like shiny balloons whenever they had to stretch for the ball. I watched Glorie toss the ball high in the air and reach to slam it over the net for another ace. I felt sorry for the girl from Jennings County.

When the second set was 3-0, I hopped off the back of the bleachers and joined our coach, Pete Bledsoe. He was standing behind the fence on a grassy rise where he could watch all five matches at the same time. When Pete was in high school, he had advanced to the state finals his senior year, and though he was slightly paunchy now, he was still said to be the best tennis player in the county. We talked about the team in between his occasional shouts of encouragement to the girls:

"Come on, Tammy. You can do it."

"Nice work, Denise."

Glorie ran to the net and smashed her opponent's feeble return past her, then waited there to shake hands. The other girl barely touched fingertips, but Glorie didn't seem to mind. She wiped her face with a towel, picked up her water jug and tennis bag, circled around the end of the fence, and reported to Coach Bledsoe.

She had short auburn hair, gray eyes, and sharp features, which gave her face a Swedish quality.

"Good job," Pete said. "What was it, 6-0, 6-0?"

"Uh-huh, she's only a freshman." Glorie pulled off her headband and used it to wipe her face.

"That's all right," Pete said. "You took care of business."

With a quick, self-effacing smile she said, "All I had to do was get it over the net." I liked her smile. She didn't show a lot of teeth.

"Give yourself more credit," Pete said in his slow, encouraging voice. "Sometimes when you have a weak opponent, it makes you play poorly yourself. You didn't fall into that trap. You put her away."

"She put herself away."

The number-2 singles match was in the third set, and the Campbellsville girl was complaining about the last line call her opponent had made. Pete ran down and called her over to the fence. Glorie headed for the bleachers, and I tagged along.

"You're a friend of Kelly Marcott, aren't you?" I said.

She looked at me as if I had accused her of something. "So?"

"So nothing. I saw you at his grandfather's place at the lake about a week ago. You dropped Kelly off there."

"He needed a ride. His bike got wrecked."

"Do you have any idea where Kelly is now?"

"No."

"Do you know the police are looking for him?"

"Who doesn't? It's all everybody's talking about."

One of the girls on the bleachers yelled, "Glorie, come on! Hurry up! We can't win without you!" The JV girls erupted in laughter. They sounded like a gaggle of geese.

"When was the last time you saw Kelly?" I asked.

"Excuse me," she said. "Coach wants us to watch the other matches." She ran to the bleachers. The short skirt flapped gently as she ran. She had nice legs, nice everything. I felt like a dirty old man watching her.

As she approached the girls, some loud-mouthed boy said, "Of course he done it. The cops are searchin' for him as we speak."

Glorie dumped her things on the ground and said, "Shut up, Raymond Surenkamp. You don't know what you're talking about."

"Oh don't I? Your Mr. Hollywood is a convicted drug dealer—in case you don't know."

Another girl shot back, "You just don't like him because he said we should drop basketball."

Raymond forced a laugh and said, "They'll drop math and English before they drop basketball. At least basketball makes money. How much money does tennis make?"

"Just ignore him," a third girl said.

Coach Bledsoe ambled over. "Hey, keep it down, okay?" he said. "They're still playing out there."

In lowered voices the boys went on badmouthing Kelly. One of them said, "When they catch him, he should be tried as an adult and get ten years."

After a couple more minutes of this, Glorie picked up her things and said she had to go.

"You can't leave," one of the girls said. "The match isn't over yet."

"I've got stuff to do."

"Let's sit somewhere else—away from the Three Stooges."

The Stooges laughed. In a mocking, high-pitched lilt Raymond Surenkamp said, "Bye, Glor-i-aaaa."

She lugged her water jug, tennis bag, and a stack of books toward the student parking lot alongside the school. Under a rosy sun her long shadow trailed on the grass. As she reached the lot, a husky, dark-haired young man in a tight black T-shirt got out of a pickup truck and yelled, "Hey, Glorie, c'mere. We need to talk." She glanced at him but did not stop. He ran after her, grabbed her arm, and swung her against the side of a car. Her books went flying, and sheets of paper exploded from them like birds. I started up the hill.

The guy held her by the shoulders against the car and got in her face. She glared back at him. Then he pulled her away from the car and shoved her against it again.

I broke into a run and yelled, "Hey, knock it off!"

He turned on me and waited. "Who the shit are you?" he said with a South Hoosier redneck twang.

I was pumped. "Leave her alone," I told him.

He was taller than I was and a lot more muscular. If it came to a fight, he'd win. Even if I was in shape, he'd win. "Get lost before I call the cops," I said.

He sized me up and sneered. "Screw you." He gave Glorie a disgusted stare and said, "You better wise up, that's all I can say." He glared at her, then went back to his truck and drove away.

Glorie dragged a wisp of hair out of her eyes and stooped to pick up her books. Several written sheets of paper swirled around like litter. I chased them down and carried them back to her.

"Thanks," she said.

"Are you all right?"

"Uh-huh."

"What was that all about?"

"Nothing."

"Then I'd hate to see *something.*"

"We used to go together. He thinks he owns me."

"Watch out for that kind."

"No kidding."

"Who is he?"

"His name's Curtis Davis. He graduated last year."

She looked at her reflection in a car window and raised a shoulder to wipe sweat off her face. Then she went to her car, the yellow Beetle, and I went to the Focus wagon, the company car I was using.

I followed her out of the parking lot. I wanted to see if Curtis Davis was lurking up the street, waiting to follow her. I also wanted to see if she would lead me to Kelly.

She led me a couple of miles to 24 Persimmon Trace at the Shale Creek Golf Course. She lived in a large colonial-style home surrounded by shade trees alongside a manicured fairway. I wondered how much the house had cost. Why wonder, Larrison? You'll never make enough money to live here.

CHAPTER 18

PIZZA TIME

"Hi, it's me," the message from Angela said. It was waiting for me in my voice mail after the tennis match. "I see you called a couple of times. I just wanted to let you know I'm back."

I returned her call right away. "It was good to hear from you," I said. "How'd the visit with your parents go?"

"Not too great. Mom was all worked up about Kelly. Dad kept telling me to get a lawyer. I wished I hadn't gone to see them."

"You did the right thing."

"Then as soon as I got back here this afternoon, I wished I had stayed in Martinsville, because my ex-husband showed up to tell me he's going to contest Chester's will."

"That doesn't surprise you, does it?"

"No, it doesn't surprise me." A note of defeat crept into her voice: "But it's one more headache. I swear, I think he came out here just to get on my nerves. I didn't want to hear it. I told him to get out of my house."

"Your father was right—you're going to need a lawyer."

She inhaled with a soft whistling sound. "Dale said I have no right to be here. He said he would kick me out of the house. I told him to get out before I call the police. I thought he was going to hit me—it wouldn't have been the first time—but he just called me a bitch and left. I locked the door behind him. When he heard the click, he kicked the door so hard I thought it would come off the hinges. He acted like a spoiled brat."

"Maybe you should get a restraining order to keep him away."

"Yeah, right, like that would stop him."

"Do you know where he's staying?"

"I didn't ask. But wherever it is, I know one thing, he'd rather be here. He can't stand it that Chester cut him out of his will."

"I bet."

In the silence that followed, I heard faint, faraway voices on the line. They were barely audible, but I thought I might be able to understand them if I listened hard enough. It made me wonder if someone was listening to *our* faraway voices. Then I remembered what the exalted cyclops had told me about Chester. It tied in with something Angela had said in an earlier conversation.

"Speaking of Chester," I said, "you once told me he used to send Kelly a gold coin every now and then."

"That's right. For his birthday and at Christmas. Why?"

"I was talking to someone over the weekend, and he said Chester had a collection of gold coins. I was wondering if you had come across it."

"No."

"Did Chester have a safe-deposit box at a bank?"

"Not that I know of. When the will was read, the lawyer gave me a list of Chester's assets—his real estate, insurance policies, CDs, all that stuff. There was nothing about a safe-deposit box."

"Have you found any keys around the house?"

"A few in his bedroom, but not the kind that open a lock-box." Her voice rose: "Why? Do you think that's why Chester was killed—for a coin collection?"

"It's something to think about," I said. "All along I've felt that the killer was looking for something. A lot of rooms were torn up, but not every room. If it was a burglary, maybe the crook found what he was after and got out of there."

"That makes sense."

"Or maybe he heard me coming. In that case, whatever the killer was looking for may still be in the house, if it was there to begin with."

"I've been all over the house—the attic, the cellar, everywhere. I haven't found any gold coins."

"Would you mind if I took a look around sometime?" I asked.

"You'd be wasting your time. I've seen every square inch of this place."

"What about the barn?"

"I looked around in there a little, but I can't say I searched it. I'm afraid of snakes. And rats. And spiders." She laughed at herself. "I don't belong in the country. If Kelly wasn't in trouble, I'd go back to LA and take him with me."

"I don't think he'd go."

"I'd make him."

"He'd probably run away first. He's got unfinished business here."

"I know. I know. He wants to put some hundred-year-old men in jail."

"He wants justice."

"So do I. But that's what the police are for. Kelly's just a kid."

She was getting upset. I quit arguing and took a different tack: "Are you hungry?" I asked.

"Huh?"

"How about if I pick you up and we get something to eat?"

"Now?"

"It's supper time—for me anyway."

"Thanks, Phil, but I'm too tired to go out. I feel like a dish rag."

"Then how about this? I'll pick up a pizza and deliver it, with a bottle of wine."

She didn't answer right away. I waited for the final no. Then she said, "You know what? That sounds awfully good."

"Fantastic. What do you like on your pizza?"

"Oh, I don't care. . . . Whatever you like—except anchovies."

"No problem. I'll be there in about an hour."

With a smile in her voice, she said, "Okay. That'll give me some time to fix myself up."

I needed fixing up too. I devoted half an hour to that, and then I phoned in my order to the Brooklyn Pizza Company. While the pizza was baking, I picked up a bottle of Chianti at the Happy Hour Package Store.

I didn't get out much since my wife left me for greener pastures. I could count my so-called dates on the fingers of one hand.

There was a spring in my step as I walked to my car.

• • •

It felt amazingly good to be driving through the country on a balmy spring evening with a pizza on the seat beside me. I kept wanting to snitch a slice. Instead, I popped a few tic tacs in my mouth and tried not to chew them. I wondered if they would set off a chemical reaction with the Listerine I had gargled before leaving. Probably not. My breath was in tiptop condition. What was not in tiptop condition was the rest of me. I needed to lose more weight.

Giant spaniels floated in the soft blue sky. What would Angela say if I asked her to marry me? She'd say, "You're nuts, you idiot." She'd think I was after her inheritance. I could offer to sign a prenup.

I caught myself driving too fast on the country roads. Cool it, Larrison. Keep to the right on the rises. I went up and over the long hill before Zumma.

Angela was rocking on the glider as I approached the house. She stood up when she saw me coming and smiled as I got out of my car. I held up the pizza and wine.

"It's about time," she said. "I'm starving."

"Me too. You're lucky I didn't eat half of it on my way here."

She held the door open for me. I caught a touch of perfume as I passed her.

The gouges in the walls were still there, broken plaster clinging to old brown slats. Angela was wearing dark blue jeans and a plain violet blouse that revealed a tiny chink of cleavage. She looked gorgeous.

I handed her the pizza and trailed her to the kitchen. A vase filled with daisies stood on the table, which was covered with a red-and-white checked cloth.

"Do you think I should warm this up?" she asked me.

"Sure, go ahead. I'll open the wine. Do you have a cork-screw I hope?"

"It's in the cabinet next to the sink, top-right drawer."

She turned on the oven and stooped to get a baking pan out of the bottom of the stove. Her jeans curved snugly around her shapely behind. The banging and clattering she made sounded like a kitchen band tuning up. She pulled out a blackened cookie sheet with orange rust streaks on it. She covered it with a sheet of aluminum foil. The large pepperoni-and-green-pepper pizza hung over the sides of the cookie sheet.

"This looks good," she said. "What a great idea, Phil."

"That's me, always thinking."

She laughed. I hadn't seen her laughing and smiling like this. I popped the cork on the bottle and poured the wine. Our eyes met as we took our first sips. I wondered if she was thinking the same thing I was. Dream on, Larrison, said the voice in my head.

As soon as the aroma of pizza began seeping out of the oven, Angela took it out. "I don't want to burn it," she said. "I'd rather eat it cold than burn it."

We sat at the table with the flowers between us. I slid the vase to one side. I made myself look at her eyes when she spoke. I had a habit of looking at people's lips when they talked. It was a dumb habit that I was trying to break.

Her hazel eyes with their light-blue eyeshadow had no trouble looking into mine. The eyeshadow was the same color as my Accord. She seemed relaxed. I was always on edge, looking ahead to the next thing I had to do. She was beautiful. I believed in love at first sight. In fact I took it a step further: if it wasn't love at first sight, it wasn't love.

"This is good," she said. "Is it hot enough for you?"

I nodded, chewing, thinking, yearning, burning.

"I wish Kelly was here," she said.

I thought about saying, *So do I,* but I didn't want to lie. I made the mistake of saying, "He shouldn't have run from the police."

"He *stopped* running!" she exclaimed. "He was starting to come back. Then that stupid cop started shooting."

That was her take on it. I wasn't sure Kelly *was* starting back. I agreed with her as much as I could: "It wasn't very smart of the deputy to fire his gun."

"It was totally stupid! He ought to be fired!" She seemed to realize she sounded strident. She pushed the reset button: "It scared me half to death," she said in a softer tone. "I'm worried sick about Kelly."

"Do you have any idea where he is?"

"No."

"Do you think he's with his father?"

She shook her head. "I doubt it. Dale might be helping him with money, but . . . I don't know. I imagine the police are watching Dale just like they're watching me."

"How do you know they're watching you?"

"I see them driving by once in a while. Sometimes they stop down the road and sit there. It happens at night too. I *assume* it's the police, but I can't say for sure. It's scary. I hear noises at night, like somebody's walking around outside. I guess it's deer. The house makes noises too. It's gotten to the point where I'm afraid to go to sleep."

"You ought to get yourself out of here."

She shook her head emphatically. "Not as long as Kelly's on the run. One of these days he'll be back. He has to. He'll need clothes, food—everything. He's going to get sick."

"Someone must be helping him."

"I don't know who."

"Do you know any of his friends?"

"No."

"Has he got a girlfriend?" It was a disingenuous question. I just wanted to see if she knew about Glorie.

"If he does, he hasn't told me."

"What about back in Los Angeles?"

She cocked her head as if she hadn't thought of that possibility. "There were girls in his crowd, but they were just friends," she said. "He wasn't serious with any of them. At least I don't think he was."

I chomped into another slice of pizza and debated whether to tell her about Glorie. I decided against it. Angela was getting desperate. I was afraid she would get in touch with Glorie and grill her about Kelly. I didn't want Glorie to get spooked. I was thinking about following her after school, or after a tennis match. She might lead me to Kelly, or Kelly might come to her—but not if either of them thought she was being watched.

After supper, we sat in the living room. The fireplace caught my eye. "Do you ever make a fire?" I asked.

"I think about it," Angela said, "but I'm afraid of burning the house down. It's so old, the chimneys might be clogged with soot."

"Hire a chimney sweep. It'd be nice to have a fire on a chilly night."

"That's a good idea. Maybe I will, when I can afford to."

She turned on the TV to *Wheel of Fortune*. I was pretty good at the word game, but Angela was better. She said she watched it every night.

"I watch it once in a while," I said, "usually with the sound off. I can't stand the screaming contestants."

She laughed and said, "What a grump you are."

"Now you know."

After five minutes or so, I began to feel sleepy. My mind wandered to Kelly. Where was he? Was Glorie helping him hide? Why did I want to find him? I had to stop and think. The wine must have fogged my brain. . . .

I listened to Angela guess at the puzzles. She was really into it.

I remembered what I'd been thinking about. I wanted to find Kelly so Angela could stop worrying about him. I wanted to persuade him to surrender to the police. . . .

I woke up with a start. Angela was tucking a quilt around my shoulders. "What time is it?" I blurted out. I felt kind of grumpy. I always did when I woke up after a nap.

"It's going on 9:30," Angela said.

"That late? I've gotta get to work."

"Work? Tonight?"

"Yeah. I should be there already." I stood up, stiff and groggy. "I'm sorry I conked out. I'm lousy company."

"No you're not."

"Did I snore?"

"A little bit." She smiled. "It was nice."

"Yeah, I bet. I probably sounded like a horse."

She laughed. "I had a good time, Phil. I'm glad you came."

"So am I."

As I started my car, I saw her standing in the doorway. The lonely scene made me sad. I hated to leave her in that house by herself.

CHAPTER 19

LASHING OUT

THE Reverend Mr. Harnish walked into my office the next morning. "Hey, Phil," he said, "have you seen this?" He handed me the latest issue of *Mothermucker*.

"Thank you, Father Bob," I said.

"Phil! You know what the Lord said. Call no man Father. You've got to get over that Catholic stuff."

"I can't help it, Bob. I went to Catholic school."

"I understand. You've got to get over that Catholic stuff."

Kelly's latest gem was a single sheet of typing paper with the *Mothermucker* logo across the top of the front page. The issue was devoted to a single article under a screaming headline printed in red:

Marcott Offers to Surrender
If Judge and Sheriff Resign

I read the headline out loud and groaned a long groan.

Bob said, "Hey, at least he isn't demanding the governor's resignation. Mitch would come down here on his motorcycle at the head of the National Guard and declare martial law till Kelly is hunted down."

Kelly had written a news story about himself under his own byline. I read the first paragraph out loud:

> Kelly Marcott, on the run from the police, has issued a statement calling for the resignations of Judge Vernon Maxwell and Sheriff Carl Eggemann because of their family ties to the Ku Klux Klan. According to Marcott, these relationships were only recently discovered.

I looked up at Bob and said, "He attributed the statement to himself. That's good. Without saying *According to Marcott,* it would be the reporter who's claiming that the ties to the Klan were "only recently discovered." Of course, Kelly Marcott *is* the reporter, so it doesn't make much difference."

"It must be your mentoring, Phil."

"Or yours."

He held up his hands, which looked as big as Ping-Pong paddles. "Don't look at me," he said. "I would never say Vern and Carl should resign. I have only the highest respect for our elected leaders, as long as they're Democrats."

"How do you keep your job, Bob? Most of the people in your church are Republicans, aren't they? Do you have some strange power over them? Are you running a cult?"

"Presbyterians are broadminded people. Even you would be welcome in our midst."

I said, "Do you happen to know where Kelly got his new information about Judge Maxwell and Carl?"

"Me? How would I know? *You're* the detective."

"Yeah, right." I resumed reading in silence. I skimmed Kelly's rehash of his original story about the lynching of Abner Richards. Then, "Here we go," I said. I read the following paragraph to Bob:

Marcott has been running for his life since the sheriff tried to arrest him for the murder of his grandfather, Chester Marcott. "The reason I ran," Kelly Marcott said, "was because I thought my life would be in danger if I got locked up in the Meridian County Jail. I found out that some of the deputies in the sheriff's department had ancestors who were members of the Ku Klux Klan when Abner Richards was lynched in 1936 behind the Meridian County Courthouse in Campbellsville. I could see myself getting lynched if I went to jail, so I ran when the sheriff and his men tried to serve me with a warrant for my arrest for the murder of my grandfather. "Some people say I should have let the sheriff arrest me instead of runnibng away," Marcott said. "They say running made me look guilty. But it's a good thing I escaped, because at that time I didn't know about the sheriff's ancestors being in the Klan." he said. "I ran because I was afraid I would be killed if I went to jail. If the sheriff and the deputies whose relatives were (and maybe still are) in the Klan will resign along with Judge Maxwell, I will turn myself over to the Indiana State Police. I did not murder my Grampaw, and I am willing to stand trial to prove it, as long as as I can get a fair trial somewhere outside Meridian County," he said.

I stared at Bob in disbelief. I couldn't believe Kelly had written such a long, runny paragraph. What had started out as a news story had deteriorated into a frenzy of blame and self-justification, with obvious typos that should have been corrected. I leaned forward and let my forehead clunk on the desk. A giant scratchpad made of sheets of blank newsprint softened the clunk.

Bob said, "It gets a little sloppy there at the end. Kelly got in a hurry. He should've asked you to take a look at it before he published it."

With my forehead and nose still on the pad, my incredulity turned to hysteria, and I started laughing. "Good grief," I said, "did he really write that, or is somebody trying to frame him for murdering the AP Stylebook?"

"I knew you'd like it."

I sat up and stretched. "I need a cup of coffee. You want to go to Mackey's?"

We crossed the square under a high blue sky in which you could still see a faint moon. Suddenly the entire sky seemed to crack into a pattern of fine lines, like a crazed piece of pottery. I wondered if it was a new kind of migraine aura. Or perhaps it was a vision of the impending destruction of the galaxy.

Speaking seriously for the first time that day, Bob said, "I'm worried about Kelly. He's lashing out. I hope he doesn't go over the edge."

"Do you have any idea where he is?"

"No, do you?"

"I'm thinking his girlfriend, Glorie, might be helping him, but it's just a guess."

"It's a thought," he said. "*Somebody* must be helping him hide somewhere."

I gave him an insinuating stare over the top of my glasses.

Bob said, "Don't look at me. I'm not hiding him."

I followed up with: "Where'd you get the latest *Mothermucker?* Did you help Kelly write that story?"

"Damn it, Phil, now you've gone too far. If you're not careful, I'm going to quit giving you my tips and take them to the radio stations."

"Where'd you get the *Mothermucker?*"

"I found it stuck in the screen door this morning."

"Why didn't I get a copy?"

He tossed his hands in the air and said, "How would I know? Maybe Kelly doesn't trust you. Or maybe he doesn't like the way you write."

CHAPTER 20

A HIKE IN THE HILLS

WHEN I finished my fourth or fifth coffee of the morn-ing—I had lost count—I called Angela to ask if she had seen the latest issue of *Mothermucker.*

"No," she said. "Why? What's in it?"

"Kelly's offered to turn himself in, provided Sheriff Eggemann and Judge Maxwell resign their jobs."

"Oh my God! Why did he say that?"

"He says some of their ancestors were in the Klan, but as usual he doesn't give any proof."

She sighed and said, "Oh Kelly."

I went on: "And even if their ancestors *were* in the Klan, it doesn't mean the sheriff and the judge are guilty of anything."

"I know. I'm sure Kelly knows it too, but—I don't know. Can you imagine how scared he must be?"

"Yes," I said, but at the same time I couldn't help wondering if my original impression of Kelly had been wrong. Maybe he wasn't so smart after all.

Angela said, "I feel like going to bed and not waking up."

"How about if I come out? I'll show you what Kelly wrote." Another idea popped into my head: "And I'd like to see if I can find that treehouse of his. Maybe he's been using it. Are you up for a hike in the hills?"

"I don't know. Will we get lost?"

"Probably."

She laughed. "In that case, sure, I'll go with you—but not right now. Can we do it this afternoon?"

I glanced at my watch. It was 9:25. "I've got things to do too. I'll be there around 1:30."

As soon as we hung up, I called the jail to get the sheriff's reaction to Kelly's offer. Carl wasn't in. I wondered if he was just not in for me. He was probably upset with my reporting that his cruiser had got stuck in the mud.

I spent the next hour editing two stories that were waiting on my computer. After that I called a quick staff meeting to see who was covering what tonight. Then I went to Walmart to buy an iPhone. My BlackBerry was old and weak, and I had to have a reliable phone if I was going to search the Hoosier National Forest. I picked out the latest version and let the Walmart "associate" give me a lesson in how to use it.

Back in the car, I thought of Angela again. I was getting obsessed. *Night and day you are the one, only you beneath the moon and under the sun.* I had visited Cole Porter's grave once. My parents made me go with them. We drove from Greencastle up to Peru. Dad said the locals pronounced it Pee-ru. The ride was his idea. It was a kind of pilgrimage. We took the back roads. He liked them better than the interstates. I got carsick and nearly threw up. Mom let me sit in the front seat. Dad was afraid I'd barf all over the car. . . .

Angela was mowing the front lawn, or rather the front meadow, when I arrived. It was a nice day, with fluffy clouds alternately hiding and unveiling the sun. She turned off the mower as I got out of the car.

"How are you at catching moles?" she said, stretching an arm at the ragged network of molehills the lawn mower had chewed through.

"I'm just the paperboy," I said. "Here." I handed her the latest issue of *Mothermucker,* all one sheet of it.

She held it stiffly in the breeze and read her son's offer to surrender. Her forehead creased as she read. When she finished, she looked at me and said, "Does he really expect them to resign? It's—" Instead of coming up with a word, she fluttered her lips:"*p-p-p-p-p-p-p-p-p-p-p-p.*" She finished reading and dropped her hands. "How could he do this? What was he thinking?"

"I could use a cup of coffee," I said. "You got any of that instant left?"

"No, but after you got off the phone I went into town and bought a new coffee maker—and real coffee."

"Thank you."

She led the way inside. I followed the back of her neck. Long ago I realized that every part of a woman's body could turn me on.

I sat at the kitchen table while Mr. Coffee rumbled, then gurgled. Then he sounded as though he was taking a pee.

There was a knock on the back door.

"Now who could that be?" Angela said. She opened the pantry door, and the outside door opened with a screech at the same time. "Dicey," Angela said as if scolding her, "you don't have to come around to the back of the house."

Dicey said, "Your best friends always use the back door. I brought you a little somethin' I made."

"Oh, how nice! Thank you. Come on in. Have some coffee."

"No. I know you have company. I seen the car. Here, I just want to give you this pumpkin bread I made."

"I didn't hear you drive up. Did you walk over?"

"I did. Gas is so expensive these days, $3.89 a gallon now. I can remember when it was 17 cents."

I got up and went to the door. "Hi, Dicey," I said. "Come in. I'm the 'company.'"

"Phil! I didn't know it was you. Well, in that case I *will* stop and visit awhile." Dicey bustled through the pantry, and Angela set the loaf of bread, which was wrapped in aluminum foil, on a plate. "Oh, I see you've been fixin' up the place. The last time I was here it looked like a tornado hit it, didn't it, Phil? What brings *you* here?"

"The latest news from Kelly." I picked up the *Mothermucker* and showed it to her.

A look of concern grew on her face as she read. When she finished, she gave the paper back to me and said, "I don't think they'll quit."

"Neither do I."

"Kids—they think the world revolves around them." She turned to Angela and said, "I think I *will* have a little coffee after all."

"Sure," Angela said. "Sit down. I'm going to slice the pumpkin bread."

"I hope you like it."

"I'm sure I will," Angela said.

"I'll give you the recipe if you want it. I know it by heart."

The discussion went on. When I had learned all I needed to know about pumpkin bread, I asked Dicey if she could tell me how to find Kelly's treehouse.

"More or less," she said. "Chester and me walked up there once. There's an old logging trail that starts on the west side of the stone fence at the county road. The trail's actually on Chester's land—oh! I'm sorry, Angela, I mean *your* land. Your property doesn't end right at the wall, like you might think it does. It ends at the border with the National Forest. There's a sign at the entrance to the forest. The trail goes up and down over the knobs. It's a long hike, but if you keep to the trail, it'll take you to where you're close to the treehouse. It's not far from a cliff where you first see Lake Monroe off in the distance."

"How far is it?" I said.

"I'm not sure. A couple miles or so."

"How did Kelly build it if it's that far away?"

"Chester said his son, Dale, built it when he was a boy. He said Dale carried lumber back in there a few boards at a time. He built it all by himself. Chester said he used cedar so it wouldn't rot. It's in a big old oak tree. It's hard to see it, especially when the trees are in leaf like they are now."

Angela piped up: "I want to see it. Maybe that's where Kelly's been staying. Do you want to go with us, Dicey?"

"I can't. I got work to do. I got *two* houses to take care of now. I've been spendin' most of my time at the lake, fixin' up the place Chester left me. I get real emotional when I'm there." She raised her eyes to Angela's. "I hope you don't feel like I cheated you out of what should be yours."

"Don't be silly," Angela said. "Chester left me so much, how could I feel cheated?"

Dicey's lips trembled. "He was a good man. I miss him a lot. He didn't deserve what happened to him."

• • •

AFTER Dicey left, Angela and I went looking for the treehouse. We took Chester's dog with us. The field between the house and pond was buzzing with bees. The pond held a reflection of blue sky and bright clouds, but when the breeze touched the surface, the reflection turned into a grid-like image that resembled a bit-mapped photo on a computer screen. Beyond the pond was the thick crop of wheat. We waded through the trampled area that the sheriff's posse had made when it galloped after Kelly. Sadie bounded through the field ahead of us.

We climbed over the stone fence where the horses had jumped it. Soon we found the logging trail that Dicey had mentioned. It came from beyond the west side of the farm through a narrow hollow formed by a foothill on one side and the first knob on the other. We followed the trail through some new-growth forest to the foot of the knob. We stepped across a trickle of water in a creek and began angling up the steep hill, which was a few hundred feet high.

Soon I was puffing and sweating. I couldn't keep up with Angela. "Hey, slow down," I said. "You're in better shape than I am."

She waited for me to catch up. "I'm sorry. I'm not used to walking with someone else," she said.

I asked her if she was a jogger.

She nodded. "Uh-huh. I like to run, but I haven't done any running since I got here."

"Do you miss Los Angeles?"

"Only because Kelly got in trouble here. I like being near my mom and dad. They're getting up in years. They were pretty old when I was born. Mom says I was a little bundle but a big surprise."

"How old was your mother?"

"She was forty-three when she had me. She's seventy-six now."

So Angela was thirty-two or thirty-three. She looked more like twenty-three. I was going on thirty-two, but, unlike her, I did not look ten years younger. I was really out of shape. I'd have to start running up and down the knobs with her.

The trail, which was more like a gully in spots, zigzagged uphill. Rain had washed away dirt, exposing loose stones that were hard to walk on. I should have known better than to go hill climbing in street shoes. Fallen branches and piled-up leaves littered the trail. Sadie kept running ahead and loping back.

It took us about twenty minutes to reach the top of the knob. There the trail narrowed and went west along the ridge through an area that appeared to have been clear-cut several years ago. For a while, walking was easy, until our path went down the other side of the hill. It was worse walking down than going up. The hill was so steep and I walked so stiffly that the muscles in my legs began to ache. Then we climbed another hill that was just as steep as the first one.

As we hiked along the second ridge, I began looking for the treehouse. I wondered if we had already passed it, but then I remembered what Dicey had said about Lake Monroe.

The trail went down again, then up another hill.

"I wonder how far it is," Angela said. "Maybe we ought to go back before we get lost."

"We won't get lost," I said. I took my iPhone out of my pocket and asked it a question: "Siri, where are we?"

The know-it-all replied, "You're at Hoosier National Forest, Story, Indiana."

"*She's* a big help," Angela said.

We made it to the top and went down the other side, sometimes lunging from tree to tree. Then we tackled the next knob. At the top we could see Lake Monroe shining like a silver mirror miles away. We couldn't tell where the trail went from here, so we started looking for the treehouse.

After five minutes of fruitless searching, we sat down on a boulder that bulged out of the top of the hill. A light breeze rustled the trees.

"That feels good," Angela said. She lay back and closed her eyes. I sat near her and listened to her breathe. Her chest rose and fell. Staring toward the lake, I noticed a huge tree about fifty feet away. Through its leaves, some of the branches seemed to form a square. That's weird, I thought—until I realized I was looking at the treehouse.

"There it is," I said.

"What?" Angela sounded half asleep.

"The treehouse."

She pushed herself up. "Where?"

I pointed.

She stared where I was pointing. Then she scrambled to her feet and walked in that direction. When she was nearly under the treehouse, she laughed and said, "Now I see it!"

The treehouse had been built on the tree's second tier of branches. Its weathered boards were concealed by the tree's own leaves and by some thick cedars that had grown up into the oak's branches. Some of its massive roots clung to the ridge and snaked down the side of the hill.

I stood beside her, looking up. As the branches had grown over the years, they had pulled the boards apart, even off their bolts in some cases, leaving rusty holes in the lumber. These boards had been reattached to the branches once or twice. I assumed that the latest generation of bolts—the bright silver ones—had been screwed into the tree by Kelly.

What looked like the bottom rung of a rope ladder dangled from a closed trapdoor in the floor of the treehouse. It made me wonder if Kelly, or someone else, was in there right now and had pulled the ladder up. If it was Kelly, he already knew we were there, but I yelled anyway: "Kelly! It's me, Phil Larrison. Your mother's here too. Are you in there?"

There was no answer, so Angela shouted, "Kelly, are you there?"

The gears in my head were turning: I couldn't climb the tree. I wouldn't be able to get my arms around it—it was way too thick. And even if I did somehow manage to reach the two main branches supporting the treehouse, I'd have to turn into a squirrel to get across one of those branches. What's more, there was only a small slit for a window on that side of the treehouse, so I wouldn't be able to get in. But maybe I could get up on the roof. Maybe I could drop down onto it from the branch above it. It was a nearly flat roof with black shingles, and it extended over the sides about a foot all around. If I were Tarzan, I could hang from the edge of the roof with one hand and try to raise one of the wide wooden flaps with the other. Yeah, and then I could fall and break my neck.

"I don't think he's in there," I said to Angela. "See that rope ladder up there sticking out below the trapdoor? Why is it hanging out like that? If Kelly's in there, he probably would've pulled the whole thing in. I bet there's a long branch around here that he uses to put the rope ladder up there when he leaves, and then he lets the trapdoor down on it. When he comes back, he pushes the trapdoor up with the branch and pulls the ladder down. Let's see if we can find a long stick."

"Good luck to us," Angela said. "There are branches on the ground everywhere."

We began wandering through the dead leaves and fallen branches that covered the forest floor. A few minutes later we had covered every inch of ground under the branches of the oak tree. Maybe I had the wrong idea. If there was a long branch or stick, maybe Kelly kept it somewhere else, where he could pick it up on his way here and hide it when he left.

"Phil!" Angela shouted. "I think I found it."

She was bending down underneath the low branches of a cedar tree, looking up into it and reaching for something. I went to help her and saw that she had found a long bamboo pole that was somehow suspended in the tree, no doubt so the bottom of the pole wouldn't be seen standing on the ground. The tree's needle-like leaves fell on her as she struggled to pull the pole out of the tree. When she raised the pole a few inches, it came free.

"Good job," I said.

"Yuck, I'm covered with icky stuff."

"You smell good. And you *done* good." I kind of liked *done good*. It made me sound like a real man.

Angela stood up straight and used the top of her fingers to flick the leaves out of her hair. Then she pulled her shirt out of her jeans and shook off more leaves. I brushed some off her back. Then I carried the bamboo pole to the treehouse. The pole was at least fifteen feet long, with a four-inch hook attached to one end. I reached up and hooked the rope ladder, but I couldn't pull it out from under the trapdoor, so I placed the top of the hook against the door and pushed it up. The hinged trapdoor rose and fell backward onto the floor. Then I used the hook to pull the ladder down.

I had never climbed a rope ladder, but how hard could it be? Answer: very hard. Up I went, twisting and swinging. Sadie began barking at me. I struggled to stay vertical. Angela grabbed the bottom of the ladder and tried to keep it taut. When I finally got myself inside the treehouse and looked down through the trapdoor, it seemed twice as high as it did when I was on the ground.

The treehouse was dim inside, with just a few planes of light seeping in between the boards. I pushed one of the heavy wooden flaps up, then used a couple of 2x2s lying nearby to hold it open. Angela was watching me.

"Do you want to come up?" I said. "I'll come down and hold the ladder for you."

"Uh, I don't think so. What's it like up there?"

"There's not too much stuff. A few posters. A wooden crate and a chair. Some wasp nests. Not much else."

The crate served as a table. A wooden, curved-back kitchen chair stood next to it. I sat down and opened the crate. It contained a clear, zippered storage bag with a rolled-up sleeping bag inside. It also contained a metal cookie can with several packs of peanut-butter crackers. In a corner of the treehouse was a rusty hibachi that looked as if it hadn't been used in years. A stack of magazines that were wrinkled from getting wet and drying out stood in another corner. Three active wasp nests were attached to the ceiling a few inches above my head. The only other items in the treehouse were some faded posters of old rock bands—the Eagles, the Doobie Brothers, and Dire Straits—and a five-gallon plastic orange bucket with a lid. I figured the posters had belonged to Kelly's father when he was a kid. The bucket, which was new and came from Home Depot, was being used as a trash can. Inside it were some ketchup- and mustard-stained wrappings from McDonald's, a few bits of French fries, an empty box of Tylenol caplets, and an empty bottle of Robitussin. The trash did not look as if it had been there a long time.

I stuck my head out the window and called down to Angela: "It looks like Kelly *has* been here."

"I'm coming up."

"Wait, I'll help you."

I went to the trapdoor, but she was already a quarter of the way up. She was afraid to look down. When she reached the treehouse, I took her hand and helped her in. "My legs feel like wet noodles," she said.

I opened the only other window flap. This one provided a long view of the forest. Sadie began whining because both of us were in the treehouse. I pictured Kelly up here by himself. What a change it must have been from Los Angeles.

I gave Angela the tour. I thought about not showing her what was inside the bucket. I knew she'd get upset if she thought Kelly was sick. She took the decision out of my hands by pulling the lid off.

"Tylenol . . . Robitussin. . . . At least he took some medicine."

"Right."

"But he's sick. He must be. He's living in a tree in the woods, in the cold." She shook her head. "I have to find him. I'll make him give himself up. He didn't kill Chester, so the police can't prove he did. How can they prove it when he's innocent?"

"I agree," I said. "He ought to give himself up."

Angela peered out the window I had just opened. This side of the treehouse was near one edge of the hill, which fell steeply down to Salt Lick Creek, a squiggly ribbon far below. Angela gazed into the distance. She wants to see what Kelly sees when he's here, I thought.

Angela said, "Maybe I should stay up here in case Kelly comes back."

"Bad idea," I said. "It's dangerous out here. There are coyotes. And feral hogs—wild pigs. They attack people."

"If it's so dangerous, why did we come?"

"Because we're idiots," I said.

"Kelly should have a gun to protect himself. I can give him the shotgun."

I didn't think that was a good idea. What if the police found the treehouse and Kelly felt he had to protect himself from *them?* I kept the thought to myself.

While Angela took a last look around, I lowered the window flaps and psyched myself up for the climb down the rope ladder. A short 2x2 was lying next to the trapdoor. I figured it was a prop to hold the trapdoor up while the last person descended the ladder. I thought I would be that person, but Angela was afraid to go first.

I wasn't eager to go first either, but someone had to, so down I went, swinging and hanging almost horizontal half the time. Somehow I managed to get down alive and undamaged, and I held the ladder to keep it steady for Angela. When both of us were on the ground, I went back up to the treehouse. With my head, arms, and shoulders inside the house, I raised the trapdoor on its hinges and lowered it onto my head. Then I went down a couple of rungs and propped the door open with the 2x2. Now Angela held the rope more or less steady for me, and when I reached the ground again, I used the bamboo pole to raise all but the last rung of the ladder up into the treehouse. Then I knocked the prop aside and let the trapdoor fall on the end of the ladder. After we hung the pole in the cedar tree, things were pretty much the way we had found them.

It was going on four o'clock. It would take us at least an hour to get back to the house. I had hardly accomplished anything at work today.

On the way back, Angela said, "I'm glad we did this, Phil. My knees are still shaking, but now I know where Kelly might be, at least some of the time. I'm still worried about him, but I'm not as scared as I was before." She turned around to face me. "Would you like to stay for dinner?"

"Yes I would," I said, "but I can't." I told her what I had to do that evening: three meetings were scheduled, and I had to cover one of them. "May I have a raincheck?" I asked.

"Sure."

We held hands as we walked down the steep hills.

CHAPTER 21

DEAR KELLY

A FTER the hike in the knobs, I faced a long night at the *Gleaner.* Denny Abramson, our news editor, had the flu, so our next-best reporter, Judy Wirth, covered the Campbellsville City Council. Madison got to do the Meridian County School Board for the first time, and I took the County Plan Commission, which had a controversial issue on its hands: the homeowners in a new subdivision on the east side of town were fighting to block a farmer from starting a 25,000-hog confinement operation a mile away from them. They were afraid the odor would be intolerable and would destroy the value of their property.

I did not get home till midnight. I felt pleasantly exhausted, pleasant because we had ended up with a good front page. I poured two fingers of Scotch and turned on *Law and Order.* A cop's face filled the screen and frowned in disapproval to make sure viewers understood that a man should not beat a woman to a bloody pulp. I switched to an old Perry Mason episode and sipped my drink.

I slept straight through till 8 a.m., when the telephone rang. I tossed the covers off and staggered to the living room. "Hello?" My voice sounded scratchy from sleep.

"Did I wake you up?" Angela said. "I'm sorry."

"That's okay." I coughed the scratchiness away. "I overslept."

"Oh." She paused, then started afresh: "Phil, the reason I called is I want to get a lawyer for Kelly."

I wondered if he had been caught by the police or turned himself in. If so, Angela should have called me last night. I would have got it in this morning's paper. . . . Knock it off, Larrison—you're acting like a selfish pig. "Is Kelly in jail?" I asked.

"Not that I know of," she answered, "but I was up all night worrying he might be sick. He could catch pneumonia or something, sleeping out in the woods. And what's he eating? He's got to see a doctor. I got an idea—maybe you would put something in the paper saying his mom wants him to turn himself in."

"Sure, why not? If you want to make a statement, I'd be happy to run it."

"And what about the radio stations? Will they carry it too? Kelly might not see the paper."

"I'm sure they will."

"And I want to hire a lawyer. I want Kelly to have one if he turns himself in to the police. I thought you could tell me who I should get. The only lawyer I know is Clyde Goen, Chester's lawyer. Should I call him?"

I said, "If I were you, I'd get M. L. Dunn II."

"Is he a good lawyer?"

"No. *She* is."

"She? You said M. L. Dunn the second."

"Her name's Mary Lou Dunn, but she goes by M. L. Dunn II. Her father was a lawyer. She's the son he never had. Once she gets her teeth into something, she's like a bulldog. 'M. L. Dunn gets the job done.' That's her motto."

"Okayyyyy." The way her voice tailed off, she sounded dubious, but she said, "I'll give her a call."

"Let me know what she says."

"I will. Thanks, Phil. I'm sorry I got you out of bed. Bye."

I had met M. L. Dunn at a party once. She was not your typical Meridian County attorney. She had a petite figure and a girlish, oval-shaped face. The way her chin-length brown hair enclosed it made her face look even more oval than it was. She struck me as the quiet, bookish type—until she opened her mouth and morphed into a fervent feminist, a member of the ACLU, and an outspoken supporter of Jill Stein, who was running for President. Pastor Bob admired her, "even if she is a Quaker," as he put it. He told me that most of her clients were too poor to pay her fees, but she took their cases anyway, especially if they were illegals from south of the border.

I turned on CNN, then went hunting and gathering. I came up with a bowl of Cocoa Puffs, two stale sweet rolls, and an overripe banana. I heated the rolls in the microwave and made a pot of coffee in my French press. It was Wednesday, one of my make-believe days off. The talking heads on TV got on my nerves, so I hit the mute button.

After another cup of coffee, I went to the bathroom and did my routine. I brushed my teeth, gargled with Listerine, shaved, and took a shower. After that, I made myself change the sheets on the bed. They were starting to reek. Then I straightened up the apartment a little bit and took the garbage out back.

At 11:30 the phone rang again. "Hi, Phil," Angela said. "I tried to get you at work, but you weren't there."

"It's my day off. I thought I told you."

"Oh, I'm sorry. You said I should tell you about my meeting with Mary Lou."

"That's right. Did you talk to her already?"

"Sort of. She had another client in her office, but I made an appointment with her for 1:30 this afternoon."

"Good."

"I'll let you know what happens."

"Very good. Call me at the *Gleaner* after your meeting."

"You just said it was your day off."

"It's supposed to be, but I hang out there anyway."

"I think you're a workaholic."

"It's not that. I just don't have enough outside interests."

• • •

I PIDDLED around at my desk for the next hour or so. Then I had another cup of coffee and drove to the *Gleaner,* where I piddled around in my office. Every few minutes I glanced out the window to see if Angela had arrived. On about the fifth glance I saw her pull up to the curb in Chester's old green truck. The door opened with a clunk and a screech. She should have been getting out of a Lexus, not a bulbous-fendered pickup that looked like something out of an old cartoon. Her hair fluttered in the breeze as she climbed out. She was wearing a gray-and-white striped suit and high heels. The driver of a UPS truck did a double take as he drove by.

Angela asked someone in the front office if I was in.

A few seconds later she was standing in my doorway. "Hi," she said. "Are you busy?"

"No." I stood up. "Come on in." I felt ashamed of my office. Two of the panels in the drop ceiling had brown water stains, and every now and then a fluorescent tube flickered.

Angela settled onto a wooden armchair in front of my desk. She was wearing a blue top and blue eye shadow to match. She had cut back on the eye shadow since the first time we had met. Her lips were glossy pink. "Well, here I am," she said.

"Here you are." I thought about saying how nice she looked, but that might imply that she didn't always look nice, and it wouldn't be professional either. "How'd the meeting with M. L. Dunn go?" I asked.

"It went well," she said. "I like her. But when I first saw her, I felt huge." She spread her arms. " She must be a size two, at most."

"Don't let her size fool you," I said.

"I won't. She may be small, but she struck me as being very sharp and tough." Angela's tone turned serious: "I told her what happened last week—how Kelly ran into the forest when the sheriff came to arrest him. I told her the sheriff said the murder weapon that killed Chester had Kelly's fingerprints on it. I said it's an old baseball bat that was upstairs in Kelly's room. I said it must have belonged to Kelly's father when he was a kid. Kelly could have picked that bat up a hundred times since he came here. Just because his fingerprints are on it doesn't mean he used it to kill Chester."

"What did Mary Lou say to that?"

"She said I had a point. She said the best thing Kelly can do for himself is surrender to the police. If he does that, she said she'd be happy to represent him. So then I told her what I talked to you about this morning—putting an open letter from me in the newspaper and on the radio urging Kelly to give himself up. Mary Lou said if I can't get in touch with him any other way, that might be a very good idea."

"I'm glad to hear that."

"So when do you think you can you help me write it?"

I said, "Whenever you like. Right now, if you're in the mood."

"Thank you, Phil." Her voice rose: "I'm so excited! For the first time I feel like everything's going to be all right. I'm practically shaking."

I drummed the palms of my hand on the arms of my chair and said, "So let's do it. Would you like to sit here at the computer and type, or would you rather dictate to me?"

She shook her head. "I can't type. I don't even know what I should say."

"It'll come to you. Pretend you're talking to Kelly. Tell him what you think he should do. Just speak from your heart."

Her eyes began tearing up. "I'm sorry," she said. "I'm a nervous wreck. I'm always on the verge of crying."

I slid a box of Kleenex across the desk. "Cry all you want."

She sniffled twice. "All right. I'll 'dictate' something." She blew her nose and crumpled the tissue. She looked down at her lap and concentrated. Then she got rolling. I did not change a word she said. I wanted her letter to sound like her. My only contributions were the punctuation marks.

> Dear Kelly,
>
> My dear son, I hope you are reading this letter. I want you to know I can't believe that the police think you murdered Grampaw, but they don't know you like I do. I am your mother, and I know you better than anyone in the world. I know you could never kill anybody. When they read this, people might say, "Oh, that's just his mother talking," but they need to know I know my son. And I know you could never do such a terrible thing.

The words came faster as she spoke. I raised a hand to stop her so I could catch up.

"I'm sorry," she said. "How does it sound?"

"It sounds good. You're doing fine."

"Am I? I doubt it." She slipped out of her jacket and let it hang over the back of the chair. She shook the front of her blouse to cool her chest. When I stopped pounding the keyboard, she said, "What should I say next?"

"It's your letter. I'm just the typist." That sounded indifferent, so I added, "You're doing fine, Angela You're speaking from the heart. Keep it up." I leaned back in my chair. Our eyes met, and something clicked. Suddenly we seemed close, very much at ease with each other. I had a dreamlike sense of walking across a wide flat field between the high walls of a canyon. Somehow the letter seemed irrelevant, until Angela said, "Should I tell Kelly I hired a lawyer?"

"Why not?" I said. "Or maybe first you should encourage him to turn himself in and then say you got a lawyer. . . . No, do what you said—tell him you hired a lawyer."

"Okay. What's the last thing you typed?"

I read the last few sentences back to her. Her brow furrowed, and she dictated again:

> Kelly, honey, I want you to know I've hired a lawyer to help us. Her name is Mary Lou Dunn. She's listed as M. L. Dunn II in the phone book. You can call her up and talk to her. She told me you can turn yourself in to her, and she will go with you to the city police or the sheriff's department or the state police, wherever you'd be more comfortable.
>
> Please, Kelly, stop running and hiding. It's not helping your situation. It's making people think you're guilty. We'll get through this together, you and me. Don't be afraid. I love you. You know how much I love you, Kelly. Please, my dear son, do this for both of us. Please!
>
> —Your Mom

She began to cry in earnest. She took another tissue and blew her nose. Then she tossed her tissues into the wastebasket next to my desk and pointed toward the computer screen. "Can you fix it up?" she asked.

"It doesn't need fixing."

"Hah! That's a laugh."

I asked if she'd mind if I held the letter until tomorrow before giving it to the radio guys, and she said, "That's up to you."

I considered offering to take her to the radio stations to introduce her, but I decided not to overdo my generosity to their news departments. If the self-styled *Number-One Station for News* and the *First-with-the-News-Always!* gang wanted to talk with her on the air, they could set it up for themselves.

"You going to be all right?" I asked.

"Yes. Don't worry about me." She got up to leave.

I felt six pairs of eyes on us as I walked her out to the car.

After she drove away, I went back inside and moved her open letter to our website. Then I went home to wash my car. The Accord still looked as good as it did when I bought it around eighteen months ago. After that, I did some food shopping at JayC and picked up a couple of hamburgers at Rally's. I gobbled them up while I watched CNN. Finally, I set two alarm clocks and took a nap on the sofa for an hour and a half.

That night I went back to the *Gleaner* to help design the front page. I had something special in mind for Angela's letter. I wanted it to look like an actual letter on a piece of stationery, so I had it tilted twenty-five degrees to the right, with a drop shadow on the right side and bottom. I kicked myself for not thinking of having her write it in longhand.

Never satisfied, Larrison.

Never happy.

CHAPTER 22

WEAK EVIDENCE

I HAD a good night's sleep, and the next morning I woke up fresh and clear. My head felt as if all the garbage had been flushed out of it.

I went to Mackey's for breakfast. Sheriff Eggemann was in his favorite spot in the back. A copy of today's *Gleaner* lay on the table. It was quarter-folded, with Angela's letter face up. I slid into the empty seat across from him and asked how he was doing. I hadn't seen him for a few days. He went on eating his biscuits and gravy as if I weren't there.

I put my arm on the back of my seat and looked around. The place was busy, and nearly every table had someone who was reading the paper. I turned back to the sheriff and said, "Hey, Carl, what do you think of Angela Marcott's letter to Kelly?"

He raised his thin, close-shaven face and leveled his eyes at me. "Did you put her up to writing it?" he asked.

"No, sir, it was her idea."

"It was, was it?"

"Yes. Why? What's the problem?"

"No problem. I just can't help wondering why it's on the front page of the paper."

"It's news," I said.

"Is that what you call it?"

"You bet. Look around. Nearly everyone's reading it."

He sopped up gravy with a buttermilk biscuit and said, "Is it also front-page news that she hired M. L. Dunn to represent her son?"

"Sure, why not?"

He shrugged. "I don't know. I'm just wondering why we don't read about it on the front page when other people hire a lawyer."

"What have you got against Mary Lou Dunn, Carl?"

"I don't have anything against her. It's her clients that I generally have something against."

This wasn't like Carl. I had never heard him complain about Mary Lou Dunn. I concluded that he must be angry with me. "Come on, Carl, what's bugging you?" I said. "Are you mad at me?"

He faked a laugh. "Now why would I be mad at you? Everybody knows it's front-page news when a police cruiser gets stuck in the mud."

Okay, it was out now. Lowering my voice, I said, "You told me you didn't want to see a photo in the paper. There is no photo of your cruiser in the paper."

He shot back, "Just a story on the front page is all."

"If I hadn't said the car got stuck, don't you think people would have wondered why you didn't go after Kelly right away when he started running? They'd have asked why you waited till the posse got there." I let that sink in, then added, "My boss wanted to know why I didn't get any photos of the car. Not running a photo made us look bad."

"So you had to make us look bad. Thanks." His slack cheeks made him look like a tired hound dog. A waitress showed up, and I ordered eggs over light, toast, and coffee. That's all. I was trying hard to lose some weight.

Carl ate the last few bites of his breakfast in silence. Then he wiped his mouth with a napkin and said, "You think that letter's going to make the boy give himself up?"

"I don't know. Maybe. He *has* offered to surrender, you know."

"I do? How do I know that?"

"It was in the latest *Mothermucker.* Didn't you see it?"

"I don't subscribe."

"Oh, I thought you got a complimentary copy. It came out the day before yesterday. It was a special issue, just one sheet of typing paper with an article by Kelly saying he'll turn himself in if Judge Maxwell and you resign. He claims your families had ties to the Ku Klux Klan."

The normally mild-mannered sheriff slammed both hands on the table. "Gol durn it, Phil, why didn't you tell me?"

"I phoned you Tuesday as soon as I read it. I was told you weren't in."

"You should've called again or left a message."

So Carl really was out when I called that day. Maybe. No, he wouldn't lie. I was the dissembler, not Carl. "I *should* have called again," I said. "I guess I got busy and forgot."

"Uh-huh." He stared at me, fuming. I sensed I was losing his trust, if I hadn't lost it already.

He stared past me. Then his eyes moved slowly back to mine. "I did say I'd never talk to you again if you put that picture in the paper. I shouldn't have said that. I was out of line. You were just doing your job."

He was still annoyed with me, but not quite so much. I wasn't expecting what he said next. In a whisper, he said, "My dad *was* in the Klan for a while, but he got out. He said it was a mistake to join. He told me he thought it was a patriotic organization." Carl gave me a long hard stare. "Phil, I just want to say that nothing I've ever done or not done as sheriff had anything to do with the fact that my father was in the Klan. Nothing. Not one thing. And it never will!"

"I know that, Carl," I said. "You didn't have to tell me."

He began to slide out of the booth, but I stopped him by saying, "You don't really think Kelly murdered his grandfather, do you?"

He glowered at me as if he were fed up, but he didn't seem angry. "It doesn't matter what I think," he said. "That's the job of the jury. We identified the murder weapon—a baseball bat with Chester's blood on it. We had the DNA checked. The bat's also got Kelly Marcott's fingerprints on it. I can't ignore that kind of evidence."

"Were there any other prints on the bat?"

"A few. Partials. Smudges. Nothing we can identify with certainty."

"Did you find any prints elsewhere in the kitchen?"

"We did. Most of them belonged to Chester, of course. And his friend Dicey. And Kelly Marcott. We also found *your* prints in the kitchen, Phil . . . but we know how *they* got there, don't we?"

"Did you find any other prints that you couldn't identify?"

"Certainly, but it's not just about fingerprints. There's other evidence that points to Kelly Marcott as the killer."

"What evidence, Carl?"

He stood up and laid a tip on the table. "You have a good day, Phil," he said. It was a parting jab—he knew I hated that line. He walked to the cash register to pay his bill. Some guy on a stool at the counter started talking to him.

I was still waiting for my breakfast to come. While I sat there, I thought about the baseball bat. It seemed like weak evidence to me. The fact that Kelly's fingerprints were on it did not prove he killed Chester. I wondered if Carl had charged him with murder in order to put him in jail, or rather the juvenile center, to prevent him from leaving the county. Would Carl actually do such a thing? I didn't think so, but it was a moot point because Kelly was not locked up. He already might be out of the county. He might be in California right now, smoking pot or riding a wave.

No, not possible, I told myself. Kelly is still here, trying to get justice for Abner Richards. I'd bet on it.

CHAPTER 23

VOODOO

I WENT to work early the next day. Eighty-five pieces of spam were waiting for me, along with fifty-four pieces of regular email. I began skimming the titles in the spam to make sure it was all junk, and while I was doing that, Edward strolled in and sat down. He belched silently, begged my pardon, and leaned forward to set his coffee mug on the edge of my desk. "Do you think the kid will turn himself in?" he asked.

I shook my head. "Not really. Do you?"

"Nah. He's probably not even here now. I bet he's gone. I think his mother's blowing smoke. She's using us to make herself look good."

"I don't think so."

"Both of the radio stations did a piece on her letter this morning."

"Did they? Did they have her read it on the air?"

"No. They just reported what she said in the letter. At least they mentioned the name of the paper. Maybe it'll help us sell a few copies. The way our circulation is falling, we need all the help we can get."

Like most newspapers, the *Gleaner* was hurting. Advertising was way down. The paper was shrinking, not only the number of pages but also their size. If the *Gleaner* kept shrinking, it would soon be a tabloid. All because of the Internet. I tried to convince myself that small papers would be all right—there was nowhere else people could get in-depth coverage of local news. But not many people wanted in-depth coverage. They were satisfied with snippets. I was beginning to worry about my job.

"Ed," I said, "we need to do more with our website. Obits and a few stories aren't enough. We need an electronic edition of the paper—an *e*-dition that people must subscribe to."

He reached for his coffee and took a big gulp. Then he said, "I'm thinking about it, Philip."

"Good."

"What have we got for the front page today?"

"The murder weapon in the Marcott case has come back from the DNA lab," I said. "I thought we'd lead with that."

"Okay. It still points to the kid, doesn't it?"

"The sheriff thinks so," I said.

I wondered if Ed was thinking of selling the *Gleaner*. It was one of the last independent dailies in the country. Maybe it was the only one. We could boast about that. TV stations were always bragging about themselves. Why shouldn't we?

A better idea popped into my head. It was 7:55. There was a chance that Glorie Kovacs was still at home. I could call and ask her if she saw Angela's letter in this morning's paper. I could say I hope Kelly sees it.

I phoned the Kovacs home. Glorie's mother answered with her three-syllable "Hel-lo-o."

"Hi, Mae," I said. "This is Phil Larrison at the *Gleaner*."

"Good morning, Phil Larrison at the *Gleaner*. What can I do for you?"

"Is Glorie there?"

"No. She left for school already."

"Oh. Okay. I thought she might still be at home. Sorry I bothered you."

"It's no bother. Can I help you? Oh, by the way, that was quite a picture you had of Glorie in the paper the other day."

The color photo showed Glorie at the net, winding up to smash a winner. Her breasts pushed against her shirt. Her short plaid skirt revealed the bottom edge of her tights.

"That *was* a good shot, wasn't it? Our sports editor, Steve Carpenter, took it."

"My husband said it was too sexy."

"I'm sorry he thought so," I said. Actually I wasn't a bit sorry.

Mae said, "Glorie's not on the tennis team anymore, you know."

"No, I didn't know. Why? What happened?"

"Coach Bledsoe kicked her off the team for missing practice too often. He warned her about it before."

"That's too bad. She's the best player."

"It's her own fault—she should have gone to practice like the other girls."

"Why didn't she?"

"She's lost interest in tennis—and everything else. It's all because of. . . . Oh never mind."

"Because of what?" When she didn't answer, I said, "Because of Kelly?"

Her breath fluttered through the line. Then she said, "She's being very foolish."

"How do you feel about Kelly, Mae?"

"How do *I* feel?"

"Do you like him?"

Long pause. "I hate to say it, but I do." Short pause. "Yes, I like Kelly. He's a rebel. That's refreshing compared with some other boyfriends she's had. But he's trouble."

"Is she still seeing him?"

"She says she hasn't seen him since he got suspended from school."

"Do you believe her?"

"I want to. I have to. I don't want to think about the alternative."

"Are they very close?"

This time she made a breathy sigh. "I'm afraid so. I'm afraid she's in love with him."

"You said you like Kelly."

"That's the problem. I do. But he's dangerous. . . . I don't mean *dangerous* dangerous. I mean. . . . You know what I mean."

"Sure."

"Kelly's not a bad kid. That idiot sheriff says he killed his grandfather, but he doesn't know what he's talking about. He's just looking ahead to the next election."

"He can't run for sheriff again," I said.

"Then he'll run for something else. He's a career politician. It's time he retired."

I steered the conversation back to Kelly: "Have you seen the letter from Kelly's mother in today's *Gleaner?*"

"I haven't read the paper yet."

"She wrote an open letter pleading with Kelly to give himself up to the police."

"I hope he listens to her."

"So do I. When will Glorie get home today?"

"She's supposed to come home right after school. Since she's not on the team, she won't have to practice."

"Would you mind if I called her?"

"Wait—I almost forgot. She'll have to do her homework as soon as she gets home from school. She has a wedding rehearsal to go to this evening—plus the rehearsal dinner. She's a bridesmaid in Christine Gasaway's wedding tomorrow night."

"Where's the wedding going to be held?"

"Campbellsville Nazarene Church. Then there's a reception at the National Guard Armory."

In the background a man's voice shouted, "Who you talking to, Mae?"

She shouted back, "I'm on the phone, Ted."

"Who *is* it?"

She muffled the phone, but I could still make out what they were saying: "Phil Larrison from the *Gleaner.*"

"Hang up," he ordered.

"We're almost finished"

"Hang up!"

She said, "Bye, Phil. I have to go," and hung up.

T. Preston Kovacs sounded like a control freak. I wondered what he did for a living. He must pull down a nice paycheck if he owned a house at the Shale Creek Golf Course. I looked up his name in the Chamber of Commerce directory and learned he was the owner and president of Meridian Steel Tubing, Inc.

I felt as if I had done a full day's work already. I shouldn't have come in so early. I pushed back from my desk and stretched. Then I went to the break room for a cup of coffee.

When I returned to my office I found a stack of mail in the tray. I sat down and began tearing it open. One of the envelopes was stuffed with the front page that featured the first article I had written about Chester's murder. Scribbled over the story in huge letters made with an orange crayon were the words "VOODOO VOODOO VOODOO." I didn't know what to make of it. Was it a threat? A curse? Criticism of the Klan? Or was it simply a rant by some nut?

An hour later I called Angela to see if she had seen today's paper.

"Yes," she said. "I hope Kelly sees it."

"Both of the radio stations did a report on it."

"Good. Maybe Kelly heard it."

"He'll get the word somehow," I said.

"I hope so."

"What are you going to do today?" I asked.

"I don't know. Wait and see if Kelly calls, I guess."

"Do something, Angela. Don't just sit there waiting for the phone to ring."

"I've got to be here for Kelly."

I heard a faint sniffle. "Are you okay?" I said. "Would you like me to come out there for a while?"

"You don't have to do that. I'll be all right."

"You sure?"

"Yes. I have to be—for Kelly's sake."

She sounded depressed. I wondered if something had happened that she hadn't told me about.

Suddenly she said, "Thanks for calling, Phil," and hung up.

I stared out the window. The trees behind the courthouse glowed green and golden in the morning sun.

I wondered what Angela would do if something happened to Kelly. She wouldn't stick around here, that's for sure. Maybe she'd sell everything Chester left her and go back to California.

To stop thinking negative thoughts, I looked up Christine Gasaway's wedding announcement in the paper. It was scheduled for 6:30 p.m. at the Campbellsville Church of the Nazarene, with a reception to follow at the National Guard Armory starting at 7:30. "Invitations will be sent," the article stated, "but all friends and relatives are invited to attend."

Christine and her fiancé had just made a new friend.

CHAPTER 24

BECAUSE HE LOVES ME!

THE armory was located in the Meridian County Airport
and Industrial Park. A cube-shaped, yellow-brick gym was
flanked on both sides by flat-roofed, one-story attachments
that included offices, meeting rooms, a kitchen, and window-
less storage rooms, which I assumed were for weapons.

The large parking lot in front of the building was nearly
full. I parked just inside the entrance to the lot so I could get
some exercise hiking to the armory. The high, narrow windows
of the gym glowed with a cold white light. The office windows
were dark.

I fell in behind a chubby couple in cowboy shirts and jeans
and followed them inside, where we joined a winding line of
guests in the lobby, a wide but narrow area between the front
doors and the gym. I did not see anyone I knew. As we inched
along toward the inner doors of the gym, I saw the bride in the
receiving line.

Christine Gasaway was a tall young woman with dark Pre-
Raphaelite hair and a low-cut gown. She gave guest after guest
a wide-eyed, delighted welcome as they exchanged a few words
and laughed and smiled and hugged and patted each other on
the back. The groom was a foot taller and about as thin as his

bride. He had short sandy hair and a bronze tan. He looked like a farm boy.

I didn't see Glorie until I was inside the gym. She was the fourth bridesmaid in the receiving line. The cowboy and cowgirl in front of me were yukking it up with the first bridesmaid, so I went around them to get closer to Glorie.

She and the other four girls were decked out in lavender gowns and floppy peach-colored hats. Their décolletage was as revealing as the bride's.

Glorie saw me coming, and for some reason she pretended not to recognize me. All right, Glorie, we'll play it your way. When we were face to face, I said, "Hello, Miss Kovacs. I'm Phil Larrison. We met at a tennis match."

"Oh . . . yeah . . . that's right. How are you?"

"I'm fine. How are you?"

"Couldn't be better," she said. Her eyes looked past me to see who was in line behind me.

"Big wedding, isn't it?" I said. "Looks like half the school's here."

She forced herself to look at me again. "Just about."

I laughed as if she had said something funny. I started to say something else, but she was already listening to the person behind me.

I drifted off, avoiding the bride and groom because I couldn't remember which one was supposed to be congratulated and which one should get best wishes. Besides, I didn't know either one of them.

This was the first wedding reception I had attended since my own, and I hoped I wouldn't bump into my ex-wife. I probably should have moved to another part of the country after our marriage died, but I was still here.

I passed the bandstand, where a DJ was blasting out old rock tunes. Then I crossed the gym toward the food lines. Walking on a basketball court in street shoes always made me feel as if I were breaking the law. Many guests were already eating at long rows of tables covered with lavender paper. Adorning each table was a round peach candle encircled by a small wreath of spring flowers.

Through the hubbub I heard someone call my name. I saw a pair of arms waving at me. The arms belonged to Jimmy Dobbs. He looked like an overweight referee calling timeout at a football game. "Sit with us," Phil," he shouted over the din. "Get yourself some chow, then come an' join us." I waved back and shouted, "Okay."

The next five minutes of my life were spent standing in line and deciding what I would eat. I settled on chicken cordon bleu, succotash, Caesar salad, fried biscuits—the groom's favorite, someone told me—and a cup of coffee.

My arrival at Jimmy Dobbs's table caused a great deal of shifting and squeezing to make room for another chair, which had to be passed over the top of the table. "I can sit somewhere else." I said.

"No no no. No problem." Dobbs erupted from his seat to grab the chair by its front legs. "Here. Sit yourself down. Take a load off." Wheezing from the slight exertion, he introduced me around the table as I wedged myself in between him and his wife.

Katie Dobbs was a great deal thinner than her husband. She had sharp angular cheeks, wore frameless glasses, and talked fast. She had a habit, or affectation, of narrowing her left eye when she looked at you. It was a sultry half wink, sort of a come-on, though not enough of one that she couldn't deny it. I had previously decided she was a tease, the prim, bookish type who would take a flirtation only so far.

Jimmy's right shoulder overlapped my left, and his wife, who was left-handed, kept bumping my right side with her elbow. She apologized, jauntily wagging her head as she lamented the problems of lefties. I got another half wink.

"I see they've still not caught the Marcott kid," Dobbs said, sticking a golfball-sized biscuit into his mouth. "You still think he's innocent, Phil?"

"Till proven guilty."

He laughed, shoulders and belly shaking. "That shouldn't be hard to do, if they ever nab 'im. He's probably back in lala land by now. I heard he stole a car."

"Where'd you hear that?" I asked.

"On the radio. A car was stolen this afternoon at the Toyota plant."

"Why do they think Kelly stole it?"

"Somebody seen him in the area."

Katie said, "I told Jimmy he'd better watch out—that boy will be after him with a baseball bat next." I thought I sensed a note of hope in her words.

"So you think Kelly's guilty too?" I said to her.

In a hurry to answer, she chewed her food quickly, dipping her chin and patting the top of her chest. "It sure looks that way, doesn't it?"

"Looks can be deceiving."

Her husband said, "Phil's sticking up for the kid because he calls himself a journalist—the kid, I mean, not Phil." He chortled again as if proud of himself for hitting both of us with one punch.

I saw Glorie and the other bridesmaids scurry across the basketball court. The food lines had shrunk, and the girls quickly filled their plates and found their seats at the head table on a long dais.

I asked Jimmy if he had any idea who might be helping Kelly hide from the police.

"I couldn't say for sure," he answered with his mouth full. "Maybe one of the kids that help him put out that rag he publishes. But I don't want to accuse them of harboring a fugitive."

"What are their names?" I asked.

"They're juveniles. I can't release the names."

"Why not?"

"It's against policy."

"Off the record then."

"Sorry, Phil. No can do."

I turned to his wife. "Do you know Kelly Marcott?" I asked her.

Her lips parted, and her tongue slid from side to side. I suspected she knew I was on to her, but she was secure in her defenses. "No, I'm afraid not," she replied. She turned to the faces across the table.

I finished eating while Jimmy discussed corn and soybean prices with a farmer on his right. Then I pushed my chair back to give myself more room and waited for the toasting and roasting to begin. I found myself studying the back of Katie Dobbs's neck. Its graceful arcs made me think of Angela. I squeezed out of my chair and abandoned the Dobbses.

I went out to the lobby and found a quiet spot in the hallway where the offices were. I almost phoned Angela again. An old urge to bite my fingernails came back to me. Why? Must be some connection between the armory and the gym where I played basketball once when I was in the sixth grade. I broke the nail-biting habit that year.

I stuffed my hands in my pockets and read the notices on a bulletin board. I looked in the offices through the glass in old oak doors. I obsessed about Angela. What did she mean to me? Did I want to get seriously involved with a woman again? Did I want a wedding reception of my own at the armory? Did I want a seventeen-year-old kid for a stepson, or did I just need a roll in the hay?

I returned to the lobby, where I heard the after-dinner speeches starting in the gym. I walked down the hallway on the opposite side of the building. I tried the locker-room doors. They were locked. The storage rooms were locked too, and there were no windows in these doors. I read a recruitment poster. Back in the sixth grade, I wanted to be a fighter pilot in the Air Force. Somewhere along the line I dropped the idea.

To kill some more time, I went out front and watched a spectacular purple, golden, and salmon sunset taking shape amid low flat clouds. The only things missing were choirs of angels. When I went back inside, the DJ's loud, hip voice was booming. I went to the restroom, and by the time I returned to the gym, the music was going full blast and a few couples were dancing on the basketball court.

I saw Glorie trying to talk to an old lady in a wheelchair. The woman motioned Glorie to stoop down so she could say something in her ear, but the noise was too loud. The woman shook her head hopelessly. Glorie gave her a little squeeze and spun away.

I caught up with her near the free bar. "Hey, Glorie," I shouted over the throbbing amplifiers, "got a minute?"

She did not appear anymore thrilled to see me than she had before. She waited for me to say something else.

I had to shout to be heard: "This is great, isn't it? It almost makes me want to get married."

"There you go," she said.

"But I tried that once."

"Did you?"

"Yeah. It didn't work out."

"That's too bad."

"I thought so too."

She began to inch away.

"Have you heard anything from Kelly?" I asked her. When she ignored the question, I said, "Did you see the letter his mother had in the paper yesterday?"

"No, I was on the moon."

To my own surprise, I felt tempted to ask her to dance, even though I was a rotten dancer. I wondered who was at the controls in my brain. "Have you heard anything from Kelly lately?" I asked.

"If I had, I wouldn't tell you. You'd put it in the paper."

"No I wouldn't."

"Yeah, like I believe you."

"I wouldn't. Seriously. I mean it. Listen, I'm on Kelly's side. I'm trying to help him. If you know where he is, please tell me. Or tell him to get in touch with me."

"I don't know where he is."

"Maybe not this minute you don't, but I have a hunch you know how to get in touch with him."

I expected her to bolt, but she didn't go anywhere. The music stopped, and we stood there like a pair of dancers waiting for the next song.

"Come on, Glorie," I said. "We're on the same side."

The music started up again. She did not speak. Her eyes were on three boys who had just entered the gym. I recognized two of them: Troy Roberts, who played center on the Campbellsville High School basketball team, and Chad Williams, the son of a local bigwig who was rumored to have gotten the former basketball coach fired for not playing Chad enough. The three kids surveyed the raucous dance scene for a minute or so before heading for the bar.

"Aren't you worried about Kelly?" I asked Glorie.

She looked at me as if she could not believe her ears. "Of course I am! The police are after him, aren't they?"

"Are you and Kelly going together?"

"That's none of your business."

"You're right, it's not, but I like Kelly, and I'd like to know who his friends are . . . if he still has any."

Tears began to form in the corners of her eyes, and she looked away.

I watched the three boys try to get the bartender to give them beers. The youngest of them—the one I didn't recognize—looked under sixteen. The other two were older. I read the bartender's lips: "Sorry, guys. I wish I could."

The kids worked on him until an out-of-uniform city cop came over and said something. Roberts, who was taller than the policeman, laughed in his face and walked away, followed by his friends.

"Kelly's mom is afraid he might be sick," I told Glorie. "Is he?"

She didn't answer.

I said, "If he's sick, you ought to make him go to a doctor."

"I can't make him do anything he doesn't want to."

"Then at least tell him he ought to talk to his mother."

"You act as though I know where he is and I can talk to him anytime I feel like it. We don't live together, you know."

I saw a familiar face watching us over the shoulder of the girl he was dancing with. "Curtis Davis is watching you," I said.

"So?"

"You're not still friends with him, are you?"

She forced a laugh and said, "Gimme a break." She fanned a fly away from her hair. "Look, Mr. Larrison, I wish you would stop asking me questions. Just leave me alone, okay?" Without further ado, she whirled away and joined the other bridesmaids near the head table.

I got myself a cup of coffee. It was too strong. While I was looking for a place to ditch it, I saw Glorie and another girl leave the group and circle around the dance floor. The other boy who had come with Williams and Roberts yelled at her to wait up. She ignored him and went with her friend to a restroom at the far end of the gym. The boy ran after them and barged into the ladies' room. A few seconds later three women came out laughing their heads off. I set my coffee down on the salad table and raced across the gym. Just before I reached the restroom, the door flew open again and Glorie came out. The boy was right behind her.

I asked Glorie if she was all right.

"Get lost," the boy told me.

Glorie said, "Shut up, Michael."

The kid was about eight inches shorter than I was, but he had a tough, cocky face. He looked like a surly thirteen-year-old. Maybe fourteen. Maybe fifteen.

I said, "You mind your business, buddy, and I'll mind mine." Alliteration worked well to belittle and insult, but I regretted taking the low road.

"Fuck you," he said.

He looked as though he wanted to punch my face in. I was ready for a punch, but I didn't mind that it didn't come. It would have been a tad unseemly to get in a fight with a kid in the middle of a wedding reception.

He gave me a shoulder as he brushed past. I laughed it off. I watched him rejoin his friends. The three of them gazed through the crowd at me as he gave his report. Then he and Troy Roberts disappeared into the lobby. I figured they were going out for a smoke.

Williams walked over to Glorie and began talking to her. She looked up at his face but said nothing. I began working my way toward them, but before I was halfway there, Williams flipped both hands in the air and walked away.

The music was even louder now that dinner was over. Senior citizens were starting to leave. I thought about going back to work, but I wanted to have another go at Glorie. I got a fresh, more drinkable cup of coffee and stood watching the kids dance. The bride, in her long white gown, was rolling around on the floor with other dancers doing the old alligator.

Williams was heading into the lobby when Roberts came running back into the gym and nearly crashed into him. Roberts said something, and they took off together. Glorie, who had been watching, raised her gown a few inches and ran after them in high heels.

I caught up with her outside. She was gnawing on some of her knuckles. The two boys had already disappeared, but from the office side of the building, someone yelled, "There he is! Get 'im. Kick his ass."

"What's going on, Glorie?" I said.

She spun around and screamed in my face. "They're after Kelly! They'll beat his brains out!" She pulled off her shoes and began running in the direction of the shouts, one shoe in each hand.

I went after her. "Did you see him?" I aimed my words at the back of her head.

The kid named Michael came tearing around the north side of the building. When he saw Glorie, he stopped and said, "Get your ass home, or I'll tell Dad you're with him."

So Michael was Glorie's brother. He raced by us toward the opposite side of the armory.

Glorie turned around and started to go after him, but I grabbed her arm. "Are you sure it's Kelly?" I said.

"Let go of me!"

"I bet it's not," I said. "Why would he take a chance on coming here, with all these people?"

She stared into the darkness. The streetlights cast an amber glow against the cloudy sky. She was like a spring about to be sprung. Suddenly a broken cry burst out of her throat: "Because of me! Because he loves me!" She started to cry.

In the parking lot, boys were running back and forth between the rows of cars. Their yells seemed to bounce off the low clouds:

"Anybody got a flashlight?"

"Look under the cars."

"Try the doors. Look in everything ain't locked."

"Get the cocksucker!"

"I think I saw him go over the fence."

"It's barbed wire. He didn't go over no fence."

"Anybody call the cops?"

"Screw the cops. I get him first."

The last voice, which had a farm-boy twang, belonged to Curtis Davis. Troy Roberts loped toward us. Every few yards he peered inside a vehicle, then went down on his hands and knees to look underneath it. At the end of the row of cars and pickups, he veered past us with his shirt hanging out and sweat running down his face. He looked as if his heart wasn't in the search. Another boy climbed on top of a van and scanned the parking lot. In the light mist, he stood out as a faintly purple silhouette. People leaving the reception stopped and stared at the goings-on. Some of them hurried to get away.

Jimmy Dobbs came out. He shrugged when someone asked him what was going on. Curtis Davis came running, and Dobbs grabbed his arm and asked him the same question.

"It's Marcott," Davis said. He ran off shouting orders: "Don't let him get away. Check every car."

Across the road at one of the old barracks still left from World War II, a motorcycle started up. Seconds later the kid on top of the van yelled, "It's him—Mr. Hollywood! Get the prick."

The motorcycle sped out to the road and swerved toward Main Street. I saw Kelly leaning over the handlebars. Under the eerie streetlights, his long hair blew in the wind like an orange flame.

Several of his pursuers ran to their cars, but by the time they got going, Kelly was almost on Main St. Two cars peeled out of the parking lot, but they weren't going to catch him.

Michael Kovacs strode up to Glorie. "You glad he got away, slut? You happy now?"

Her jaws tightened, and she tried to slap him on the face, but he was too quick for her. He grabbed both of her hands and squeezed them hard. Her knees buckled, and her eyes closed in pain.

I walked over and said, "Let her go."

He released her hands, and in the same motion he spun around and swung at me. I saw the punch coming and leaned back, but his fist grazed my chin. I wrapped my arms around him. He tried to knee me in the groin. I was taller than he was and heavier—with fat, not muscle—but I managed to trip him backwards and take him down. He tried to bite me, and I used my arm to press one side of his face against the blacktop.

The cop I had seen in the armory came running. "Break it up," he shouted. "Come on, guys, that's enough."

He sounded too calm. My heart was racing. The cop and some other guy separated Michael and me. I couldn't believe I had won the fight.

Yeah, big deal, Larrison, you kept a fourteen- or fifteen-year-old kid from beating you up. Maybe you'll get a medal.

CHAPTER 25

AN UNEXPECTED GIFT

WHEN I got back to the office, the light on my phone was blinking. It was a message from Angela: "It's me, Phil. I've got something to tell you. Talk to you later." My guess was she had heard from Kelly. I called her back right away. Her hello sounded far away, as if she had just woke up.

"Hi," I said. "I just got your message. Did you hear from Kelly?"

"No."

"Oh, I thought that's what you were going to tell me. . . . Guess what."

"What?"

"I saw him tonight, less than an hour ago."

"You did?" she said, surprised. "Where? Is he all right?"

"He was all right when I saw him. He was riding a motorcycle."

"A motorcycle? He doesn't own a motorcycle. Are you sure it was Kelly?"

"Yes."

"Oh God, Phil, thank you. At least now I know nothing's happened to him. I've been sitting here going nuts. Where was he? Where did you see him?"

"At a wedding reception at the National Guard Armory. He was outside. A gang of high-school kids was chasing him in the parking lot. I didn't see him till he was getting away on the motorcycle."

"I didn't know he could drive a motorcycle." She acted perturbed, then exclaimed, "What was he *doing* at a *wedding* reception? What was he *thinking?* He's lucky he didn't get beat up or killed!"

I decided it was time to tell her about Glorie. "I think I know why he was there," I said. "His girlfriend was in the wedding party. She was a bridesmaid."

"He never told me he had a girlfriend here. Who is she? What's her name?"

"Glorie, spelled I-E, not Y."

"Glorie? I never heard of her. What's her last name?"

"Kovacs. I wouldn't get in touch with her, if I were you. You'll get her in trouble. Her father doesn't want her to go with Kelly."

"You know all about her. I don't know a thing."

"I get around."

"What else do you know that you haven't told me?"

"Glorie told me Kelly came to the reception to see her. She said he's in love with her. From the look on her face, I'd say the feeling's mutual."

"Oh jeez, I wish I could talk to him. Why doesn't he call?"

"Maybe he hasn't seen your letter, Angela, and if he has, maybe he's afraid your phone is bugged. Maybe he thinks the police are watching your house."

"I told you I've seen police cars around here, but I haven't seen anyone watching the house. Do *you* think they're watching me?"

"I doubt it. I don't think Carl has enough deputies to stake out your house 24-7. And you want to know something else?

I don't think Carl really believes Kelly killed Chester. I may be wrong, but I think he charged Kelly so he could arrest him and lock him up and keep him from going back to California, where he might never be able to find him."

"It sounds like you're saying that Kelly should go back to California and the sheriff might stop trying to catch him."

"I'm not suggesting that Kelly flee the state. I'm just telling you what I think might be going on in Carl's mind."

"I like that idea, especially the part where you said the sheriff doesn't think Kelly killed Chester."

"Don't quote me on that. It's just a feeling I got while I was talking to him."

"I hope you're right."

"Me too. Well, I'd better get to work here. I just wanted to let you know I saw Kelly."

"Okay. Thanks, Phil. That makes me feel a little bit better." Suddenly she shrieked: "Oh my God! I almost forgot what I wanted to tell you. I had a call from Mary Lou Dunn this evening. She said a big black guy walked into her office this afternoon and handed her a $500 check to help pay for Kelly's defense. He said he read my letter in the newspaper. That's how he got Mary Lou's name. She told me she asked him why he wanted to help Kelly, but he didn't give her a reason. All he said was, 'I just want to help Mr. Marcott's grandson,' and he left. Isn't that something! What do you make of that?"

"I don't know." The wheels in my brain were turning. "There was a black man at Chester's funeral," I said, "but he never got out of his car. It was an old hulk. From the looks of it, I wouldn't have thought he could afford to contribute $500 to anything. It's probably not the same guy."

"Mary Lou gave me the name and address on the check: Andreas Pluckett, 1028 E 950 N, Campbellsville. She thought I might want to send him a thank-you note. You know, I really don't need the money, thanks to Chester's will. Maybe I should tell Mary Lou to send him his check back."

I scribbled the name and address on my desk pad and said, "Let him help if he wants to. He must have a reason. I wish I knew what it is."

"All right, if you say so."

"I'll call you in the morning, okay?"

"Sure. I'll be here, hoping Kelly calls."

I got back on the computer and batted out a short item for the front page about Kelly's showing up at the wedding reception. I didn't bring Glorie into it—I didn't want to get her in trouble with her father. After that, I began going over everything else for the front page. I had trouble concentrating. I couldn't stop thinking about Andreas Pluckett. At the same time, I was afraid I was missing things in the stories I was editing. Why was I editing them anyway? Denny had already gone over them. He was a good editor. I ought to trust him. I had trouble delegating responsibility. I'd punch myself on the head if a single typo appeared on the front page. I obsessed over everything. Get over it, I told myself for the thousandth time. You can't be a perfectionist in the newspaper business. Not when you've got deadlines to meet. So get over it. Nobody's perfect, Larrison, least of all you.

In spite of this brilliant insight, I went right on looking for mistakes, questioning every phrase, nitpicking like a nitwit.

When I finished nitpicking, I sat down alongside Melissa, our best page designer, at her computer in the makeup room. We laid out the front page, and then I went back to my office to wait for the press to start. All of a sudden I felt tired. I got a cup of coffee to keep me awake.

I was tired, but it was a pleasant feeling, the kind where you know you're not going to have any trouble falling asleep tonight.

CHAPTER 26

CONSCIENCE MONEY?

NEXT day I went looking for Andreas Pluckett.
It wasn't hard to find him. He lived eleven miles from Campbellsville in a small subdivision called Cowper Acres in the northeastern corner of Meridian County. Its name was on a small sign along the highway, but some wiseguy had painted over two of the letters, changing the name to Cowpie Acres. As soon as I turned into the subdivision, I knew I had the right man. An old Pontiac—the same one I had seen at Chester's funeral—was parked in front of a one-car garage that was attached to a house. The faded maroon Bonneville looked too long to fit in the garage. The small ranch house had brick wainscoting on the front and faded white siding everywhere else. Two car tires painted bright blue lay on the front lawn with daffodils growing out of them. A second car, a bulbous Hudson without tires, stood on concrete blocks near a metal storage shed.

A black man in a dark-green T-shirt was sitting on a church pew on a narrow porch like mine. A concrete goose stood next to the pew, and a little girl sat next to the man, swinging her legs. There was no curb or sidewalk, so I parked as other drivers had done, half on the street and half in the grassy swale of a drainage ditch. The man and the girl watched me get out of the car.

"Mr. Pluckett?" I called.

"That's me," he called back. "What can I do for you?"

I introduced myself as I crossed the lawn. Unlike the next-door neighbors' yard, his lawn was nearly free of dandelions. The girl, whose hair was styled in perfect corn rows, pushed herself off the pew and ran into the house. The man chuckled at her shyness and stood up as I approached.

The house was full of noise. A baby was crying, and hip-hop music blasted through the screen door. Over the frantic beat, a woman shouted, "Kiesha, you get your fingers out of that dish—*now,* girl!" A teenage boy appeared at the screen door, looked at me, and lingered in the shadows. Mr. Pluckett and I shook hands.

"Nice to meet you, Mr. Larrison," he said. "I've got a feeling I know what brings you here. News travels fast in a small town, don't it?"

"It sure does," I said.

He was tall and broad-shouldered, with thick arms that looked like a wrestler's. I put his age in the early fifties.

"May I get you something to drink?" he said. "Lemonade? Ice water?"

"Lemonade sounds good."

He started for the door, saw the boy standing there, and said, "Charles, get Mr. Larrison a glass of lemonade, would you, please."

The boy vanished, and I said, "Is that your son, Mr. Pluckett?"

"Call me Andy."

"Thank you. Call me Phil."

"Good. Got that over with." He laughed and then answered my question: "Charles is my grandson. And that little cyclone you scared away is my granddaughter—one of 'em." He hooked his thumbs in his pockets and stared across the street at a white boy who was washing a high-riding pickup truck with oversized tires.

"How many grandchildren do you have?" I asked, just to be asking.

"Six and counting. One boy and five girls. I have four daughters, but no sons." He put on an act of checking the doorway for eavesdroppers and whispered, "After our fourth daughter was born, my wife said to me, 'That's it. I'm done. You are not going to keep getting me pregnant because you want a son.' So Charles is like my son. He's special to me. But don't tell my granddaughters I said that."

The lemonade arrived, and I thanked the boy, who started to go back inside, but Andy told him to sit down with us. He plopped down on the right side of his grandfather, and I sat on the left. I took a long, ear-clicking drink. When the next song began, Charles tapped out the beat on his thighs.

A parade of giggly faces appeared at the screen door and in the picture window behind the pew. Andy called his wife to come out, but instead of her, one of his daughters showed up.

"Hello," she said to me, then turned to her father. "Mom's in the basement. What do you need, Dad?" She was tall and thin, a striking woman who looked like a model. She was wearing dark-blue jeans and a light-green polo shirt. Andy introduced us to each other, and we shook hands. Then one of the kids started screaming. Something crashed, and she ran back inside. Andy told me she worked as a lineman at the Meridian County Rural Electric Membership Corporation.

"Really?" I said. I was thinking feature story. She might be the only woman in the state working as a lineman for an electric utility.

I asked Andy where he worked, and he said he was at the Lowe's distribution center near North Vernon. For the next twenty minutes I learned what his wife, his other three daughters, and his four sons-in-law did for a living. Charlie asked if it was okay if he went inside. Reluctantly Andy nodded. He seemed disappointed in his grandson, but at the same time he seemed to realize that we had been boring the kid to death.

During the ensuing pause, I asked him why he had contributed $500 to Kelly Marcott's lawyer.

His eyes narrowed. His lips protruded like the mouthpiece of a horn. He nodded slowly and said, "It's just somethin' I felt like I had to do."

"That's a lot of money," I said.

He gazed at the high blue sky, where the contrails of three jet planes were forming a giant H. "It is," he agreed. "It *is* a lot of money, though $500 don't buy what it used to."

"That's true. So why did you decide to make a donation to Kelly's defense, if you don't mind my asking?"

His head popped up. "On account of you, Phil. I have been reading your stories in the paper." He waved a fly away from his face. "You showed that the boy has a good heart. You made it clear—at least to me—that he is no murderer."

"Not everybody would agree with you there," I said. "I've been told that some of my stories make Kelly look guilty."

"Not to me." He leaned closer. "Why would Kelly kill his grandfather? It is a ridiculous charge. Your stories show that all the boy wants is for the truth to come out. Perhaps there are some people who would rather not see that happen."

"Are you related to Abner Richards?" I asked.

He tilted his head sideways and stared at me. Then he straightened up and said, "Half related, you might say. Abner Richards was my mother's first husband." His large hands began rubbing his knees. "She was still a girl, just sixteen, when they got married. He was at least ten years older than her. My mama told me he was not sure how old he was. He did not know the year he was born, not even his own birthday. They was married five years when the Klan dragged him out of his house and lynched him." He nodded as if agreeing with his own words. "He wasn't my papa, but I've always felt a bond with him. Ever since I was a boy, Abner Richards has been like a spiritual father to me." He began to choke up, which he tried to hide by clearing his throat. "He never raped no white woman. My mama told me. He never done what they said he done. It was all trumped up. He was with my mama the night they said he raped a white lady. My mama told me so herself. The Klan had a lust for blood. They wanted to hang a black man on a tree, and they got themselves one."

"What was your mother's name?" I asked.

"Lila Johnson was her name before she married Abner Richards. He was hanged in 1936. In 1949 my mother married William T. Pluckett, and I was born the following year, 1950."

So Andreas was sixty-one or sixty-two—around ten years older than my guesstimate. "Are your parents still living?" I asked.

He stuck out his lower lip and shook his head. "No. My father was killed in a farm accident. He was working alongside a tractor that tipped over on him 'cause it run into a big ground-hog hole. I was only four years old at the time. My mama's gone too. She had a hard life. She lost two husbands and had to work like a slave the rest of her life to support her children and stepchildren. There was five of us in all. I had two half-sisters, a half-brother, and a sister." A wan smile stretched his fleshy lips, which seemed glazed with silver. "So you see, Phil, I never got to know either one of my fathers—not my real father nor Abner Richards neither."

"Your family's had way more than its share of trouble."

"Perhaps. But not more than it could bear. My mama bore up under her troubles, and she made sure the rest of us did too. She was as tough as an alligator, and she never did give up despite all that happened to her. After the county took her farm away from her, like you said in the paper—or like Kelly Marcott said—after they sold the farm out from under her, she had nothin' left but the clothes on her back. She told me those were the darkest days in her life. She had to work like a horse day and night, doin' whatever work she could find. She even scavenged in the dump. But she never gave up. She made sure her children amounted to somethin'."

"She sounds like quite a woman," I said.

"That she was. For years she kept after the county to find the murderers who lynched her husband, but nobody paid attention to her, not even the newspaper you work for, I'm sorry to say."

"I'm sorry too. How much do you know about the death of Abner Richards?"

"Not much. My mother never told us kids much about it. I didn't even know he'd been lynched till I was in school and learned it from my classmates. I still remember the time I first heard of it. I felt like I'd been lynched just like he was. He seemed that close to me. For a long time I had trouble fallin' asleep at night. I relived the whole thing in my mind. I cried my eyes out. What they done to Abner Richards was a terrible, terrible thing, and they got away with it. I thought of ways to get even with them. I wanted to kill them one by one. I was filled with meanness and hate, just like them. My mama got me over it. She told me I mustn't be as bad as them. I must grow up to be big and strong, not a killer, not a coward who has to hide his face under a hood. 'Don't let hate control you,' she said. 'It will wear you down. It will turn your heart into a stone.' She said, 'They will be punished for what they did someday. Mark my word—they will be punished.' "

He stopped talking and stared at the concrete floor. Then he turned to me and said, "I didn't believe her. I never thought it would happen. But it's happenin' now. That's why I done what I could to help Kelly Marcott. That's why. He wants people to know what happened. He wants everybody in Meridian County to know what the Ku Klux Klan done to Abner Richards, and I for one am grateful to him for wanting that."

A car came up the street with its windows open and a loud, throbbing five-note melody pouring out over and over. I shouted above the din, "When did your mother die, Andy?"

"In the year 2000, just a week away from her eighty-fifth birthday."

"It seems strange that she stayed in this area after Abner was killed. I'd have wanted to get as far away as possible."

"She probably couldn't afford to go anywhere else." Andy stared at the bright blue sky. The enormous H was fuzzy and bloated now. "You know, Phil, Campbellsville was always a bad place for black people. I have heard it said that right up into the 1960s a black man had to be afraid to stop overnight in Campbellsville. If you was black, you had better keep on movin'. You had best not stop for gas or a bite to eat, and definitely not a motel, 'less you wanted to get beat up real bad, maybe even worse. Back in the 1920s and '30s the Klan was thick in this county. Indiana was a hotbed of Klan activity, and nowhere was it any hotter than here."

"There are black people in Campbellsville now."

"I know. Times have changed. But the changes do not go deep. I know from what I hear at work that the old attitudes are still there."

"Why did you go to Chester Marcott's funeral?"

His head jerked up in surprise. "You saw me there, did you? See what I mean—a black man in Campbellsville still sticks out like a sore thumb."

"It's just that you were the only black person at the funeral."

"Is that right?" he said with a knowing chuckle.

"Were you a friend of his?" I asked.

"I never met the man."

"Then why did you go to his funeral?"

"I went to say goodbye to him. And I wanted to thank him for something."

"What?"

His eyes creased shut until they nearly disappeared, then popped open. "I suppose Mama won't mind if I tell you, now that both her and Mr. Marcott are gone. He made her promise not to tell anybody, but she thought somebody should know what he done. That is why she told me—but not until she was dying. Now that the two of them are both in a better place, I suppose it's all right for me to talk about it, especially since it puts Mr. Marcott in a good light."

He took a long breath and continued: "I went to his funeral to thank him for what he done for my mama and her family, including me." He paused, then added in slow, portentous syllables: "He gave her a lot of money. Not cash. It was old gold coins—several twenty-dollar gold pieces. They was worth over $5,000 back then. She sold them to a coin dealer in Salem, and that's what she got for 'em."

"Did she say why Mr. Marcott gave her the coins?"

"No. I asked her that question, of course. I asked her more than once. All she ever said was, 'That is between me and our benefactor.' I did not even find out who he was until after she passed away. I found an envelope in the chest of drawers in her bedroom where she kept important papers—that is, papers that was important to her. Her will was there, along with a letter to me. It said Mr. Chester Marcott helped us get through some hard times after my papa died. That was in 1990. That was the first time I ever heard of Mr. Marcott."

"Did her letter mention the coins?"

"No, sir. It did not."

"Is it possible—" I stopped and started over: "I hope this doesn't offend you, Andy, but is there any chance that your mother and Chester were romantically involved?"

He clenched his jaws and shook his head stiffly, from side to side, just once. "No sir, it is *not* possible. My mama was not a loose woman. She made us go to church with her every week at the AME Church there in Campbellsville. No, Mr. Larrison, there is no chance they was lovers. You should apologize to her for even thinkin' such a thing."

"I'm sorry," I said. "Do you know who she sold the coins to?"

"All I know is it was a dealer in Salem. She did not sell them all at once. She sold them one at a time over the next few years. She told me she got $200 for each one."

I wondered if she had gotten a fair price. Gold was worth about $1,700 an ounce right now, but I had no idea what it was worth in the 1980s and '90s. What's more, these were old coins we were talking about. No doubt they had a value to coin collectors over and above the value of the gold itself. Oh well, even if the collector took advantage of her, whatever he gave her for the coins was pure profit as far as she was concerned.

I rephrased my question again: "Andy, why do *you* think Chester gave your mother those coins?"

He scrunched up his lips and inhaled. Then he stared at the floor. After a long pause, his head came up slowly as he said, "I hate to say this of Mr. Marcott, I really do, but the only thing I can think of is it might have been conscience money."

"Conscience money," I echoed. "Hnh. Do you think it had something to do with the lynching of Abner Richards?"

He looked me straight in the eyes. "Your guess is as good as mine. But Mr. Marcott could not have had anything to do with that. He would have been too young. But I have often thought maybe his father had something to do with it. He could have been in the Klan, and it could be that them coins belonged to him and they got passed on down to Chester when he died. Maybe Chester wanted my mama to have them to make up for what his father done to her first husband. I can't rightly say that's what happened though, because I just don't know for sure."

Before I left, I asked if he would mind if I wrote an article about what he had told me.

"I have no objection," he said. "Only please do not give people the idea that I have a stash of gold coins in the house. Those coins would be worth a lot of money today, a lot more than they was worth when Mr. Marcott gave them to my mama. It would be an invitation to thieves to break into my house."

"I'll make it clear that your mother sold the coins years ago."

"I'd appreciate that."

"One other thing," I said. "I'd like to get a picture of you."

"No you don't. That ain't necessary."

"I need a photo to go with the story. All you have to do is sit on the porch, or stand by your old Hudson over there."

"No. Forget the photo. I don't want it to look like I think I'm somebody important."

His wife came out to the porch scolding: "Andreas Pluckett, you let the man do his job. There's no reason in the world why you shouldn't have your picture in the paper." She was a handsome woman with a serious face and a white bandana wrapped around her head, which appeared to be bald. Chemo, I figured.

"All right," he said to me. "Her ladyship has spoken. You can take my picture. But fix it up some. Make me look like Denzel Washington."

CHAPTER 27

THE GLORY SUIT

BEFORE I could get away, Andreas Pluckett told me more about himself. He said he wanted to be a good role model for his kids and grandkids. He said he took in foster children in emergency situations. He said he was a Big Brother to a middle-school boy who had gotten himself in trouble with drugs. He said he was helping to put a new roof on his church. He said he wanted to "give something back" for what the Lord had given him. From the looks of his small house, the Lord had not given him very much.

On my way back to Campbellsville, I began to get sleepy. It was a bright, warm day with small, fluffy clouds spaced out widely across the sky. To keep from nodding off, I phoned Angela to tell her what Mr. Pluckett had told me about Chester. Before I opened my mouth, I got the Caller ID treatment: "Phil! I was just getting ready to call you! Are you busy? Can you come out here?"

"What for? What happened?" I wondered if Kelly had shown up.

"I found something! You need to see it!"

"What'd you find?"

"Can you come?"

"Sure. I'm on my way."

I pulled into a driveway to dig out the county roadmap in the glove compartment. I plotted a course across the northern end of the county to the Zumma neighborhood.

There was no direct route from here to there. Some of the back roads ended at T intersections, which meant I had to take a road that went in a different direction. It was a series of zigs and zags through farms and hills. Some roads were unpaved and either pot-holed, washboardy, or both. I wished I was driving a company car.

Naturally the trip took longer than I had expected. Soon my eyes were glazing over. I stretched out my arms and made myself sit up straight. I tried to shake the drowsiness out of my head, but every minute or so I felt my eyes glazing again. My face felt numb. I opened the windows and turned the radio up. Golden oldies. I sang along when I knew part of the song. I blinked. I rocked back and forth. I clutched the wheel. Orange dust enveloped the car. Watch me plow into a tractor. Watch me hit a cow. Watch me wipe out a family with four kids and two dogs in the back of a pickup truck. . . .

When I got to Angela's house, I was still alive and awake, more or less. She was sitting on the front porch with a gray tiger cat standing on her lap.

"Where'd you get the cat?" I asked as I got out of the car.

The cat was pressing its front paws against Angela's belly, first one paw, then the other. It looked as if it were kneading dough. I started toward the steps, and suddenly the beast freaked out. It jumped off Angela and ran to the far end of the porch. Except it wasn't really a run. It was more like a fast, stiff-legged walk.

"That cat runs funny," I said. "What's wrong with it?"

"Poor Puddybaby," Angela replied. "She doesn't know how to run very fast. She's never been outside before. She just came from California."

"How'd she get here running like that?"

She laughed. "FedEx brought her this morning. A friend of mine, Mollie, was watching her for me while I'm here, but I didn't expect to be away this long, so I had Mollie send her overnight express."

The cat, as if afraid to jump off the porch, did its quickstep back to the door and began clawing the screen. Angela hopped up and opened the door. The cat hunkered down, then slithered under the door and disappeared inside.

"Is that what you wanted me to see—the cat?"

"Don't you like Puddybaby?"

"Of course I do. I like cats. But I tend to like squirrels and raccoons and chipmunks more—things I don't have to feed."

She made a face and said, "Well, I missed her." She opened the screen door again. "Come on in. I'll show you what I found. It gives me the creeps."

"What is it?"

"You'll see."

I followed her inside the house and up to the second floor. She turned left and led the way through the hall. The rooms we passed no longer looked as though a tornado had hit them. "I see you've been busy up here," I said. "You've got the place looking a lot better."

"Thanks." She glanced over her shoulder at me. "There are still some big holes in the walls that need to be patched, but you can't see them much from the hall. I patched the small ones myself. I haven't made up my mind whether to have the rooms repapered or painted. New wallpaper would probably look best, don't you think?"

She showed me into a large bedroom with windows on two sides. "This was Chester's room," she said.

Huge holes in the walls showed a smashed latticework of old narrow brown boards from which pieces of plaster dangled like broken teeth. The newly patched areas resembled baby ghosts.

"There's still a lot of work to do in here," Angela said. "I'd say whoever tore up the house when Chester was killed spent most of their time in here."

"What did you find that they didn't?" I said.

"It's on the bed." She pointed to a short stack of bedsheets. "They were on a shelf in the closet. They looked like they hadn't been touched in years. I was looking for clean sheets to make the beds." She lifted all the sheets except one off the stack. "This is where it was, on the bottom of the pile. I put it back just the way I found it. I wanted you to see how it was."

She laid the sheets that she was holding on a dresser and began unfolding the last sheet in the stack. After a few unfolds, what I thought was a pillow case appeared inside the sheet. She walked around to the other side of the bed and unfolded the rest of the sheet. Then she unfolded what I had taken for a pillow case. It looked like a small, old-fashioned nightshirt—until she picked it up to reveal a cone-shaped hood underneath.

"I'll be damned," I said.

It was a child-sized version of the robe and hood of the Ku Klux Klan, the so-called glory suit. On the left breast of the robe was a round red patch with a white X on it. There was a small K at each end of the X and a red spot in the middle of it. The four Ks obviously stood for Knights of the Ku Klux Klan, but I had no idea what the red spot signified. It resembled an upside-down apostrophe or a bloated number 6 with a filled-in loop. There was also a plaque attached to a long cord. The plaque was at least twice the diameter of the red patch and bore the image of a crusader's shield with a cross on it and a curved row of stars on each side of the shield.

Angela said, "It gave me the creeps when I found it." She leaned over and spread out the small white robe on the bed and placed the hood above the neck. Both items were sharply creased and slightly yellow. "Do you think it was a Halloween costume?" she asked me.

"No, it looks authentic," I said. "My guess is a member of the Klan had it made for a three- or four-year-old kid maybe. The guy probably thought it was cute." I arranged the cord like a belt across the waist and placed the plaque in the middle of it.

Angela shook her head fast and shivery. "It's not cute. It's spooky. I wish I hadn't found it."

"I wonder who it was made for," I said.

"It must have been Chester's. Why else would it be in his room? Why else would he have kept it?"

"You're probably right," I said. "Maybe Chester's father had it made for him. Maybe Chester's father was in the Klan."

"Oh my God, you think so?"

"Seems plausible, doesn't it?"

"I don't know," Angela said. "This is going to give me nightmares. I'll be afraid to go to bed."

"I don't blame you. This house is full of ghosts."

She poked me on the arm. "Thanks. That helps a lot."

"Sorry, but if I were you, I'd be out of here."

"Believe me, if it wasn't for Kelly, I would be."

We stood there staring at the robe.

"What should I do with it?" Angela asked.

"Fold it up. Put it away someplace where you won't see it again."

"Like in the trash?"

"No. Hang onto it. It may turn out to be important."

"I'll put it upstairs in the attic."

"There you go."

She started to yawn, but I happened to catch her, and she stopped. "Would you like a cup of coffee?" she asked.

"Sounds good."

We went to the kitchen. She turned on the radio, and I listened to the news that the station had gleaned from the *Gleaner*. I watched Angela fill Mr. Coffee. As I sat there eyeballing her curvy figure, I told her about my visit with Andreas Pluckett. I told her about the gold coins that he said Chester had given his mama. I told her he said he thought it was conscience money. "If it was conscience money," I added, "what was on Chester's conscience? What did he feel guilty about? Was it something he did, or what?"

Angela whirled around, but instead of coming up with a response to my questions, she said, "Maybe Chester played being in the Klan when he was little. Oh God, Phil, maybe Chester's father was in the Klan. Maybe he helped lynch the black man Kelly wrote about."

"Could be," I said. "And it also explains the $500 you said Mr. Pluckett gave Mary Lou Dunn to defend Kelly. It might be his way of supporting Kelly's effort to get justice for Abner Richards."

We drank our coffee on the front porch and gazed at the fields and sky. I watched a pair of buzzards circling high over the farm. Buzzards are good birds—they take care of road kill—but right now they seemed like an unfavorable omen.

I turned toward Angela and caught her watching me. She gave me a little smile. "What are you looking at?" I said.

"You," she said with a little laugh. "Aren't I allowed to look at you?"

I hated *Aren't I,* but coming from her, it was okay.

CHAPTER 28

SHACKED UP

THE next morning I woke to the sound of bells from the church up the street. It was Sunday, a regular workday. Except for coffee, I skipped breakfast to lose some weight. Then I took a shower and shaved.

On my way to the *Gleaner,* I saw Dale Marcott pumping gas at the Marathon station on Main St. He was the only customer. He had a dented brown Chevy that looked as if it had been washed with paint thinner. I drove about fifty feet past the station and pulled over to the curb.

I wondered what he was doing out on Sunday morning. I decided to follow him and find out. Maybe I'd get lucky and he'd lead me to Kelly.

I squirmed around sideways and looked out the back window to watch him. When he finished pumping gas, he went inside to pay his bill. A few minutes later he came out with a bag of Krispy Kreme doughnuts. I wished I had a bag too—half a dozen Bavarian creams.

He pulled out of the station and came in my direction. To avoid being recognized, I leaned over as if getting something out of the glove compartment. I let him get a block away from me, and then I followed his car.

He stayed on Main St. for several blocks. I hung back, hoping I wouldn't get stopped by a red light. There was hardly any traffic, so as long as he stayed on Main, I could keep him in sight, and if a light did turn red, I'd go through it, unless I saw a cop.

He made a right turn at the Meridian Park Shopping Center. I stepped on the gas and reached Meridian Park Drive just in time to see him make a left into the Longview Trailer Park behind the stores. Cemeteryview would have been a better name for it. Apartment buildings had gone up on two sides of the trailer park, leaving a long view only in one direction, south, where a cemetery was. Every week or two the *Gleaner* carried a story about the latest meth lab to be busted in one of the trailers.

I drove over two speed bumps and spotted the brown Chevy on the second street on the right. It was parked at the picture-window end of a green-and-white mobile home. I parked on the curbless street and got out. The smell of burning garbage hung in the air. I knocked on the narrow metal door.

A busty, heavy-set woman with frizzy orange hair opened the door and seemed astonished to see me, which made me wonder if I should know her. "Good morning," I said. "I'm looking for Dale Marcott. Have I got the right place?"

"Yes. Who may I say wishes to see him?" She laughed at her put-on formality. She had a wry smile and a round, friendly face. She was wearing tight yellow capris and a sleeveless, dark-blue top. The sides of her bra showed through the oversized armholes.

"Who's there?" Marcott shouted from deep in the trailer.

"What's your name?" the woman asked me.

I gave her my name, and she relayed it to Dale with a yell over her shoulder.

"What's he want?" Marcott yelled back.

She made a face and rolled her eyes. "Why don't you come here and find out," she shouted. She held the door open for me. "Come on in."

I went up three rickety metal steps. Inside, the trailer was perfectly neat, but the furniture was cheap and shabby. I sat on an upholstered recliner that began to recline as soon as my rear end touched it. I held myself up by clutching the front of both arms.

The woman said, "I'm Jo, short for JoElla. Can I get you a cup of coffee?" She seemed happy to have a visitor. I wondered if she was preparing the soil for a possible next boyfriend.

Down the hall, a door squealed, and Marcott came out drying his hair with a pink towel. When he saw me, he stopped in his tracks and said, "What are *you* doin' here?"

"Good morning," I said. "I came to see you. I'm wondering if you've heard anything from Kelly."

"No. Have you?"

"No. But I saw him the other night—Friday. He was on a motorcycle. You don't happen to own a motorcycle, do you?"

"No—not that it's any of your business."

"You sure you don't own one?"

He turned to Jo. "Do I own a motorcycle, babe? Tell him."

"If he does, I've never seen it," she told me.

"Did you see the letter to Kelly that his mother wrote him?" I asked Marcott. "It was on the front page of Thursday's *Gleaner*."

"I seen it. That was stupid of her."

"She's worried about him."

"She oughta be. She's the one that got him in the mess he's in."

"Do you know where he is?"

"I wish I did."

He went on drying his hair. He had very long fingers. When finished, he folded the towel and laid it over the back of a barstool at the kitchen counter. Next he took a silver metal comb out of his back pocket and leaned over to peer at his reflection in the window of a built-in oven. Very carefully he combed his hair. Then he put the comb back in his pocket and took a can of Budweiser out of the refrigerator. He held it up and said, "Either of you want a beer?"

"No thanks," I said.

Jo said, "It's too early for me."

"Suit yourselves." He came into the living room and plopped on the couch. Jo sat on an armless rocking chair that looked too small for her.

A motorcycle came rumbling up the street and pulled in next to the trailer.

It's Kelly, I said to myself. A perfect coincidence. Must be fate. I thought I was about to catch Marcott in a lie.

The horn beeped twice, and another door in the hallway opened. A young girl came running toward us.

"This is Ginger, my daughter," Jo said as the girl passed the kitchen counter and veered toward the front door. "Hey, what's the hurry, Ginge? Don't you say hello when we have company?"

"Hi," the girl said, barely glancing at me. She looked anorexic. Her face seemed small, probably because it was surrounded by a cloud of rose-colored hair with silver highlights, which she began tying in a ponytail with a rubber band. An airbrushed T-shirt was stuffed lumpily into her jeans.

"Hey you, just a minute!" Jo said.

The girl stopped. With a sullen expression, she cocked her head and bent one knee. "What," she said without a question mark.

"Where do you think you're going? It's Sunday morning."

"So? Greg and me are goin' to Luh'vulle." The way she pronounced *Louisville* made me wonder if they were transplants from Kentucky.

"On a motorcycle? Oh no you're not."

"Why not"

"It's too dangerous, that's why."

Marcott was grinning like the evil landlord in a silent movie. Ginger fired back, "What am I, a prisoner?"

"You know what I said about Greg—he's too old for you."

"He is not."

The horn tooted again. The engine revved.

"Yes he is."

"No he's not."

Marcott said, "Let her go. Let her have some fun."

"Thanks a lot," Jo shot back. "You're a big help." She jabbed a finger at Ginger. "You are not going to Luh'vulle on that motorcycle. I want you to stay home and do your homework."

Ginger started toward the door again. "Get off my back." Under her breath she muttered, "Fat cow."

Jo catapulted herself out of the rocker. "Don't you talk to me like that! You're lucky we have company, or—"

Ginger stood her ground. "Or what?"

"Go to your room."

"Screw you."

"That's it! I've had all I'm going to take from you."

I thought Jo was going to smack her on the face, but instead she tried to stare the girl into submission.

Ginger leaned forward and stared back.

Jo said, "I told you to go to your room. Now do it!"

Ginger stood there defiantly a few more seconds and then stomped back to her room. She slammed the door so hard that the whole trailer seemed to shake.

"Good!" Jo yelled. "Lock yourself in while you're at it." Wagging her head, she took a deep breath and gave instructions to Marcott, "She is not to go out today. She's to stay here and do her homework. Don't let her get on that motorcycle, okay?"

He laughed. "You better go tie her up before she climbs out the window." He took a swig of beer.

The motorcycle revved up again, but this time it began moving away. Jo panicked. "If she's out there, I'll—" She flung the front door open and stuck her head out. Then, with a victorious smirk, she said, "He must have heard us fighting. He went off by himself."

"I hate you!" Ginger screamed from the bedroom. "I hate you! I wish you was dead!"

"She's only thirteen," Jo said to me. "He's too old for her."

Marcott laughed again. "Maybe *she's* too old for *him.*"

"I know, she's thirteen going on twenty, but I'm still her mom."

"What were *you* doing when you were thirteen?" Marcott said to her.

"Just because I was young and dumb doesn't mean she has to be dumb too."

"It's in her genes," he said. "It's all your fault." Another laugh.

"I'm doing my best to bring her up right. I'm trying to be a good mom." Her lips tightened. She was on the verge of tears. She went to the kitchen sink, leaned over the spout, and dabbed water on her eyes.

"Happy you came?" Marcott asked me with his ever-present grin.

"I'm not unhappy."

"Good for you. Then why don't you buzz off."

"I will. But I have another question for you. Did you know that some twenty years ago your father gave $5,000 worth of gold coins to the woman who had been married to a black man who was lynched by the Ku Klux Klan in 1936?"

There was a brief delay as he digested my runny question. Then he laughed like a maniac and said, "Gold coins worth $5,000? Who the fuck told you that?"

"Someone in a position to know."

His temples pulsed ever so slightly. "Whoever you been talkin' to doesn't know his ass from a hole in the ground. It's bullshit. My dad was as tight as a tick. He wouldn't give $5,000 to anybody."

"I understand your father was a coin collector."

The grin turned into a sneer. "That's more bullshit. He was no coin collector. He had a few old coins that used to belong to *his* old man, that's all. He sent one to Kelly every now and then."

"From what I've been told, he had more than a few."

"I believe I would know what he had better than you would, and I'm tellin' you he was no coin collector."

"More than one person has told me he was. Why would they make that up?"

"How should I know? Maybe they wanted to get their names in the paper."

"I don't think so."

"I don't give a rat's ass what you think. It's none of your business anyway." He stood up and glared at me.

I said, "Why are you so insistent that Chester didn't collect coins?"

"Because it's none of your damn business if he did."

"I understand you're contesting Chester's will."

"Damn right I am. I'm not giving up what's rightfully mine." He stopped and looked at me. I was sick and tired of the grin. "Anyway, what's it to you, Larrison? Are you cookin' up somethin' with my former wife?" His lips parted, exposing his straight white teeth.

I didn't answer.

"You after the farm?" he went on. "If you are, you'll never get it, because *she's* not gonna get it."

Jo rejoined us in the living room. She looked red-eyed and weary. "I've got to get ready and go to work," she announced.

"Where do you work?" I asked her.

"CVS."

"Well, I'll get out of here," I said. "It's been nice meeting you, Jo."

"Nice meeting you, Phil."

As I was leaving the trailer, Greg returned on his motorcycle, a black and silver Harley. At the same time Ginger came running from the front end of the trailer near the street and hopped on the bike. Jo screamed at her from the front door, but Ginger wrapped her arms around Greg's waist, and they took off in a cloud of dust, with their hair blowing in the wind.

"Stupid kids," JoElla said. "They don't even have helmets on."

CHAPTER 29

VISITORS

I WENT back to the office and wrote a feature about Andreas Pluckett for tomorrow's paper. After reporting what I had learned from him, I inserted a few of my own thoughts:

> Chester's gift raises some questions. Why did he give gold coins worth thousands of dollars to the widow of a man who had been lynched 53 years earlier? And does the fact that he owned a sizable number of gold coins support the theory that he was murdered by someone who was searching his house for the "treasure" that was rumored to be hidden there.

The story also reminded readers that Chester, a few years after the death of his second wife, had sold her farm to Walmart, enabling the company to build a supercenter in Campbellsville.

It took me almost as much time to write a headline for the story as it did to write the story itself. I wasn't thrilled with what I finally came up with, but it was the best I could do:

Chester Marcott's Gift of Gold Leads
County Man to Support Kelly Marcott

I wished I could make a connection between Chester's gift and the money he had received for the land he sold Walmart. It would have been a tiny bit of poetic justice if some of that money had gone to Andreas's mother. But why would Chester give her gold coins instead of currency? That didn't make sense, unless it was the only money he'd had at the time. But he would have had a lot of money after selling the farm to Walmart. Furthermore, Chester had given her the gold coins in 1989 and his deal with Walmart did not take place till 1993, so there was no connection between the two events. Too bad. It was unfair that Lila had lost the farm in a sheriff's sale after Abner was lynched.

I finally let go of the article and keyed in a skimpy summary of it on our website. When I hit the publish key, it made me feel good to know that the story was already in people's homes, or on their smartphones or other devices. Unfortunately it also reminded me, once again, that the print version of the *Gleaner* was probably doomed.

I sat back and peered out the window. I found myself staring in a trance at what was most likely the hanging tree behind the courthouse. Maybe I should launch a campaign to have it cut down. No, it wasn't the tree's fault it had been used to kill a man. The tree didn't deserve to be punished. Men did.

I felt my pants sticking to the chair. I peeled myself off and took a hike to the coffee machine.

As I watched the golden-brown liquid gurgle into my mug, it occurred to me that Chester may have given Lila more than one valuable gift. Maybe Andreas didn't know everything that had gone on between them. But if *he* didn't know, then who did? Or what if he just didn't want to tell me everything he knew? Now that I thought about it, he had protested a bit too much when I asked him if Chester and his mother may have had a romantic relationship.

I went back to my office and checked to see how many stories were waiting for me on the computer. There wasn't a single one yet. Thank God I had my feature on Pluckett. While I was congratulating myself, the phone rang.

It was Angela.

"Phil!" she burst out frantically, "I'm sorry to bother you again, but Dale was just here."

"He was? I just had a talk with him this morning."

"You did? Why?"

I wondered if it was my visit that had inspired Dale to return to the old home place. Instead of sharing that thought with Angela, I said, "I spotted him at a gas station and followed him. I wanted to see where he's been staying."

"Was Kelly there?" she asked.

"Not while I was. What did Dale want at your place?"

"I don't know. He was looking for something. He got into a storage space under the stairs in the living room. I didn't even know there was a storage space there. You can't see the door to it. It blends in with the paneling. I'm standing in front of it right *now,* and I can't see the edges. Dale peeled back the carpet to open it. There's a hidden latch or something, I don't know." Her voice rose: "Whatever he was looking for, it wasn't there. It made him mad. I mean he was *furious.* I think he must've been been drinking. He accused me of stealing his property. He said it didn't belong to his father, so it wasn't part of my inheritance. What was that all about? Not that I'm ever going to inherit anything, according to him. He screamed at me like a crazy man—'It's not yours! It's mine!' He scared me half to death. I thought he was going to kill me."

I said, "Take it easy, Angela."

"How can I take it easy?" she said as if pleading to be understood. "He was in the house! Dummy that I am, I let him in." She began to cry. "I need to get out of here! I can't stay here. If it wasn't for Kelly, I'd be gone. I have to go. I'm going to my parents' house."

"Not now," I said. "You're too upset. You might get in a wreck. If you want me to, as soon as I'm through here tonight, I'll come out and stay with you. I'll sleep on the sofa. In the meantime, you can stay here in my office with me while I'm working."

"What if Dale comes back before I leave?"

"Where's your shotgun?"

"In its usual place, next to my bed. I thought about getting it when he came earlier, but I knew it would make him mad, and then who knows what would happen. I don't know if I could shoot Dale. After all, he *is* Kelly's father."

I told her what else I had learned that morning: "Dale's living in a trailer with a woman named JoElla and her daughter, Ginger. It's a dumpy-looking trailer on the outside, but inside it's neat and clean."

"It better be," Angela said. "If JoElla leaves a dirty dish in the sink, Dale's liable to throw her through the wall. How old is the girl?"

"Thirteen."

"Is she pretty?"

"Yes, but way too skinny."

"She'd be better off if she was ugly."

"Why do you say that?"

"For her sake. Dale's got a thing for pretty young girls. That's probably why he's shacked up there—so he can get close to Ginger. Did he say anything about Kelly?"

"Just that he hasn't heard from him and doesn't know where he is."

"I don't believe that."

"Neither do I."

"Somebody must be helping Kelly," she insisted. "He's got to be eating *somewhere!* And what's he doing for money? I swear to

God, it's like I'm in a nightmare that won't end. I don't know what to do! Why hasn't he called me? It's been three days since I put that letter in the paper. Something must have happened to him."

Just like that, she was depressed again. Up and down—I knew the drill. She needed to get out of that house. I thought about inviting her to stay at my place. "Angela," I began, "how about if—"

She cut me off : "Somebody's at the back door!"

The dog was barking. She took her phone with her and ran through the house. The floor squeaked. She opened a kitchen drawer and fumbled for something. Then she entered the pantry and screamed with joy.

"Hi, Ma," Kelly said. "Whadaya gonna do with that knife?" He sounded hoarse.

Angela's joyful sobs and Kelly's protests told me she was hugging and kissing him.

"You're thin as a rail," she scolded. "When was the last time you had something to eat?"

A raw, raspy cough came out of his throat.

"Oh, Kelly, you sound *awful!*"

"It sounds worse than it is," he said.

"You sound like you have pneumonia. You need to see a doctor."

"I don't need a doctor!" he said. "I just want to wash up and get some clean clothes. Then I'm outta here."

"You're not going anywhere. You sound terrible!"

"Thanks a lot."

I stopped listening. I hung up the phone and ran out to my car.

CHAPTER 30

EVERYTHING WILL BE ALL RIGHT

I MADE it to Angela's place in record time. I was happy to see that no police cars were there. I took it as a good indication that her phone wasn't tapped.

As I pulled up to the porch, the screen door opened and Angela came out. I got out of the car, and she said, "I knew you were coming when you weren't on the phone. I guess you know Kelly's here."

"Yes. I wanted to get here before he took off again."

A pretty smile lit up her face. "Phil, I can hardly believe it. I feel like I'm dreaming, but he's upstairs in the tub this very minute." Her smile faded. "He's sick though. He has a bad cough and a sore throat. I think it's the flu. I gave him some cough medicine, and he drank a glass of orange juice."

"I'm glad he's here," I said.

Angela went on: "He looks terrible. He's lost weight. He hasn't shaved. His clothes are *filthy.*" She shook her head. "And he smelled something awful. I made him take a hot bath."

We sat on the rocking chairs and stared toward the county road. A blue tractor sped past the stone fence. A minute later Angela stood up and said, "I'd better check on Kelly and make sure he's all right."

We went inside. She asked if I'd like some coffee, and of course I said yes. I followed her to the kitchen and sat at the table. She filled the coffee machine and set a mug in front of me. Then she hurried upstairs and knocked on the bathroom door. "How you doing in there, Kelly?" she called. "You okay?"

In a grating voice he called back, "I'm still here, if that's what you're worried about."

"Good. Don't fall asleep in the tub."

She came down laughing to herself. When she saw me watching her, she stopped and said, "What are you thinking about?"

"You," I said. "And Kelly. I'm thinking maybe you should call the police and tell them he's here."

"Don't rush me, Phil. He just got here." She brushed past me and went to the kitchen.

I remained in the living room. I wanted to have a look at the storage space that she had mentioned on the phone.

The triangular wall below the banister on the living-room side of the stairs was paneled in dark wood all the way to the floor. I could not see a door, and there was no baseboard at the bottom of the triangle. If there had been a baseboard, it would have been attached to the paneling all the way across and there would have been two vertical cuts in it, revealing a door. This made me wonder if the entire triangle might be a door, but it would have been awfully big. I noticed that the bottom of the paneling appeared to be behind the edge of the wall-to-wall carpet. That explained why Dale had to peel the carpet back to open the door.

I moved a small table with a lamp on it away from the wall. Then I knelt down and pushed against the wall in several places, but the paneling did not give. I felt around the edge of the entire triangle and slid my fingers up and down the grooves in the wood.

"What are you doing?" Angela said. She was staring at me from the dining room.

"Checking the wall," I said. "I'd like to take a look inside the storage space, if you don't mind."

"Dale said there's nothing in there but some dusty old boxes of dishes and glasses, but you can take a look if you want to."

"I'm trying to figure out how to open it."

"I don't know, but the door is right in the middle there, where you are. Dale had to pull the carpet back to open it."

I knelt down again. This time I pushed my fingers behind the edge of the carpet and immediately pricked two of them on a tack strip. I sucked the dots of blood on my fingertips, then wiped my mouth and tongue on my shirtsleeve. Carefully this time, I raised the edge of the carpet, exposing an old wooden tack strip that was nailed to the floor next to the paneling. It ran the entire length of the triangular wall, including where the door must be, but, as close as I was to it, I still could not see the door.

"Did you notice how he opened this thing?" I asked Angela.

"No."

I ran my fingers up and down the grooves in the paneling again, but there was no latch or push button or anything else that would open the door. Then I noticed that a two-foot section of the tack strip had a half-inch triangular point at both ends, which fit snugly into notches in the adjoining parts of the tack strip. Unlike the rest of the strip, the pointed section was not nailed to the floor, and with some prying and wiggling I worked it up out of the notches. This revealed a narrow space under the door. It was just big enough to slide a small screwdriver blade or Popsicle stick back and forth. I figured the door would be hinged at the taller side on my right, so I looked for some kind of hook or latch at the bottom-left corner of the door, about two feet from the bottom of the stairs. I found a sliding latch, which I managed to move with a corkscrew, and the short side of the door popped open.

"Good job, Phil!" Angela said.

I stuck my head into the secret storage room, but it was too dark to see much of anything, and there was no light switch, so I took the lamp off the table that I had moved, switched it on, and set it inside. There were several boxes of china and glassware, but nothing else. I asked Angela if she was sure Dale hadn't removed anything.

"Absolutely," she said. "He dragged those boxes out, and I watched him all the time."

"Did he say what he was looking for?"

"No. I asked him, but all he said was, 'It belongs to me.'"

I said, "Maybe it was the so-called treasure Chester was believed to have."

"Yes," she said, and maybe Dale knows something about it."

"You be careful—he might come looking for it again."

"It wouldn't surprise me."

Water from the bathtub began draining through a pipe in the wall. We heard the bathroom door open, and Angela called upstairs, "Kelly, should I fix you some lunch, or would you rather have breakfast?"

He coughed hoarsely and said, "Whatever's quicker."

I joined his mother at the foot of the stairs and shouted, "Hey, Kelly, you've got company—me."

He appeared at the top of the stairs. "Phil?" he said. "What are *you* doin' here?"

Angela said, "Phil was on the phone with me when you got here. He heard us talking."

"What are you doin'?" he asked me. "Lookin' for a story?"

"Always," I said.

He came down barefooted. He was wearing a clean pair of jeans and a gray T-shirt. His damp hair draped over his back. He made a hard, dry cough and grimaced as though it hurt.

Angela said, "You're going to catch pneumonia. Here, dry your hair." She tossed him a dish towel.

I said, "How are you, Kelly? It's good to see you again."

He made a loud snotty sniffle and swallowed the snot. When he spotted the storage-room door standing open, he said, "Whoa, I didn't know about that. What's in there?"

"Nothing important," Angela said. "Your father was here earlier today. He was looking for something in there, but he didn't find it, whatever it was."

Kelly got down on his hands and knees and peered inside. The lamp was still on. He pulled off the shade and held the lamp like a flashlight. "Cripes," he said, "I wonder how many other hiding places there are in this house. Those photos of the Klan could be anywhere."

Angela went to the kitchen, but I waited for Kelly to finish his search. His head got tangled in a cobweb, and he crawled out backward, using his fingers to rake the cobweb out of his hair. When he stood up, he began coughing loud, long, hard, dry coughs.

He went on hacking and coughing all the way to the kitchen, where Angela was making grilled-cheese sandwiches in a large cast-iron pan. She shook her head hopelessly and said, "Kelly, you sound *awful!* As soon as you eat, I'm taking you to the emergency room."

"No you're not. I'm okay. It sounds worse than it is." He went to the refrigerator, grabbed a half gallon of milk, and took a gulp out of the plastic bottle.

"Drink some more orange juice," Angela said. "It'll help your throat."

"This helps."

I asked him if he had seen his mom's letter in the *Gleaner*.

"What letter?"

"She wrote you an open letter urging you to turn yourself in to the police."

"What'd you do that for?" he asked her. Then he paced back and forth like a wolf in a cage.

Angela said, "You can't keep running, Kelly. You're ill. You may have the flu."

"It's just a cold." He began coughing again.

"You need to see a doctor," Angela said. "Then I want you to give yourself up."

"You want me to get lynched? Once I'm in that jail, I'm dead. They'll lynch me and call it a suicide."

I said, "That won't happen, Kelly. Believe me."

"Ha! There'll be a rope around my neck the first night I'm in jail."

"How about this?" I said. "I'll ask the sheriff to let me stay with you overnight." That was the second time today I had offered to stay with a Marcott overnight.

A phony laugh burst out of his mouth. "Why? So you can get a picture of me hanging in my cell?"

"You won't go to jail," I said. "You're only seventeen. You're still a minor. You'll go to the juvenile center."

"Forget it!" he croaked, which generated another coughing fit. When he finished coughing, he looked so weak and haggard that I thought he was falling asleep.

"Sit down," his mother said. "I'm fixing you some lunch. You too, Phil."

Kelly plopped onto a chair at the table, and I sat across from him. He stared past me out the side window. There were enormous bug bites on his arms and neck.

I asked him where he had been staying.

His head cocked to the side, and one corner of his mouth opened.

The expression implied that I must be crazy if I expected to get an answer to my question, so I tried another one: "How did you get here today?"

"No comment," he said.

Angela set our sandwiches in front of us. Kelly picked up half of his, and it disappeared in two bites.

"When was the last time you had something to eat?" Angela said.

He didn't answer.

With what was getting to be a permanent look of concern, his mom said, "You must be starving. I'll make you another sandwich."

"He can have mine," I said, sliding my plate across the table.

Kelly pulled it toward him. "You sure you don't want it? Thanks."

While he devoured my lunch, I said, "I saw you at Christine Gasaway's wedding reception Friday night."

"Oh yeah?" he said, chewing and talking.

"Uh-huh. You're lucky you had a motorcycle, or you would've got caught."

"No shit, Dick Tracy."

"Kelly," Angela said, "must you talk like that?"

"Yeah, I must," he said.

"Where'd you get the motorcycle?" I asked.

"I borrowed it."

"Does that mean *borrow* as in *borrow* or *borrow* as in *steal?*"

"I'm not a thief."

"I'm glad to hear that. What were you doing there? Why'd you take a chance on getting caught?"

No answer. Just another bite of the sandwich.

"Was it because you wanted to see Glorie?"

He leveled his eyes at me and said, "Leave Glorie out of it."

"Has she been helping you hide?"

Slowly he repeated, "Leave . . . her . . . *out* . . . of . . . it!"

"She doesn't want to be left out. I had a talk with her at the reception. She's worried about you."

"I think I know that."

Angela reached across the table and touched his hand. "Are you and Glorie going together?" she asked.

He pulled his hand back and stared at the table.

"Kelly," his mother prodded, "is it serious?"

I expected him to tell her to shut up, but instead he took a long, deep breath and said, "We were talkin' about goin' to Southern Cal together after we graduate, but that was before I got kicked outta school and—" He left the thought hanging.

"And what?" Angela asked.

He seemed to debate with himself. Finally he finished his sentence: "—before Glorie told me she's pregnant."

Angela looked wiped out. "Oh God," she said miserably. "You wouldn't joke about something like that, would you, Kelly? It's not something to joke about."

"You don't have to believe me if you don't want to."

She put her hand on top of his. "When it rains, it pours. Does she think you're the father?"

"I *am* the father."

"Are you sure?"

"Yes. I'm sure. We've been going together since the middle of January. She hasn't gone out with anybody else. She told me she missed her period last month. She said she's never missed one before."

Angela put her elbows on the table and rubbed her eyes. Her lips were so tight they seemed to have disappeared. Finally, in a low, grim voice she said, "What are you and Glorie going to do?"

"What do you think we're going to do? We're going to get married."

"How old is Glorie?" Angela asked.

"Seventeen, a month younger than I am."

"Do her parents know she's pregnant? Has she told them?"

"She's afraid to. She thinks they'll want her to get an abortion, and she doesn't want to. I don't want her to either."

Angela sprang off her chair and threw her arms around Kelly's neck. Tears ran down her cheeks as she pressed the side of his head against her breasts. "I love you, Kelly," she said. "Tell Glorie not to be afraid. . . . Tell her everything will be all right."

Kelly went on: "Glorie said she's gonna wait and see if she misses her next period. If she does, then she'll tell her mom."

Angela kissed Kelly on top of his head. Her tears ran into his long tangled hair.

CHAPTER 31

THE PURPLE BAT

D ESPITE her last words to Kelly, Angela did not look as if
she believed everything would be all right. She looked
absolutely miserable. She seemed drained, as if she had no tears
left. By a quirk of association, it reminded me of a sign I had
seen once—the name of a beauty shop, *Curl Up And Dye,* outside a house in the country.

When Angela stopped crying into her son's hair, I said,
"Kelly, how would you like some free advice?" The question
made me think of my father. He used to ask me if I wanted
some dadvice. I never did.

"No thanks," Kelly said.

"I'll give you some anyway," I told him. "You need to turn
yourself in to the police."

His mouth twisted as if I had said something stupid. "What
I need to do is find out who killed Grampaw," he insisted.

"Is that what you've been trying to do?"

"Yeah."

"How's that going for you?"

"Not great. The system's rigged. I tried to get the names of
the descendants of the creeps that lynched Abner Richards. I
thought I could do it at the genealogical society, so I went there

with Glorie one day. There was only one person there. She said her name was Veevee." He began coughing again.

I said, "I know Veevee. Vivian Velmann. She was society editor at the *Gleaner* when I started working there."

"That's nice to know," he said. He coughed some more. It sounded painful. In a voice that sounded as if he had sandpaper in his throat, he said, "She wasn't much help. I told her we were working on a school project where we had to trace the descendants of some people who were born around a hundred years ago. I didn't tell her they were in the Ku Klux Klan. I thought that might tip her off as to who I was."

He had another coughing attack, and Angela said, "Wait a minute, Kelly. I'll get you something for that cough." She ran upstairs and returned with a nearly empty bottle of Vicks cough syrup. She couldn't get the cap off, so she ran it under hot water. "Go ahead, I'm listening," she said.

Kelly seemed ready to nod off, but he went on with his story: "Veevee said she couldn't let us have any information about the people on our list unless we could prove we were closely related to them. She said she couldn't even tell us if any of their descendants were dead or alive. She said it was because of federal privacy laws. The government wants to prevent identity theft. She said, 'I'm surprised your teacher doesn't know this.' It was like she knew who I was but was afraid to say so. She probably thought I'd kill her."

"Or maybe she doesn't think you're guilty," I said.

Kelly made a loud sniffle and said, "You know, you might be right. She did help us a little. She said I could trace a family tree by looking up obituaries in old newspapers. She said I should start by looking through back issues of the *Gleaner* to see if I could find the obits of the guys on my list. The obits would tell if they ever got married and had children. Then I could look up the children's obits and see if *they* got married and had kids, and keep goin' like that up to now. Then I would have to try and find out if any of them are still alive." His bloodshot eyes met mine. "The *Gleaner* has all its old issues, doesn't it, Phil? Can I access them on a computer?"

"No," I said. "Only the past ten years or so are available on our website, but all the earlier issues are on microfilm."

"They all should be on the computer," he said.

"Tell Ed Wylie—he owns the paper."

"Could I come in during the night and look at the microfilms when nobody's around?"

"You want me to get fired?"

"Or maybe *you* could do it."

"It would take too much time," I said. "You've accused a lot of people of lynching Abner Richards three-quarters of a century ago. Who knows how many descendants there are, and how many have moved away? It would take forever to research them."

"I'm not asking you to look at every newspaper in the United States. Just the *Gleaner*. I want to find out which ones are still alive and if they live around here. They're the most likely ones who killed Grampaw. Maybe you could put a reporter on it."

"We don't have the staff to do genealogical research."

"Why not? This is investigative journalism, not genealogy. It's about tracking down the guys who lynched an innocent man and think they got away with it."

Angela piped up: "Maybe I could help. Are the microfilms anywhere besides the *Gleaner?*"

"Yes," I said, "the Campbellsville Library has them. So does the Indiana University Library, and the Indiana State Library. But it would take a ton of work."

"What else have I got to do?" she said. "I could do it in Campbellsville."

"Yeah," Kelly said, "and I can go up to IU. Nobody would recognize me there, I don't think. But the first thing I got to do is search this place from top to bottom. I need to find those photos of the Klan."

"If they're still here," I said. "Whoever killed Chester might have them."

"In that case, I'm screwed."

I thought about telling Kelly and Angela that they should start by talking to the old Klansmen who were still alive, as I had done, but that could be dangerous, so I didn't suggest it.

Angela said, "Kelly, I just remembered, I found something you'll be interested in."

"What?"

"Come with me. I'll show you."

She led the way to Chester's bedroom. The bed sheets that she had shown me yesterday were no longer on the bed. They were back on the shelf in the closet where she had found them. She got them down and unfolded the bottom sheet again.

When the little white robe appeared, Kelly erupted: "Holy shit! Was that Grampaw's?"

"I don't know," Angela said. "Maybe. Or maybe his father had it made for him. Maybe your great-grandfather was in the Ku Klux Klan."

"Or maybe Grampaw had it made for Dad."

Angela cringed. "I didn't think of that," she said.

I said, "Maybe your grandfather was against publishing the photos because he didn't want it to come out that any Marcott had been in the Klan."

Kelly spun around on me. "Our name wasn't on any of the photos I found."

"Maybe he was afraid that if you published them, someone would reveal that one or more Marcotts used to be in the Klan too."

"I gotta see those photos again," Kelly said. "I have to find them! I'll tear the place apart if I have to."

Angela said, "You don't have to wreck the house, Kelly. I'll help you look for them. If they're here, we'll find them."

I felt a slight tickle in my throat. I wondered if I was getting Kelly's sore throat. He was a walking germ machine. My back was getting sore too. I stood up and tried to work the kinks out as I said, "Kelly, the best thing you can do for yourself is surrender to the police. I don't think they have enough evidence to convict you of murdering Chester. All they have is a baseball bat with your fingerprints on it."

"I can explain that," he said. "The bat belonged to my dad. I found it in the attic. I thought it was cool. It's purple. I never saw a purple bat before. It's got a shallow cup hollowed out at the top. Grampaw called it a cup bat. And yeah, it's got my fingerprints on it. That's because I used to hit hickory nuts with it out in the yard. Grampaw called them pig nuts. They're all over the lawn out there."

"Did anyone ever see you do that?" I asked.

"Grampaw did. He told me not to break any windows."

Angela's face lit up. "Kelly, you should tell the police. It explains how your fingerprints got on the bat."

"It wouldn't matter," he said. "They have their 'proof.' My prints are on the bat. To them it means I killed Grampaw. They're gonna believe what they want to believe."

I said, "At least you have a good explanation for how your prints got on the bat. And besides, if you used it to kill Chester, you would have wiped the fingerprints off, wouldn't you?"

"Of course," he replied, "but the cops would say I panicked or something and forgot."

"You don't want to agree with anything I say, but your explanation about the bat raises a reasonable doubt. If your case were to go to trial—and I'm not saying it will, but if it *would*—all your lawyer would have to do is get one juror to doubt that you killed Chester, and you'd be acquitted."

"I can't take that chance," Kelly said. "If I walk into that jail and give myself up, I'll never walk out again."

"You have that fixed in your head," I said. "You're wrong."

"That's what you think." As if tired of arguing, he turned away and said, "I have to go to the bathroom."

Angela and I stared at each other as he tromped away. I waited for the bathroom door to close. As soon as it did, I asked if she wanted me to call the police.

She hung her head. "I don't know. What if he's right and something happens to him while he's in jail?"

"He won't be in jail. He'll be in the juvenile center."

"Whatever," she said. "If anything happened to him, I couldn't forgive myself. I couldn't live with myself."

"You said he should turn himself in."

"I know what I said! But I'm not sure now."

Kelly began coughing again.

Angela went down the hall and knocked on the bathroom door. "Are you all right, Kelly?" she asked.

"I'm on the john," he shouted. "Gimme a break!"

I debated whether to call the sheriff. I wasn't a cop, but I wanted to maintain a good relationship with Carl. If he would find out I had been here with Kelly, he might think I was helping him evade arrest. I wondered if it was a crime to fail to report the whereabouts of someone who was wanted for murder. I might lose my job. On the other hand, I wouldn't even know Kelly was here if I hadn't just happened to be on the phone when he showed up, or if Angela had hung up on me before letting him into the house, or if I had hung up instead of eavesdropping on her. . . . I went on rationalizing: It was just a coincidence that I knew Kelly was here. I wasn't entitled to the information. It wouldn't be fair to turn him in. What's more, if I did turn him in and he ended up getting lynched, Angela might blame me for it. That would be the end of our budding romance, if that's what it was.

Vickie used to say I thought too much. Stop thinking, Larrison. Get out of here. Go back to work.

The bathroom door opened, and Kelly yelled, "Oh *shit!* Whadaya *doin'* there, Mom?" She was standing right in front of the door.

"I'm sorry," Angela said. "I thought something was wrong."

"So you decided to give me a heart attack?"

"I want to take you to the emergency room. We'll go to the hospital in Bedford. I don't think anybody would recognize you there."

"I gotta search the house." He squeezed past her and walked toward the far end of the hall.

"Kelly!" Angela pleaded.

He opened the last door on his right and tromped upstairs. Angela just stared.

In a feeble effort to make her feel better, I said, "I guess he's going to search the attic. Maybe he'll find what he's looking for."

"Will it do any good if he does?"

"It might. If he can shine enough light on the lynching, one of those old KKK guys might break down and confess before he meets his maker." *Meets his maker*—did you really say that, Larrison?

Kelly was banging around in the attic. I thought about helping him with his search. I felt as if I shouldn't leave the house as long as he was there. But what would I do when he decided to leave? Try to stop him? Tie him up? "I'd better get back to work," I said.

Angela nodded.

"What are *you* going to do?" I asked.

"I don't know," she said. "I'm thinking about calling Mary Lou Dunn and asking her to come out here and talk to Kelly."

"That's a good idea."

She started downstairs. She seemed to carry the weight of the world on her back. When we reached the front door, she turned to me and said, "What do you think Mary Lou will say?"

"I think she'll tell Kelly to give himself up."

"I mean do you think she'll come?"

"Oh. I don't know. I think she will, if she's not busy."

She began biting a fingernail.

I said, "Would you like me to stick around?"

"No. You have to go to work." She hesitated, then said, "Phil, you won't put it in the paper that Kelly came home, will you?"

"No. Don't worry about that."

"Thanks."

"I'll call you later, okay?"

"Okay."

I let myself out, and she followed me onto the porch. As I pulled away from the house, she was biting her nails again.

CHAPTER 32

LEAFY SHADOWS

B Y the time I got back to town, it was going on five o'clock. I was hours behind on my work, so instead of going home I went to the *Gleaner*. I found a ton of stuff waiting for me.

Roberta Akin, who had been working at the *Gleaner* longer than I'd been alive and who liked to needle me, poked her head into my office and said, "Where have you been all day, Phil? Up to no good again?"

"No," I said. "I was just minding my own business. How are things in Akin Bottoms?"

She laughed and announced to the newsroom, "He's back. Better pretend you're doin' somethin'."

The next few hours flew. When I got caught up on the computer, I sat back and folded my hands on top of my head. The nice thing about Sunday was there were no late local stories to wait for—no meetings, no sports. Barring a fatal wreck, there probably would be nothing else we'd have to write up. And unless the Associated Press moved a major story, I had everything I needed for the front page.

I treated myself to a pack of cashews, and after prying the bits out of my teeth with my tongue, I called Angela.

"It's me," I said. "What's going on out there?"

"Ohhhh nothing," she said in a slow, tired voice. "I was just sitting out front watching the grass grow."

"Sounds like fun," I said.

"I wasn't having fun." She paused before adding, "Kelly's gone."

So she wasn't tired. She was depressed. I had some Prozac in my medicine cabinet. I thought about offering to bring her some, but then she might think I had a depression problem, and right now I didn't. "Did you talk to Mary Lou?" I asked.

"Yes, I got her on the phone, but she wasn't at home. She was in New Harmony. She won't be back till tomorrow."

"That's too bad. I was hoping she'd talk Kelly into turning himself in."

"Me too, but he wouldn't have done it, I know that. He wants to find those photos he's after. I think he would have gone on looking for them all night, but his girlfriend showed up and he went somewhere with her."

"Is he coming back?"

"I don't know. I don't think he did either."

"Did you talk to his girlfriend?"

"Just a few words. Kelly said she didn't want to come in, so I went out and introduced myself. She stayed in her car. She seemed real nervous. I think she was afraid of me."

"Did Kelly talk to Mary Lou?"

"No," she said feebly. "I tried to get him to, but he wouldn't. He wanted to keep searching. He didn't find anything in the attic, but at least he got it straightened up a little. Next he went through the bedrooms. He pulled everything out of the closets. He had boxes and clothing all over the rooms." Her voice rose in distress: "I'm worried about him. He was—I don't know— sort of obsessed." She sniffled and said, "Excuse me." She laid the phone down and blew her nose. When she picked up again, she said, "I'm worried, Phil. I've never seen him like this."

"I'm worried about *you,*" I said. "Listen, I should be able to get out of here early tonight. I could come out there and keep you company."

"Are you sure you want to? In case you can't tell, I'm not in a very good mood."

"I know the feeling. I'll be there as soon as I can."

· · ·

I HELPED design the front page, and I hung around to check the paper as it came off the press.

The Pluckett story looked good. It started in a blue-bordered box on the bottom of the front page and ran over to the back page of section A. I grabbed a copy for Angela. I had wanted to get to her place sooner, but I felt sticky, and my hair curled up on the sides like the roof of a pagoda, so I went home and took a quick shower.

Drying off, I pictured Angela waiting for me. Vickie had stopped waiting up about a month after I got my job at the *Gleaner.*

Watch out, Larrison. Forget Vickie. Think of Angela. She's out there waiting for you. She needs you.

It was a pretty night. Halfway to Zumma, a layer of mist hung over the fields, and I went in and out of it as the highway rose and fell. The moon seemed to race me through the trees.

When I drove up the lane toward Angela's house, the porch light was on, glowing through the mist. The scene imprinted itself on my brain. I knew it would come back to me at random moments the rest of my life.

I rolled to a stop in front of the porch and got out of the car. The front door opened as I went up the steps, and I saw Angela silhouetted behind the screen door.

"Here I am," I said. "And here's tomorrow's *Gleaner.*"

"Thanks." She pushed the screen door open and took the paper. She seemed ready to conk out. She was wearing a light-gray top that zipped up the front and a dark-blue skirt. I hadn't seen her in a skirt or a dress since Chester's funeral.

"How ya doing?" I said.

"I've been better."

She flapped a hand at the moths fluttering around the porch light. I followed several of them into the living room. Every light was on, and all the drapes were closed. She swung the door shut and fastened the locks.

"Would you like something to drink?" she asked. "Coffee? Tea?"

"You know what I could go for—a cup of cocoa, if you have some." Weirdly, I felt like a traitor to coffee.

"That sounds good," Angela said. "I think there's some in the cabinet."

I followed her to the kitchen. She found a box of Swiss Miss, and she heated milk instead of water. While she stirred the powder in cups of hot milk, she said, "I feel like I'm in a haunted house. It makes noises. Every time I hear a noise I jump."

"You've had a rough time," I said.

"I wish Kelly hadn't run off again. But he wanted to be with Glorie. I can understand that, especially if she's pregnant."

She set the cups of cocoa on the table and used a knife to scrape a gob of marshmallow creme into each one. She plopped down on a chair across from me and gazed across the table with a look of hopeless acceptance.

It was nice sitting in the kitchen with her. It would have been even nicer if she hadn't been in such a down mood.

"What'd you do after I left?" I asked.

"Not much. I called Mom and Dad and told them Kelly had been here. I didn't say how sick he was and how his girl-friend might be pregnant. They would have freaked out."

"Wait till you know for sure that she's pregnant."

"Oh, she's pregnant all right. Why should anything good happen? Everything just keeps getting worse. One of these days Dale's going to come and beat the hell out of me. I'm surprised he hasn't already. Maybe he's afraid it would hurt his chances of winning his lawsuit if I have him arrested."

"How's his suit going?"

"It's going nowhere. Nothing's happened. Everything's tied up in probate. I'm surprised Dale hasn't tried to have me evicted."

"I'm not. Chester left the house and farm to you. Dale's challenging the will, but I doubt that he'll win. Chester was in his right mind. I met him shortly before he was murdered, and he was not incompetent. I'll testify to that if you want me to."

"Thanks. I might take you up on that."

I said, "I don't think Dale has a snowball's chance of winning his suit."

She frowned, unconvinced. She stared into her cup as if it were a crystal ball. The marshmallow creme had dissolved, and a ring of light had formed in the cocoa. Without looking up, she said, "I'd let Dale have everything if I could just take Kelly back to LA with me."

"You don't mean that. Kelly got in trouble with drugs out there."

"He's in a lot worse trouble here. Here he's wanted for murder."

I leaned forward and said, "Angela, I just can't take the murder charge seriously. Kelly didn't kill Chester. I can't believe a jury would convict him."

"I can."

"No way."

She sipped her cocoa and stared at me over the top of the cup. When she lowered it, a tan smear covered her upper lip.

She licked it away. I wished I had thought of licking her lip. There was a time when I would have. That was long ago, when I was going with Vickie. That was then. This was now. Let Vickie and her husband, the daring anesthesiologist, go rock climbing on El Capitan. Let them fall off the mountain and land on their heads.

Don't be bitter, Larrison. You've got to get over Vickie, or she'll go on haunting you the rest of your life. Look across the table. That's Angela sitting there. She's beautiful. She's gorgeous. She's the one.

The old stirrings were back. I hadn't slept with a woman since Vickie left, and that was five years ago now.

But why would Angela want me? I was overweight. I was nobody—a small-town newspaper editor in a failing industry. One of these days I'd be out of a job. If I made a play for Angela, she'd think I was after the money Chester had left her.

I made an effort to stop thinking about myself. I asked Angela if she wanted to watch TV.

"What's on?" she said.

"I don't know. Does it matter?"

"Kind of."

"Let's go see."

We went to the living room. I clicked through the channels and found an old episode of *Perry Mason* in black and white. We sat on the sofa next to each other. After a few minutes I held her hand on her lap. She put her other hand on top of mine.

When Perry Mason and his secretary, Della Street, drove through a neighborhood of small houses and tall palm trees, Angela said, "This reminds me of Los Angeles. I think I was on that street once."

Uh-oh, I said to myself, the next thing she's gonna say is she shouldn't have sent Kelly here. "You want me to turn it off?" I asked.

"No. I like seeing how Los Angeles used to be, and I'm glad you're here with me."

"So am I." I was tempted to unzip her top.

As if reading my mind, she said, "Phil, we're both in our thirties, aren't we?"

"That's my biological age," I said. "Emotionally I'm only twelve."

"Whatever. Legally, we're both adults, right?"

No more wisecracks, Larrison. Go for it. What's one more mortal sin?

I turned sideways and kissed her. It was a series of light kisses on her forehead, her eyebrows, her lashes, her eyelids, her nose, her ears, her chin.

Should I tell her I loved her? Did she expect me to say it? But *was* I in love? I had quit believing in love. It used to mean something permanent to me. I had quit believing in things that were supposed to last forever. Love is just a word, just a sound. . . . I was thinking too much. *Shut up,* I told the voice in my head.

"I love you, Angela," I said. "I fell in love with you the first time I saw you."

"At the funeral home?" She laughed. "How romantic."

"I'll show you how romantic." I slid the zipper on her top halfway down.

"Let's go upstairs," she said.

She turned off the kitchen and living-room lights, and I zapped the TV. We held hands going up the wide steps.

In the bedroom, moonlight cast leafy shadows on the walls. I put my arms around her and kissed her again. She undressed down to her panties and bra. She started for the bed, but I stopped her and finished undressing her. Then I took off my clothes and sat on the edge of the bed. Standing between my legs, she ran her fingers through my hair as I kissed her breasts.

"Watch Kelly come back now and catch us," she said.

"I'll hide under the bed," I told her.

She laughed, and we got under the covers.

I felt like an oversexed kid, all charged up, but I didn't rush her. I kissed and caressed her. At first she simply lay there, still and quiet, letting me play with her, but when I climbed on top, she ran her fingers up and down my sides and wrapped her legs around mine. The passion in her kisses surprised me.

"God, you're wonderful," I said.

Her heart beat against my chest. Her fingernails glided up and down my back. Her breath fluttered in my ear. I wished I was twenty pounds lighter—I didn't want to squash her.

When I finished, she was breathing as hard as I was. She went on squeezing me as if she didn't want to let go. She gave me a long, tender kiss.

We lay together like a pair of spoons.

I held her breasts as we fell asleep.`

CHAPTER 33

LOVE IN THE MORNING

I DIDN'T wake up till eight in the morning. Angela was still asleep, lying on her side with her back toward me. I listened to her breathe. Now and then there was a light flutter of a snore. I rolled onto my side and put my arm around her. She pushed back against me. Then I nudged her onto her back and drew her nightie up.

We kissed as we made love. Long slow kisses. I held her face between my hands. I kissed her eyes, her ears, her breasts. I had forgotten how much I enjoyed making love in the morning.

While Angela was taking a shower, I got dressed. I hated putting on yesterday's socks and shorts, but I hadn't expected to spend the night.

I went down to the kitchen and scared the wits out of the cat, who made a tailback's cut around me and fled through the dining room. I fixed myself a mug of instant coffee and carried it out to the porch.

It was a mild, sunny day. The air was filled with chirps, whistles, and trills. I sat on a rocking chair and watched the sun rise above the knobs. I felt like a decadent aristocrat. I could get used to this, I said to myself.

A few minutes later, Angela came out in a white terry-cloth robe. "There you are," she said with a cheery smile. "I wondered where you got to."

I set my coffee on the floor. "C'mere."

She stood in front of me, and I put my hands on her hips. A long-ago feeling came back to me—a pull, a yearning, a desire to possess and protect, the obsessive sensation of being in love. "I wish I didn't have to go to work," I said.

"I wish you didn't have to, too." She began sliding her fingernails up through the hair on the back of my neck. "It was nice last night. For the first time since Kelly ran away I had a good night's sleep."

I pulled her closer.

Her face turned serious. "Would you like to move in, Phil?" she asked.

"You read my mind," I said.

She leaned over, and we kissed each other as hard as we could.

• • •

My life entered an idyllic phase.

When the weather was nice, we'd have breakfast around 7:30 in the kitchen. Then we'd move to the porch for a second cup of coffee and watch the sun burn off the mist hanging over the fields. In the evening we'd take Sadie for a walk around the pond or the stone fence. We stayed off the road so Dicey wouldn't see us and figure out that we were living together, though we knew she'd find out sooner or later. Sometimes we'd sit on the porch and watch the shadows on the knobs, or we'd sit in in the living room and watch TV or read.

I hadn't read a book in years, but now I started one about the rural revival that was supposedly taking place in the so-called Heartland, thanks to fracking oil out of shale. Angela read the *Gleaner* or *Cosmopolitan, Glamour,* and *Marie Claire.*

At least five nights a week I still had to work late. It got harder and harder for me to leave the house and go to the paper. And when I was at the *Gleaner,* I couldn't wait to get back to Angela again.

On Friday night, just when I was starting to psyche myself up to go back to the *Gleaner,* I heard loud thumps on the porch. Angela and I looked at each other, and just then the screen door opened, and someone ripped it off the door frame. Then the front and back doors came crashing in.

Boots. Shouts. Broken glass.

Angela screamed. I wished the shotgun was here in the living room instead of up in our bedroom, but it wouldn't have made any difference because two guys wearing forest camouflage were already in the house, waving assault rifles at us and screaming like idiots. Another two came charging through the kitchen and dining room, and as soon as they reached the living room, one of the first two sprinted upstairs. Each of them wore a black plastic tag with his name in white letters. I might have thought they were real soldiers if one of them hadn't been ridiculously overweight. He was also sporting a bushy black beard that made him look like a mountain man.

Angela was trembling. I tried to get up to go to her, but the mountain man leveled an AK-47 or whatever it was at my chest. The name on his tag was Jakes, and he had a surprisingly soft voice: "Whoa, easy tharrr, buddy."

"What the hell is this?" I said as fiercely as I could.

"If yuh wanta keep them purty white teeth in yuh mouth, yuh bettuh keep it shut," he said.

A fifth man strutted into the house. He was in his late fifties, early sixties maybe. His name was Bickerstaff, and he reminded me of a British officer in an old war movie. He was the only one without a rifle, but he had a holstered handgun on his belt. "Good work, gentlemen," he said with a light southern accent. His eyes rested on Angela briefly, then shifted to me. I thought he was speaking to me when he said, "Go upstairs," but his next words were, "Private Cullman, and see if Lieutenant Trotter needs some help."

"Yessuh, Colonel!" the so-called private shouted. He sounded like a country boy. Skinny and acne-scarred, he appeared to be in his mid-twenties. He had a toothpick in his mouth, and he kept flicking it up and down. He tapped the banister with the bottom of his fist as he climbed the stairs.

The colonel barked again: "Corporal Jakes, you and Private Smedley secure the prisoners. Wrap 'em up good and tight." He took his pistol out of its holster as Jakes and Smedley set their rifles down. The pistol looked like an antique German Luger. I wondered if he was a Nazi.

Jakes grabbed Angela from behind by her arms.

"Take your hands off me!" she screamed as she tried to break away.

He pulled her hands behind her back.

"Oww! Are you trying to break my arms?"

He lifted her a few inches off her feet and swung her to the floor. He held her down as Smedley bound her wrists and ankles with pieces of clothesline.

Smedley was the youngest member of the squad. His head looked as if it had been shaved a few weeks ago. As he finished tying Angela, he jutted his chin at her backside and glanced at Jakes, who did not play along.

"Let's stay focused, Private," the colonel said to Smedley.

"Sorry, Cunnel," Smedley said with a stupid smile on his face.

I toyed with the idea of jumping the colonel and grabbing his Luger while two of his "soldiers" were busy with Angela, but he never took his eyes off me. Besides, even though he was probably twice my age, I wasn't sure I could take his gun away from him. He appeared to be in good shape. He was a solid square-faced guy with a craggy face and gray flattop. He stood very straight. He had a two-day-old beard and the beginnings of a turkey neck.

Over our heads, boots stomped from room to room. Doors banged into walls. Clothes hangers jangled and fell. Either Trotter or Cullman went up the steps to the attic. About ten minutes later both of them returned to the living room.

"Nobody's up there, sir," said the lieutenant, "but we found this." He handed Angela's shotgun to the colonel. "There might be more weapons," he added. "We didn't search every nook and cranny."

The lieutenant looked too old to be a lieutenant—he was at least forty-five. He stood about five-feet-ten, and his nearly bald head was shaped like a football. A long nose curved downward and inward. His thinning black hair looked as if it had been drawn on his scalp with India ink. The way his eyes darted around the room made him seem wary of everything.

The colonel said, "Thank you, Lieutenant. You and Private Cullman may go and check the cellar now."

The two of them went to the kitchen but came back almost immediately. Without stopping in the living room, Lieutenant Trotter reported, "There's no door to the cellar in the kitchen or dining room, Colonel." His eyes scanned the living room as if searching for a door he had overlooked. He and Jakes proceeded to the parlor on the other side of the stairway.

In the parlor, a door opened and closed. Trotter and Cullman spent less than a minute there before returning to the living room.

"All we found over there was a little john. There's nothin' but a commode and a dinky little sink in it. If there's a cellar, there must be an outside entrance to it."

The colonel said, "I did not see an outside entrance to a cellar. But I did see a 500-gallon propane tank to the west of the house. And I see hot-air registers in this room. There must be a furnace somewhere. Find the furnace, or find me a cellar."

"Yes, sir!" said the lieutenant.

"Yessuh," said the private.

I tried not to laugh at the make-believe army. And I didn't laugh. I barely snickered. But the colonel heard it.

He came toward me with his gun pointed at my face. "You think it's funny, mister?"

I shook my head and said, "No, sir." I was still on the sofa. I could kick him in the nuts. But I had to stay alive—for Angela's sake, if not my own.

The colonel poked his Luger against the middle of my forehead. His finger tightened on the trigger. I felt the blood sink out of my face.

Angela yelled, "Don't shoot him! There's a cellar! There's a door to it in the toilet in the parlor."

The colonel said, "You go through a toilet to get to the cellar?"

"Yes," Angela said. "It's just a partial cellar. There's nothing down there except the furnace and some old canning stuff."

This was news to me—I hadn't known about the door to the cellar.

"Thank you, ma'am," said the colonel. "I'm glad one of you appreciates the gravity of the situation." He lowered his pistol. I thought he was finished with me, but he went on: "You could learn something from the lady, mister." Then he struck my left ear with the barrel of his gun. It felt as though my ear was on fire. He whacked it again.

Angela yelled, "Stop it. Why are you hitting him?"

The colonel sidled over to her and wagged his head. "Ma'am, I'd keep my mouth shut if I were you."

Trotter and Cullman went back to the parlor. We heard a door open. A light clicked on. Then another door opened.

Cullman radioed, "Well, ah'll be damned. Lookie here. There *is* a cellar. Them steps don't look too safe, if ya ask me."

On his walkie-talkie the lieutenant added, "We're goin' down, Colonel."

A few minutes later the pair returned to the living room.

Trotter said, "There's not much down there, Colonel. Like the lady said, it's not a full-size cellar. It was dug out sometime after the house was built."

Cullman said, "I seen that door when we first found the toilet, but I thought it was a linen closet. It ain't a reg'lar-size door."

Trotter said, "There's nothing down there but the furnace and some canning supplies. There's no foundation under the house. The walls and floor are dirt. You can see where they dug outside to excavate the cellar, but they didn't put an outside door in. They just filled up the hole they dug next to the house."

"Thank you, Lieutenant," the colonel said.

Cullman said, "You want me to stand lookout now, Colonel?"

"Yes, Private. Patrol the perimeter of the yard about a hundred feet out. Is your walkie-talkie on?"

"It will be, suh." Cullman saluted from his eyebrow and went out past the shattered front door, which was hanging from a single hinge. Frogs were calling in the pond.

The colonel turned to me again. "I haven't forgotten you," he said. "I won't have you laughing at us." He told his gang to tie me up.

Smedley let out a whoop and said, "Git on the floor, smartass."

When I didn't move, he gave me a side-handed chop in my Adam's apple. My eyes nearly popped out of my head. While I was gagging, he grabbed one of my legs and pulled me off the sofa. He twisted me around so I was lying on my chest. Jakes, the big guy who looked like a mountain man, sat on my head while Smedley and Trotter tied my hands and feet.

"Don't hurt him!" Angela pleaded.

Smedley laughed and pulled the rope tighter. Then he stood up and gave me a kick in the ribs.

"Leave him alone!" said Angela. "He didn't do anything to you."

The colonel said to the lieutenant, "The lady talks too much, doesn't she?"

"Yes, sir," said Trotter.

Colonel Bickerstaff yanked a curtain off a window, tore it in half, and told Angela to open her mouth.

"Go to hell," she said.

He grasped her cheeks in one big hand, pushed her down on her side, and rolled her onto her back.

"Ow!" she cried.

"Oh, did that hurt?" the colonel said. "How does this feel?" He squeezed her nostrils together.

Angela swung her head from side to side trying to shake off his hand, but he did not let go, and when she tried to roll away from him, Smedley sat on her ankles and pressed her legs down at the knees. She held her breath as long as she could but finally opened her mouth, and the colonel stuffed a wad of curtain fabric into it.

"I thought you had better sense, ma'am," he said. "Now we'll have some peace and quiet in here."

Angela turned toward me. Tears ran out of her eyes. The cream-colored curtain looked like a stream of mayonnaise pouring out of her mouth. The grotesque sight made my heart ache.

The colonel batted at the bugs flying around his head. "Lieutenant Trotter, find something to cover up the doorway," he ordered.

Trotter ran upstairs to find a blanket, and Corporal Jakes ripped the door off its remaining hinge and leaned it against the open side of the stairway in the living room. The colonel then told Private Smedley to "run out to the van and get the toolbox out of the Hummer." By then all kinds of bugs were batting against lightbulbs and climbing the walls.

A couple minutes later, Trotter came back with a blanket and a patchwork quilt, and Smedley returned with the toolbox. They nailed the quilt over the front entrance and the blanket over the kitchen doorway.

While this was going on, I realized that, despite all the racket in the house, Sadie wasn't barking. I remembered hearing her bark just before the goon squad invaded the house, but at the time I didn't think anything of it. Now I assumed that the dog must be dead. Poor Sadie. She had tried to warn us.

I wondered if these guys had killed Chester too. If so, they'd have no qualms about killing Angela and me. They weren't wearing masks. They had name tags on their uniforms. Obviously they weren't worried that we could identify them. That worried me.

"Colonel," I said, "may I ask you a question?"

Through her gag, Angela mumbled, "Ill, uhht uh!" which I translated as *Phil, shut up!*

The colonel gave me a sick-and-tired look. "You have a learning disability, don't you?" he said.

"Who are you?" I asked him. "What do you want here?"

The colonel ignored me, but Smedley said, "Yuh want I should bust 'im one, Cunnel?"

"No thank you, Private." The colonel turned to his second-in-command. "Check in with Private Cullman, Lieutenant. See if we've attracted any attention from the neighbors."

Trotter unclipped a walkie-talkie from his belt and said, "Watchdog, Watchdog, come in, Watchdog."

Private Cullman's voice crackled, "Watchdoag here."

"How's it look out there, Watchdog? Any problems? Over."

The watchdog barked, "No, sir. Nothin' ta worry about."

"Colonel Bickerstaff wants to know if we've attracted any attention. Over."

"It don't look like it, sir."

Trotter gave a brief report to the colonel, even though he had heard every word.

"Very good, Lieutenant," Bickerstaff said.

He went to the dining-room and dragged one of the chairs from the table into the living room and set it next to me. Then he sat on it and looked straight down at me.

"Now, Mr. Marcott," he said. "I will tell you why we're here. I believe you have something that belongs to us. We would like to have it back."

CHAPTER 34

A LIGHTLESS PLACE

"My name's not Marcott. It's Larrison," I said. "And I don't know what you're talking about."

The so-called colonel seemed speechless. He tried to hide it with a fierce command: "You got any ID?"

"In my wallet," I said. "It's in my back pocket."

Corporal Jakes rolled me over, pulled the wallet out of my pocket, and tossed it to the colonel.

The colonel flipped it open and removed my driver's license and Social Security card. "I'll be damned," he said. "His name's Phil Larrison. That sounds familiar."

Trotter replied, "Larrison was the name of the reporter who wrote the article we got, Colonel."

"What's *he* doin' here?" the colonel asked, but without waiting for an answer he pulled the gag out of Angela's mouth and said, "What's *your* name, sweetheart?"

"None of your business," she said.

"Don't make me mad again."

"Get out of my house, dammit!"

Smedley said, "You gimme the order, Cunnel, and ah'll make sure she don't cuss at ya no more."

"Simmer down, Private," the colonel said.

Lieutenant Trotter spotted Angela's handbag on the dining-room table. He picked it up and dumped the contents on the table.

Angela twisted her neck to see what he was doing. "Leave my things alone," she said.

Trotter opened her checkbook and told the colonel, "Her name's Angela Marcott. Her address is in Los Angeles."

The colonel said, "Tell me, Angela, how are you related to Chester Marcott? Are you his daughter?"

"That's none of your business."

"I understand Chester Marcott was murdered not long ago."

"Oh really? Are you the bastards who killed him?"

The colonel leaned over her again and said, "No, ma'am. Chester is no good to us dead. And don't call us bastards. We're all legitimate." He slapped her once, twice, three times, harder each time and pausing after each slap. "Let me know when you're ready to answer my question," he said.

Angela's cheeks were red. "What question?" she muttered.

"Are you Chester Marcott's daughter?"

"No. I was married to his son, but not anymore. We're divorced."

"And what is the name of his son, please?"

She spat out the name as if it were a piece of dirt: "Dale Marcott!"

"I see. How many children did Chester have?"

"Just the one I was dumb enough to marry."

"Where is your former husband now?"

"I don't know."

The colonel pursed his lips and moved them from side to side. His nose moved with them. "You wouldn't be trying to protect him, would you?"

"Hell no."

"When was the last time you saw him?"

"At Chester's funeral. That's why I'm here. I came from LA for the funeral."

The colonel paced back and forth, scratching the back of his neck. Angela was lying on her back with her bound hands beneath her. She squirmed uncomfortably, then raised her knees and tried to roll onto her side.

"Corporal Jakes," the colonel said, "help the lady onto the sofa, please."

The mountain man lifted her onto her feet and supported her as she hopped to the sofa, where she turned around and plopped down.

"Would you like some water?" the colonel asked.

She started to say no but changed her mind and nodded.

"Get her a glass of water, Corporal," the colonel commanded.

Jakes lumbered to the kitchen and returned with a glass of water, which he held up to Angela's mouth. She drank about a third of it, then turned her face away.

The colonel stepped in front of Angela and said, "Tell me this, ma'am. If Dale is Chester's only child, and if you are no longer Dale's wife, then how is it that you are living in this house—with Mr. Larrison, it seems—and Chester's son is somewhere else? Now that Chester is deceased, doesn't your former husband own this house?"

"Chester left it to me," Angela said.

"Oh really? Why did he do that?"

Private Smedley chortled. "Mebbe he was doin' *her*, Cunnel."

Angela shouted at him, "He wasn't *doin'* me, you idiot!"

Smedley rushed forward and grabbed both of her cheeks with one hand. He squeezed so hard I thought he meant to break her jaws.

Angela moaned in pain.

Smedley said, "If ya talk ta me like thet again, lady, ah'll pull yer tongue outta yer mouth." He glared at her like a snarling dog.

"That's *enough,* Private!" the colonel said. "I'd like Mrs. Marcott to be able to tell me why her father-in-law bequeathed her his house."

Smedley gave Angela's face one last squeeze and let go.

As if testing her jaws, Angela opened and closed her mouth a few times. In a barely audible voice, she said, "Dale cheated on me. Chester didn't like it. He was a good man."

"Good to *you,* maybe," the colonel said, "but he may not have been as good as you think."

I butted in: "Why do you say that? What did he do?"

"I'll ask the questions, Mr. Larrison."

"When you called me Marcott, you said you thought I had something that belonged to you. What is it?"

The colonel said, "You're getting on my nerves, Mr. Larrison."

"Let's make a deal," I said. "You tell me why you're here, and I'll tell you where Dale Marcott is."

"You are in no position to make deals."

"I'm just trying to save you some time," I said.

"In that case, just give us the man's address. We'll pay him a visit and see if he can help us get what we came for. If we do, we will have accomplished our mission, and we'll be on our way."

"On your way where?"

"The less you know about us, Mr. Larrison, the better off you will be."

Trotter said, "Maybe *she* knows something, Colonel."

The colonel seemed annoyed with the lieutenant for speaking. Even so, he took the lieutenant's advice and turned to Angela. "When did you and Dale Marcott get married?" he asked.

"Why?" she shot back.

"Answer the question." He waited a few seconds, and when she still did not answer, he took two quick steps and gave her a hard slap on the face.

Angela uttered a soft cry and said, "After I graduated from high school."

"What year was that?"

"1996."

"Were you and Dale in the same class?"

In a dull, lifeless tone, she said, "He graduated the year before."

"How long did you know him before you got married?"

"About a year and a half. But we didn't go to the same school. We met at a basketball game in Martinsville, where I grew up."

"Martinsville, Indiana?"

"Yes. It's about fifty miles from here."

"Did he ever say anything to you about something very valuable that his father unexpectedly came into possession of?"

"Like what?"

"Old coins," the colonel said. "More specifically, old gold coins."

Smedley said, "She might be lyin', Cunnel."

"I'm aware of that possibility, Private." The colonel walked back and forth, then asked, "When were you born, ma'am?"

"1978. What's that got to do with anything?"

"So you're now thirty-four?"

"I will be, next month."

The colonel said, "Lieutenant Trotter, check on that. See if you can find her driver's license in those things on the table."

The lieutenant returned to the dining room and picked up a red leather wallet that had been in her handbag. He found the license inside. "It says she was born May 27, 1978," Trotter reported.

The colonel said, "She would have been eleven years old in 1989. If she knows anything about the gold, it must have come either from the man she married or his father, in other words her father-in-law."

"Ya lost me, Cunnel," said Smedley.

Angela said. "I never heard either Chester or his son talk about old gold coins."

The colonel said, "We lost certain assets in 1989. Since Chester Marcott is dead, we'll have to talk to his son. He may be the only person alive who can tell us what happened."

"Are you saying Chester stole your gold coins?" Angela asked. "That's crazy. Chester wasn't a thief. He never would have done such a thing."

"I did not accuse him of stealing our assets," the colonel replied. "I said we have reason to believe they came into his possession."

"What's that supposed to mean?" Angela said.

"Suffice it to say we have a theory—a theory that is supported by what Mr. Larrison wrote in his newspaper."

"Colonel Bickerstaff," I said, "how much money are you talking about?"

He seemed surprised that I had used his name. "A lot," he said.

"How did you find my articles? You don't subscribe to the *Gleaner,* do you?"

Smedley said, "You want me ta shut 'im up, Cunnel?"

"No, Private, I do not want you to shut him up," said Bickerstaff. "I'm questioning him." To me he said, "Tell me where we can find Dale Marcott."

I took this as an indirect acceptance of the deal I had offered him. "He lives in the Longview Trailer Park in Campbellsville," I said. "It's behind the Meridian Park Shopping Center on Main St. That's US 50. Look for an old green-and-white trailer. It's not far from the entrance to the trailer park. At the second cross street, turn right."

The colonel took a deep breath and said, "Lieutenant Trotter, you and Private Cullman stay with the prisoners. Corporal Jakes, Private Smedley, and I will try to find Mr. Marcott. If we succeed, we'll bring him back here for interrogation."

Without further ado, the three of them slipped outside through the quilt. They reminded me of Arab terrorists leaving a tent.

I figured it would take them at least an hour to get Dale and bring him back here—that is, if he's in the trailer. That gave Angela and me an hour to escape—but how? I wondered how Chester had gotten tangled up with this bunch of crackpots. And where were they from? Somewhere down south, from their accents. Brilliant, Larrison!

A few minutes after Bickerstaff, Jakes, and Smedley left on their kidnapping mission, Lieutenant Trotter called Private Cullman on his walkie-talkie and told him to return to the house. The private reappeared almost immediately.

Trotter ordered him to check the ropes on our hands and feet. "Make sure they're good and tight," he said.

Cullman went straight to Angela. "She ain't bad lookin, is she?" he said. He bent down and squeezed one of her breasts. "Nice tits," he said.

"Keep your hands off me, you goon!" she said.

He felt her up again. She tried to bite his hand. He laughed and reached inside her shirt.

"Leave her alone!" I said.

He straightened up and walked over to me. "Make me?" he said. It sounded like something a little kid would say. His toothpick flicked up and down.

Angela said, "I need to use the bathroom."

"Hold it in," Trotter said.

"I have to pee."

Trotter heard something outside. "What's that, Delmar?" he asked the private.

"What's what?"

"That noise. Listen."

It was a loud peeping sound.

Cullman said, "Them's frogs."

"Frogs? You sure?"

"Yeah."

"Frogs don't sound like that."

"Yeah they do. They's little frogs—spring peepers. There must be a pond around here."

Trotter headed for the doorway, followed by Cullman. Their boots crunched on the broken glass. Trotter raised one side of the quilt, and they went outside.

"Phil, who are they?" Angela whispered.

"A gang of idiots," I said. "Some kind of wacko militia, I guess."

"What are they going to do to us?"

I didn't answer. I was thinking if I could get myself up on the sofa, maybe one of us could untie the other's hands. No, it would take too long. We'd get caught. I had a better idea. I began rolling toward the glass on the floor. If I could get a piece of it, maybe I could cut through the clothesline on my wrists. I started rolling.

In a few seconds I reached the closest pieces. I twisted myself around to line up my hands with a knife-like shard that was about three inches long and one inch wide.

"What are you doing?" Angela asked me.

"Shhhh!" I raised the small of my back and tried to pick up the piece of glass. It wasn't easy. It was taking too long. I gave up and rolled back where I'd been.

The nutcakes must have heard us.

They charged into the house, and the quilt came down on their heads. They struggled against each other to get it off. I warned myself not to laugh. When they escaped from the quilt, they were furious. "What's goin' on in here?" Trotter demanded.

"Nothing," I said.

"Ya think it's a joke?" Cullman said.

"Why would I think what's a joke?"

He came at me with a comic-book snarl on his face.

I raised my feet to hold him off. He sidestepped my two-footed kick and stomped on my balls. It hurt big time. I thought he was going to do it again, but instead he went to the fireplace and grabbed an iron poker that was standing on the hearth. He dropped the poker on my chest, then stormed out of the room and came back with a kitchen chair, which he placed sideways in front of my feet.

He tried to lift my feet by the clothesline that bound my ankles, but I kicked at him. He evaded the kick, then wrapped his arms around my legs, and lifted them onto the chair. "Hold 'im down, wouldya, Lieutenant," he said.

I thought Trotter would put an end to this, but instead he turned around and looked at me. He stepped over my chest and adjusted the position of the chair so that my forelegs rested on the seat and my feet extended a few inches over one side. Then he sat on my forelegs, straddling the chair and resting his arms on the back. I thought the bones in my legs would crack.

Cullman pulled off my shoes and socks and said, "I always wanted to do this."

Angela screamed at the top of her lungs, "Stop it! Don't hurt him!"

I said, "You gonna let him torture me, Lieutenant? What about the Geneva Convention?"

"You're not covered by it," he said. "You're a civilian." To Cullman he added, "Make sure you don't miss him and hit me with that poker."

"Don't hurt him!" Angela screamed again. "He didn't do anything to you."

Cullman reared back and swung the poker against the soles of my feet. A dizzying pain shot up my legs. My eyes began to water. "I give up," I said. "I'll talk. What do you want me to say?"

"He thinks he's a comedian," Trotter said.

Cullman swung again . . . and again. . . .

Don't scream, Larrison.

My legs shook uncontrollably. My whole body was shaking. Trotter's mouth opened in a slow, wide yawn. Angela was crying, begging them to stop.

I heard someone yelling.

The yells were coming from me. I must be dreaming, I thought. Faces were watching me. They heard me screaming, but they didn't care. This is what hell will be like for you, Larrison. Maybe you're there already. Maybe you died and went to hell.

Angela was crying, "Stop it! Stop it! Stop it!"

Cullman said, "Shut up, ho, or yuh'll get it too."

He stopped hitting me, but the blows seemed to go on. My feet were throbbing. I wondered if any bones were broken. Would I be able to walk again? Was I awake or asleep? I told myself I had to stay awake. I had to protect Angela.

Right, I was doing a great job of protecting her.

The wacko whacked me again.

I had never wanted to kill anyone—until then.

As if he knew what I was thinking, he hit my feet again. My hands felt wet. Was it sweat or blood? Had I cut them on a piece of glass?

I was in a dark, twisting tunnel. . . . It twisted like a snake and kept getting longer. . . . But it wasn't a tunnel. . . . It was alive. . . . It was a giant snake twisting back and forth. . . . It was swallowing me whole. . . .

Don't pass out, Larrison. Be a man. Show them what you're made of. Take whatever they dish out.

I shouted in pain. It seemed to help. I shouted again and again and again. . . .

CHAPTER 35

MILITARY DISCIPLINE

THE rattle of gravel startled me out of a morbid sleep. Tires churned to a stop. Muffled voices drifted through the quilt, which covered the doorway again. Boots scraped across the porch.

They dragged Dale Marcott feet first into the house. Like Angela and me, his hands and feet were bound with clothesline, but his mouth was covered with duct tape. He strained to hold his head up off the floor as they pulled him over the broken glass.

It was almost 11:30. I was startled to see how late it was. I felt as if I had been asleep just a few minutes, but more than an hour had passed. I had been drifting in and out of a weird dreamland of everyday faces that were completely indifferent to what was happening to me. They knew I could see them, but they were completely indifferent. When I tried to speak to them, however, their faces began to melt. Their lips peeled away to reveal enormous brown teeth. Tentacles grew out of their fingers. . . .

"How'd it go?" Cullman asked the militiamen who had dragged Dale into the house.

"We got him," the colonel said. "He didn't want to come with us, but he had no choice."

Marcott tried to sit up, but Lieutenant Trotter put a boot on his face and pushed him back down.

Private Smedley laughed. It sounded like three giddy hiccups.

I felt as stiff as a board. My legs were no longer on the kitchen chair. I wondered if Trotter and Cullman had done anything to Angela while I was unconscious. I twisted myself around to look at her. She was still on the sofa. She was staring at her ex-husband as if in a trance.

"Untape him," the colonel ordered.

Smedley grabbed one end of the duct tape and yanked it off Dale's lips.

Dale yelped as if his skin had come off with the tape. As he grimaced in pain, he saw me watching him. "What the fuck are you doin' here?" he demanded.

Smedley answered the question: "It luks like he's been screwin' yer ex-wife."

"No shit?" Marcott said. "She must be desperate."

"Screw you, Dale," Angela said.

"Watch your mouth," the colonel said. "That's no way for a lady to talk."

She shot back, "Don't tell me how to talk in my own house. Go away, and take him with you!"

Dale yelled, "Your house? You bitch, it's not your house."

"Keep telling yourself that."

The colonel approached her. For several seconds he stood there without speaking, but suddenly he grabbed her by the hair and pulled her head back to make her look up at him. "I didn't come here to listen to you squabble with your ex-husband," he said. "Now be a good girl and keep your mouth shut."

"Drop dead," she told him.

Bickerstaff turned to his men and shook his head as if he pitied her for being so obstinate, then spun around and slapped her, first on one side of her face with the back of his hand, then on the other side with his open palm.

I caught a strong whiff of urine.

Angela began to cry—from embarrassment rather than pain, I thought.

"How about letting her go to the bathroom to clean up," I said to the colonel.

Smedley laughed and said, "Ah'll help her clean up, Cunnel."

Angela's face was crimson. I thought she was going to spit at the colonel. She trembled with anger but did not spit.

Marcott was grinning. It was not his habitual grin. It was hateful and contemptuous.

I said to the colonel, "She asked to go, but your lieutenant wouldn't let her."

"That's enough out of you," he said. "Lieutenant Trotter, take her upstairs and let her wash. Let her change her pants and undies as well, but don't let her out of your sight."

Trotter took out a pocketknife and went down on one knee to cut the rope around Angela's ankles. As he rose, he reached for her upper arm, but she pulled it away from him and stood up by herself.

The back of her pants was soaking wet, as were two seat cushions on the sofa. The air reeked.

With a desolate, fixed expression, she started toward the stairs. At the same time Puddybaby came out from behind the sofa and did one of her weird slow-motion runs toward the door. Smedley drew his pistol and shot the cat in the side.

For a moment I thought Angela was laughing, but it was a hysterical cry. "Why? *Why? WHY?*" she screamed at Smedley.

"Ah shot me a cat," he boasted.

The cat panted a few times, then lay still. Angela fell to her knees beside it. She obviously wanted to hold the cat and pet it, but her hands were still tied behind her back. She glared at Smedley and said, "Damn you, you're worse than an animal. I hope you rot in hell."

"Oh yeh? Mebbe ah will, but yu'll be theh too, ho."

The colonel said, "Put the cat outside, Private Smedley."

Angela cried out, "No! Some animal will get her. I want to bury her!"

The colonel did not rescind his order, and Smedley picked up the cat by its tail and tossed it out into the front yard.

Angela said, "What's wrong with you people? What's the *matter* with you?" Her voice was almost normal, which gave her words more power.

"Take her upstairs, Lieutenant," the colonel ordereed.

"Ah'll do it," Smedley said.

Angela whirled around. "Stay away from me, you pig." She looked as if she wanted to claw his eyes out.

"Look who's talkin'," he said. "Ye're the one thet smells like a pig." He raised his hand to hit her, but the colonel stopped him.

"That's enough, Private," the colonel said. "Go outside and stand guard."

Smedley stiffened. I thought he was going to challenge the order, but he merely said, "Yessuh." As he left the house, his eyes moved up and down Angela's body in a silent threat.

As Trotter escorted Angela upstairs, Dale said, "What the hell's goin' on? Why'd you bring me here? Whadaya want with me?"

The colonel turned to Corporal Jakes and Private Cullman. "Help Mr. Marcott onto the sofa," he ordered. "Put him where the lady was sitting."

"No!" Dale shouted.

Jakes rolled him over with his foot, then grabbed the back of Dale's belt and lugged him like a suitcase toward the sofa.

Dale yelled, "No, put me down!"

"Why?" Jakes said in his soft voice.

"The couch has been pissed on. Put me down."

"Squeamish, isn't he?" the colonel said. "Sit him in the piss on the couch. Let him soak it up."

Dale squirmed and kicked. Jakes wrapped his arms around Dale's chest and plopped him down where Angela had been. Dale struggled to get up, but Jakes held him in place. Dale went on yelling and cussing until the colonel threatened to tape his mouth again.

In the ensuing silence, the colonel paced back and forth as if deep in thought. Finally he stopped in front of Dale. "Mr. Marcott," he said, "we have determined that your father came into possession of certain assets that belong to us. Unfortunately your father is no longer alive, but you are. We expect you to return our assets to us."

"What fucken 'assets' are you talkin' about?"

"I'm talking about a great deal of money, Mr. Marcott— money in the form of gold coins minted by the government of the United States of America."

I watched for Dale's reaction. There was none. All he did was try to raise his rear end off the wet part of the sofa.

"Think about it," the colonel said. "I'm going to get something to drink."

The colonel took his time in the kitchen. Meanwhile, Trotter returned with Angela. She had washed her face and changed her clothes. Her ankles were no longer bound, but her hands were tied behind her back. I wondered if Trotter had changed her pants and washed her up, or if he had untied her so she could do it. He sat her in an armchair next to the fireplace.

I was amazed when the colonel told Jakes and Cullman to take me to the toilet. Jakes untied my ankles, then short-roped them so I could halfway walk on my own. My legs had fallen asleep. They tingled so much they hurt as I shuffled across the room and climbed the stairs.

In the bathroom they untied my hands so I could take a leak. Then they watched me take it. I was tempted to turn around and hose them.

Jakes read my mind. His lips barely moved as he said, "I wouldn't try it unless you're itchin' to be a eunuch."

When I was finally finished, they tied my hands behind my back again.

As we went downstairs, I heard the colonel saying, "You'll be better off if I don't tell you where we're from."

Dale said, "Let me guess—Alabama."

"If I tell you, we'll have to kill you. We don't want to do that. All we want is our assets to be returned to us."

Angela looked scared but angry. I mimed the words, "You okay?" and she puckered one corner of her mouth as if I'd said something stupid. Cullman saw her and blurted out, "They're plottin' somethin'."

Angela fired back, "We are not!"

"Yeah you are," Cullman said. "I seen ya."

The colonel said, "My men don't lie to me, ma'am." He crossed the room and loomed in front of her again. He scratched his Adam's apple in one direction only, from bottom to top. Then he placed a finger against her lips. When she jerked her head away, he clutched her chin and said, "You need to show respect, little lady."

I said, "She didn't do anything. Leave her alone."

The colonel squeezed her lower jaw until her mouth opened like a hideous flower. It must have hurt something awful because tears streamed down her face onto his hand. He released her and wiped his hand on her shoulder. Then he hit her again, left side, right side.

Her head swung from side to side. A drop of blood appeared in the corner of her mouth. There was a faraway look in her eyes.

The colonel wasn't finished. He grabbed the front of her shirt and yanked it down, ripping the buttons off. Then he took out a switchblade. He opened the knife and put the tip of the blade between her breasts. Angela was trembling. "Don't," she blubbered. "Please don't cut me."

He cut the front of her bra between the cups. He spread the shirt and bra to expose her breasts. She tried to lean forward to hide them, but the colonel said, "Sit up before I give you a mastectomy." He laughed as if he had told a good joke.

Cullman said, "Before you operate on her, Colonel, let us have her."

The drop of blood became a scarlet worm crawling down Angela's chin. Her mouth hung open. A look of surrender came over her face.

Silently I formed three words with my lips: "I love you."

"Isn't that sweet?" Dale said with a triumphant laugh.

CHAPTER 36

THE MYSTICAL NUMBER

"GIVE Mr. Marcott a dry seat," said the colonel. Lieutenant Trotter picked up the chair on which the soles of my feet had been beaten and planted it in front of Dale. Corporal Jakes then let Dale get off the urine-soaked sofa cushion.

"How 'bout letting me change my pants," Dale said.

"Put some paper towels on the chair for him," the colonel directed.

"I'd rather stand than sit in piss," Dale said.

Jakes grabbed the back of Dale's shirt collar and pulled him down onto the chair. Private Cullman then put Dale's bound hands over the curved back of the kitchen chair and wrapped another piece of clothesline around Dale's ankles and the front legs of the chair.

"Feel better now?" the colonel asked.

"Fuck you," Dale said.

"Good," the colonel replied. He lapsed into thought, then continued: "Now, Mr. Marcott, as I told you earlier, we have reason to believe that your father came into possession of a large number of gold coins that belonged to us. We want you to tell us what you know about that."

For several seconds Dale said nothing. Then: "That's what I know about it."

The colonel laced his fingers together, bowed his head, and placed his thumbs against his chin. In this meditative pose, he walked back and forth in front of Dale. When he stopped, he said, "Pardon me, but I find it hard to believe that you know absolutely nothing about the gold." He lowered his hands and cracked his knuckles. "When were you born, Mr. Marcott?"

Dale did not answer.

"I'm not going to play games with you," the colonel said. "Answer my question."

When Dale still didn't answer, the colonel asked Angela when he was born.

Her chest was still exposed. She was clearly unwilling to answer but was afraid not to. "In 1976," she said.

Dale shouted, "Shut your face, bitch."

Angela shouted back, "Stop calling me a bitch, you—"

The colonel stepped over my head and stared at Angela. She sat back as if trying to put more distance between them.

The colonel gazed at Angela's chest. "Ain't that a sight?" he said, shaking his head in disbelief. "It's easy to see why men fall victim to creatures like her."

"Not all men,"Private Cullman said. "Some of us know how to avoid their traps."

The colonel began calculating again. "Now then," he said to Dale, "if you were born in 1976, you would have been thirteen in 1989."

"Did you figure that out all by yourself?" Dale asked.

"Be careful, Mr. Marcott," the colonel said. "I was merely establishing that you would have been old enough to know what happened here in 1989. It was an extremely difficult year for us. We suffered devastating losses." He made a loud belch. I wondered if he had belched because he thought it would irritate Dale, and as a matter of fact Dale did look irritated. The colonel went on: "We lost our air force that year, our plane and our pilot—a small air force, yes, but only the beginning. In addition to which, we lost our entire treasury, which consisted of $125,000 in gold coins. That's what the gold was worth in 1989. It would be worth four times as much today." He looked at his troops. "As you've all heard me say, men, the losses we sustained in 1989 nearly destroyed our movement. It was our darkest hour and our greatest challenge. But we survived, and we shall rebuild. We shall be stronger than ever."

"Amen," Lieutenant Trotter said.

Dale said, "So what the fuck does all this have to do with me and my father? I never heard of your 'movement,' and I doubt if my father did either."

The colonel spotted a bug flying around in front of him. He raised his hands slowly and clapped them together. "Got 'im!" he boasted, spreading his palms to display a large mosquito that was bent out of shape. He flicked it off his hand and went on with his history lesson:

"True, Mr. Marcott, you knew nothing about us in 1989. But in that year our plane disappeared, and our destinies were linked." Thumbs on chin, fingertips tapping in front of his mouth, he paraded around the room as his mind took off on a flight of fancy: "Since then 23 years have passed—23, a mystical number. Do you know there are 23 sets of chromosomes in the human genome? Do you know that the earth's axis is tilted at a 23-degree angle? Do you know that William Shakespeare was born on April 23? We lost our plane on April 23, 1989, and next Monday will be April 23, 2012. It's no coincidence that it's almost 23 years to the day that our plane was lost."

Dale broke into the colonel's reverie: "Why do you think your plane came down here?"

"I'll tell you why," the colonel said. "We have Mr. Larrison to thank for it. It was his articles in the local newspaper that brought us here. They led us to conclude that this is where our plane went down—right here on your family farm, Mr. Marcott."

"You're full of it," Dale said.

Corporal Jakes looked at the colonel, who nodded once. Jakes then wrapped his left arm around Dale's neck and began drilling the knuckle of his right index finger into the top of Dale's skull. "If I was you, man, I'd be thinkin' about apologizin' to Colonel Bickerstaff," Jakes said.

Within seconds Dale was apologizing for his insult and promising not to wise off again, but Jakes went on drilling into his skull as if he didn't hear him. The torture lasted another minute or so. Then the colonel motioned for Jakes to stop.

Dale was in agony. He leaned forward in his chair, with his head hanging down. Eyes closed, he swung his head from side to side.

"Our airman set out to fly to northern Illinois that day," the colonel continued. "The weather report called for clear skies over Indiana, but isolated thunderstorms popped up in this part of your state. No doubt Captain Murphy tried to fly around them: however, he was never heard from again. We now know that he went down in this area, most likely on this very farm." The colonel stopped speaking and approached Dale. "Surely a boy of thirteen would have known if a plane crashed on his family's farm."

Dale muttered, *"Maybe* he would, *if* it crashed, but you're just guessing." Every word was an effort. He stopped to clear his throat, then went on: "The plane could've crashed anywhere. It could've crashed in the Hoosier National Forest. . . . There's a wilderness area out there too. . . . Or it could've gone down in Lake Monroe, the biggest lake in the state."

"Mr. Larrison also reported that your father gave away a substantial amount of gold to a poor black woman. That suggests our plane came down here."

"Then ask *him* where your gold is," Dale said. "You're pickin' on the wrong guy. I don't know where it is. I don't know anything about your damn gold."

I said, "I wrote what Mr. Pluckett told me. I didn't make it up."

"Thank you, Mr. Larrison," the colonel said, "and what you wrote was that a certain Negro named Pluckett—interesting name, isn't it? It sounds like he came from a family of chicken pluckers. Pluckett told you that Chester Marcott gave his mother gold coins worth thousands of dollars beginning in 1990. That was not long after our plane and the assets that it was transporting vanished without a trace." He leveled his eyes at Dale again. "Tell me this, Mr. Marcott, was your father in the habit of giving gold coins away *before* the year 1990?"

Dale said, "I don't think he ever gave a gold coin away his whole life."

He was lying, of course. Angela had told me that Chester used to send a gold coin to Kelly a couple times a year. Dale would have known that, but under the circumstances a lie was understandable.

With a sarcastic smile the colonel said, "So you think the chicken plucker made up that story, Mr. Marcott? Why would he do that? What would he have to gain? People might think he *stole* the gold from somebody. Why would he draw attention to himself with an unlikely story that a white man gave Pluckett's mother thousands of dollars' worth of gold, if it wasn't true?"

"I don't know," Dale said. "Why don't you ask him?"

The colonel stared at Dale in mock disappointment. "Mr. Marcott," he said, "I rather admire your brazen stubbornness, but I believe that what Mr. Larrison wrote in his paper is absolutely true. His articles ring true, whereas nothing you say does." He turned to Cullman and said, "Private, put Mr. Marcott on the floor, please, on his back."

Cullman, who was sitting on a windowsill, jumped to his feet as if he had been caught napping. He grasped the back of Dale's chair and braced his foot against the bottom rung connecting the back legs. Then he jerked the chair backward and let it fall on the floor.

Dale gritted his teeth as his full weight fell on his bound wrists. "Lemme go," he said. "I don't know what happened to your gold."

The colonel gestured at Dale's feet, which were pointed straight up. They reminded me of the ears of a deer on high alert. Cullman yanked Dale's loafers off his feet.

"No!" Dale shouted. He tried to roll sideways while still tied to his chair, but Corporal Jakes dragged him and the chair back across the room and wedged it between the dining-room archway and an end table that stood next to the sofa. Cullman pulled Dale's socks off and waved them in the air as if they stank.

Private Smedley came running into the house. He was out of breath but said, "Whaat's goin' on in heeah?" He sounded as if he thought he had been cheated out of something.

"It's party time," Cullman said. He looked around for something and picked up a splintery split log from a small stack next to the fireplace.

Dale looked scared. "Why're you doin' this? I don't know where the fucken gold is."

"Perhaps the gold is gone," the colonel said. "Perhaps your father gave it all away. But you have been lying to us, Mr. Marcott. Our aircraft came down somewhere around here. I'm certain of it, and I am equally certain that you *know* where the plane came down. You *must* know. You were living here at the time. How could you not know?"

Dale tried to shift his weight off his hands. "I don't know where it is. I don't know anything about it!"

"If the plane crashed, Captain Murphy must have been in it. He would have fought to the end to save the plane. Where is it, Mr. Marcott? Where is our comrade? We must take his remains home with us."

"I don't know! I don't know! I don't know."

The colonel nodded at Cullman, who swung the log against Dale's feet. "Aaaarrrrrhhhh!" he cried. His whole body jerked. His voice strained as he yelled, "Stop it! If I knew, I'd tell ya."

Cullman hit him again. This time a dry sob came out of Dale's throat. The third blow made him shake. "I don't know where your gold is," he yelled. "I swear I don't."

Smedley said, "Gimme thet wood. Ah'll make 'im talk."

He wrenched the board out of Cullman's hands and caught a splinter under his thumbnail. "Damn fuck it!" he yelled. He took his anger out on Dale and began slamming the log against his feet.

The colonel watched the torture as if in deep thought. For a couple of minutes he said nothing, Then suddenly he grew furious and screamed at Dale: "Talk, Mr. Marcott! Talk! Where is our plane?" He picked up an assault rifle and sprayed the ceiling and walls with bullets.

The house seemed to shudder. The bullets tore through the plaster. Chunks of it rained down on our heads. Along with the plaster in the ceiling came a glittering shower, which at first I thought was water from a broken pipe.

It was not water.

A bright golden shower fell out of a hole in the ceiling. Gold coins gleamed as they fell, shining, twirling, jingling, jangling, ringing, spinning, bouncing, rolling. . . .

With a beaming smile the colonel spread out his arms and laughed. "We are blessed," he said. "The good Lord has blessed us."

His men cheered. They grabbed their rifles and joined their leader in blasting away at the ceiling and walls. The noise was so loud I thought everyone for miles around would hear it. I wouldn't have been surprised if the entire ceiling collapsed and the furniture in the room above us fell on our heads.

The gang went on shooting until their guns were empty. Then they hugged and squeezed one another. They hooahed and laughed. They jumped up and down and danced with joy on the fortune in gold on the floor.

CHAPTER 37

SQUEAMISH

THE troops went on celebrating by raiding the refrigerator and liberating several cans of Budweiser. After five minutes of drinking and back-slapping, Bickerstaff and Trotter went upstairs to find the place where the gold coins had been hidden.

As they tromped around in Chester's bedroom, plaster dust drifted down on us from the bullet-riddled ceiling. We heard them shove the bed across the room. Then they dragged the rug into the hall, rolled it up, and let it slide down the steps and crash into a small table near the front door.

"Oops," the colonel said from the top of the stairway. "Lieutenant Trotter wants to take that moth-eaten old rug home with him, don't you, Cletus?"

"Yes, sir, I do," Trotter replied. "It's not moth-eaten. It'll look real nice in our family room."

Angela shouted, "It's not yours to take!"

"Spoils of war," the colonel said.

It didn't take them long to find the hiding place under the hardwood floor. It turned out that only about half the coins had fallen through the ceiling. The colonel carried the rest down in an antique washing basin. He also had two cream-colored cloth bank bags that must have originally contained the coins. Grinning from ear to ear, he said, "Look what we found, men." He let their eyes feast on the bowl of gold. "Most of our assets have now been recovered," he said. "This proves beyond the shadow of a doubt that our plane came down somewhere around here, most likely right on this farm."

"Hooah!" Smedley shouted.

The others erupted in cheers, whistles, and a chorus of hooahs.

"Ah'd say ye're right, Cunnel," Smedley said. He gulped down the rest of his beer and threw the can at the fireplace. Cullman pulled out his handgun and fired more bullets into the ceiling.

The colonel raised his hands for quiet. When the noise died down, he said, "Do you know what else this proves? It proves our friend here—Mr. Marcott—has been lying to us. He *had* to know that a plane came down." The colonel bent over and patted Dale on the cheek several times. Each pat was progressively stronger. "How are you feeling, Mr. Marcott? I bet your feet are just killing you, aren't they?"

Trotter said, "Somebody must've found the plane and took the gold." Staring at Dale, he said, "It had to be him or his father, or the two of 'em."

"I never saw your fucken plane," Dale said.

At Dale's words, the colonel's mouth fell open in mock surprise. He gaped at his men, drawing wild laughter, but when he spoke again, he was deadly serious: "It also means I must make a confession. I owe an apology to Captain Randall P. Murphy. All these years I harbored a dark suspicion that he was a traitor who made off with our assets. I have been guilty of doubting a loyal member of our force, a trustworthy airman who gave his life for our cause. I deserve to be horsewhipped for believing that he could betray us. *I* am the traitor. I betrayed his friendship and loyalty. I have dishonored him. Before God and man I apologize to our fallen hero. I submit myself to your judgment, gentlemen. I submit to whatever punishment you decide I deserve."

"I'll be glad to oblige," Dale said. "Untie me and give me the horsewhip."

The colonel set his jaw and nodded. "He mocks me. The fool mocks me. He lies there with his feet in the air, and he has the nerve to mock me."

Like the colonel, I found it hard to believe Dale's denial. A plane crashes on the family farm, and he knows nothing about it? And I didn't want to believe that Chester had found the gold and kept it as his own. But the room above the living room was the master bedroom, Chester's room. Even if he himself hadn't found the gold, it couldn't have been hidden under the floor without his knowing it.

After the colonel's confession to his men, wrinkles of concern appeared on Lieutenant Trotter's face. "Don't be so hard on yourself, Colonel," he said. "It's understandable that you had some doubts about Captain Murphy. The plane was never found. We checked the news every day—newspapers, radio, TV. You even paid for a news-clipping service out of your own pocket, but we never got a good lead on a plane that went missing around the time Captain Murphy was in the air. Even those Google alerts we signed up for nine or ten years ago didn't do any good until now. It was Google that put us onto the Campbellsville newspaper and the stories about some fella in southern Indiana who gave away thousands of dollars in gold coins to a needy woman. It sounded like a long shot, but it turned out to be true. But not till we came here did we discover that Captain Murphy did not betray us. We all thought—those of us who were in the movement back in '89—we all thought he made off with our assets. If you deserve to be punished for thinking he was a traitor, then so do I and the others who used to be with us."

Dale began laughing. It was a nutty kind of laugh.

The colonel gazed at him in silence, as if accepting the mockery.

Smedley said, "You ain't gonna take that from him, are ya, Cunnel?"

"Let's pick up the coins," the colonel said. "Put them on the table in the dining room."

The coins had bounced and rolled all over the place. A few had even made it as far as the parlor and kitchen.

The colonel sat at the dining-room table. As his men delivered the coins to him, he arranged them in stacks of ten. When all the coins were on the table, he had a total of 319 gold pieces.

"These coins are worth a lot more today than they were in 1989," he said. "Gold is worth over $1,600 an ounce today. In 1989 an ounce of gold was worth less than $400." He seemed to bask in the glow of the gold. "And that's just the value of the bullion," he added. "These coins are collector's items. Each of these $20 gold pieces—they're called double eagles, by the way—each double eagle contains nearly an ounce of gold, so each one of them is worth more than $1,600 now, and depending on the date and condition, they're worth even more than that to a coin collector."

Cullman said, "We're rich!"

"Not us, Private. Our army is rich. We will be stronger than ever. This gold is our future, men. We must guard it with our lives."

Lieutenant Trotter said, "Do you think we got it all, Colonel?"

"No. Some of them are missing. Mr. Larrison reported that some of the coins were given away. But we have two bags here." He held them up, one in each hand, and continued: "Originally each of these bags contained exactly 205 double eagles. There are only 319 of them here, but, as I said, the coins have appreciated in value. They're worth a lot more today than they were in 1989. I know there were no really rare coins among them, but I'd say what we have here on the table is worth well over half a million dollars."

They cheered. They laughed. They hooahed.

Smedley, who was still looking for more coins, said, "Mebbe we can make the ho pay back what's missin', Cunnel."

"Good thinking, Private," the colonel replied. "Mrs. Marcott did say that her father-in-law left the farm to her. Perhaps she would be good enough to borrow against the farm and repay what was stolen from us—at present value, of course."

Angela said, "If something was stolen from you, you can have it back. I don't want it. But the property isn't mine yet. It's tied up in probate court." I half expected her to say that Dale was responsible for tying it up, but she didn't.

"I see," said the colonel. "Well, I suppose we can wait a little while longer. After all, we've been waiting twenty-three years."

I said, "What do you plan to do with the gold, start a revolution?"

He replied, "That's precisely what we plan to do. But it won't be the kind of revolution you may be thinking of. We have declared war on those who are destroying the fabric of our nation—the drug dealers, the homosexuals, the abortionists, the illegal aliens, as well as the ultra-liberal politicians who control Washington. We saw what was coming decades ago. We were preparing to fight them when we lost our assets. It was an enormous setback, but now we have the means to fight again, and our fight will spread like wildfire across the land." Moved by the sound of his own words, he choked up and stopped talking.

I said, "Who's gonna get blown up first—some gay guys in a bar?"

Lieutenant Trotter said, "We have plenty of options. It's a target-rich environment."

The colonel nodded and said, "Gentlemen, we will begin planning our next mission as soon as we get home, but there's one more thing we need to do while we're here. One of our men is missing in action. We need to find Captain Murphy's remains, if possible, and take them home with us. We must give what's left of our MIA a proper burial."

He marched over to Dale, who was squirming around to relieve the pressure on his arms under the back of his chair. "What happened to Captain Murphy's body?" the colonel asked him.

"How should I know?" Dale said.

The colonel tapped Dale's bare feet with the side of his boot. "I'm sure you know something about it. Why not make it easy on yourself and tell us?"

"I told you—I don't know!"

"This is extremely important to us, Mr. Marcott. As I said earlier, I feel very bad for doubting the loyalty of Captain Murphy all these years. All this time he was missing in action. I want to do what I can to make it up to him. I want to give him a decent burial. But I need you to tell me what happened. Did the plane crash and burn? If so, what became of the wreckage, and what became of Captain Murphy's remains?"

"Maybe he bailed out," Dale said. "Maybe he's still alive. Maybe he took some of your gold."

"No. If he survived the crash, he would have contacted us immediately."

"Cunnel," Smedley said, "ye're bein' too nice to this guy. Let us have at 'im. We'll make 'im talk. We'll start pullin' teeth. Or we'll honey-dip 'im."

The colonel smiled and nodded. "Very good, Private Smedley. I think you would make an excellent interrogator."

He chuckled softly. "Mr. Marcott *is* a bit squeamish, isn't he? A dip in the septic tank might do more to loosen his tongue than anything else we could do to him. I'd like you and Private Cullman to find the tank. It's probably not far from the side of the house where the bathroom is—a few yards maybe. Go down in the cellar and see if there's a pipe that goes out through the wall. But more likely, since the cellar was dug out after the house was built, the pipe may come out of the bathroom on the second floor and then down the outside of the house. Look where it goes into the ground, and then find a stick or something and jab it in the ground till you hit the top of the tank. It's prob'ly no more than a few inches underground. Drive the vehicles around to the side of the house and use the headlights to give you some light."

Dale said, "Come on, you're not gonna do this. I don't know anything about your plane and your pilot. My father must've found the gold. I don't know what happened to the plane."

"You are our only hope of finding Captain Murphy's body," the colonel said. "If you can't tell us where our MIA is, who can? Mr. Larrison wouldn't know. I don't believe your former wife knows either. And your father's dead. So you're the only one who can help us." There was a brief pause before he added, "But if you won't help us—if you won't tell us what happened to the plane and our pilot— you're going to spend the last minute of your life swallowing piss and shit in a septic tank."

CHAPTER 38

THE SINS OF THE FATHERS

SMEDLEY woke me with a kick in the ribs shortly before dawn. I was surprised I had been asleep. Most of the night I couldn't get to sleep. It was cold on the floor, and I was sore all over. Whenever I started to fall asleep, some ache or pain would wake me up.

I smelled bacon. I heard voices in the kitchen. I smelled coffee. Angela said something. She had been put to work making breakfast for the colonel and his men. Dale was still tied to his chair, but now he and it were on their sides. He was snoring in loud bursts. He sounded as if he had sleep apnea.

"You make a very good breakfast, ma'am," the colonel said. Knives and forks clinked on dishes.

The colonel added, "Private Smedley, tie the lady up. We don't want her to throw a pot of coffee at us, do we?"

"No, suh, we shore don't."

With one hand on the back of Angela's neck and the other on her right arm, Smedley escorted her back to the living room. Her ankles were short-roped, and she shuffled along in jerky steps.

I said, "I'd say 'good morning' if it was one, Angela."

She looked haggard and miserable. She was wearing a white T-shirt under an unbuttoned cardigan. Her hair was in tangles.

Smedley sat her on the unsoiled end of the sofa and turned her sideways so he could tie her hands behind her back. As he finished tying, he whispered something in her ear.

"Not if you were the last man on earth," she said.

He patted her on the behind and said, "We'll see 'bout thet, darlin', we'll see."

"Did you have any breakfast?" I asked her.

"I'm not hungry," she said.

Private Cullman came through the dining room with a toothpick wagging in his mouth. "What's goin' on?" he asked.

"Nothin'," Smedley said.

Cullman gazed at Dale. "How can he sleep like that with an arm under the side of the chair?"

"I dunno," Smedley answered. "He snores like a hog though." He kicked Dale's sideways feet.

Dale's eyes popped open as one last snort came out of his nose. He seemed more asleep than awake.

"It's about tamm ya woke up," Smedley said. "Ah'm sick a list'nin' to ya snore."

"Go fuck yourself," said Dale.

Smedley's lean face flared like a cobra's. He planted a boot on the side of Dale's head, then briefly raised his other foot to add more weight. Dale closed his eyes and gritted his teeth.

The colonel strolled in and made a satisfied belch. "Looks like Private Smedley's dishing out some punishment," he said. He looked at me and asked Smedley, "How's our prisoner today? Is he behaving himself?"

"Yessuh, Colonel," Smedley said. "He ain't said much. Ah reckon he's scared shitless."

The colonel said, "He should be," and laughed. He went upstairs to the bathroom. Like his men, he preferred the big bathroom to the tiny one off the parlor.

By the time the colonel reappeared, Trotter and Jakes had joined us in the living room. The gang of five got Dale, Angela, and me on our feet. They short-roped my ankles like Angela's, but they tied Dale's tightly together.

"Whadaya gonna do?" Dale asked the colonel.

"We're going to do a little enhanced interrogation," the colonel said.

Talking fast, Dale said, "I don't know what happened to your plane. I don't know where it is. I can't tell you what I don't know."

"Take him outside," the colonel ordered. "Let's do some honey dippin'."

Jakes dragged Dale outside by his arms.

"Lemme go!" Dale pleaded. "Don't do this. I don't know anything about your plane." He twisted and squirmed.

Escorted by the two privates, Angela and I shuffled along behind Dale. Trotter and Bickerstaff brought up the rear.

It was just beginning to get light, and the fields were covered with mist. A mourning dove cooed in the field. If that had been the only sound, I would have taken it as an omen of doom, but a cardinal was whistling a loud, bright tune.

A red van and a black Hummer were parked in front of the porch. Both vehicles were facing away from the house toward the tree-lined driveway.

Angela and I followed Dale's struggling figure to the right and around toward the back of the house.

The place where the septic tank had been found was about six feet from the house, under the branches of a tall double-hickory tree. A small shovel marked the spot.

"The top of the tank's just about two inches down," Cullman said.

"That's good," the colonel replied. "Let's find the lid." He looked at me. "You dig, Mr. Larrison."

"Why me?" I said.

"Because I said so."

He picked up the little shovel and handed it to me. It looked like the kind of shovel I had seen soldiers use to dig foxholes in old war movies.

I knelt down and began digging.

The clay was hard, but I hit concrete right away. He watched me remove dirt for a couple of minutes, then ordered Trotter to see if he could find a bigger shovel in the barn.

Trotter took off at a slow run. A minute later he called on his walkie-talkie and said, "There's a padlock on the door, Colonel."

"Damn it, Nate, use your sidearm and shoot it off," the colonel said.

The crack of a pistol shattered the calm morning air. I wondered if someone in the neighborhood might have heard the gunshot. If so, it was nothing they'd call the police about.

A few minutes later Trotter returned with two shovels, one long, one short.

"There's all kinds of tools in there," he reported. "I'd like to liberate a few of them."

The colonel ordered Smedley and Cullman to help me uncover the tank. Their shovels had standard blades. I got to keep the miniature one.

As the three of us tossed dirt aside, the colonel asked Dale if he was ready to talk. Dale said, "Don't do this. If I knew where the plane is, I'd tell you." His voice was weaker. He shook as if shivering in the cold, but it wasn't really cold.

"When are you going to stop lying, Mr. Marcott?" the colonel said.

"I'm not lying!"

"Of course you are."

Smedley said, "Why don't ya make *him* dig, Cunnel?"

The colonel said, "Because I don't want to put a weapon in his hands."

Cullman said, "I found the lid, Colonel. It's flush with the top of the tank. It don't seem very big though."

"That's an inspection hole," the colonel said. "We need to find the main lid. It'll be about the size of a manhole. Clear the dirt off the whole tank. Then we'll know what we're dealing with here."

"Smedley said, "How d'ya know so much about septic tanks, Cunnel?"

"I'd better know something about them," the Colonel replied. "I'm in the construction business, you know."

We dug and scraped. Gradually the outline of the tank appeared. It was about eight feet long and four feet wide. Before we got the top completely uncovered, Smedley discovered a rusty handle near the middle of the tank. We cleared the surrounding dirt away and exposed the top of a concrete plug that was about twenty inches in diameter. It had two rusty handles, each extending about an inch above the lid.

The colonel said, "If the tank hasn't been cleaned out in a long time, it might be hard to get the lid off."

He was right. When the lid was completely uncovered, we were unable to lift it. I couldn't raise it a hair, and the two privates strained to lift it until their eyeballs bugged out. The colonel explained that over the years dirt had settled into the little bit of space around the tapered lid. That, along with the weight of people walking on it, had wedged the lid tightly in place.

It began to look as if Dale might not get dipped after all.

"We'll have to try to winch it out," the colonel said.

"I'll get the Hummer," Lieutenant Trotter said.

He drove the Hummer around the house. It had a winch attached in front, and they tossed a hook on the end of the cable over a thick tree branch above the septic tank. Next they tied a piece of rope about six feet long to both handles on the lid and hung the middle of the rope over the hook.

The winch strained and groaned. It looked as if the lid was not going to come loose, but suddenly it popped out like a cork and nearly hit the colonel in the face.

The overpowering stench of sewage filled the air.

"Peeeuuweee!" Smedley said. "It shore is ripe!"

Trotter hurried to the van and returned with five gas masks, one of which he already had on. He distributed the others to his fellow warriors, but Colonel Bickerstaff was content to breathe through a black ski mask, which he folded in half and held against his nose and mouth.

Unnoticed by anyone, Dale had crawled about fifteen feet away toward the pond. Corporal Jakes went after him and dragged him back. The colonel ordered Cullman to attach the hook to the rope around Dale's ankles.

"No!" Dale shouted. He raised his feet to fend them off, but Cullman simply hooked the cable to the rope while Dale's feet were in the air. "Please," Dale begged. "Don't do this. I don't know where the plane is."

"Take him up," the colonel ordered.

As the winch raised his legs off the ground, Dale began cursing. Then he started to cry.

I knew Dale was big on neatness and order. His anal personality recoiled from what was about to happen. He thrashed like a fish on a hook as Jakes pulled the cable along the tree branch to position him over the middle of the septic tank.

The stench was unbearable, but the thought of what was about to happen to Dale helped me ignore it.

Slowly spinning, Dale went on blubbering while Smedley and Cullman laughed. "No, no, no," he begged as they lowered his head toward the opening. The airspace at the top of the tank became an echo chamber.

"Hold it there, Privates," the colonel said.

Dale squirmed and twisted. He gasped for a breath of clean air.

The colonel said, "I'm going to give you one more chance, Mr. Marcott. Where is our plane? What happened to Captain Murphy?"

I began to think Dale was going to tell them what they wanted to know, but instead he said, *"I don't kno-o-o-o-ow."*

"Dip 'im!" the colonel commanded.

Dale's head inched slowly toward the tank. A foamy crust had formed on top of the wastewater. Angela shut her eyes. Dale squeezed his eyes and mouth shut as his head approached the crust. He went on struggling but stopped shouting.

I figured he had filled his lungs with one last breath of air. His head disappeared in the crust. The colonel and Trotter stepped back from the opening so their uniforms wouldn't get soiled.

I counted the seconds in silence . . . fifteen . . . thirty . . . forty-five. . . . There was a burst of bubbles, and the colonel said, "Pull him up."

Gagging, coughing, choking, Dale's face emerged from the foamy filth. His head and shoulders looked as if they were covered with papier-mâché. Black water dripped from his nose and mouth. As soon as he could speak, Dale began begging them to stop.

"Ready to talk, Mr. Marcott?" the colonel asked.

Dale coughed so hard it sounded as if a lung would come out of his mouth. Private Smedley laughed like a lunatic.

"Dip him again," the colonel said. "Stir it up good this time. Get him down in the muck."

The smell that Cullman and Smedley stirred up burned my eyes. I breathed through my mouth instead of my nose, but it barely made a difference. The stench was so strong I thought I was swallowing it.

The colonel noticed that Angela wasn't watching what was happening to her ex-husband, so he clutched the back of her neck and made her look. I was afraid to tell him to take his hand off her. I was as squeamish as Dale when it came to getting dunked in a septic tank.

When Trotter raised Dale out of the tank again, he was covered with the filthy crust. A clump of soggy toilet paper hung from one ear. He was spitting and gagging. He twisted slowly on the hook.

"Had enough, Mr. Marcott?" the colonel asked. "Are you ready to tell us where our airplane is?"

Dale mumbled something.

"What did he say, Corporal?" the colonel asked.

Corporal Jakes was standing closer to Dale than anyone else. He seemed to want the best view and worst smell of the event. As if out of respect for the colonel, he removed his gas mask and said, "I couldn't hear him, sir."

"Speak up, Mr. Marcott," the colonel said. "You sound like your mouth's full of shit." His men laughed, except for Jakes, who was all business.

Dale coughed something up and spat it out. In a halting voice he said, "My father . . . buried it . . . back by the woods."

A broad smile lit up the colonel's face. "So, you admit that your father buried the plane! Very good, Mr. Marcott."

Dale kept trying to spit things out of his mouth.

"Did it make a safe landing?" the colonel asked him.

Spitting as he spoke, Dale said, "No. It crashed. It nearly hit our house."

"Did the plane explode?"

"No. The engine quit. The damn plane came down with a thud. My old man turned on a hose and wet down the engine. The plane could've blown up and killed him. He risked his life to try to save the pilot, but it was too late."

The colonel took a deep breath through his ski mask and pondered what Dale had told him. He circled Dale, whose face was now as red as a kidney bean from hanging by his heels. Finally Bickerstaff said, "So your father tried to save Captain Murphy's life, but he didn't bother to call an ambulance or the police. He simply buried the plane, you say."

"Yeah," Dale replied. "That's what he did."

"Did he bury Captain Murphy with the plane?"

"I don't know," Dale said.

"What do you mean you don't you?"

"I had to go to school. When I got home, the plane was gone."

The colonel stopped and stared at his men. Their gas masks made them look like giant insects. "That sounds strange, doesn't it?" he said. "But I think I know why your father did what you say he did. He probably found the gold and decided to keep it for himself instead of trying to locate its rightful owner. That's what happened, isn't it, Mr. Marcott?"

"I don't know," Dale said. "The plane nearly hit the house. It could've killed us."

"That was an accident. It was no excuse for hiding the plane and Captain Murphy's body and stealing our assets."

"It's not what I would've done if it was up to me. But you've got your gold now, so what difference does it make?"

"We don't have all of it," the colonel said. "Some of it is missing. And our military operations have stagnated for a quarter of a century."

"That's not my fault. Why are you taking it out on me?"

"The sins of the fathers, Mr. Marcott. The sins of the fathers. . . ."

"I didn't bury your plane and your pilot. I didn't know where my old man hid your gold. I was as surprised as you were when it fell out of the ceiling."

"Oh you were, were you?"

"Yeah," Dale insisted. Still spinning, he ran his tongue around his teeth and spat out what looked like a piece of excrement.

"You're going to show us where your father buried the plane," the colonel said.

"I'm not sure exactly where it is."

"The general area will be good enough for starters."

"It's probably covered by trees by now."

"I'll give you a choice, Mr. Marcott. Help us find the plane, or enjoy another dip in the septic tank. Which will it be?"

Trotter turned the winch on and off, dropping Dale's head a foot closer to the opening.

"Okay! Okay!" Dale yelled. "I'll try to find it for you."

"We're not playing games," the colonel said. "The plane better be where you say it is, or you're going back in the tank, permanently. . . . Untie him, men."

They lowered Dale to the ground and replaced the lid on the tank. I told them there was a hose hooked up behind the house.

Private Cullman was ordered to get the hose. He returned spraying water into the air, as if trying to wash away the stench.

"Clean him up," the colonel ordered, and Cullman aimed the nozzle at Dale.

Dale shivered in a stinging rod of cold water. As he spun above the tank, he kept trying to catch water with his mouth to rinse out the filth.

CHAPTER 39

THE MUMMY'S SECRET

Aftter hosing Dale off, the colonel's men cut the clothesline off his ankles and replaced it with a looser piece so he could walk in baby steps like Angela and me.

"How far is the plane?" the colonel asked him.

Dale was shivering. He was dripping wet. He still smelled like the septic tank. "It's at the back of the farm, just over the first rise," he said.

"Let's get some exercise," said the colonel. "Bring those shovels, Private Smedley."

"We gonna dig up the plane, Cunnel?"

"That's the idea, Private."

Smedley picked up the shovels and carried one on each shoulder, with his assault rifle slung across his back.

As we marched around the side of house, the colonel said, "Lieutenant Trotter, you stay here and keep an eye on the gold in case somebody happens to show up."

"What should I do if they do, sir?" Trotter asked.

"That all depends. As soon as you see somebody coming, give me a call on the walkie-talkie."

"Yes, sir!" Trotter said with a smart salute.

As we approached the dog pen, Angela froze.

Sadie lay on her side with her paws outstretched. She looked like a dirty mop soaking up blood.

Smedley laughed at Angela. "Aw, poor little girl, did yer doggie get hurt?"

A few steps ahead of me, Angela raised her shoulder to wipe tears off her face.

Cullman took a deep breath of the cool fresh air. "This ain't bad," he said. "I could get to like it here. I could go huntin' or fishin' every day."

"You want to be a Hoosier, Delmar?" the colonel asked him.

"No, sir. I ain't turnin' into no Hoosier. I'm just sayin' it ain't bad here. It's pretty country."

We staggered toward the back of the pond. The ground was punctuated with crawdad holes topped with conical "chimneys" that were several inches high and made of small mudballs. I could hear the crawdads splash inside their watery homes as we approached.

We shuffled through the wheat field toward the stone fence on the west side of the farm. Because our hands were tied behind our backs, Dale and I rolled over the fence on our chests, and Corporal Jakes picked up Angela and lifted her over, which brought wisecracks from Smedley and Cullman.

We turned right on the logging trail that ran between the stone fence and the edge of the woods. The overgrown trail was littered with fallen branches that kept snagging the ropes on our ankles.

"Where are you taking us?" the colonel shouted at Dale.

"We're almost there!" Dale said.

At the back of the farm, the fence made a ninety-degree turn to the right, but the logging trail continued straight ahead for another hundred feet or so before turning to the right as well. As soon as we made the turn, we were in the narrow hollow that I had seen when Angela and I went looking for Kelly's treehouse. The hollow was like a small valley nestled between the high, steep knob on our left and the low foothill on the right. At ground level the "valley" was only about a hundred feet long and forty feet wide.

"Is this where our plane is buried?" the colonel demanded.

Dale spat something out of his mouth and muttered, "Yeah, unless my old man moved it somewhere else."

"You better hope he didn't," the colonel said.

Jakes walked on by himself, studying the ground. He stopped in the middle of the overgrown field and waved at us to come ahead. Then he pointed at the ground and said, "Ya see how the land's sank here, Colonel? I'd say this is where the plane's at."

"Then this is where we dig," the colonel said. "Good work, Corporal." He turned to Dale and said, "How deep is the plane?"

Dale blew at a bug that was trying to get into his eyes. "I don't know," he said. "I didn't bury it."

"You'd better hope it's not too far down, or you and Mr. Larrison will be digging a long time."

Smedley said, "What we need is a backhoe, Cunnel."

The colonel said, "I've got one back home, but that won't help us now." He studied the sunken area, then said, "Okay, let's see if it's here. Untie our friends. Give them the shovels."

Smedley said, "Mebbe we cud rent a backhoe from one a them rent-all places, Cunnel. It would save a lotta time."

Irritated, the colonel said, "Let's see how our prisoners do with their shovels, Private."

"Yessuh."

I got the short shovel this time, but it was better than the small foxhole shovel that I had used earlier.

As Dale and I went to work, the colonel said, "Watch 'em, men. We're all tired, but we can't afford to get careless. Keep some distance between you and the diggers. If they come at you with those shovels, shoot them."

A couple of hooahs went up, but Cullman said, "Cunnel, what about the gold that's missin'? Are we just gonna fergit about it?"

"No, Private. Didn't I say we will have to work that out with Chester Marcott's heir before we leave?"

Dale said, "My old man didn't leave me a dime. Everything went to my ex-wife, the bitch. So get your money from her."

The colonel said, "Start digging."

Fortunately the soil was a mixture of clay and sand. If it had been solid clay, it could have been as hard as concrete. Even so, as soon as I began digging, my arms felt weak. They weren't used to this. And my feet were still sore from the beating they had taken last night.

The colonel ordered Cullman to tie Angela to a tree at the edge of the woods. A few minutes later I heard her yell, "Take your hands off me, you pig."

Dale was already a foot or so down in the hole he was digging. I felt like telling him to slow down. He was making me look bad.

We worked about five feet apart, but gradually the holes we were digging came together. Despite the chilly morning, I began to sweat. I felt hot and cold at the same time. It occurred to me that I might be digging my grave. Maybe once we found Captain Murphy's body, they'd bury us alive, along with Angela. I imagined how it would feel to be lying next to Angela as the dirt hit our faces and blocked out the light.

Smedley and Cullman talked and joked as if they were sitting around a campfire. I whispered to Dale, "How do we get outta this?"

Barely moving his lips, he murmured, "There's a gun in the plane. If it still works, I'm takin' one or two of these bastards with me."

I went on digging as if he hadn't said a word, but my brain began buzzing. If he knew there was a gun in the plane, he must have helped bury it. If he could get that gun, maybe he could take out the two privates and Dale and I could get their assault rifles. That would make it two against two.

I began to admire Dale. I didn't want to elevate him, but look what he had been through. He had managed to survive the septic tank. He had endured way, way more than I could have. He kept battling, kept lying through his teeth. . . .

"Hey, newspaperman, keep that shovel movin'," Cullman said. "Put your back into it."

Smedley said, "Ah wish ah had me a bullwhip," and both of them laughed.

As the hole grew deeper, it got harder to dig. We had rocks and roots to contend with. I was already sweating. I took off my shirt and stuck it inside my belt so I could use it to wipe my face. Smedley and Cullman laughed at my bulging gut.

Exhausted to begin with, I was beyond exhaustion now, but I kept digging. Sweat streamed down my forehead and stung my eyes. The sun climbed higher. Whenever I slowed down, the slave drivers hurled threats. Sweat felt like it was boiling on my back. I wasn't used to physical labor. Make a virtue of necessity, Larrison. Dig. Lose some weight.

I kept my eyes open for something I could use as a weapon. A good-sized rock maybe. It would take a perfect throw. Every now and then a mini-avalanche occurred, burying our feet in dirt. There was no breeze in the hole, and as we got closer to the center of the earth, the temperature increased. My skin was streaked with orange mud.

The sun rose higher and inched across the sky. I estimated that an hour had passed. The holes we were digging were a few feet down. Dale's was deeper than mine. The colonel and his men looked nice and cool. All they had to do was keep their eyes on us.

We kept digging. I had a rhythm going. I consoled myself with the idea that the plane couldn't be too far down. But what if the plane wasn't here? In that case, they'd make us dig some-where else. They'd make us dig up the whole field. Then, if we still hadn't found the plane, they'd kill us. Why would they let us live to tell the police about them? Why would they let me live to write about them? So maybe I should be hoping we wouldn't find the plane. The longer we took to find it, the longer we'd stay alive.

I began to wonder if there really was a plane. Why had Dale waited to tell them about it until he had been dipped in the septic tank? I recalled what he had told me about a gun in the plane. If he knew there was a gun there, why hadn't he told them where the plane was right away instead of going through his ordeal? It was nuts. You'd think he'd want to get to the plane as soon as possible to get his hands on the gun. So maybe there *was* no gun. Maybe he was afraid to lead them on a wild-goose chase. They might shoot him.

Thwank ka-reeee.

Dale's shovel scraped metal. We scraped away a few more scoops, and a flat white surface began to appear.

Above us, Cullman said, "I think we found somethin', Cunnel."

Four silhouettes gathered around the top of the hole.

"Looks lakh a wing," Smedley said.

"Keep digging," the colonel ordered. "Dig out under the wing. That's where the doors are."

While Dale and I cleared off part of the wing, the colonel called Lieutenant Trotter on his walkie-talkie to tell him we had found the plane.

Trotter congratulated him.

The colonel said, "We all deserve congratulations, not just me. After a quarter of a century, the maggots have had a lot of time to do their work. There's not likely to be more than a skeleton and some clothing left, but whatever there is, we'll take it home with us. We'll give Captain Murphy's remains a proper burial."

Cullman said, "It's a damn shame he was buried here 'stead of back home."

"I agree with you, son," the colonel replied, "but look at the bright side—he'll be going home."

Smedley said, "Ah hope the skeleton don't fall apart."

Growing impatient again, the colonel instructed Dale and me to clear off more of the wing to find the front and back of it. Then we should dig out underneath it on both sides, using it as a roof over our heads while we excavated a door to the cabin. "If you can't tell which way the door is, locate one of the struts," he added. "It'll slant down toward the fuselage, not away from it."

"No shit," Dale said under his breath.

Smedley spat on Dale's head. "Shut yer face," he screamed, "unless ya wanna git dipped some moah."

Dale stared at the ground with murder in his eyes.

It turned out we were at the far end of the starboard wing. We worked on opposite sides to tunnel toward the fuselage. It took hours. We couldn't just throw dirt behind us. We had to toss it out of what was now a deep hole.

It was hot in the hole. Sweat dripped off us and made mud around our feet. Bending and twisting, we'd scoop out a shovelful of dirt, then back out and stand up and catapult it out of the hole. Sweat flies tried to get in our eyes.

Above us, the excitement grew. Soon the make-believe army would have its MIA as well as its gold. It was their shining moment.

Lieutenant Trotter radioed every hour or so to check in and get a progress report. He said he wished he could come and see what we were doing, but the colonel ordered him to stay at the house and guard the gold. It made me wonder if Trotter was the only member of the militia that the colonel thought he could trust.

Dale reached a door to the cockpit before I did. He raised a finger to his lips and laid his shovel down. He was chopping away at the last foot or so of clay at the bottom of the door when the colonel slid into the pit behind me.

"You're relieved, Mr. Larrison," he said. He stuck his pistol in my back and took my shovel, which he passed up to one of his men. I glanced up and saw two gun barrels staring at me like a pair of eyes.

The colonel said, "Private Cullman, get down here and tie him up."

Cullman slid down and screamed at me, "Turn around an' put your hands behind yer back." He pressed my face into the wall and wrapped a piece of clothesline around my wrists.

It was a tight fit for three of us on my side of the hole, so the colonel ordered Cullman to climb over the wing to the other side.

All this time Dale had been working frantically to clear the door.

I heard the colonel say, "That will do, Mr. Marcott. I'll take over now."

Dale went on digging and scraping. "Just give me another minute and I'll have it cleared," he said.

"Now means *now*," the colonel said. "It doesn't mean a minute from now. It means *now!*" He shot a round into the wall of dirt. "Put the shovel down. There's not enough room over here for you. Crawl out to Private Cullman. Don't try anything. I'll be right behind you."

Dale crawled out of his tunnel under the wing.

The colonel shouted, "Private Smedley, get down here and assist Private Cullman. Bring some rope with you."

"Ah ain't got none," Smedley said.

"Then use your belt."

"Ah'll use his," Smedley said.

He jumped onto the wing, then to the ground.

"Take off yer belt," Smedley ordered Dale, and when Dale did not immediately comply, Smedley hit him on the side of his head with his gun and said, "If ah hafta tell ya again, ah'll put a bullet in yer head."

In a calm, sinister voice, the colonel said, "Mr. Marcott, if I were you, I would remove my belt," and Dale took it off. Smedley wound the belt around Dale's wrists in both directions behind his back and buckled the ends together.

The colonel knelt down and crawled into the tunnel. He was taller and heavier than Dale, and I wondered if he'd be able to get to the door of the cockpit. Dale's tunnel was only about five feet long, but it was low and narrow, and it had to be expanded in order to open the door.

The colonel insisted on digging it out by himself. I heard him tossing dirt into what had been my tunnel on the other side of the wing. Smedley asked if he was all right. Cullman asked if he needed help. Bickerstaff told them to stay where they were and watch the prisoners.

After a while Trotter whispered to Jakes, "He's been in there over an hour now."

Finally Bickerstaff announced, "I can see Captain Murphy through the window on the door. Damnation, he looks like a mummy. His skin is all brown. Wait a minute! What the hell?"

"What's the mattuh, Cunnel?" Smedley called.

Without answering, the colonel scraped at the door and struggled to pull it open. Next we heard him prying at it with the tip of his shovel. The door opened with a screech of metal against metal. Silence followed.

I wondered if Bickerstaff was paying his respects to what was left of the pilot.

Cullman said, "You need any help, Cunnel?"

I inched closer to the tunnel to see what the colonel was doing. I could see him leaning inside the cockpit and fumbling with something. He was half inside for another ten or fifteen minutes. Finally he came backing out of the tunnel on his hands and knees, dragging something in front of him. When he reached us, he stood up holding a .22-caliber rifle.

Smedley said, "Where'd ya find thet gun, Cunnel?"

Bickerstaff looked furious. Sweat dripped off his face. His chest heaved as he glared at Dale and said, "Captain Murphy did not die in the crash. He was shot. He was murdered. There are two bullet holes in his forehead. I suspect that this is the gun that killed him, and I have no doubt that you're the rotten bastard who did it."

Dale, who was still on his knees, insisted, "It wasn't me!"

With both hands, the colonel raised the .22 over his head. "Look at the name on the stock—Dale Marcott! This is your rifle. You're the son of a bitch who killed Captain Murphy."

"I didn't do it. I swear."

"Liar!" the colonel shouted as he unholstered his Luger.

"My old man shot him, but it was self-defense—the pilot shot first."

The colonel said, "Captain Murphy managed to get the plane down in one piece, only to be killed by you, you pig."

Dale said, "You weren't there. You don't know what happened. I didn't kill him!"

"Then how'd your gun get in the plane?"

"My father must've put it there."

Smedley piped up: "You don't hafta argue with 'im, Cunnel. Just put a bullet in his head."

Dale yelled, "The pilot shot first. My dad shot back."

The colonel scoffed. "If Captain Murphy fired first, he would not have missed. He was a crack shot. He was a Green Beret in Vietnam."

Smedley said, "Let's put 'im back in the shit tank, Cunnel."

Smedley and Cullman debated how to execute Dale. Drown him in the septic tank? Shoot him in the head "jest like the pilot got it"? Bury him alive in the plane?

"Here's what we're going to do," the colonel said. "We're going to—"

A shotgun blast came from the side of the hill on the north side of the little hollow. It was very loud and very close. As soon as the echoes faded, a boy's voice that was meant to sound like a man's shouted, "That's just a warning! Give up! You're surrounded!" It was Kelly.

As if to prove the militia was surrounded, a second shotgun blast came from the low hill on the opposite side of the field, even closer to the pit we were in. This time Dicey Cockerham yelled, "Come out with your hands up, or we'll blow your damn heads off."

"That's a woman," Smedley said. "I ain't never fought against no woman before."

"Don't let it bother you," Bickerstaff replied. "She's an enemy. Take her out."

CHAPTER 40

NEVER SURRENDER

As the two shots echoed off the big hill, Corporal Jakes rolled sideways into the pit and fell on Dale, who made a sound like soggy cardboard being torn apart.

The walkie-talkie crackled, and Lieutenant Trotter said, "What's goin' on out there, Colonel? Over."

"We've got a situation here, Lieutenant," the colonel said. "Stand by."

"Do you need my help, Colonel? Over."

"We're assessing the situation. Sit tight. Stay with the gold. But in case we need you here, put the gold in the Hummer and lock the doors."

"Will do," Trotter said. "Then what? Over."

"Keep an eye on it. I'll call you if we need you."

"Yes, sir. Out."

The colonel, Jakes, Smedley, Cullman, Dale, and I were crammed together in one side of the pit, so the colonel told Jakes and Smedley to get up on the wing. "Sneak a peek and see if the shooters are moving closer," he said, "but don't poke your heads up. Damn, I wish we had our helmets."

I was standing against the slightly sloping wall opposite Dale. His eyes were shut, and his mouth hung open like a fly trap. His lips were dirty, and he had a purple blood blob on the tip of his tongue.

The colonel asked Jakes and Smedley if they could see anything.

Smedley said, "Not too much. The view's blocked by the dirt piles them two piled up."

"Don't stand there gawking," the colonel warned. "The shooter on the high side might be able to see you."

Smedley stooped on the wing.

The colonel said, "I wonder how many of them there are."

"At least two," Smedley said.

The man knew how to count.

The colonel reviewed the situation: "They've got us pinned down, and we don't have a great deal of ammunition with us, just what's in our gun belts. We are not in a favorable position. That's my fault, men. I failed to anticipate an enemy action. The enemy used the element of surprise, but the good news is we have him outgunned. Their shotguns are no match for what we've got. On the other hand, they hold the high ground, and we're stuck in here like sitting ducks."

"Cunnel," Smedley said enthusiastically, as if he had a brilliant idea, "why don't we use our prisonuhs as shields and march outta here with one of 'em on each side of us? The enemy won't risk shootin' at us with them scatterguns they got, or else they'd hit the prisonuhs."

"Thank you for your suggestion, Private, but no thanks," said the colonel.

"Beggin' yer pardon, sir, but ah think it's worth a try. We got what we come for—the gold. Why don't we just git outta heah?"

In a slow burn, the colonel said, "First of all, your idea works only if the hostages are too stupid to drop to the ground, leaving us completely exposed to their buckshot. And second of all, we are not leaving this place without taking Captain Murphy with us."

"Beggin' yer pardon ag'in, Cunnel, but if Cap'n Murphy's been buried here ovah twenty years, mebbe we should leave 'im be."

Slowly the colonel said, "I'll pretend I didn't hear that, Private. We're not leaving here without Captain Murphy. He's one of us."

Dale laughed at their bickering.

"Shut him up," the colonel said.

Cullman cracked Dale on the head with the barrel of his gun, and Dale tipped over, apparently unconscious.

I was surprised to hear Jakes speak up: "Why don't we find out what they want, Colonel? Maybe we can make a deal with 'em."

The colonel seemed stunned that his men were challenging him. He started to say something, stopped, and started over: "Very well, if that's what you want. Let's see what happens." He raised his face toward the sky and shouted, "Hey out there, who are you? What are you shooting at us for? What do you want?"

Kelly shouted back, "Who are *you,* the freaken Ku Klux Klan?" This time his voice came from a different spot on the big hill.

The colonel laughed. "The Ku Klux Klan?" he shouted back. "Where'd you get that idea?"

Kelly did not answer.

I was surprised that Angela hadn't called out to him. I thought by now she would have warned Kelly not to mess with these guys. She's probably dying to do just that, I told myself, but she doesn't want the colonel to find out she's Kelly's mom. He could use her as a bargaining chip—he could threaten to kill her unless Kelly would withdraw.

When Kelly still didn't reply, the colonel shouted, "Nobody's gotten hurt. You fired at us, but we haven't fired at you. So before somebody gets killed, why don't we agree to a truce so we can talk face to face and clear things up. I don't see why we have to shoot at one another." He stopped, then added, "And I ought to warn you—we have some serious weapons at our disposal. If it comes to a fight, unless you have more than a couple of shotguns, you won't win."

Kelly replied from a different location, nearer his mother. "Throw your guns out and give up. Then we can talk."

I inched up the wall backward and glanced in Angela's direction. She was staring toward the trees. I wondered if she was looking at Kelly. Another warning shot—from Dicey, I assumed—peppered the ground between Angela and me. A flock of crows took off squawking. Jakes and Smedley opened up with their assault rifles, raking the woods where the shot had come from.

"Cease firing!" the colonel ordered after they had peppered the hillside. "Save your ammunition." He contacted Trotter on his walkie-talkie. "Situation critical, Lieutenant," he said. "We're running out of ammunition, and we're pinned down. We need you to bring us some ammo."

"Will do, sir. Where are you? How do I find you?"

"There's a lane just past the stone wall on the west side of the farm. The lane bends to the right beyond the farm and goes between the first two hills. We're pinned down in there by two shotguns. They've got us in a crossfire."

"Can I drive in there, Colonel?"

"Don't. You'd have to go out to the county road first, and somebody might see you and wonder what you're up to. *Walk* to the lane I told you about, but be careful. Stay low. We'll use what ammo we've got left to cover you."

"I'm on my way, Colonel. Out."

Next, the colonel tried to make contact with the enemy again. "Are you still there, fella?" he called. "What are your terms for surrender?" He winked at his men to show he wasn't serious about giving up. "If they respond, fire in the direction of the voice," he said. He sounded jolly. He could have been playing cowboys and Indians with his grandchildren.

"Throw your guns out," Kelly repeated.

Jakes, Cullman, and Smedley opened fire.

Again, when the AK-47s started blasting blindly into the trees, the shotguns went silent. The *bam-bam-bam* of the semiautomatics opened a hole in my belly. I wondered if Smedley or one of the other nutcakes would take a shot at Angela. Or she might catch a stray bullet.

As soon as the AK-47s stopped shooting, there was another shotgun blast. Buckshot swished over our heads. I hunkered down, and the colonel called Trotter to ask where he was.

"I'm on my way, Colonel. I hear your weapons firing." He sounded out of breath, as if running.

"Tell us when you get near our location," the colonel said.

"Will do, sir."

A few minutes later Trotter said, "I see Mrs. Marcott tied to a tree, Colonel."

The colonel told his men to fire, and the corporal and privates shot blindly into the trees again. My eyes inched up over the top of the wall and peered out between the dirt piles. I saw Trotter lugging an old-fashioned piece of brown leather luggage that looked like a huge gym bag. As if using it to protect his chest, he carried it with both arms under it. His assault rifle was slung over his shoulder, and he was moving as fast as he could.

Smedley's assault rifle ran out of ammunition.

Then Cullman's.

Then Jakes's.

Finally the colonel's Luger.

Trotter was about ten feet from the pit when the next shotgun blast came from farther up the higher hill.

"I'm hit!" Trotter cried out, but he managed to stay on his feet. He tried to run with his bag of ammo, but a few feet short of our hole he stumbled and fell.

The colonel and Smedley crawled halfway out and pulled Trotter in by his arms.

"Get that bag," the colonel said. "Without it, we're dead meat."

Kelly and Dicey weren't shooting. I wondered if they were out of ammunition too.

"Where are you hit?" the colonel asked Trotter.

"In the ass," he said. "It feels like it's on fire. It feels like half my ass is shot off."

The colonel said, "It just feels that way, J.T. You're still in one piece."

Smedley reached out for the leather bag, but a blast from Dicey's side of the battlefield turned his face into a bloody pudding. That horror and the much louder blast from her gun meant that she had moved a lot closer to us.

"They got Smed," Cullman said. He sounded shocked and angry. He jumped up on the wing and crawled out of the hole. With some difficulty, he managed to get most of his body under Smedley's. Balancing Smedley on his back, he used him as a shield to reach the bag of ammunition.

The next blast peppered the leather bag and Smedley but did not hit Cullman. Another blast hit Cullman's boots but did not penetrate the leather.

Cullman dragged the ammunition back to the hole. Smedley's body slid off him like a heavy quilt and fell on the wing. His arms hung down dripping blood.

Kneeling next to Trotter, the colonel shouted at his men, "Reload! Reload! Kill the bastards. Kill 'em all! No mercy. No prisoners!" He turned back to Trotter and said, "You'll get a medal, J.T. You'll get *two* medals—one for bravery under fire and one for your wounds."

Trotter sucked air through clenched teeth. "I hope I live to see them, Colonel."

"You'll live. I don't think any of your vital organs got hit."

"I'm bleedin' bad," Trotter said.

"We'll get you to a hospital. Thanks to the ammo you brought us, we're going to win this fight."

Closer now, but still on the steep hill, Kelly yelled, "If you're not the Klan, then why'd you murder my grampaw?"

The colonel looked confused. "What'd he say? He thinks we killed his grandfather? He must mean Chester Marcott. That means this piece of garbage"—he jutted his chin toward Dale—"must be his father."

Trotter groaned and said, "It hurts. God, it hurts. I'm gonna die." He pleaded with the colonel: "Put a bullet in my head, Hank. I don't want to lay here pissin' and moanin'."

The shotguns began firing again. Jakes and Cullman, who had reloaded their weapons, began shooting back. Over the din the colonel shouted at them, "We've got to get out of here. We've got to take the hill." He reloaded his pistol.

Cullman said, "You can use Smed's gun, Colonel. It's good to go."

"Good. The next time they take a shot at us, you two strafe the mountain. I'll suppress the shotgun on the other side."

Jakes and Cullman stooped on the wing and waited for the next shots to come. Their eyes were at ground level as they peered out between the piles of dirt.

The next two shots from Kelly's double-barrelled shotgun sprayed a blizzard of pellets across the wall above Dale.

Jakes and Cullman fired back as they scrambled out of the pit. The colonel emptied Smedley's gun into the trees on the other side of the clearing, even though no shots had come from that direction. Either Dicey is out of ammunition or she's dead, I said to myself.

Jakes and Cullman made it to the woods. The colonel put his rifle down and returned to Trotter.

"Hang on, J.T.," he said. "Don't you go dyin' on me."

Dale, who had not really been unconscious, reached up and grabbed the colonel by his hair. With his puffy, bruised face, Dale looked like an eyeless monster.

The colonel raised his Luger, but Dale yanked his head back. The colonel stretched his arm around his chest and shot behind himself, twice. The first shot thwunked into the ground, but the second one hit Dale in his left side. Despite the wound, Dale sliced the colonel's neck with a jagged tin-can lid that he must have found in the hole we had dug. A wide Muppetlike mouth opened in Bickerstaff's neck, and blood poured out like water overflowing a bowl.

Trotter cried like a baby as the life drained out of the colonel's face.

I thought Dale was going to cut Trotter's throat too, but he plopped on the ground and raised his shirt a few inches. He pulled off the shirt and tried to stop the bleeding with it.

"Are you okay?" I asked him.

"I don't know," he said.

"Can you cut the rope off my hands?" I asked.

He nodded slowly.

He used the tin-can lid to cut through the clothesline around my wrists. Somehow he must have cut through the belt around his own wrists too, while I thought he was out cold.

"Thanks," I said. "I'll try to get you some help."

He nodded again. He was sitting with his back against the wall. His chest rose and fell as he breathed through his mouth.

I heard Cullman trying to contact the colonel by walkie-talkie. I clipped the colonel's device onto my belt in case I might want to talk to Cullman later.

I also took the colonel's Luger and climbed out of the pit.

When Angela saw me, her face lit up. I ran toward her as fast as I could. I was amazed that Jakes and Cullman weren't firing at me. Any second I expected to be cut down. The only reason I'm still alive, I thought, is they're hunting for Kelly and Dicey, and they don't want to reveal their positions.

"Thank God you're alive!" Angela said as I dove behind her.

"Yeah," I agreed, though there was no reason for God to want to keep me alive.

I knelt behind Angela to untie her from the tree. Blisters from digging had sprouted on my fingers and palms. It was hard to get a grip on the knots. A burst from an AK-47 ripped through the hill where Kelly was.

"Oh Jesus, poor Kelly," she said. "And poor Phil. How'd you get away?"

I summed up what had occurred in the pit.

A shiver ran through her. "That sounds dreadful," she said. "Is Dale still alive?"

"Uh-huh. He got shot, but the last time I saw him he was still alive."

She said nothing. I wondered what she was thinking . . . and feeling.

I finally got the rope off her hands, and we hid behind a clump of scrawny trees and blackberry bushes.

"You have a gun," she said.

"Yes. It belonged to the colonel. I thought I'd keep it as a souvenir on the chance I live through this."

"Really? You want to remember this day?"

I was trying to come up with a clever comeback when a burst of bullets tore through the leaves above our heads. I got on the walkie-talkie and said, "Hey, Cullman, are you there? Listen, let's quit playing soldiers. The colonel and Smedley are dead, and Trotter's in very bad shape. How 'bout putting an end to this so Trotter doesn't die too."

There was no reply, so I said, "Look, Delmar, you and Jakes haven't killed anyone as far as I know, so use your head. Quit shooting. The game's over."

Gunfire came at us from two directions. Jakes and Cullman had us in a crossfire now. Angela lay on the ground and covered her head with her arms. I lay beside her and put an arm over her back. Blood pounded in my ears like a drum.

Somehow Dale got himself up to the top of the pit. Cullman charged out of the woods with his gun blazing, and Dale dropped out of sight. Cullman dove behind a pile of dirt.

Higher up the hill a girl screamed, "Kelly, watch out! Behind you!"

"Is that Glorie?" Angela asked. Her mouth hung open in amazement.

An AK-47 opened up, and either Kelly or Glorie came sliding down the slope through the underbrush.

"Oh God!" Angela screamed. "No! No! No! No!" She tried to get up, but I held her down. She jerked up and down as she sobbed.

I caught a glimpse of Kelly sliding feet-first down a scrubby, eroded section of the hill. He was struggling to break his fall. He slid another thirty feet and disappeared in a thicket of bushes at the bottom.

A shotgun blast came from Dicey's side of the battlefield. The buckshot sliced through the trees on the hill behind us.

I wondered what Dicey was shooting at. Then I saw Jakes coming down a mostly bare, rocky area halfway up the hill, maybe fifty feet or so above Kelly. He lunged from one scraggly tree to another.

Dicey fired again. She's a lousy shot, I said to myself. Jakes was a big target, but she missed him.

The bushes where Kelly had vanished were moving. "I think Kelly's okay," I told Angela. "He might be caught in those bushes. I'm gonna try to get him out of there before Jakes finds him."

"I'm going with you," she said.

"Stay here." I stared into her eyes. "Promise me you'll stay here, or neither of us is going."

She didn't promise, but she said, "Be careful," which was almost as good.

I ran toward the moving bushes. Jakes was having trouble standing on the slippery slope. When he saw me, he planted one foot against the bottom of a scrawny tree and raised his gun. I dove into high weeds near the bushes.

Two shotgun blasts boomed not far away. The pellets whooshed over my head and hit Jakes. He fell and rolled down the hill until he crashed into a dead sycamore tree. I took back what I had thought about Dicey's marksmanship.

Cullman let out a fierce cry and ran toward the woods where Dicey the sniper was.

Angela screamed, "Dicey, look out!"

Kelly began cussing as he tried to pull the long, thorny stems off his clothes. His arms were covered with cuts and bruises.

"Kelly, are you all right?" I called. "Any bones broken?"

"Nah," he said. "I'm just banged up a little."

"Good. Stay down," I said. "There's still one of them left. He's after Dicey."

"I lost my gun on the way down," he said.

"Go help your mother. I'm going to see if your father's all right."

I crawled through the high weeds toward the airplane pit. Cullman fired a short burst, and Dicey responded with another blast. The weeds ended not far from the pit. I crawled between the piles of dirt, rolled onto my side into the pit, and came down on top of Trotter. He howled in agony and tried to raise a pistol. I planted my knee on his arm. Two rounds from his gun went into the dirt. He was weak. He could barely move. I pulled the gun out of his hand.

Dale was nowhere in sight.

"Dale, where are you?" I yelled.

"In here," came from the tunnel he had dug.

Cullman fired, and one of the good guys shot back.

I unclipped my walkie-talkie and pressed the send button. "Hey, Delmar, you and Trotter are the only ones left. Trotter needs a doctor. He's lost a lot of blood. It's time for the white flag."

Cullman didn't answer.

"Trotter," I said, "tell Delmar it's time to surrender. Then we can get you to a hospital."

Shaking, Trotter muttered, "Gimme the walkie-talkie."

I handed it to him.

With some effort he held the device up to his mouth and said, "Private Cullman, this is Lieutenant Trotter. Do not surrender. I repeat, do not sur—"

I yanked it out of his hand.

Cullman let out a rebel yell.

I got up on the wing and saw him charging toward me. I fired at him with what was now my AK-47, but I missed because I failed to hold the gun steady.

I saw Dicey. She was lying in the weeds not far from Cullman, maybe fifteen feet away. She took aim with her shotgun and fired both barrels. His head sailed through the air like a soccer ball trailing blood.

There were shots below me—a short burst from Trotter's rifle and a single shot that sounded like a firecracker.

Lieutenant Trotter's eyes were fixed on the sky. His lips were parted. Blood streamed out of his right eye.

Dale Marcott was sitting under the airplane wing with his old .22 in his hands and a grin on his face.

He was grinning, but he was as dead as the five men who had dipped him in the septic tank.

CHAPTER 41

THE GAME CHANGER

ANGELA squealed with joy when Kelly stood up and began trying to pick his way out of the thorn bushes at the bottom of the hill. She ran through the weeds and tried to help him peel away the long wands that clung to his clothing.

"Stop it, Mom," Kelly said. "I'll do it."

As soon as he freed himself from the brambles, Angela smothered him with kisses.

He didn't look good. Besides being bruised from his slide down the hill, his face had broken out in pimples and he had lost a lot of weight. His long hair had grown even longer and was now tied in a stringy ponytail.

Glorie was having trouble descending the steep hill, but when she saw that Kelly was okay, she screamed, "We won, we won!"

Kelly poked two thumbs in the air.

From the weeds behind me Dicey called out, "What about them in the hole with you—are any of 'em still alive?"

"I don't think so," I shouted back.

She slowly got to her feet. "Lordy Lordy, what a day," she said, wiping her brow. She propped her shotgun against her hip, then bent over and raised the bottom of her shirt to wipe her face.

Angela and Kelly emerged from the tangle of briars. Kelly's face, neck, and arms were covered with scratches and bug bites. He looked at me and said, "Where's my dad? Is he all right?"

I didn't want to be the one to tell him that his father was dead, but I was the only one who knew. "I'm sorry, Kelly," I said. "He didn't make it, but he finished off the top two bad guys."

Angela tried to put an arm around him, but he ran to the edge of the pit and looked down. He did a double take when he saw his father sitting there.

Glorie made it down the hill without falling and then ran to Kelly. She was wearing a Purdue University sweatshirt, which was much too big for her, and a ragged pair of jeans. They hugged and kissed. When she saw the bodies in the pit, she gasped and covered her mouth with both hands.

Kelly pointed and said, "That's my father. He's dead."

"Oh, Kelly, I'm so sorry," Glorie said. She put her arms around him. She seemed excited and exhausted at the same time.

I followed Angela and Dicey to the edge of the pit. We peered at the bodies. Flies buzzed around Dale Marcott, Bickerstaff, Trotter, and Smedley. Sitting with his back against the orange-gray wall, Dale's ever-present grin made him look like a late-night comedian who had just told a good joke.

Angela turned away.

Glorie began rubbing Kelly's back in a slow circle. They were only a few steps from Cullman. Flies and ants crawled on his face. Dicey stepped between Glorie and the corpse as if to shield her from the sight.

Gazing at his father, Kelly said, "He used to say life is shit. He got that right."

"No he didn't," Glorie said.

"It's nothin' but one piece of shit after another."

332   *John Pesta*

Glorie gave him another squeeze. "I love you," she said. "Your mom loves you."

Dicey said, "A day like this'll get anybody down, including me. I never shot nobody before. Today I shot—I'm not sure how many. At least two of 'em, maybe three. But in spite of all the bullets that were flyin', we're still alive. I'll take that any day instead of the alternative."

She looked fresher than any of us. Her flannel shirt was dirty and sweaty, but her face glowed with satisfaction. She could have been on her way up from the pond with Chester and a mess of bluegills.

"Let's go back to the house," Angela suggested. "This is a nightmare. All these bodies. One without a head."

"We need to call the police," I said. "I'm surprised they're not here already after all that shooting. You'd think somebody in the neighborhood would have called them."

Dicey said, "Not this neighborhood. Somebody's always shootin' out here."

"Not assault rifles," I said.

"That's what you think. They've got everything. One guy's got somethin' that sounds like a bomb."

It occurred to me that I had a story to write. Six men had died in a gunfight today. I wondered if that many people had ever been killed in a shootout in Meridian County. I'd have to find out.

Suddenly Kelly jumped into the pit. He pulled off his shirt and draped it over his father's head to keep the flies off. As he did this, he began to cry. Bare-chested, he looked seriously underweight. I left him grieving over Dale and rejoined Angela, Glorie, and Dicey.

When Kelly climbed out of the pit, we all plodded back toward the house. Glorie took Kelly's hand. It was a silent procession until I said, "It's a good thing the three of you showed up today. I hate to think what would have happened to us if you hadn't."

"We didn't save my father," Kelly said.

"You tried!" Glorie told him.

"Big deal."

"How'd you know we were in trouble?" I asked. "What made you come and save us?"

Kelly said, "Glorie and I need to talk to Mom about somethin'. It's bad."

Angela's face swung from Kelly's to Glorie's. "What happened, honey?"

"Her brother beat her up," Kelly said.

"Oh no. Are you all right, Glorie?"

"I told my mom I'm pregnant. She told my father, and then my stupid brother heard them talking about it. Dad got real mad, and when he went outside with Mom, Michael came to my room and started punching me in the belly." Tears streamed down her face as she said, "He punched me so hard I could hardly breathe. He did it again and again. He was trying to make me have a miscarriage."

Angela put her arms around Glorie. "You poor girl!" she said. "Are you all right? Do you need to see a doctor?" Angela's lips were tight and small.

Glorie sniffled and said, "I'm okay, I guess, but I don't know about the baby."

Angela stepped back a few inches and looked into Glorie's eyes. "How far along are you, Glorie?"

"Ten or eleven weeks, I think."

"It's probably all right," Angela said. "Your baby is still so small your brother probably didn't hurt it."

"How big is it?" Kelly asked.

"An inch or so long," Angela said.

"Is that all? Are you sure?"

"Yes. It's still very tiny."

"Damn it, if he killed or deformed our kid, I'll kill him."

"No, Kelly!" Glorie burst out. "They'll put you in prison. I need you to be with me."

"They'll put me in prison anyway, if they catch me." He turned to his mother and said, "I want Glorie to stay here with you before her stupid brother kills her and our kid."

"I can't stay here," Glorie said. "I'll get your mother in trouble. My dad'll say she helped me run away."

"You can't go home," Kelly said. "It's too dangerous."

Glorie began to cry. "I know. . . . I don't know what to do."

"I do!" Kelly said. "You're going to stay here."

With tears dripping off her face, she went to him, and they embraced again.

Angela began crying too. "Where did you two stay last night?" she asked.

"We camped out in the woods," Kelly said.

"In your treehouse?"

"No. Somewhere else. Then we hiked here at dawn."

"Oh, Glorie," Angela said, amazed. "How did you do that? Do you feel all right?"

"I'm okay," Glorie said. "I haven't had any morning sickness at all."

"That's good. You're lucky."

Kelly said, "We came down a trail near Dicey's house. We heard something goin' on over here. I heard somebody yelling and screaming. It sounded like Dad's voice, but I wasn't sure. I had to see what was happening, so we cut through the fields across from Dicey's. Then the yelling stopped. I made Glorie stay behind the stone wall. I crawled over it and snuck up close to the house. I crawled through the weeds so nobody would see me. I heard some guys laughing. Then I saw them hoist Dad up by his feet, and he started screaming again. At first I didn't know what they were doing, but then I caught a whiff of the septic tank—it stank like hell—and I realized what they were gonna do. I nearly puked just thinkin' about it."

Kelly snorted as if trying to blow the stench out of his nose, then said: "I was close enough to hear what they were saying. I saw you, Mom. You too, Phil. And I saw them lower Dad into the tank to make him talk. I didn't know what they were trying to get out of him. There was something about a buried airplane. I never heard Dad cry until they broke him and made him talk. When he led the gang and the two of you to find the plane, I went back to Glorie, and we went to Dicey's for help. Dicey wanted to call the police, but I didn't want her to. I was afraid the cops would show up with their sirens going and get my mom and dad killed, as well as Phil. And I didn't want the cops to catch me. Dicey had a couple of shotguns and some ammunition. I thought we had a better chance of saving you by ourselves."

"We whupped 'em," Dicey said. "There was five of 'um, and they had machine guns. All we had was a couple of shotguns."

Kelly said, "But we had the high ground. We had the advantage of shooting down at them. Most of them were trapped like rats in a hole." He turned to me and said, "What's the deal with the plane? What's that all about?"

I filled in the background, recapping what the colonel had said about the plane's mission and the gold they lost in 1989. Then I described how the militia found the gold in the house. "It was an accident," I said. "They started shooting like crazy in the living room, and the gold fell out of the ceiling. It rained down on us. So they found what they came for—the gold, or rather some of it, because, according to the colonel, it wasn't all there. I had a story in the *Gleaner*—an interview with Andreas Pluckett. His mother was the widow of Abner Richards. He was her first husband. Later she married a man named Pluckett. Her son told me Chester gave her several thousand dollars' worth of gold coins to help her keep from losing her home. The colonel had read that story, and he said it might explain why some of the gold was missing."

I was talking too fast. I caught my breath, then went on: "After the gold came out of the ceiling, they went up to Chester's bedroom and found more gold under the floor beneath the bed. The leader of the gang—they called him Colonel—said they found the original bags the gold was in. He took that as an indication that the plane hadn't been completely destroyed in a crash, and since the wreckage had never been found, he figured that someone must have taken the gold and got rid of the plane. The so-called colonel, whose name was Bickerstaff, said he thought there was a chance the pilot's body might still be in the plane. He said they had to find it and, if the pilot was still in it, they had to take his remains 'back home for a proper burial.' That's where they made their mistake. They'd probably still be alive if they had just taken the gold and gone home."

Dicey said, "You sound like you think it *was* their gold. How do you know they just didn't *say* it was theirs after it fell outta the ceiling? I say it belonged to Chester. It was in *his* house, up in *his* bedroom." She stopped but immediately had another thought: "And how do you know they weren't the ones that killed Chester? Maybe they read about them rumors that there was a fortune hidden in the house and they came after it a couple or three weeks ago, and that's when they killed him."

I took a deep breath and said, "Several things, Dicey. First, they said they were here to get their gold *before* they shot up the living room and it fell out of the ceiling. Second, they said it was the stories in the *Gleaner* that brought them here. Those stories didn't appear till *after* Chester's death. One of the stories mentioned the rumor of a hidden treasure in the house. If they suspected that their plane had crashed in this area, and if they learned of the treasure rumor *before* the story appeared in the *Gleaner,* they probably would have shown up long before now. Third, they said they had lost a plane and a pilot. They said the plane was carrying gold to buy weapons for their military operations. They thought Dale must have known where the plane was, and they dunked him in the septic tank to make him tell them where the plane's been buried since 1989."

Dicey nearly jumped down my throat: "Chester wouldn't've shot the pilot and stole the gold. He wasn't a murderer and a thief."

I felt tired, limp. "I didn't say he was," I replied. "Maybe Dale shot the pilot. I don't know."

"And Chester never said nothin' to me about findin' a plane with bags of gold in it. He would've told me if he had."

"I hope you're right," I said. "I hope the gold did belong to Chester all along. But that's for the police to decide. Speaking of which, we have to call the sheriff."

Kelly said, "If you do, I'm outta here."

"I think you and your mom should tell the police what happened today," I said. "Dicey and I will have to make statements too, but I think it would do you a lot of good if you talked to the police first."

"Leave me out of it," Kelly said. "Listen, you don't have to call them right away, do you? I want to see where that gold was stashed. Maybe that's where Grampaw hid the photos of the Klan after he snatched them out of my room."

I said, "You really should turn yourself in, Kelly."

He forced a laugh. "Forget it."

"Look at it this way," I said. "You're not the only suspect in Chester's murder anymore. Maybe Dicey's right—maybe the five-man militia unit did come here a few weeks ago. The sheriff has to consider the possibility that they killed Chester. This is a game changer for you."

"I can't turn myself in," he said. "It's too big a risk. The cops don't believe anything I wrote about the Klan, so why should they believe a 'militia' killed Grampaw?"

I said, "There's more room than ever for a jury to have a reasonable doubt that you killed your grandfather."

Wearily Angela said, "Let's go back to the house. I'm thirsty and hot. I think I'll ask Mary Lou Dunn what we should do about the gold."

"Don't bother," Kelly shot back. "I know what she'll say."

Angela said, "Phil, don't you think there's a chance it was these guys that killed Chester?"

"I could be wrong, but, no, I don't think they did it. I think it was Chester's murder that *brought* them here. The colonel—their leader—said that after the plane disappeared, they subscribed to a clip service that was supposed to send them any news articles about a plane that crashed on the day it took off. Then years later they signed up to get Google alerts, and that's how they learned about my stories in the *Gleaner*—the ones I wrote after Chester was murdered. The first story mentioned the rumor that there was a treasure hidden in his house, and it raised the possibility that he was killed by someone who was trying to find that treasure. Then last week we ran a story that said Chester gave a woman named Lila Pluckett $5,000 worth of gold coins. That was the value of the gold he gave her back in 1990, the year after the plane crashed. The colonel put two and two together and concluded that the plane came down here and that Chester found the gold in the wreckage. That's why they showed up last night—to get back what was left of their gold."

"Who's Lila Pluckett?" Glorie asked.

"Her maiden name was Lila Johnson. She was the widow of Abner Richards. Lila and her second husband, William Pluckett, were the parents of Andreas Pluckett, the man who donated $500 to Kelly's lawyer to defend him against the charge that he murdered Chester."

"Why did he do that?" Dicey asked.

"Because he admires what Kelly is doing—telling the world who lynched Abner Richards and—"

Kelly interrupted me to say, "And I'm not done yet. I want the lynchers who are still alive to go to prison. I want the truth to come out. They've gotten away with it too long."

Proudly Glorie said, "And if it wasn't for Kelly and what he wrote in the *Mothermucker,* they would have got away with it forever."

CHAPTER 42

CRAZY KIDS

A DAZZLING silver-white sun gleamed high in the sky.
I thought about whether to tell Angela, Kelly, Glorie, and
Dicey what the colonel said he discovered in the plane: the .22
rifle with Dale's name on it and the bullet holes in the pilot's
skull. I could also tell them what Dale said when we were digging down to the plane—that he knew there was a rifle in it.
These facts suggested that Dale may have killed the pilot, but
he told the colonel that Chester had done it.

I'd write it all up for the *Gleaner,* but for now I thought it
would be better to keep my thoughts to myself. Why? Because
I didn't want to upset Kelly by suggesting that his father had
murdered the pilot and tried to save his own skin by telling
Bickerstaff and his men that Chester had done it.

Other possibilities popped into my head. Suppose the plane
was struck by lightning and its radio was knocked out, making
it impossible for the pilot to report his position, and then the
plane came down on Chester's farm. Suppose Dale, who would
have been only twelve or thirteen at the time, heard the plane
crash land and found the pilot unconscious in the wreckage,
with bags of gold in the cockpit. Thinking the pilot was dead,
Dale may have taken the gold home, but then the pilot came

to and discovered it was missing. He may have made his way to Chester's house and accused him of stealing the gold. Perhaps the pilot pulled a gun on Chester and threatened to kill him if he didn't return the coins. Dale may have heard the threat, grabbed his .22, and shot the pilot to keep him from shooting Chester. Then Chester and Dale may have put the pilot's body back in the plane and buried it, hoping it would never be found.

No, Larrison. No way. For Chester to have done that, he would have had to be a fool. The plane had recently crashed. Chester wouldn't have known that its radio had been knocked out. And the plane may have been tracked by radar. The Federal Aviation Administration may already have known approximately where it went down. It wouldn't take long to find it. Then they'd find the bullet holes in the pilot's head. By trying to hide the pilot's body and the plane, Chester had changed an accident investigation into a criminal one.

On the other hand, the fact is the plane had been missing since 1989. It could have gone down in the Hoosier National Forest or the Charles C. Deam Wilderness Area, a massive number of acres. Neither the FAA nor anyone else had found the plane until Bickerstaff and his men made Dale show them where he and Chester had buried it.

Would Chester really have buried the plane and its pilot? I didn't know him well enough to say what he would or would not do. I didn't know what the truth was, and now that both Chester and Dale were dead, I doubted that anyone would ever find out if Chester had committed a serious crime.

I wanted to believe that he was innocent. I found it easier to believe that Dale was solely responsible for the pilot's death and for taking the gold. But could Dale, who would have been only twelve or thirteen years old at the time, have managed to bury the plane by himself, without his father's knowledge? Perhaps he could, but could he also have hidden the gold under the floor in Chester's bedroom without his father's discovering it? No, there was absolutely no way he could have accomplished that, unless. . . .

Maybe Dale found the gold in the plane and did not immediately tell Chester about it. Perhaps the pilot was injured in the crash, and Dale buried the plane by himself and kept the gold. Sometime later Chester or his wife may have found the "treasure" in Dale's room or another hiding place, such as the barn. Maybe then Dale admitted to Chester that he had killed the pilot, and maybe Chester sought to protect him by not revealing the murder and the bags of gold coins. Was this the beginning of Chester's disappointment with Dale, and did it ultimately lead to his decision to leave Dale out of his will?

• • •

IT felt odd to see the screen door lying on the front lawn. I hadn't noticed it when we were marched out early that morning. The doorway was now wide open.

Dicey said, "I hope no critters got in the house."

"Like what? Angela said.

"Raccoons. Coyotes. Snakes."

"Oh God," Angela said. "Don't even think it."

Dicey said, "Now that it's over, I feel like I just woke up from a bad dream."

"It wasn't a dream," Angela said. "It was a nightmare."

"So it was," Dicey agreed, adding, "Do you mind if I use the bathroom before I have an accident? I told Chester he should've kept the old privy, but he didn't want to. He said it was full of termites, so he burned it down."

"I'm glad he did," said Angela.

Dicey stepped over the quilt and hurried upstairs as fast as she could.

Angela stared at the living room. "God, just look at this place. I no sooner get it fixed up than five nitwits with machine guns shoot it all to pieces again."

Kelly said, "They weren't machine guns, Mom. They were assault rifles, submachine guns." He squeezed past her and whistled. "Holy crap, it's another war zone."

Glorie peered inside, and Angela moved out of her way.

I followed Glorie into the living room, where Kelly stood staring at the ceiling. Shattered plaster, chunks of wood, and pieces of wallpaper dangled from the ceiling. White dust covered much of the room.

Kelly pointed at the largest hole and said, "I guess that's where the gold came from, huh?"

"Yes," Angela said. "It came pouring down, but not all of it. The men went upstairs and found more gold hidden under the floor."

"I'm gonna see if there's anything else in there," Kelly said. He started upstairs, and Glorie and I followed him. Dicey was in the bathroom, humming a song.

There were no bullet holes in Chester's bedroom, but his heavy walnut bed had been pushed up against the front windows. An old rug was rolled up beside it, revealing a rectangular hole between two floor joists. A wooden lid that matched the hardwood floor lay next to the hole. Despite the shooting spree, the lid was still in one piece.

"Hi, Mom," Kelly said, looking down through the hole.

Angela said, "Be careful you don't fall. The floor might be weak."

"It's good and solid," Kelly said. He dropped to his knees and felt around under the floor. His scruffy ponytail lay draped on his back. Then he stretched out on the floor and stuck his head into the space between the bedroom floor and the living-room ceiling. "It's too dark," he said. "I can't see anything."

He got up off the floor and unplugged a reading lamp that stood on a night table. He yanked off the shade and replugged the lamp into a socket that was closer to the hole in the floor. Holding the lamp like a flashlight, he switched it on, lay down on his chest again, and shined it between the joists in both directions.

"Bingo!" he said.

From down below, Angela said, "What do you see?"

"A box."

He squirmed to one side and reached as far as he could under the floor. "Shoot!" he said, "I can't reach it. Grampaw didn't want this to be found."

"We can always knock another hole in the ceiling if we have to," Angela said. "What difference does one more hole make?"

Kelly said, "I might be able to get it. Glorie, get me a clothes hanger—a wire one, if you can find one."

Glorie ran to the closet and pushed clothing aside until she found an empty wire hanger. She brought it to Kelly, and he untwisted the wound-up hook and straightened the rest of the hanger. Then he lay on the floor again and used the hook to pull the box toward him.

Down below, Angela hollered, "Where's the gold? It's gone!"

I leaned over Kelly and called down, "I heard the colonel tell one of his men to put it in the Hummer."

Kelly dragged the box until it reached the edge of the hole in the ceiling. Then he let the wire hook fall into the living room, and he lifted the box out. It was an old cigar box. He set it on the bed and flipped the lid back. Several old photographs lay inside. He began placing them on the bed, and as he uncovered the fourth one, he muttered, "Oh shit, look at this!"

The photo showed six members of the Klan in their robes and pointed hoods standing around their victim. Under his hanging body were the words, "Abner Richards, Raper of White Woman, Gets What He Deserves!!!" The night scene was illuminated by a burning cross on the left and car head-lights in the background.

Kelly said, "This photo looks like one of those I found in the attic, but there weren't any words on the front of that one." He turned the photo over and showed me the Klansmen's names, which were written in skinny, leftward-leaning letters. "It's the same handwriting that was on the back of the other ones," he said.

"Who are they?" I asked.

He read five names out loud: "J. D. Nonnemaker, Kelvin Kantner, Ray Hartsel, Tony Smith, John Worman." I had never heard of any of them. Kelly looked at me and said, "There's one more. Are you ready for this? It says, James T. Wylie, owner and editor, Campbellsville Gleaner newspaper."

"You're joking," I said.

Kelly held up the photo to show the names on the back.

"Wow," I said, "I wonder if my boss knows his father was in the Klan."

The next photo was vertical instead of horizontal, and it was the only one with deckle edges. It showed a little boy in a miniature glory suit. He was standing in front of an adult dressed in full Klan regalia. The bottom of the boy's hood was folded up at his eyebrows, making it look a bit like a sailboat and showing his face from the eyes down.

Angela entered the room as Kelly was staring at the photo. She looked over his shoulder and said, "That looks like the little Klan costume I found in the closet."

Kelly turned over the photo and read the words on the back: "Chester Marcott Sr. with little klucker, Chester Jr., four years old."

"Oh hell," Angela said in a breathy whisper.

There were nine photos in all, and in every one of them the Klansmen were wearing robes and hoods. The only exposed face was little Chester's.

Kelly said, "We've got to publish these, Glorie. We have to get another *Mothermucker* out."

Glorie said, "You're not going to publish the one with the little boy in it, are you? Isn't that your grandfather?"

"If we publish some of them, we have to publish them all. It wouldn't be fair otherwise."

"Then maybe we shouldn't publish any of them," Glorie said.

"We've got to. We have to show who was in the Klan. We can't exclude anyone just because of who he is. We know the Klan lynched Abner Richards. The photos prove it, but the Klan's gotten away with murder since 1936. And besides, Grampaw told me he didn't join the Klan when he grew up. I'll make it clear in my story that he never joined."

Angela said, "But Chester Sr. is in the photo too. That must be your great-grandfather."

"I realize that, but I can't cover it up."

Glorie said, "It might not be safe, Kelly."

"Life isn't safe."

"We're going to have a baby. I don't want anything to happen to you. I want you to be there for our baby."

"I do too," Kelly said. "But if *we* don't show what the Klan did, who will?" He looked at me.

I knew what he was thinking: *The Gleaner sure as hell won't.*

I said, "The *Gleaner* will publish the photos and the names right after *Mothermucker* does."

"Will it publish the one of James E. Wylie?"

"If I have anything to say about it, yes, we'll publish it."

"I'll hold you to that," Kelly said. He put the photos back in the box. "Let's go, Glorie."

"Where?"

"To get another *Mothermucker* out, like I said."

Glorie said, "I really don't think you should publish those pictures, Kelly. It's too dangerous. It'll make some people real mad."

Kelly said, "We have to expose them. I want people to see them in their clown suits—spelled K-L-O-W-N. We'll show the names on the back of each photo too."

"It's too *dangerous,* and besides, how are we going to publish another *Mothermucker?* We can't do it at school, and you don't have a computer anymore—it got smashed. And we don't have the money to pay Staples to do it."

Kelly flashed the grin he had inherited from his father. "I know where we can get all the money we need," he said. "Phil said the gold coins are in the Hummer. I think we deserve at least one of them for what we did today."

Angela said, "You mustn't take that gold, Kelly. I want you to turn yourself in to the police. I'll call Mary Lou Dunn and ask her to come out here. Then we'll go to the police together."

"Bye, Ma," Kelly said. "Come on, Glorie." He bolted out of the room with the box of photos in his hand.

Glorie yelled, "Kelly, wait for me!" and ran after him.

Angela and I followed her into the hall.

Dicey came out of the bathroom looking fresh and clean. "My word," she said. "What's all the racket about? What's goin' on out here?"

Glorie ran down the steps. Angela, Dicey, and I went after her.

Out front Kelly was dashing around the Hummer, trying to find an unlocked door. When he saw us on the porch, he stopped running and said, "I have to break a window." He looked around for a rock or something.

"No!" Angela screamed. "That gold doesn't belong to you. I'll give you some money." She ran back into the house.

Glorie put an arm around Kelly's waist and rested her head on his shoulder.

Angela returned with two twenty-dollar bills. "Here, Kelly, take this," she said.

Kelly took the money and said, "Thanks, Ma. Is it all right if I borrow the truck?"

"The keys are in it," Angela said. "Just be careful."

Glorie said, "Give your mom a kiss, Kelly."

Kelly gave Angela a peck on the cheek and ran toward the green pickup. Glorie ran after him.

We watched them drive out the lane between the long rows of pear trees.

"Crazy kids," Dicey said.

CHAPTER 43

17.4 Pounds of Gold

Sheriff Eggemann had the fed-up look of a man who had seen and heard much more than he wanted to in one day. He had crawled through the small tunnel under the wing of the Cessna to see the remains of the pilot, and now his uniform was smeared with dirt. A drop of sweat trickled down the high slope of his forehead, and in the dazzling sunlight the stripe of sweat gleamed like the silvery trail of a snail.

We stood at the edge of the hole and watched Deputy Bruce Chastain snap photos. I had already grabbed some of my own before the sheriff and his men arrived. I had a grisly shot of the pilot, a brown mummy in a blue flannel shirt. He was sitting upright at the controls, and I could make out the two small bullet holes in his forehead. If we ran the picture in the paper, we'd get some angry calls and cancelled subscriptions. Ed wouldn't want to run it.

Hearses from three funeral homes were standing by to carry seven bodies to the hospital for autopsies. The deceased included Dale Marcott and the five militiamen who died today, as well as the mummified remains of the pilot who died twenty-three years ago. Coroner Travis Baker had arranged with two pathologists to perform autopsies.

"Don't let anyone touch the bodies till the coroner and Jim Simpson sign off on them," the sheriff told Deputy Chastain.

Flies buzzed over the corpses, which were covered with sheets of black plastic. Some of the flies were more than an inch long.

We walked back toward the house. I smelled of sweat.

Carl said, "I wish you hadn't let the Marcott boy leave."

"What was I supposed to do, Sheriff, shoot him?"

"You shouldn't have let him run off again."

"I didn't 'let' him. He just went." I didn't mention that Angela had let him take her truck.

"I'm not sure we're on the same side, Phil," Carl said.

Earlier I had told him about everything that happened since last night, including the fact that Kelly found more photos of the Klan under the floor in Chester's bedroom. Now I said, "Kelly ran off to publish the new batch of photos in the *Mothermucker*. By the way, the original photos that Kelly found were not with these. So maybe whoever killed Chester found those somewhere else in the house the day Chester was killed. Kelly thinks it was the Klan who killed Chester to keep the photos from being published. He thinks they may have stolen the ones he wrote about in the first place, and now they might come after the ones he found today."

"And then what?" Carl asked.

"He's hoping they'll get caught in the act. Maybe he'll try to record it, I don't know. He's trying to clear himself."

"Where's the gold that fell out of the ceiling?" Carl asked.

"In the Hummer, right over there."

"How much gold are we talking about?"

I said, "According to the so-called colonel, Bickerstaff, the guy who ran the operation, the coins that fell out of the ceiling are worth around $500,000. Bickerstaff said that's just the value of the gold itself. The coins would be worth even more to collectors."

"So Eli was right," Carl said. "There was a treasure hidden in the house."

"Yep. I saw it rain down out of the ceiling."

"I'd like you to put all this in a written statement."

"Sure," I said. "I'll do it back at the office. It'll be easier to write it up on the computer."

"No. You might get yourself killed on the way to town. Do it for me now."

"I need to write my story first, Carl. I don't want to get beat on a story I was right in the middle of."

"What's the rush? Tomorrow's Sunday. There's no paper on Sunday."

"I want to put something on our website."

"I see. Well, first write a statement for me. Then you can go to the paper and write your story."

"I'll do it as soon as I get something online. I have to get a story out before the radio stations get wind of it."

His eyebrows rose as he said, "How about this? You sit down like a good, cooperative citizen who wants to help the police, and I won't release the news to my friends at the radio stations until your story's online. On the other hand, if you prefer not to cooperate with your county police force, then I'll have to call my good friends at the radio stations and—"

"It's a deal, Carl."

"Thank you, Phil."

Deputy Jesse Holsapple was standing on the porch with a white plastic toothpick poking out of his mouth. I figured he was listening to whatever Angela and Dicey were talking about inside.

The quilt was hanging over the doorway again. Holsapple led the way through. He held the quilt for the sheriff and continued holding it—with a smug grin—for me.

The sheriff looked at the hole in the ceiling. Then he went to the bedroom for a look from above. Instead of tagging along, I went to the kitchen.

Angela and Dicey were eating cheese and crackers. For some reason I didn't feel hungry, but I poured myself a cup of coffee and joined them at the table. While I was having my caffeine fix, there was a crunch of gravel as a car pulled up out front.

"That'll be Mary Lou," Angela said, getting up. Dicey and I followed her to the living room.

M. L. Dunn II rapped on the door frame and used the back of her arm to push the quilt to one side. She looked even shorter than I remembered. I glanced at her feet and saw they were in running shoes. The only other time I had ever talked to her they were in stiletto heels. Carl came downstairs as she stepped inside.

"Good morning, Sheriff," she said in a strong, confident voice. "How are you today?"

"Could be better, Counselor," he said.

Carl was a successful politician who was on a first-name basis with everyone he knew. The fact that he didn't address Mary Lou by name meant he really didn't like her. They were both Democrats, but Carl was an old-fashioned Roosevelt Democrat while, in his eyes, Mary Lou was a wild-eyed leftwing radical.

Mary Lou said, "I understand there was a big shootout here today and several men were killed. Can you tell me how many died, Sheriff?"

"Ma'am, I just got here," he said. "Anything I tell you would be hearsay. Ask the people in the room. They were *in* the shootout."

"Thank you, Sheriff." She wasn't the least bit flustered; however, the tone of her voice indicated she knew where she stood with him.

Carl started to go outside, but Dicey spoke up: "Phil said I need to give you a statement, Sheriff. Can I do it now, or do you want to come an' see me later? I'd like to go home an' get some o' my reg'lar chores done. You know where I live. That's where I'll be. I'll not be goin' anywhere."

"I didn't see your truck outside, Dicey," Carl said. "Do you need a ride home. I'll have one of my men take you. Then I'll drop by later and get your statement."

"That'll be fine and dandy," Dicey said.

She followed Carl outside, and through the front windows I saw him talking to Holsapple, who led Dicey to one of the cruisers and drove away. Meanwhile, Carl tried the doors of the Hummer. All of them were locked. He went to his cruiser and came back with a long thin tool, which he used to unlock the passenger-side door.

I sat on the porch and began scribbling my statement. I heard Angela telling Mary Lou about the events of the past nineteen hours.

I went inside and reported what the sheriff was doing. "Is he allowed to confiscate the gold?" I asked Mary Lou.

"If the gold belonged to Chester, it belongs to Angela now," she said. "If it was in the Hummer, it was put there illegally. We'll tell the sheriff you want it back."

I said, "The militia claimed it belonged to them."

"Oh really? Then let them prove it."

"They're all dead—the ones who came here, I mean—but there may be more of them wherever this gang came from."

"They can come forward if they want to file a claim."

Angela asked, "What if the sheriff insists on taking the gold?"

"We'll demand an itemized inventory," Mary Lou replied. "We'll tell him we want a list of every coin."

"Good luck with that," I said.

I went back outside and resumed scribbling.

The sheriff had no trouble finding the gold in the Hummer. Angela told him that the colonel had claimed the gold belonged to him and his men, but Carl said he had to consider the possibility that they had stolen it. "I'll have to hang onto it until we do an investigation and determine who it belongs to," he said.

He agreed with Mary Lou that the gold should be inventoried before it leaves the house, so he dumped the coins on the dining-room table and photographed them with his smartphone. Then he put all the gold in an evidence bag and weighed it on a digital scale that Angela brought down from the bathroom. He photographed the bag on the scale, which showed the weight as 17.4 pounds, and he promised to give her copies of the photos as soon as possible.

Mary Lou wasn't satisfied with this arrangement. She said, "If you need the gold for evidence, then give Angela a list of each and every coin, including its date, mintmark if any, and condition. If you're unwilling to do that, then leave the coins here with Angela. Until a judge rules that they are not legally hers, they ought to stay with her."

"I don't have time for that, but I'll give you a receipt." Carl said. "I assure you that nothing will happen to the gold while it's in my hands."

"That's not good enough, Sheriff," Mary Lou said. "Some of the coins might just happen to disappear. I'm not saying I think *you* would take them, but someone else might."

"I'm sorry, ma'am," Carl said. "You'll just have to trust me. The coins are going with me." He was losing his cool.

Mary Lou raised her voice: "It's not a matter of trust, Sheriff. It's a matter of proper procedure."

Angela waved a hand and said, "Oh, let him take it. I don't care. It's caused nothing but trouble. Chester was probably killed because of it." She turned to Carl and said, "My son certainly didn't kill him, whether you believe it or not."

"It doesn't matter what I believe, ma'am," Carl said. "I've just got to do my job and go where the evidence takes me."

Mary Lou shook her head and said, "Evidence isn't a road map. It can take you in the wrong direction." She looked up at him with a stony expression on her face. Then she said goodbye to Angela and went to her car.

It was late afternoon. I went back to writing my statement, and when it was finished, I went looking for Carl. I found him talking to a state trooper who had just arrived. I handed him my three scribbled pages.

Carl looked at it and griped, "You ever learn penmanship, Phil?"

I said, "The story in the *Gleaner* will be easier for you to read—if I ever get to write it."

I saw Angela in the backyard, out beyond the dog pen. She had a long shovel and was struggling to dig a grave for the dog and the cat. I went to help her.

She stopped digging as I approached. She looked miserable. Her shirt was wet with sweat.

"Let me do that," I said. "After this morning, I'm an expert digger."

"Thanks," she said as I took the shovel.

My arms felt stiff, but I figured they'd limber up soon enough. I plunged the shovel into the hole she had started.

Angela stared at Puddybaby. The cat lay in the grass with its mouth open. Flies crawled on its face.

"Why don't you go back to the house," I told her. "I can handle this."

She raised her head and said, "Is it okay if I stay at your place tonight? I'm afraid to stay here. I don't want to spend another night in this house. There must be a curse on it. I feel like burning it down."

"Carl will want a statement from you," I said. "I'll take care of Sadie and Puddybaby. Then we'll get out of here."

"Wonderful," Angela said.

CHAPTER 44

A GORGEOUS EVENING

"WHERE are *you* going?" Carl asked when he saw me carrying a small suitcase out to my car.

"This is Angela's," I said. "She's afraid to stay here, so I'm taking her to my place." I wondered what he'd think of that.

Angela came out of the house with a bag of groceries and a small travel bag.

Carl said, "Phil tells me you'll be staying at his place, Ms. Marcott."

"Do you mind?" she replied.

"No, ma'am. Here's your receipt." He handed Angela a note about the gold he had confiscated. "If you decide to leave the county, I'd appreciate it if you'd let me know where I can reach you."

"I won't be leaving till Kelly can go with me," she said.

I didn't like the sound of that. I didn't want her to leave, period.

Carl said, "If you won't be here, ma'am, I reckon we ought to board up the doorways when we're through today."

"I'd appreciate that," she said. "Send me a bill."

"We'll see what it takes," Carl said.

I put Angela's suitcase in my car and went back to the house to collect my stuff. Some of my clothes were in the hamper. Angela put them in a plastic bag for me.

When we came back outside, Carl was talking to a couple of deputies about sealing the house.

"I'll check with you later, Carl," I said.

"What for?" he demanded.

"Any new developments."

"Don't call me. I'll call you."

I opened the car door for Angela, and she slid inside. One of the deputies said something, and the other one laughed. I wished I had heard what was said. I glanced at them as if I had.

As we drove out the lane, Angela put her head back and said, "I am so glad to get out of that house. I never want to see it again."

I held her hand on her lap.

We drove in silence until we were through Zumma and starting up the steep hill. Then Angela said, "I feel like I'm in a dream. Did all that shooting and killing really happen today?"

"I'm afraid so."

"I can't believe Dale's dead."

I said, "He looked as if he died happy. He got his revenge on the colonel and the lieutenant for what they did to him."

Staring straight ahead, she said, "I guess it's up to me to bury him. As far as I know, he doesn't have anyone else, except Kelly."

When we got to my place, the two sisters who lived across the street were sitting on their porch. The only parking space on the street was in front of their house, and as we got out of the car, one of them said, "Hello, Phil. Nice day, isn't it?"

"Yes it is, Reva. How are you today?"

"Oh, I'm in pretty good shape for the shape I'm in," she said.

As I lifted Angela's suitcase out of the trunk, Phoebe said, "Looks like you have a visitor, Phil."

Angela turned to them and said, "Yes, he does. I'm Angela, Phil's friend."

Soon the whole town would know we were sleeping together.

"Come see us sometime," Phoebe said. "Both of you."

I said, "Thank you," which didn't commit us to anything.

Inside my apartment, Angela said, "So this is your man cave."

I didn't like the term, but all I said was, "If I'd known you were coming, I would've left the vacuum cleaner in the middle of the floor so you'd think I was getting ready to clean."

"Hah! Your place looks a lot better than mine."

She plopped on the sofa and crossed her legs. Her swinging ankle turned me on—it didn't take much. I felt like feeling her up, but I told myself to act like a gentleman. I turned myself off and said, "I'd better go to work. I've got a story to write."

"Can't you do it tomorrow?"

"I want to get it online today."

"Oh, okay."

"Will you be all right here by yourself?" I asked.

She nodded. "I'm going to take a nice long bath."

"Uh-oh, the tub might be . . . kind of contaminated."

"I'll uncontaminate it. Do you have any cleanser?"

"In the kitchen, under the sink. But *you* don't have to clean it. I'm the one who grimed it up."

"No. I have to earn my keep. You go to work." She was in a better mood. Her eyes were soft.

Here's what you do, Larrison. Tonight, after you take a shower, you ask her to marry you.

I can't. I don't have a ring.

You don't need a ring. You can get one later.

People will think I'm after her money.

Since when do you care what people think?

She doesn't need me. She could have any man in the galaxy. It's only a matter of time before she finds someone else.

You're a coward, Larrison.

"What's the matter?" Angela asked.

"Nothing," I said. "Just stressing over my story. I'll feel better when I get it done."

"Then go do it."

On my way to work, I felt tension building. I really didn't feel like writing a story after all I had been through. I told myself it's no big deal. Just bat it out. How many people will read it anyway? The online *Gleaner* had fewer than 700 subscribers, and how many of them would be on their computers on a Saturday afternoon? Approximately one maybe. Why even bother posting it? I had all day tomorrow to write it. That was stressing me out too. I wasn't sure how I should do it. Should I make it a straight news story so it would read as if someone else had written it, or should I write it in the first person, since I had been directly involved in everything? I didn't like to write about myself. I was supposed to be the medium, not the message. Maybe I should do two articles—an objective news story and a subjective sidebar. I could leave my byline off the news article. But that would violate *Gleaner* style.

When I got to the office, I was happy to see I had the place to myself. I got a cup of coffee, thought for a minute, and began hacking away: "Six men died in a gun battle this morning on a farm in Salt Lick Township in northwestern Meridian County. . . ."

• • •

WHEN I finished the article two hours later, my neck was stiff, my eyes were sore, and my back was killing me. I had set out to write a bare-bones piece, like the statement I had given the sheriff, but this story demanded more details, both past and present, if I wanted my readers to understand it. What made it even harder to write was that I was in too much of a hurry. As a result, many sentences were too long, and some parts were too sketchy. It was good enough for our website, but I'd have to rework it for Monday's paper.

I almost forgot something. I inserted a paragraph saying Sheriff Eggemann took possession of the gold coins until their legal owner could be determined. I didn't want any potential burglars to get the idea that the gold was in Angela's house and tear the whole place apart again.

I tapped a few keys, and just like that the article was available to our online subscribers. No papers to print. No bundled copies for paperboys and route men to deliver. No wonder newspapers were in trouble.

I got up to go home but immediately thought of something else. I wrote myself a note to replace phrases such as *last night* and *this morning* with days and dates. Ideally I would do this at midnight tonight, after everything else I had to do.

Then it occurred to me that I should have mentioned that Kelly was still wanted by the police for Chester's murder. I wondered if I had subconsciously omitted that fact. I sat down to stick it in the story somewhere, but the voice in my head screamed at me: Larrison! Get out of here! Go home! Any people in Meridian County who don't know that Kelly is wanted for his grandfather's murder must be brain dead. You don't have to worry about them.

I shut down my computer, turned off the lights, and left the building.

It was a gorgeous evening. It felt good to be going home knowing Angela was there . . . if she still was.

CHAPTER 45

LIKE FATHER, LIKE SON

WHEN I got back to the apartment, Angela was watching TV. She zapped it with the remote and said, "Guess who I talked to today."

"Who?"

"Glorie's mom. I called her up to talk about Glorie and Kelly."

"Did you tell her about the gunfight?"

"No. I told her that Glorie brought Kelly to see me, and I told her Glorie said her brother punched her in the belly to make her miscarry. She started crying—just like that. She fell to pieces. I think she had been drinking."

"I've talked to her on the phone," I said. "She was very nice, but then her husband made her hang up. I think she's under his thumb."

"I know what that's like." Angela hesitated, then said, "Phil, I want to go and see her."

"Now?"

"Yes. May I borrow your car?"

"How about if I go with you?"

"I wish you would."

"Is it okay if I wash up first?"

"Certainly. Go ahead."

I took a quick shower. Then I put on my best pair of pants, meaning the only pair that wasn't wrinkled, and a red polo shirt because my mother said I looked good in red.

Angela said, "Do you think I ought to call Mrs. Kovacs again and let her know we're coming?"

"No. She might tell you not to come."

As we walked out to my car, I felt as if everyone on the block was watching us. It was like a flashback to grade school when I was super-self-conscious, always thinking people were watching me. No one's watching you, Larrison—except maybe the two old biddies across the street.

Shale Creek Golf Course could have been a gated community. If so, it would have been the only one in Meridian County. As we wound between the fairways and mansions, I caught up with a bright-red BMW roadster whose license plate was BMWMD. I hated vanity plates, especially this one.

Dropping back, I said, "That's my ex-wife in front of us. She's married to a doctor now."

Angela's ears perked up. We stared at Vickie's short hairdo blowing in the wind. Her hair used to be brunette, but now it was strawberry blonde. We were divorced so many years now—more than a sixth of my life—that our marriage hardly seemed real anymore. Even so, I didn't like thinking about it. Seeing her was a bad omen. I was glad when she turned in at the next driveway. She was probably going to a Tri-Kappa meeting or something. Or maybe she was cheating on her husband. I hoped she was.

Angela said, "Why'd you get divorced, Phil, if you don't mind my asking?"

"We're looking for 24 Persimmon Trace," I said. "Who dreams up these names?"

She tapped herself on both cheeks and said, "I'm sorry. I shouldn't have asked that question."

I exhaled slowly and said, "That's okay." Then I told her about Vickie: "We lasted a couple of years, but she finally figured out I wasn't going to be a millionaire, so she dumped me for a doctor—an anesthesiologist with a beard. Why do you need a medical degree to put people to sleep?"

"Maybe so they wake up."

"Whose side are you on?" I was straining my eyes to read the low wooden street signs. "This is it, Persimmon Trace. What kind of street is a trace?"

It was the kind that winds between huge homes on huge lots with a few fortunate trees that had been spared when the forest was bulldozed into submission.

"Wow," Angela said as if exhaling the word. "Look at this place."

The Kovacs house was a two-story colonial mansion made of used bricks and lined with rose bushes. The high roof was studded with dormer windows. A concrete driveway curved past the front of the house and back to the trace. There was a two-car garage attached to the near end of the house, but another garage with five doors stood beyond it in the backyard. I parked in front of the front door.

I pressed the doorbell, which set off a chime inside. Someone must have seen us coming, because the door opened the instant the chime sounded.

Michael Kovacs, wary and furious, glared at me. "Whada *you* want?" he demanded. He had recently had a haircut, and now his head seemed too small for his body. Too small a brain, I decided.

I stared into his hard little eyes and said, "Hello. We'd like to talk to your mother."

He looked at Angela as if asking her name.

"Hi," she said.

He must have seen the resemblance to Kelly, because he said, "Is your name Marcott?"

"Yes. I'm Kelly's mom."

His father's voice, loud and fierce, came down a curved stairway: "Who's there, Michael?"

Smirking, the boy said, "It's Kelly Marcott's mother and a guy from the *Gleaner.*" His eyes and mine locked in a staring contest.

His father stomped down to the foyer. T. Preston Kovacs had a handsome, sharp-boned face that looked as angry as his son's. He was about five years older than I was and about the same height, but he had a better tan, better fingernails, and a better haircut. The only thing worse about him was that his hair was prematurely gray. His wife stopped on the bottom step right behind him.

Mae Kovacs was quite attractive, and she had an athletic aura. My guess was she jogged around the golf course every morning. Her hair looked like cinnamon, and her eyes were slightly red, which made me wonder if she had been crying and had splashed some water on her face before coming downstairs. She stood next to her husband in the wide doorway.

T. Preston looked down his nose at us. "Yes?" he asked coldly.

Angela stepped forward and said, "Hello, Mr. Kovacs, Mrs. Kovacs. I'm Angela Marcott, Kelly's mother. I think it's time we met. Glorie came to see me today."

He nearly jumped down Angela's throat: "Where's Glorie now?"

"I don't know," Angela said. "She went somewhere with Kelly."

T. Preston's head seemed ready to explode. "Let me tell you something, Mrs. Marcott, if I ever get my hands on that kid of yours, I'll—."

"Ted," Mae said, "calm down."

He shot back, "Don't tell me to calm down."

"Did we catch you at a bad time, Ted?" I asked as disingenuously as I could. "You seem a bit upset about something."

If eyes could kill. . . . "I'll tell you what I'm 'upset about,' Larrison—yes, I know who you are." He jutted his chin at Angela and said, "Your son got my daughter pregnant. Now she's running around with him."

Angela said, "Who can blame her, after what your son did to her?"

"What are you talking about?"

"He tried to make her have a miscarriage. She told me he punched her in the belly with all his might several times."

Michael said, "Whaaaat?" as if he couldn't believe his ears.

T. Preston said, "That's a lie. Michael wouldn't do that."

I said, "Who are you are calling a liar—Glorie or Angela?" I knew I was supposed to say *Whom,* but I didn't want to sound like a grammar wonk just then. I was afraid it would weaken my position.

T. Preston flared up: "Michael wouldn't do that! And I don't believe he did."

I said, "You may not believe it, but it's true."

"You're a liar," Michael said.

"Like father, like son," I told him. "You guys have a bad habit of calling people liars."

T. Preston said, "I've had enough of your smart mouth, Larrison. Get off my property."

Angela said, "Mrs. Kovacs, I didn't come here to start a fight. I just wanted to talk to you about Glorie. She's a great girl, and she's deeply in love with Kelly."

T. Preston was so angry, he began to stammer: "Sh-she m-may think she's in love, but she's just a kid, and she's *not* going to have that baby! She's going to have an abortion."

Michael hung his thumbs in his pockets and said, "She's prob'ly screwin' the pothead right now."

Mae said, "Don't talk like that, Michael."

Angela looked Mae straight in the eyes and said, "Kelly is not a pothead, and he won't do anything to hurt Glorie." She began talking too fast: "And it's not just his fault that Glorie got pregnant—that is, if she still is pregnant after what your son did to her. Kelly and Glorie love each other. They want to have the baby."

"She's a slut," Michael said.

Mae slapped him on the face. Michael laughed it off.

T. Preston grabbed his wife by the arm and pulled her away from the door. I thought he was going to punch her.

Angela said, "Let's go, Phil. This was a bad idea." She called to Mae, "I'm sorry, Mrs. Kovacs."

"You *oughta* be sorry," Michael said. "You're gonna be good an' sorry when the Klan gets your kid for puttin' their pictures in that piece a shit he calls a newspaper."

I said, "What do you know about the Klan?"

"Mind your own business," he said.

His father said, "Shut up, Michael. Get in here."

Michael backed inside and slammed the door.

CHAPTER 46

UNDER THE RADAR

VOICES.

At first I thought I was dreaming. Then I thought I must have left the TV on—until I heard Angela say, "What happened to your face, Glorie?"

Glorie said, "I tripped and fell."

The window was dark. It was raining. I switched on the lamp and looked at the clock. It was 4:45.

Angela said, "Did somebody hit you?"

No answer.

"Did somebody hit you, Glorie?"

"I have to go, Mrs. Marcott. It'll be light soon."

"Is Kelly with you?"

"He's out front in the car."

"Tell him to come in. I'll fix you both some breakfast."

"We're delivering these around town. I gotta go."

"Do you need any help? I'll go with you. Just let me get dressed."

Angela came into the bedroom.

I whispered, "What's going on?"

"Glorie's here. Kelly's outside in her car. They're delivering the *Mothermucker* around town."

The front door opened with a squeak.

Angela called, "Glorie, wait a minute," and ran out of the room.

I got out of bed in my underwear and went after her. She was standing at the front door, staring outside into the gloom. "I told Glorie I'd go with her, but she wouldn't wait," Angela said.

I caught a glimpse of Glorie getting into her Beetle on the passenger side. Its high beams poked through the pouring rain.

Angela shut the door and held out the latest *Mothermucker*. "Here," she said. "Glorie gave it to me. She had a black eye and bruises on her face."

"Her brother probably beat her up."

"I heard a noise at the door," Angela explained. "I thought somebody was trying to get in, so I got out of bed and peeked out the window. I saw Glorie's car out front. Kelly was behind the wheel. Glorie put a copy of the *Mothermucker* inside the screen door and started to leave, but I opened the door and told her to come in. I waved at Kelly to come in too, but he stayed in the car. Glorie said she could only stay a minute." Angela cocked her head apologetically. "I'm sorry we woke you up, Phil. Would you like a cup of coffee?"

"Yes, please."

We went to the kitchen. Angela boiled water for the French press. It's funny how coffee always tastes better when someone makes it for you. I sat at the table and read the latest *Mothermucker*.

This issue consisted of only one article, which was on both sides of one sheet of typing paper. The front page featured a new *Mothermucker* logo in orange ink. The logo was printed sideways up the left side of the front page. This time balloonish comic-book letters were used for the logo. The lead article was printed at a right angle to the logo. The headline read:

Gold Coins Fall Like Rain;
'Honey-dipped' Man Dies;
Invaders Die in Gunfight

Under the headline was Kelly's byline in small, unassuming type. I liked that. The rest of the issue was devoted to a single article, which gave an account of the invasion of the Marcott home by a "five-man militia unit with semiautomatic weapons and heavy southern accents."

The article stated that the militia's leader, who identified himself as Colonel Bickerstaff, said he had received recent issues of *The Campbellsville Gleaner*, which reported the murder of Chester Marcott and which also mentioned the possibility that his killer was looking for "a treasure that was rumored to be hidden in Marcott's house in Meridian County."

Next Kelly wrote, "According to eyewitnesses, Bickerstaff said the *Gleaner* articles led the militia to believe that a single-engine aircraft piloted by one of its members had crashed on the Marcott farm in Salt Lick Township during a thunderstorm in 1989, when the pilot was on a mission to buy weapons in the neighboring state of Illinois. Bickerstaff said the plane was carrying two bags of old United States gold coins, the bullion value of which was approximately $125,000 in 1989. This was the militia's entire treasury, which was to be used to purchase weapons. Today the bullion value would be more than $500,000, Bickerstaff said."

Kelly explained that because the plane's flight path was over southern Indiana, "The militia suspected that its lost gold might be the treasure that a burglar was possibly searching for in the Marcott house on the day Chester Marcott was murdered." He also speculated that an advance team from the militia may have come to reconnoiter the house a few weeks earlier. "Maybe the team decided to break in and search the place but my grandfather surprised them, and they killed him," he suggested.

Kelly went on to describe the torture his father endured by being dipped in a septic tank. "After this sickening experience, my father, Dale Marcott, led the militia to a place where its airplane possibly crashed in a thunderstorm and was later buried." He did not reveal who buried the plane.

Kelly also gave an account of the gun battle:

> My grandfather's friend (Dicey Cockerham), my fiancée (Glorie Kovacs), and I attacked the militia to rescue my father, my mother (Angela Marcott), and my friend (Phil Larrison). It was our shotguns against their AK-47s. We were badly outgunned, but we held the high ground and shot down at the militia from two hills that were close to a deep hole that my father and Mr. Larrison were forced to dig in an effort to find the buried plane. Unfortunately, my father was killed by a member of the militia, but not before he killed the two highest-ranking members of the five-man unit. Ms. Cockerham killed the other three invaders with her shotgun, shooting at them from close range.

• • •

When I went to the *Gleaner* that morning, things were crazy. A line of people stretched outside through the front door, and the newspaper box in front of the building was empty. Other people were reading the paper as they stood on the sidewalk or sat in their cars. The word was out. They must have heard it on the radio and wanted more than a few sentences.

I parked behind the building and went in the back way, through the pressroom.

Ed was scrounging through the papers that the press crew had discarded at the beginning of the run last night. He was looking for copies that were good enough to put in the box.

"You should've had them print more papers," he told me. "We're sold out. A couple of stores have called for more already."

"I was busy, Ed."

"Yeah, I know. You put the whole lead story on the website. You should've just written a teaser."

"We need to do more online, not less."

"There's a satellite truck from a TV station in front of the courthouse. They found out about your story already."

"Somebody's on the ball."

"You might as well have called it in to them. Billy Bob saw your story online and called them."

Billy Bob Crockett was an amateur stringer for a TV station in Louisville.

Ed raced up front with an armload of half-printed newspapers, and I got myself a cup of coffee. When I entered my office, I found the Reverend Mr. Harnish sitting there with a copy of *Mothermucker* for me. I told him I already had a copy.

"You do?" he said. "Where'd you get it?"

I sat down and looked at him. "How late were you up helping Kelly get the *Mothermucker* out last night?"

"What are you saying? Are you implying that I've been aiding and abetting a fugitive?"

Ed barged in and said, "We're selling throwaways now, dammit."

Bob said, "Hey, Ed, have you seen the latest *Mothermucker?*" He held his copy out to him.

Ed looked at it as if he didn't want to get his hands dirty.

Bob said, "Your father's mentioned in it, Ed."

Ed glared at him. "What are you talkin' about?"

"Look at the editor's note on the back."

Ed grabbed the single-sheet issue and read the note aloud:

> Another set of old photographs of the KKK was
> found by this reporter in the same place where the
> gold coins were hidden, in the living-room ceiling of
> Chester Marcott's home. These photos are similar to
> the ones that this reporter discovered a few weeks ago
> in Mr. Marcott's attic. One of those photos showed
> the lynching of Abner Richards behind the Meridian
> County Courthouse in 1936. In both sets of photos,
> the lynchers' identities are concealed by robes and
> hoods; however, the names of the Klansmen in each
> photo are written on the back. (It is not known who
> wrote the names.) Six of the Klansmen named on the
> photos that fell out of the ceiling did not appear in the
> photos that were found in the attic. Their names are J.
> D. Nonnemaker, Kelvin Kantner, Ray Savonda, Tony
> Smith, John Worman, and James T. Wylie.

"Jesus Christ," Ed muttered. "That's my dad's name. This is
defamation of character. When are the police going to catch
this punk and put a stop to it?"

Bob said, "He's helping you sell papers, Ed."

"I've never had anything good to say about the Klan," Ed
replied, "but I will say this—not everybody who belonged to
the Klan back in the 1930s was a lyncher. Most people saw it as
a civic organization."

A thunderous laugh burst out of Bob's mouth. "That's good
to know," he said. "The Klan was just like the Lions Club. Most
of them didn't *really* buy into all that racist hate. Were *you* ever
in the Klan, Ed?"

Bob had gone too far. He was an anomaly, a preacher with
a salty tongue in the middle of the Bible Belt, a fervent liberal in

a conservative area with more than its share of fundamentalists. He was a breath of fresh air, but he could get under your skin. He was haughty at times. And he didn't know when to stop pushing his point.

Ed exploded: "My dad was not a racist! You didn't know him! He was no racist!"

"Hell, Ed, he was in the damn Klan," Bob said. "How could he not be a racist?"

"He was a young man. His views were unformed."

"Come on, Ed—"

"Out!" he yelled. He looked apoplectic. "Get your. . . . Get out of here. I've had enough of this crap."

Bob raised his hands and began to say something else, but I told him to put a cork in it. I grabbed him by the arm and took him out the back way.

He snickered and said, "I've never been thrown out of the *Gleaner* before."

• • •

I HAD an extremely busy morning, but I managed to go home for lunch. When I stepped into my apartment, I was surprised to see Angela's suitcase standing by the front door.

"Would you drive me back to the house, Phil," she said. "There's so much work to do there, I should go back."

"I thought you were afraid to be there," I said.

"I feel better now."

"You sure?"

"Yes. The bad guys are all dead, and besides, I still have you to protect me."

I took that to mean she wanted me to move back to her house too. It was enough to turn me on. I felt like backing her up to the desk and unfastening her jeans, but instead, always the gentleman, I called my landlord, the owner of Tri-County

Building Supply, and asked if he could send someone to replace the front and back doors on Angela's house today. I had to yak with him for ten minutes and give him an eyewitness account of the battle with the militia before he agreed to send a man out, a house builder who had lost an arm in a farm accident.

"Can he hang a door?" I asked. I pictured him struggling to lift a door with one hand and a stump.

"I wouldn't send him if he couldn't do the job," was the reply.

Angela and I had lunch in the apartment. Then we drove back to the farm.

The carpenter was already there, removing the plywood that the police had nailed over the front doorway. He was a thin man in his early forties, and he had an old transistor radio that was blasting out country music. He was a friendly guy who hummed along with the music as he worked.

Two hours later, back at the office, I asked Ed how he'd feel if I did a story on the *Mothermucker* and mentioned the names of the members of the Klan that Kelly had named in three of its issues.

"Absolutely not," Ed said. "No way. Nein. Nyet."

"We shouldn't hide the facts from our readers," I said.

"How do you know they're 'facts'?" Ed countered.

"The *Mothermucker* says the names are on the photos."

"How do you know the names are correct?"

"Why would anyone have faked them?"

"We can't take that chance."

"Ed," I said, "what about the photo with your father's name on it? Is that one a fake?"

"I don't know. I've never seen it."

"How about if I get it from Kelly and show it to you and your mother?"

"Forget it!" he growled. "I'm not going to get my mother upset. I'm not going to slur my father just because of what some wise-ass kid says."

"I'll lay it on Kelly," I said. "I'll say, 'According to an alternative newspaper published by students,' blahdi blahdi blah."

"It's published by a kid who's wanted for murder. Let's not make a hero out of him."

I began to get annoyed. After all, I was supposed to be the editor of the paper. I thought about threatening to quit if I couldn't publish what I felt we should, but even if Ed wouldn't let me publish the Klan stuff, I'd never quit without giving notice, and I knew that if I did give my two weeks' notice, within that time I'd regret it because I loved my job, so I caved and said, "Okay, Ed, you're the boss."

"Damn right," he shot back. He reminded me of a gorilla pounding his chest.

While I was working on my emasculated story, Eunice Gormley strolled in and said, "This is something you might be interested in. I had a call from Avah Nelle Schneider this morning. She writes the Brickton items, you know, and she drives a school bus. She said she was unloading kids at the high school when a boy and a girl in a yellow Volkswagen came driving through the parking lot with the windows down, throwing flyers or something out the windows. Avah Nelle said she asked a girl who was getting off her bus if she had any idea what the kids in the yellow car were doing, and the girl said it was Kelly Marcott and Glorie Kovacs circulating their underground newspaper—that thing with the filthy name."

"Mothermucker," I said.

She covered her ears and started toward the door, but stopped to add, "Oh, Avah Nelle told me the boy took off when he heard sirens coming. Someone must have called the police on him."

I wished Avah Nelle had called me instead of the society editor. I would have jumped in my car and tried to get a picture of Kelly and Glorie littering the parking lot with *Mothermuckers.* Oh well, I had enough to do. I worked Eunice's information into the story I was writing.

Then it occurred to me to give the sheriff a call to ask if he had come up with anything on the militia.

"Not much," Carl said. "I called the FBI and told them we have seven dead men, five of them with AK-47s and various handguns, plus Dale Marcott, and plus the remains of the pilot of the plane that crashed in 1989 while on a mission to buy military weapons. I also told the FBI we're not sure where the five came from. I gave them the Tennessee license-plate numbers and the VINs on the two vehicles we impounded. It turns out both vehicles were stolen in North Carolina, but the Hummer was registered in Florida and the Dodge van was registered in Georgia. The Tennessee plates were stolen too, but they came off of two other vehicles, not the ones they stole in North Carolina. Two different ones that they stole in eastern Tennessee."

"Thanks, Carl," I said. "Maybe the gang came from North Carolina and wanted to make it look like they came from Tennessee."

"That's what I think," Carl said, "but it could be the other way around. Or maybe they came from some other state. Whatever it was, the switcheroo with the plates wouldn't have done them any good if they got pulled over for speeding or something. The license plates wouldn't have matched the VINs on the registrations. I guess they drove like good, law-abiding citizens all the time."

"Did Jim Simpson determine if the .22 in the plane was used to kill the pilot?"

"Yes. Jim found two bullets in the pilot's brain. He did a forensic analysis on them and said they came from the rifle that was in the plane—the rifle with Dale Marcott's name on it."

"Did you find out who owned the plane?"

"It was registered to a Dr. Charles C. Blackwell, a chiropractor in North Carolina, which supports the idea that that's where the militia came from."

"But Bickerstaff said the pilot's name was Murphy."

"I know," Carl said, "but Dr. Blackwell wasn't flying the plane when it crashed here. What's more, he died nine years after it crashed. The FBI is looking into his connection with the militia."

"What'd you find out about Murphy?"

"He was from Sevierville, Tennessee. The FBI is investigating him as well as the chiropractor. So far they haven't shared their findings with me. It looks like Colonel Bickerstaff and his friends managed to stay under the radar till now."

"I just remembered something," I said. "Bickerstaff told his men that he was in the construction business. That might help you get a line on him."

"Thank you."

"Did you find any documents in the plane—anything that would give some idea of how many people besides the five who came here are in the militia?"

"No, nothing that shed any light on its forces," Carl said. "There was information about the plane itself—manuals, service records, registration—stuff like that, but no personal records of any kind."

"Nothing on the pilot?" I asked.

"Nope. Nothing in his pockets or anywhere else. No wallet or billfold. No cash. No checkbook. Nothing. I'd say someone went through his pockets, either when the plane crashed or when it was searched after you and Dale Marcott dug it out."

Carl paused to think, then said, "In the statement you gave me, you said Bickerstaff spent some time alone in the cockpit. You didn't see him remove anything besides the .22, did you?"

"No I didn't."

"Could he have hidden something?"

I said, "I guess he could have, but why would he have done that? At that point he wasn't expecting to be killed or captured. There was no need for him to hide anything to keep someone else from finding it in case something happened to him. According to what I heard him say, he thought he had superior firepower and was going to win the battle."

Carl said, "That makes sense, but I'll have my men check the plane and the digging site again to see if they can find anything he hid there."

CHAPTER 47

TWO FIRES

THAT evening Angela said, "The coroner called me today. He asked me what I want to do with Dale's body."

We were sitting by the pond, watching the sun go down over the knobs. A red-winged blackbird was in a panic because we were too close to its nest.

"What'd you say to the coroner?" I asked.

"I told him it's not up to me—we're divorced—but Kelly doesn't want him to be cremated. He said he should be buried next to Chester."

"Did Dale have any life insurance?"

"He had a $5,000 policy on himself. He told me I was the beneficiary, but I doubt if he left it in my name after we split up. He probably cashed it in, or maybe he put it in Kelly's name."

"Did he have any relatives besides Kelly?"

"Not that I know of," Angela said.

"Did he have any money in the bank?"

"I hope so. I hope there's enough to bury him. I'd pay for the funeral if I had the money Chester left me, but I'm just about broke. I'm going to have to look for a job."

"That's a good idea. It might help take your mind off your problems."

"I doubt it. My biggest problem is Kelly. I worry about him 24-7."

"Well, eventually you'll get your inheritance. Dale won't be contesting the will anymore."

"That's true, but something tells me I'll never see Chester's money."

"Why not?"

"I don't know. It's just a feeling."

"You'll be rich one of these days. In the meantime, don't worry about going broke. I've got some money you can use."

"Thanks, but it's not your problem, Phil. Maybe I can get a loan."

"Suit yourself, but the offer stands."

One of my legs was falling asleep, so I stood up and tried to shake it off. About a mile away I saw a golden gleam on the top of a ridge. The gleam grew larger. It looked as though some trees on the crest of the hill were burning. "Look," I said, pointing. "Is that a forest fire?"

"Oh my God!" Angela said.

The gleam grew wider and higher until a perfect arc appeared through the thin line of trees. At first I thought it was the sun, but the sun was behind us, and it was going down, not up.

"It's not a forest fire," I said. "It's only the moon."

Reflecting the reddish gold of the setting sun, the top of the moon rose slowly behind the trees. I took it as a good omen. We walked back to the house hand in hand.

I had a cup of coffee, then left for work.

I used to look forward to going back to work at night. It helped me get through the worst hours of the day, when I needed something to keep me from thinking of Vickie, something other than Scotch or Prozac. Now I simply had to count the minutes till I could be with Angela again.

When I got to the office, I found an envelope on my desk. It was addressed to "Editor Of Gleaner"—with the quotation marks and the capital O—and inside was a letter:

Why dont you and the whore your living with go somewhere else!!! Your not wanted here!!! Kelly Marcot is a killer he killed his own granfather and you know he done it but you try to make him innacent. He should of been in jail by now, not puting peoples names in that motherfucker peice of crap. He deserves what he gets and you do to and the whore his mother!!!

PS (that means PisS on you) I use to like the Gleaner but now I dont!!!

There was no signature. Most of our letters to the editor were anonymous, and for that reason we did not publish them. I filed this one in the folder where I kept my favorite pieces of hate mail.

About an hour later I got a call from Angela. "You busy?" she asked.

"Not yet," I said. "What's up?"

"I just had a call from Glorie. She said she went home and got in a fight with her father. He was furious with her for running away from home. She said she told him she did it because her brother punched her in the belly to make her have a miscarriage—and guess what—her father took her brother's side. He said she was shaming the family and her brother wanted to protect its good name. Then he said he wanted her to have an abortion ASAP, and when she said she'd never kill her baby, he got so mad, he actually started to take his belt off to give her a whipping, but her mother stepped in between them."

I said, "He's a control freak. I'm surprised he didn't use the belt on his wife."

"Both women are at risk in that house," Angela said. "Glorie said her father grabbed her mom by the arm and pulled her out of the room, and right after that her brother came in. Glorie said he had a stupid grin on his face because he heard his father sticking up for him. She said she told him to get out, but he shut the door and pushed her down on the bed. Then he got on the bed and stuffed a rolled-up pair of gym socks in her mouth. Then he reached inside her pants—inside her panties. Can you believe it? His own sister!"

I said, "I think he's only fourteen or fifteen, but I don't know, maybe he's older. Maybe he had to repeat three or four grades in elementary school."

Angela went on: "Glorie said he threatened her. He said, 'One way or another you're gonna lose that bastard in your cunt'—his words. He said he'd use a clothes hanger to get rid of it himself if he had to. I couldn't believe my ears, Phil. That kid's a little monster!"

"He's not very little," I said. "He's only a freshman, but he's big for his age. He made the varsity football team last season."

"That wasn't the only reason Glorie called," Angela said. She took a deep breath, then explained: "She said Kelly wants her to go away with him and try to get married, but even if they can't find somebody to marry them, he wants them to live together and have the baby, and when they turn eighteen and she won't need her parents' consent, then they'll get married."

"You know what," I said, "you should have her talk to Mary Lou Dunn. Glorie and Kelly are both seventeen. She's pregnant, and Kelly wants to marry her. In light of that, I think a judge might let her get married, even though she's a minor."

"But Kelly's wanted by the police."

"He should give himself up. He doesn't want to, but maybe he would if it meant they could get married and have the baby.

Besides—you know how I feel—I don't think there's enough evidence to convict him of murdering his grandfather."

Angela said, "I don't know if Glorie will listen to me, but the next time I see her—if I ever do—I'll tell her what you said. Maybe she can talk Kelly into it."

"It's worth a try. By the way, if they run away together, what would they live on?"

"They've got it all figured out. Glorie says she has some savings bonds that her grandfather left her, and she'll get a job until the baby comes. Then she'll take a month off, and when she goes back to work, Kelly can take care of the baby and go to college."

"How could he do that?" I said. "And how could he go to college if he's wanted by the police?"

"Wait till you hear this. Glorie said Kelly plans to change his identity and get a new Social Security number so he can get a job and go to college. He says he'll either come up with a fake birth certificate or steal somebody's identity, preferably a dead man's. It sounds crazy."

"It does," I said, "but if anyone can pull it off, I guess he can. I never thought he'd be able to keep from getting caught by the police as long as he has."

"If I had the money Chester left me, I could help them," Angela said. "But it's still tied up in probate, and nothing's happening. Kelly says nothing will ever happen, because the judge's father was in the Klan, and he won't let me have the money. I'm beginning to think he might be right. I'll never get any of Chester's money."

"Yes you will. Who else could he give it to?"

"I don't know."

"If you're afraid Judge Maxwell is biased, you can ask for a change of judge. You can also try to get your case moved out of the county."

"It could drag on for years," she said. "And if I can't pay Mary Lou, she'll probably drop the case. She can't keep working for nothing."

"Maybe you should ask your other lawyer, Clyde Goen, for an advance on your inheritance. After all, Chester named you as his heir. You should be able to tap into some of the money to meet expenses."

"You think they'll let me?"

"Sure. You can't be expected to pay Chester's bills out of your own pocket."

"But they're *my* bills now. I'm living in his house, using his electricity, his water, and everything else."

"It's your house, Angela. Chester left it to you."

She took a deep breath, then closed her eyes as she let it out. "I don't feel as though it's mine. I don't feel entitled to it. I feel . . . I don't know. Grabby. Greedy."

I said, "Don't get depressed."

Right, Larrison. As if you never do.

I had a couple of front-page meetings to wait for, and both of them ran late, so by the time we got Section A made up, it was nearly eleven. As usual, I hung around to check the first copies coming off the press, just in case I had missed some stupid mistake.

The front-page headlines were all correct. The photos were in the right places. Everything looked good. I grabbed a copy of the paper and left.

In front of the building, a car and three pickup trucks were lined up side by side at the curb with their engines running. The drivers were waiting for the latest issue of the *Gleaner* to be put in the box. One of them yelled, "Hey, Phil, is there gonna be a paper tonight?"

I held up my copy and said, "Any minute now, Jeff. Good things take time, you know."

He laughed as if I had said something hilarious.

I used to get a little thrill seeing people waiting to buy a copy of the paper in the middle of the night. During basketball season there would be at least a dozen of them waiting after every Highlanders game. Now I felt a sense of loss because it no longer felt exciting.

I knew I'd have trouble staying awake, so I went to the Speedway station and bought a large cup of black coffee and a small peach pie.

I began to unwind as soon as I was in my car on the way back to Angela's. I hoped she was still waiting up for me.

I turned the radio on. An old song, "Sultans of Swing," was playing.

I was still awake when I turned onto the county road that led to Angela's house. When I was a quarter mile or so away, I came over a low rise and caught a glimpse of a fire burning off to the right. I couldn't see the house, but the fire appeared to be about where the house stood.

Suddenly I was wide awake. I was afraid the house was on fire. Angela might be asleep. I stepped on the gas.

Because of the rolling fields, I lost sight of the fire, but then the road rose and I saw it again.

The house was not on fire. What I saw was a burning cross.

CHAPTER 48

You Marcotts

INSTEAD of turning into the lane that led to the house, I drove past the farm as if I hadn't noticed the cross.

I wondered who was burning it. I thought it must be some of the Klansmen whose names Kelly had put in the *Mothermucker*. Or maybe it was just a prank—some school kids horsing around—but burning a cross was a big step up from bashing rural mailboxes.

The house was dark. How could Angela be asleep if someone was burning a cross outside? She was a light sleeper. Maybe she was hiding somewhere in the house. Maybe she was lying in wait with her loaded shotgun in case the Klan broke in.

I drove to Dicey's cottage up the road. Her truck wasn't there, which meant she was probably at her Lake of the Woods house. I thought about breaking into the cottage to see if I could find one of her guns, but I decided against it for a number of reasons. First, if she was living at the lake, she probably had her guns with her so they wouldn't get stolen out here in the boonies. Second, maybe she had hidden them somewhere and I wouldn't be able to find them. Third, I knew where Angela's shotgun was. It was leaning against the wall on her side of the bed. I had a key to the house. I could walk there from Dicey's, sneak inside, wake up Angela, and get the gun. I could run the Klan off with a couple of shots maybe.

Then again, maybe not. Maybe the Klan had surprised her in bed and had taken her prisoner to keep her from calling the police. Or maybe she had confronted them with the shotgun but couldn't bring herself to use it and they had taken it away from her. If so, I was out of luck. . . .

Quit guessing, Larrison. See what's going on over there. *Do* something.

I left my car at Dicey's place and headed back down the road. I ran for a while, walked, and ran again until I got to the stone fence. I climbed over it at the southwest corner of the field and angled toward the house.

Walking through the overgrown meadow was like wading through deep water. A pair of owls hooted at each other in the woods. I warned myself not to step in a groundhog hole. I recalled Andreas Pluckett's story about how his father had been killed when a tractor overturned and fell on him because of a groundhog hole. Now and then I heard skittering sounds. I said a conditional prayer: God, if you exist, please don't let me get sprayed by a skunk.

I couldn't see the burning cross. I was heading toward the closer corner of the front porch, and the cross was behind the house.

When I was about two-thirds of the way through the field, I saw a dark-colored van parked at the head of the lane in front of the house. No one was outside the van, but someone could be inside. I decided not to investigate.

I got down on my hands and knees and crawled through the weeds. To see what I was up against, I crawled past the side of the house where the septic tank was. When I reached the back of the house, I saw three figures in white robes and hoods standing around a burning cross made of 2x4s. It sent a chill down my spine.

I crawled to the edge of the weeds. The loud chorus of spring peepers covered the sounds I made. The cross, which stood directly behind the pantry door, was enveloped in flames. Sparks swirled in the air.

I heard Angela's voice, but I couldn't make out her words. At first I didn't even see her, but then, in the flickering light, I made out a shadowy shape on the ground. She was lying on her side not far from the Klansmen. Her hands were tied behind her back, and her ankles were also tied.

I went on crawling past the back of the house. I stopped where the weeds ended, at the side of a wide path that led to the barn.

Angela was pleading with the Klansmen: "Don't hurt him. I'll give you everything I have. I swear I will. Kelly and I will go away. We'll never come back."

So they have Kelly too, I thought. But where is he?

What to do? What to do?

Get the shotgun, Larrison.

I turned around on my hands and knees and retraced the trail I had made through the weeds. When I was on the side of the house again, I stood up and made a dash to the porch. Any second one of the Klansmen might appear at the opposite side of the yard. I hadn't seen any guns, but they could have pistols under their robes. I might get shot. I might get killed. What the hell, Larrison, nothing ventured, nothing gained.

Brilliant. Keep thinking in cliches, Larrison.

I pulled myself up over the side railing and ran past the glider. My heart sounded as loud as a drum. The house had a new screen door. To keep it from making noise, I opened it just enough to squeeze inside, then softly shut it.

The new inner door was wide open. I wondered if Angela had heard the van arrive and had gone outside to see who it was. No, she would have assumed it was me in my Accord. I started up the steps. In case a member of the KKK was using the john, I walked close to the wall, where the stairs didn't creak.

On the second floor, an elongated rectangle of moonlight projected out into the hall from Chester's bedroom. Angela and I slept in a bedroom on the back side of the house. The orange glow of the fire seeped through the windows. I saw the shotgun right where it was supposed to be, propped against the wall next to the night table on Angela's side of the bed.

I figured out how to break open the gun—there was a latch behind the barrels. The gun was loaded. Good. When I closed the breech, I noticed the sliding safety near the latch. I slid it off and on and off. A box of Winchester 12-gauge buckshot shells lay on the night table. There were five shells in the box. I put them in my pants pockets.

When I left the room, I heard voices out front. I crossed the hall to Chester's bedroom to have a look. Two Klansmen were struggling to pull someone out of the back of the van. At first all I could see of him were his legs, bending and kicking at the Klansmen. His shouts were muffled.

I couldn't see his face, but he had to be Kelly. One of the Klansmen managed to wrap his arms around his legs and pull him out of the van. The back of his head bounced off the edge of the old chrome bumper and hit the ground with a thud. Rays of long yellow hair splayed out on the ground. He was Kelly all right.

One of the Klansmen grabbed the rope between his ankles and began dragging him across the lawn. Kelly kicked at him with both feet, but the kicks were weaker now.

I went down to the living room to call the sheriff. He'd be in bed, and he wouldn't like it, but I knew he'd be even more upset if I called the state police instead of him.

His wife answered the phone with a sleepy hello.

Speaking softly so the spooks wouldn't hear me, I asked to speak to Carl.

John Pesta

"Is this Phil?" Mrs. Eggemann chided. "Don't you ever sleep, Phil?"

"No, ma'am. Never."

"Carl, wake up," she said. "It's Phil Larrison."

The bed squeaked as Carl rolled over and took the phone. He yawned in my ear and said, "What the Sam Hill have you got yourself into now, Phil?"

"Sorry to bother you, Sheriff, but I'm out at the Chester Marcott house. It Looks like some members of the Ku Klux Klan are getting ready to lynch Kelly Marcott. They've got his mother tied up too, next to a burning cross."

"How many of them are there?" Carl asked.

"I've seen three. I think that's all of them, but I can't say for sure."

"Where are you now?"

"Inside the house. They don't know I'm here."

"How'd you manage that? Never mind. We'll get there as soon as we can. Meanwhile, if they try to hang the Marcott boy or hurt his mother, do something to distract them."

"I've got a shotgun. That oughta do it."

He paused. I thought he was going to tell me not to shoot anyone, but instead he said, "Be careful, Phil. Don't let them see you."

"Hurry up, Carl."

We hung up, and I went to the kitchen. I peered outside through the edge of the curtain on the back window near the table.

Right now the only person in the backyard was Angela. Her hands and feet were still tied, but she was sitting on the ground and oomphing herself on her behind toward the pantry

I heard someone running, and in the side window on my right the third Klansman ran by in his flapping robe and floppy hood. Until then I hadn't noticed the floppiness of the hoods that the Klansmen were wearing. They were not the scary, pointed cones that the Klan wore in movies. They were more like pillow cases. And the "robes" they were wearing looked more like bedsheets. I began to wonder if these guys were really in the Klan.

When he saw Angela oomphing toward the house, Klansman Number Three, the tallest one, grabbed one of her arms and dragged her back toward the cross.

"Let go of me!" she screamed.

He squeezed her arm more tightly, and she whimpered in pain.

The other two Klansmen came around the septic-tank side of the house, dragging Kelly by his arms.

Number Three picked up a rope that was lying on the ground in a pile of loops. It was thicker than clothesline, and it had a perfect noose at the end. He was straightening out the rope by spinning it behind him as he walked. Next he held the noose by its coils and threw it overhand at the lowest branch of the tree. The branch was higher than the second floor of the house, and he had trouble throwing the noose that high. It fell far short of the branch.

I decided Number Three was the leader. He picked up the noose and threw it harder and higher this time, but again it fell short. He left the rope lying on the ground.

The shortest of the three Klansmen—cleverly I dubbed him Shorty—picked it up and flung it at the branch, but he missed too.

The remaining Klansman said something to his partners in crime. He was taller than Shorty but shorter than Number Three, so I christened him Midsize. Then he picked up the noose and tossed it overhand, as the others were doing, but his throw was the weakest of all.

During the ensuing noose-throwing contest, Kelly began rolling himself sideways toward the overgrown field where I was.

Number Three picked up the noose again. This time, instead of throwing it like a football, as they all had been doing, he held the rope about five feet from the noose and began twirling it clockwise in a vertical circle. He whirled it several times, then let it fly.

The noose sailed over the branch on the first attempt. Dangling, it swung back and forth, and the winner pumped his fist in triumph.

Shorty spotted Kelly rolling himself toward the field. Shorty moseyed after him, grabbed him by the hair, and dragged him back across the lawn.

As if trying to keep his hair from being pulled out by the roots, Kelly relieved the pressure by pushing himself forward with the heels of his sneakers.

"Please let my son go," Angela pleaded with Number Three.

He stared straight down at her face, then raised one foot and stepped on her mouth. The cowboy boots he was wearing looked as though they were smeared with cow dung. Blowing and spitting, Angela squirmed out from under the boot.

Midsize flung Kelly's head to the ground near the foot of the cross, just inches from some burning coals.

Number Three picked up the noose and slid the coiled knot to enlarge the opening. Then he put the noose over Kelly's head and slid the coils down to the back of his neck.

"Don't hurt him!" Angela begged. "Please don't hurt him!"

I began to stress out. If I shot at any of the Klansmen from the window I might hit Kelly or Angela. If I ran outside, I might be able to get two of them, but all three might run, and then I might miss all of them. Then again, if they spread out and all of them charged me at the same time, I might get one or two of them, but I wouldn't get all three and I wouldn't have time to reload . . . but I could use the gun as a club. . . .

I felt as if I were having a lucid dream. I seemed half conscious, revising my dream as it developed, putting myself in a more dangerous predicament as I went along.

You've got to do something, Larrison! Do it!

A box of matches lay on the counter. I put it in my pocket and snatched a copy of the *Gleaner* that was on the table. I thought about taking the shotgun with me, but if I had to use it, the blast might lead the Klan to finish off Kelly, so I put it behind the sofa in the living room.

I peeked through the screen door. No Klansmen were in sight, so I eased it open again. Every little sound I made seemed loud enough to give me away. I walked quickly toward the van. I could only hope there was no guard inside.

The van was a banged-up hunk of junk that was at least forty years old. The sides were rusted out at the bottom. There were no windows in the back doors or the sides of the cargo compartment.

I circled around to the driver's side, where I couldn't be seen by the cross burners. I laid my paper and matches on the ground and stuck my head through the driver's side window. In the bright moonlight streaming through the windshield, I saw that the van had an old-fashioned bench seat. A long gearshift stuck out of a hump in the middle of the floor. No headrests were on top of the seat back. On the floor of the cargo compartment were several cardboard boxes bulging with painting supplies—brushes, rollers, empty paint cans, drop covers. Lying flat were a wooden scaffold and an aluminum stepladder.

I unscrewed the gas cap and rolled up both sections of the *Gleaner,* but not too tightly. One after the other, I pushed them lengthwise down into the filler pipe. I left the second section sticking out a couple of inches.

I wasn't sure my plan would work. Would the paper burn all the way down to the gas? Maybe the tank was nearly empty and it wouldn't make much of an explosion. That's okay, I told myself. Just so it gets their attention. I struck a match, lit the paper, and ran.

I was only ten feet away from the van when the gas tank exploded. The blast lit up the night and knocked me down on the ground. As I scrambled to my feet, the lynchers were yelling and cursing. I made a wild dash to the house, where the first thing I did was retrieve the shotgun.

Seconds later the Klansman I called Midsize appeared out front. He stared at the truck, which was engulfed in flames, then ran back to his cohorts.

A blubbering, pleading *"No-o-o-o-o-o-o-o-o-!"* came from Angela"

My stomach sank. I thought they must have hanged Kelly as soon as they heard the explosion. What an idiot I was. Instead of wasting time blowing up the truck, I should have tried to save him. I went to the kitchen and peered out back.

Kelly was hanging by his neck, barely moving. I thought he was dead already—his neck must have broken—but then I noticed that the tips of his sneakers were touching the ground.

The rope was taut, but he was not dangling in the air. Standing a few feet beyond Kelly, the tallest Klansman held it with both hands, suspending Kelly on the tips of his toes. The hangman's partners were gone. I figured they were running around looking for whoever had blown up their van. They could come charging through the house at any time.

I put my finger on the trigger but hesitated. I wondered if I should hide in the house and wait for them to come inside. No. Right now only one of them was out back. I could blast him before the other two would return.

While I was wasting time trying to make up my mind, the two spooks reappeared in the backyard. The three of them put their heads together, and then Shorty took off running toward the front yard again, while Midsize started toward the pantry. I told myself they must have decided that whoever had blown up their truck must be in the house. Number Three, the hangman, bent his knees and yanked the rope with both hands.

Angela screamed as Kelly's feet left the ground. He jerked as he spun in the air.

My heart was in my throat. I charged outside through the pantry.

Midsize, who was nearly at the steps, stopped and yelled, "Shotgun!" Then he ran after Shorty.

Number Three moved to his right, keeping Kelly between himself and me.

"Let go of the rope," I shouted.

He went on pulling it.

I did not fire at him. I was afraid of hitting Kelly. I shot at the rope where it hung over the branch. The gun sounded like a cannon. Buckshot peppered the leaves and branches but did not sever the rope.

Kelly spun slowly about eighteen inches off the ground. Leaves drifted down over him. I dove onto the grass and shot under his feet at the shins of the hangman. I could only hope that none of the pellets hit Kelly.

At close range, the tight spray of buckshot knocked Number Three's legs out from under him. He let go of the rope and crumpled on the ground. At the same time, Kelly fell with a thump between us. Number Three was gasping in pain.

As I stood up, a weird calmness came over me. Small flames came and went on the cross. Somehow I seemed to see myself from above. Was I dead? Was I dreaming? Still in my hands, the shotgun stretched out like a dark line connecting me to Kelly and the hangman. Maybe the spirit *can* exist outside the body, I thought. Maybe there *is* an afterlife.

I seemed to be moving in slow motion. I watched my hand break open the shotgun. I watched the empty shells fall out. I took two shells out of my pants pocket and reloaded the barrels.

Number Three was breathing hard. It was more like panting. I stood beside him. I could not see his eyes through the eyeholes in his hood. I did a quick 360 in case his accomplices were sneaking up behind me. I thought they might come back to rescue him.

Angela was sobbing. I used the little Swiss Army knife on my key ring to try to cut the rope off her wrists. Like a faint whisper in the middle of my head I heard the words *Call an ambulance, Larrison.* The rope was thick. I was taking too long to cut it. Angela grew impatient. Finally I cut through the rope.

"Help me get up," Angela said.

I helped her stand, and she went hopping toward Kelly.

I said, "I'm going to call an ambulance. I'll be right back."

Angela sobbed as she hopped and teetered across the lawn.

I went into the house and called 911.

When I came back out, Angela burst out, "Phil! Kelly's alive!"

He was sitting on the ground, and Angela was kneeling next to him with her arms wrapped around his neck as well as the noose. She was still crying, but now her tears were tears of joy.

Kelly shouted four syllables through his gag: "Eht uhh aggh uht!"

I realized what he was trying to say: *Get the gag out.* I pulled the soggy rag out of his mouth. Angela went on squeezing the side of his head against her bosom.

"You don't hafta strangle me," Kelly said. "The jockasses did that already."

I admired how he could make a pun at a time like this.

The hangman was making a burbling sound. I noticed that one leg of his bluejeans was much darker than the other. Both legs were bleeding, but the lower part of one pants leg was literally soaked with blood. The buckshot must have hit an artery. Angela loosened the noose around Kelly's neck while I cut two pieces of rope to use as tourniquets on the hangman's legs. I picked up a couple of small sticks to use to tighten them.

Angela tried to untie Kelly's wrists, but immediately stopped and cried, "Oh shhhooot! I broke a nail." She put her fingertip in her mouth.

Kelly grouched, "Phil, untie me for Christ's sake, will you please!"

"This guy's bleeding big time," I told him. "I have to stop it, or he might bleed out." I wasn't sure where to attach the tourniquets, but I figured anywhere below the knees would do some good.

"What are you helping him for?" Kelly griped. "He tried to hang me."

"I know," I said. "I want to keep him alive so he can go to prison."

"Let him go to hell."

I knelt down to attach the tourniquets. A brilliant idea popped into my head—it occurred to me that I could take his hood off and find out if he was one of the old Klansmen I had visited. "Let's see who this is," I said.

"I'll tell you who he is," Kelly said, "He's Curtis Davis. The other two are Mike Kovacs and Chad Williams."

I pulled the pillow case off the hangman's head. Indeed, he was Curtis Davis.

Kelly said, "They brought me here to lynch me. They wanted to make it look like the Klan did it. "

"Fuck you," Curtis said, and with a trembling hand he gave Kelly the finger.

I wondered if the trembling meant he was going into shock. I remembered my half year of Boy Scout training and went back inside to get something to keep him warm. I found a patchwork quilt in the parlor, and on my way out I took a wooden kitchen chair with me. I set the chair next to Davis's legs.

When I raised his legs to elevate them on the chair, one of his feet almost fell off. It dangled as if attached by nothing but skin. I thought I was going to puke.

I straightened up and saw Angela staring at Davis's face. "Why did you try to kill Kelly?" she asked him. "He never did anything to hurt you."

Davis closed his eyes in pain. His jaws tightened. He started to say something, but stopped. He gritted his teeth. "That's a lie," he said weakly. "You Marcotts done all you could to hurt us."

"What?" Angela said in disbelief. "What did we do to you?"

Davis's mouth opened wide. He struggled to get his breath.

Angela said, "I don't have any idea what you have against us. Tell me what you think we did to you."

"It ain't what I think," he said. "It's what I know." He stopped talking. His mouth opened again, as if trying to yawn, but he was actually gasping for breath. Straining, he said, "You Marcotts put my mom and dad outta business. They lost all they had. You damn Marcotts killed my dad. He started drinkin' after they lost their store. Mom says he drank himself to death. She's never been the same since he died. You Marcotts destroyed her life."

"I don't know what you're talking about," Angela said. "What store went out of business?"

"The hardware . . . Campbellsville Hardware."

"I don't know anything about Campbellsville Hardware," she said. "I never even heard of it. Kelly and I had nothing to do with it. Nothing!"

Kelly said, "He blames me for taking Glorie away from him. That's what he's got against me. But Glorie dumped him before we started going together. He won't blame himself for losing her though. He'd rather blame me."

Curtis's lips were clenched. His eyes were tightly shut. He seemed to be struggling not to cry.

CHAPTER 49

WE JUST WANTED TO SCARE HIM

A SIREN wailed in the distance.

Kelly was frantic. "Untie me!" he yelled. "I can't stay here. I gotta make sure Glorie's okay."

Angela said, "Where *is* Glorie, Kelly?"

"Her brother and the other two dumbheads took her home before they brought me here."

"She should be all right then," Angela said.

"You hope," Kelly said. "Her brother could be on his way there right now to kill our baby."

Angela shook her head. "Her mother would never let that happen."

"How do you know?"

"I met Glorie's mom. She would never—"

"I can't take that chance. Glorie needs me. Get these ropes off me."

The worn-out expression on Angela's face made her look years older than she was.

I said, "You can't go anywhere, Kelly. You've got to tell the police how you were nearly killed tonight. Tell them Glorie's in danger. They can get to her house before her brother can."

Davis worked himself up to say, "We weren't tryin' to kill 'im." His voice was slower, weaker. "We just wanted to make 'im go back where he came from." He closed his eyes as if it hurt to talk.

"Sorry, Curtis, that won't work," I said. "You had him hanging in the air by his neck. That's why you got shot, in case you don't know it."

Kelly said, "I ought to hang *him* so he knows how it feels."

"Bite me," Curtis said.

A police car came speeding down the county road. Its siren was off, but red, white, and blue flashes streaked across the fields. It was not the car we had been listening to. That siren was still on the far side of Zumma Hill.

"Thanks a lot, Ma," Kelly said. "If Glorie's brother kills our kid with a clothes hanger, it's gonna be your fault."

"Oh, Kelly." She sounded hurt. She tried to put an arm around him, but he twisted away.

I went to meet the cop. I stood out beyond the corner of the house so he would be able to see me and I could keep an eye on things in the backyard.

The lights flickered through the pear trees. The car turned out to be an SUV. It stopped in front of the van at the end of the lane, and Sheriff Eggemann climbed out.

The van was still burning. There was no wind tonight, which may have prevented the fields from catching fire. Carl took a fire extinguisher out of the back of his SUV and hustled to spray the remaining flames. The dense smoke made a black silhouette against the starry sky.

When the last tiny flame was out, Carl hurried toward me with the extinguisher in one hand and his sidearm in the other. I briefed him on what had occurred since I had phoned him, including how I had shot Curtis to save Kelly and how I had given Curtis first aid.

Carl said, "I guess you had to shoot him." He didn't sound entirely convinced.

I thought he was going to spray the burning cross, but when he saw that the fire had burned through only a few feet of the sparse grass around it, he set his extinguisher on the ground, holstered his gun, and took pictures of the cross with his smartphone.

"Thank you for coming, Sheriff," Angela said.

"You're welcome, ma'am. This is getting pretty old, isn't it?"

"Yes it is."

Carl jabbed a thumb in the direction of the van and said, "What happened to that truck?"

I said, "You told me to create a distraction, so I blew it up."

"You're lucky you didn't blow yourself up," he said.

He unhooked a small flashlight from his belt and trained it on one person after another. "Kelly Marcott," he said, "I'm glad to see you again. I'm placing you under arrest for the murder of Chester Marcott."

The stark white beam from the LEDs in the flashlight made Kelly's face look like one of the hellish monsters that watch me in my dreams. He jutted his chin at Curtis Davis as he said, "Arrest *him,* not me. The bastard tried to lynch me."

Kelly's legs were bound at the ankles, so Carl helped him stand up. Then Carl took a switchblade out of his pocket and sprung open a four- or five-inch blade. He stood behind Kelly and sliced the rope off his wrists, but immediately he replaced the rope with a pair of handcuffs.

Angela said, "Is that really necessary, Sheriff?"

"There's an open warrant for his arrest, ma'am," Carl replied, "and I don't want him running off again." He began reading Kelly his rights.

"You happy now, Ma?" Kelly said over Carl's voice.

"Don't worry, honey. I'll call Mary Lou Dunn. In a few hours you'll be out of jail."

Carl said, "I wouldn't count on it, ma'am. First there'll have to be a hearing where the judge can set bail; however, since your son is charged with murder, the judge might decide not to grant bail. After all, your boy's already shown himself to be a flight risk. But I doubt the hearing will be held today. The law requires an initial hearing within forty-eight hours of the arrest, so most likely it will be tomorrow."

Davis was breathing harder. "Lar-Larrison shot me," he stuttered.

"There's an ambulance on the way," Carl said. "What were you doing out here tonight, Curtis, and since when are you in the Ku Klux Klan?"

Curtis seemed confused.

Kelly said, "They were trying to lynch me, Sheriff. Look, the freaken noose is still around my neck."

From behind the dog pen came a frightened shout from Chad Williams: "Hey, Sheriff, that ain't true. We wasn't tryin' to kill 'im. We just wanted to scare 'im."

"You're full of shit, you liar," Kelly yelled back.

Angela said, "Don't believe that boy, Sheriff. They wanted to hang Kelly. They wanted to make it look like the Ku Klux Klan did it."

Sheriff Eggemann called into the darkness, "Show yourself, son. What's your name?"

"Chad Williams, sir."

Kelly said, "He's in my class at school."

Carl took his gun out of its holster. "Put your hands up," he ordered Chad. "Walk toward the cross where I can see you."

Chad came out from behind the cyclone fence with his hands in the air. He was no longer wearing a sheet and pillow case. "Don't shoot," he said.

Another voice called, "I'm comin' too," and Michael Kovacs followed Chad out of the weeds beyond the dog pen.

Like Chad, he had shed his Klan costume.

"Hands up!" Carl repeated. "What's your name?"

"Mike Kovacs."

Carl waited as they approached the cross, one behind the other. Then he ordered them to sit on the ground, and he stood over them with his gun drawn.

The sound of another siren reached us.

Carl said, "That sounds like an ambulance," and he went to check on Curtis.

"How is he?" Chad asked. "Is he okay?"

Curtis was breathing even faster now. His eyes were closed, and he was starting to shiver.

Carl unwrapped the quilt I had put around Curtis. "Where'd you say you shot him?" he asked me.

"Below his knees," I said.

He pulled up Curtis's sheet and inspected the tourniquets I had tied around his shins. "Not bad," he said, fiddling with the sticks I had used to tighten the ropes. Then he came over to Angela and me and whispered, "He's shaking. He's going into shock. And he's looking pale. I imagine he lost a good deal of blood before you got those tourniquets on him. You did the right thing elevating his legs like that. But buckshot can do a lot of damage."

Chad cried out, "He ain't gonna die, is he? Give him CPR!"

"He doesn't need CPR," Carl said calmly. "His heart hasn't stopped, and he's breathing. But I'll be glad when that ambulance gets here."

Michael yelled, "It's the *Gleaner* guy's fault if Curtis don't make it, Sheriff. He didn't have to shoot him."

Kelly came to my defense. "If he dies, it's his own fault," he said. "And yours too, you stupid prick."

"Knock it off," Carl said.

A couple minutes later a box-shaped ambulance came racing down the road and turned into the lane. Carl went out front and waved his flashlight. The ambulance rumbled up the lane toward Carl's SUV, then slowed down and drove around it through the meadow toward us.

Its high beams lit up the backyard, and two emergency medical techs hopped out. Their plastic name tags identified them as EMT Ron Jackson and EMT Nora Warren. When they saw the burning cross and Curtis's long white robe, Ron said, "What's with the Ku Klux Klan? I didn't know they were around here."

"It's not the real Klan," I said. "Just impostors—two high-school kids and one of last year's grads. He's the one on the ground." I explained why I felt I had to shoot him, then added, "The buckshot caused a lot of bleeding, so I put tourniquets on his legs." I warned them about the dangling foot.

"Let's have a look at him," Ron said to his partner.

Nora asked Curtis what his name was. His chin shook as he told her.

She examined the lower part of his legs, which still rested on the kitchen chair. When she saw the damage, she made a face and looked up at Ron. "We'd better call the hospital and tell them what we've got," she said.

While Ron contacted a doctor in the emergency room, Nora checked Curtis's vital signs. She used two terms I had never heard before: hypovolemic shock and exsanguination. Then she said, "We're taking you to the hospital, Curtis. I'll give you something for your pain."

Curtis said nothing.

Nora kept talking to him. I figured she was trying to keep him from passing out. She supported his dangling foot while her partner and Carl lifted him onto a low stretcher. Ron then raised the stretcher and pushed it into the ambulance. Its wheeled legs folded underneath.

Carl had a brief confab with the EMTs, and then the ambulance plowed through the field again. It went slowly this time until it reached the county road.

Kelly was trading insults with Michael and Chad. Carl put a stop to it by telling Deputy Bobb to "take Kelly to the juvenile center."

As soon as Eli clutched one of Kelly's arms, Kelly began struggling and mouthing off. He swung his elbows from behind his back. He tried to butt the deputy in the face with the side of his head. He went limp and dropped to the ground. When Eli dragged him on his back by his bound feet, Kelly tried to kick him with the bottom of his shoes.

"Stop it, Kelly," Angela said as we followed them to the cruiser, but she flipped out when the cops shoved him into the backseat behind a steel screen. "He's not an animal," she told the deputy. "He doesn't belong in a cage."

Eli said, "If he's not an animal, he shouldn't act like one." Without further ado, Eli got in the car and headed for town.

It occurred to me that Kelly could spit at him through the steel screen. I hoped he wouldn't pick up my thought.

Angela waved at the back of Kelly's head as the car sped away.

I saw the sheriff and Deputy Holsapple taking Chad and Michael into the house. I took Angela's hand and said, "I could use a cup of coffee. How about you?"

She was glum and miserable, but she squeezed my hand. It was as if I were the only one she had left.

We caught up with the sheriff in the living room. "Jesse and the two boys are upstairs," he said. "The boys needed to use the bathroom."

"Why didn't Kelly get that opportunity?" Angela demanded.

"He didn't ask," Carl replied.

About fifteen minutes passed before Holsapple returned with Michael and Chad.

"What took so long, Jesse?" Carl asked.

"I uncuffed them one at a time, Sheriff," Holsapple said. "While one of them used the commode, I handcuffed the other one to a pipe—in case they would try something, ya know. It would've been two against one, with one of 'em unhandcuffed. Then I had to recuff the first one who used the john and uncuff the other one so he could use it."

Carl gave me a warning look in case I was thinking about laughing. Then he said, "Okay, let's get this over with. I just want to ask you boys a couple of questions. Where did you find Kelly Marcott tonight?"

"Why?" Chad asked. "What difference does it make?"

"He's wanted in connection with the murder of his grandfather," said Carl. "I'd like to know who was helping him hide from the police."

Michael said, "If we tell you where we caught him, will you let us go?"

"I can't do that," Carl said, "but I promise you this: the more you cooperate, the better off you will be."

The boys looked at each other. Since they hated Kelly's guts, whether to accept the sheriff's offer was a no-brainer. It took them about three seconds to make up their minds.

Michael said, "The Presbyterian minister has been hiding him and my sister since she ran away from home."

"Are you sure about that?" Carl asked. "If what you say is true, he could lose his job."

"He *should* lose it," Chad said. "He shouldn't be a minister. He cusses."

"Where was he hiding them?" Carl asked.

Michael said, "There's a little trailer out behind the parsonage and the church. It's got two little wings on it, like bird wings. They stick straight out at the back, one on each side. That's where we found Mr. Hollywood and my stupid sister. I don't know why she dumped Curtis for him. Yes I do—because she's *stupid!* How can she stand it in that crummy trailer with him. I bet it's fulla mice."

"Are you sure the trailer belongs to Reverend Harnish?" Carl asked.

Chad said, "Yeah, I'm sure. I asked a girl that goes to his church. She said the trailer belongs to him. He bought it at an auction. And she said her mother told her a lady friend of hers said she saw a girl come outta the trailer early in the morning, just when the sun was comin' up. The lady said the girl was real pretty and drove away in a yellow VW Beetle. Far as I know, there's only one girl in town that fits that description. So I told Mike about it, and he told Curtis. The three of us staked out the trailer a couple or three nights ago, and we saw Glorie and Mr. Hollywood go in together. It ain't got electric. They was usin' candles."

"Was that when the three of you decided to lynch Kelly?" Carl asked.

Michael shook his head sharply. "No! That's when we decided to make him *think* we was gonna lynch him. We didn't want to hang him for real. All we wanted to do was scare the crap out of him."

Carl replied, "If that's all you wanted to do, why would you run the risk of killing him by 'pretending' to lynch him? You should have called the Sheriff's Department or the Campbellsville Police Department and reported where they were hiding. The police would have gone out and arrested him."

Michael's voice rose: "Didn't you hear what I said? We didn't really want to lynch him. The only reason he almost got lynched was on account of the *Gleaner* guy. It was his fault. He comes runnin' out the back door with a shotgun pointed at Curtis. That's when Curtis pulled on the rope. It wasn't what he planned to do. It was like an accident."

"It was a reflex reaction," Chad said. "If you ask me, Curt went nuts on account of Glorie. Mr. Hollywood got her pregnant, and when Curt got a look at that dumpy trailer, he went crazy. It ain't fit for a dog to live in. Nobody wanted to kill Mr. Hollywood. We just wanted him to buzz off so Curt could get Glorie back—if he still wants her now that she's been knocked up. Mike says his dad is gonna make her get an abortion. Why did Marcott have to come here anyway? It's like he was sent here by aliens to wreck everybody's life."

"And we wanted him to quit shittin' on the sports program," Michael added. "He wants the school to dump sports, but this is a sports town."

"I've never seen a town that isn't," said Carl. "Okay, Jesse, let's get going. You take Chad in your car, and I'll take Michael."

"Hey, c'mon, Sheriff," Chad said. "We cooperated. Let us go."

"I can't do that, son. You and your two friends are in serious trouble for what you did tonight."

Chad's jaw dropped as if he couldn't believe his ears. "What'd we do?" he demanded."

"You're going to be charged with kidnapping and attempted murder," Carl said.

Chad cried out, "We didn't want to murder nobody. The only one that got hurt was Curtis, and that was the *Gleaner* guy's fault. He shot Curtis. Why don't you arrest him?" He glared at me over his shoulder as he was being pulled away.

"Yeah!" Michael yelled. "All we did was catch a wanted criminal that the police couldn't find. We oughta get a reward. We weren't tryin' to *murder* him. We wanted to teach him a lesson, that's all."

After the sheriff put Michael Kovacs in the backseat cage of his SUV, I drew him aside and said, "You don't believe that cock-and-bull story that they just wanted to scare Kelly, do you, Carl?"

"It doesn't matter what I believe," he said.

"You want to know what I think?"

"Not really, but I have a feeling you're going to tell me regardless."

I said, "I think one or more of those three kids may have killed Chester Marcott. You told me there were fingerprints on the murder weapon, the purple baseball bat—prints you couldn't identify. I think you should compare those prints with those of the three boys."

"Thank you, Phil," Carl said. "I never would've thought of that. If it wasn't for you, I'd have no idea how to do my job."

CHAPTER 50

SANCTUARY

AFTER the police left, I used the hose that was hooked up behind the house to soak the remains of the cross and the circle of glowing coals. Then I told Angela I had to go to my office to put a few paragraphs online about what had occurred tonight. I could not let the radio stations beat me on a story in which I had played a major role.

Angela threw a few things in a shopping bag and went with me.

While I knocked out my story, Angela sat on a chair in my office and fell asleep with her head against the wall. Once I got into it, I wrote more than I had intended. Because it was late at night, the story seemed better than it was. I knew I'd rewrite it in the light of day, but right now it felt good to be breaking the news.

When I stopped writing, the silence woke Angela up. We went to my place and hit the sack. Angela lay against me with her arm across my chest. It was something Vickie never used to do.

• • •

THE phone rang.

I felt as if I had just fallen asleep, but the sun was up, and through the venetian blinds thin strips of sunlight laddered the walls.

I sprang out of bed and ran to the living room. My throat felt sore, which made me wonder if I was coming down with a cold. I swallowed some saliva and answered the phone with a scratchy hello.

It was Sheriff Eggemann. "I got your two messages," he said.

"Thanks for calling back, Carl," I said. "I just wanted to ask you if you had time to check if those partial fingerprints on the purple baseball bat match the prints of any of the boys who tried to lynch Kelly."

"Yes, sir," he said as if I were acting like his boss, "I compared the prints, and none of the partials on the bat come anywhere near matching any of the alleged lynchers' fingerprints."

"Are you sure?" I said.

He sighed to show he didn't appreciate my question, then went on: "I fingerprinted Kovacs and Williams when I booked them into jail, and I compared their prints with the ones on the bat. There were no matches, nothing even close. Then I went to the hospital to see how Curtis Davis was doing. I was told he had died on the way there. He was in an unlighted room. Doctor Stone said his heart had stopped and the EMTs weren't able to get it going again. The doc got called away to another patient, leaving me alone with Curtis, so I took advantage of the situation to get his fingerprints electronically. I probably violated his rights, but I didn't think he'd mind. He was gone, and the partials on the bat are so small that I didn't expect to get a credible match, and when I went back to the jail and compared his prints with the ones on the bat, my hunch proved to be correct."

To use a word Carl might have used, I was flabbergasted. "I can't believe it," I said."So Curtis Davis died in the ambulance, and I killed him."

"I'm afraid so, Phil, but don't worry, you're not under arrest."

Things were flickering on the periphery of my vision. It was migraine time again. I focused on something slightly less stressful: "If none of the three boys' prints are on the bat, then whose are?"

"Kelly Marcott's," he said as if the answer were obvious. "As for the partials . . . I don't know. They're just traces, most of 'em. Maybe they're Chester Marcott's. Or maybe they belong to his son, Dale. I just don't know. All I've got are bits and pieces. What I do know is the prints do not belong to Curtis Davis, Michael Kovacs, or Chad Williams. The three of them are in the clear as far as Chester's murder is concerned. I can charge them with attempted murder—trying to lynch Kelly Marcott—but I doubt it would stand up in court."

"Why wouldn't it?" I complained. "I was there. So was Angela. Both of us saw Curtis try to hang Kelly. Michael and Chad were accomplices. We weren't imagining things, Carl."

Carl said, "The boys claim the lynching was a prank."

"Come on, Carl, it's more than a prank when you put a rope around someone's neck and yank him up off the ground."

"I agree with you, but you heard what they said. They said things got out of hand when you came running out of the house with a shotgun. They claim Curtis made a reflex reaction— he thought you were going to shoot him, so he automatically pulled on the rope to use Kelly as a shield."

"That sounds like Kovacs and Williams got their stories together while they were hiding in the field, and it makes me sound like a raging maniac, as if it was my fault Curtis tried to hang Kelly."

"A jury might find it reasonable to believe that Curtis was just trying to protect himself. You never know what a jury will do, especially if the defendant has a good lawyer."

"There's something else," I said. "Before you showed up at Angela's house last night, Curtis said some things that suggest he had a motive for killing Chester as well as a motive for trying to kill Kelly. He hates the Marcotts. After I shot him in the legs, he was lying on the ground, but he got in an argument with Angela. He told her the Marcotts had done all they could to hurt his family. He said, 'You Marcotts put my mom and dad out of business.' Apparently they used to own a hardware store and they blamed the Marcotts for making it fail. Curtis even blames them for his father's death. I heard him tell Angela, 'You damn Marcotts killed my dad.' He said his dad drank himself to death after they lost the store, and he said his mother was never the same after his father died. He blames the Marcotts for destroying his family."

"That's a sad tale," Carl said. "I know the Davises owned Campbellsville Hardware. It used to be on Jefferson Street, but it's gone now. And I know a good many merchants didn't like it when Chester sold Walmart the land it needed for a store in Campbellsville. But if *he* hadn't sold that cornfield on US 50 to Walmart, someone else would have sold them a piece of land. The Davises may feel Chester helped Walmart put them out of business, but Walmart hasn't put *all* the mom-and-pop stores in town out of business. As a matter of fact it seems like there are more of them today than ever before."

"That's all well and good, Carl," I said, "but the point is that Curtis thinks—I mean *thought*—Chester was to blame for the failure of his parents' business, and that is a possible motive for murder."

"I reckon it's possible," Carl allowed.

I pressed on: "Curtis had other motives too. He didn't like it that Kelly took his girlfriend, Glorie Kovacs, away from him and got her pregnant. Nor does he like it that Kelly wants the school system to drop sports in favor of the arts. Curtis was a jock, you know."

Carl yawned and said, "You call that a motive for murder? That's a real stretch. Nobody believes the school board would drop basketball, baseball, football, tennis, track, golf, swimming, and whatever else there is because some kid from California says they should. The board members would get run out of town on a rail if they pulled something like that." He chortled as he said "Bye, Phil. You have a good day."

• • •

ANGELA didn't get up until ten o'clock. The first thing she did was call Mary Lou Dunn to tell her Kelly was in jail.

I was eating breakfast—a couple of slightly stale Bavarian-cream doughnuts and my second cup of coffee. I had slept on the sofa for an hour and a half so as not to disturb Angela by getting back in bed.

Mary Lou Dunn was doing most of the talking, but I couldn't make out what she was saying. Finally Angela said, "All right, Mary Lou, will you let me know if there is? I'm at Phil's place. You can reach me here. . . . Good. Thank you."

Angela came into the kitchen. She had on a pink nightie under a baggy sweatshirt. She poured herself a cup of coffee and said, "Mary Lou thinks there might be a hearing for Kelly today. She knew he was in jail—it was on the radio, she said. I asked her if she thought the judge might let Kelly out on bail. She said I shouldn't get my hopes up."

"Good advice," I said.

"If the judge does decide to set bail, how high do you think it will be?"

I tossed my hands and said, "I don't know. Your guess is as good as mine. It's a murder case, so if he sets bail—and that's a big *if*—maybe it would be something like a $250,000 bail bond, which would mean you'd have to come up with at least ten percent of that to buy the bond."

"Hah," Angela scoffed, "$25,000. I don't have that kind of money."

I said, "You could go to a bail bondsman, but I doubt that you'd find one who'd be willing to take the risk. If Kelly disappeared again, the guy would lose his shirt."

"Maybe I could get some of the money Chester left me— like you said last night."

"I don't know if you could get it for a bail bond," I said, "but it wouldn't hurt to try."

"Now you sound like you don't think Mr. Goen would give me the money."

I took another gulp of coffee and said, "I just think Mary Lou Dunn may have been right when she said you might not be able to bail Kelly out of jail."

Angela clenched her fists on the table. "I have to do something! I can't just let Kelly sit in jail."

"It's not *your* fault he's in jail," I said. "Do you remember when Kelly put an article in the *Mothermucker* accusing Judge Maxwell and Sheriff Eggemann of being biased against him because some of their ancestors had been in the Klan? Judge Maxwell is still handling the case. Now, I'm not saying the judge is biased, but Kelly didn't do himself any good by accusing him of it."

Angela cried, "He's my son! Maybe Judge Maxwell should turn the case over to another judge. Maybe a different judge would set the bail lower."

I reached across the table and touched her hand. "There's no point in worrying about it now. Let's wait and see what happens at the hearing. It'll be either today or tomorrow."

"Do you think they'll let me see Kelly?"

"Call the jail and ask. I think regular visiting hours are on Sunday, but I bet they'll let you see Kelly today."

She drew her hand away from mine and propped her elbows on the table. She leaned forward and squeezed the flesh on her forehead as though she had a headache. "It doesn't matter," she said. "He might not even talk to me. He's probably mad at me for not untying him last night so he could try to help Glorie." She rubbed her eyes with the heels of her hands, then stood up and said, "I guess I'll go take a shower."

She looked beaten down and depressed.

• • •

I HAD another doughnut while Angela was taking her shower. Then I called the Reverend Mr. Robert Harnish.

"It's me," I said, "what's this I hear about Kelly Marcott and Glorie Kovacs, his betrothed, hiding in a trailer behind your house?"

"Who told you *that?*" Bob asked as if I had heard wrong.

"Glorie's brother, Michael," I said. "He and two of his friends caught Kelly and Glorie in the trailer yesterday evening. Then they disguised themselves as the Ku Klux Klan and took Kelly out to the Marcott farm, where they tried to lynch him in front of his mom. I shot Curtis Davis to make him let go of the rope when he had Kelly hanging by his neck. I just wanted to wound him, so I shot him down around his shins. They were burning a cross too. They were trying to make it look like the Klan lynched Kelly."

"You shot him with a damn shotgun!" Bob said. "I heard about it on the radio. They're saying you killed him."

"What? They're saying I *killed* him? I didn't kill him. I *wounded* him. He had Kelly hanging from a tree. Kelly was in front of him, and I had to shoot under Kelly to hit Curtis. I tried to hit him below his knees so it wouldn't be fatal. My shot knocked his legs out from under him, and he let go of the rope. After I shot him, I tried to help him. I elevated his legs to keep him from going into shock. When I raised his feet, one of them nearly came off in my hand."

"He's dead," Bob said. "According to the radio, he died on the way to the hospital."

I began biting a fingernail but made myself stop. "I didn't mean to kill him," I said. "I just didn't want him to kill Kelly."

"I believe you, Phil."

"How can he be dead? Jesus Christ, I was trying *not* to kill him."

"Sounds like you're talking to God, Phil. I'm glad you're a believer again."

"I have to call the hospital and find out what happened."

"The radio said the hospital will do an autopsy to determine the cause of death."

"Yes, sure, I know, but how in the world could he die from getting shot in the shins? It's ridiculous." I heard myself babbling like an idiot.

Bob said, "Before you hang up, Phil, tell me this—are you going to report where Curtis and his gang found Kelly and Glorie last night?"

"It'll be in the paper. I already put a story on our website, but it doesn't tell where Kelly and Glorie got caught. I wanted to run that by you first. So what about it—did you know they were hiding in your trailer?"

Bob hesitated before saying, "I knew Kelly was there. I gave him sanctuary. But I didn't know Glorie had moved in with him. Anyway, they're engaged to be married. They're betrothed to each other. Basically they're already married. It's not as if they're living in sin."

"Isn't it customary to give someone sanctuary in a church rather than a trailer?"

"The trailer is on church property behind Fellowship Hall."

"Does the church own the trailer?"

"I wish you hadn't asked. No, the church does not own it. It's a Shasta, a small vintage trailer that I plan to restore someday. That day may not be too far off. Once you write up that I gave Kelly sanctuary and he had a girl in the trailer with him,

I'll be out of a job. My wife and I might have to move into the trailer and hit the road."

"Didn't you tell me Presbyterians are broad-minded people? Maybe you won't get fired."

"Some of us are more broad-minded than others." He made a long sigh and said, "Oh well, don't worry about me. I'll get another gig somewhere."

I said, "Maybe you should think about making a career change."

"Yeah, maybe I should. You got any openings at the *Gleaner?*" He made a phony laugh. "Just kidding, Phil. Ed would never hire me. I'm too liberal." He laughed again and hung up.

CHAPTER 51

THE FLOWER BED

Angela was in the bedroom, getting dressed.

I was about to call the hospital to confirm that Curtis was dead, but I stopped and thought, if it's on the radio, he *must* be dead.

The old land-line phone on my desk rang. I picked up the receiver, but before I said hello, a woman with a high-pitched country voice screeched in my ear, "Are you the editor of the *Gleaner?*"

It sounded like a crank call. I hate cranks. They give you an earful, then hang up. "Yes, this is Phil Larrison," I said. "What's *your* name, please?" If she wouldn't give me her name, I'd feel justified in hanging up on her.

Silence.

I thought she had hung up. I suspected she may have called from her car to find out if I was at home before she took a chance on throwing a brick through the window. I was about to hang up when she shouted in my ear, "This is Tessie Davis! You killed my son Curtis." She began bawling. "You didn't have to kill him! He never done nothin' to you."

Her tears put me on the defensive. "I didn't want to kill him," I said. "In fact, I didn't even know he was dead until someone told me a little while ago. But he was trying to lynch a young man named Kelly Marcott. Your son had Kelly hanging by his neck from a tree branch. Kelly was twisting in the air, and Curtis was using him as a shield. I had to do something to save Kelly's life, so I shot below his feet. I shot at Curtis's legs to make him let go of the rope. I got him in the shins."

His mother cried, "I know what you done to Curtis. I seen the story you put on the computer. But Curtis didn't deserve it. He wouldn't've killed Kelly Marcott, despite everything that good-for-nothin' done to him."

I said, "I'm sorry about your son, Mrs. Davis, but he definitely was hanging Kelly by the neck."

"No! You don't know what you're talkin' about! Curtis wouldn't've killed him. Curtis was always a good boy, but now he's gone because of you. I don't know how I'm gonna live without 'im." She hesitated as if trying not to cry, but then she sobbed, and a flood of words poured out: "He was all I had. I couldn't have asked for a better son, but that . . . that lousy Kelly Marcott, he comes here from California and acts like he's better than everybody else. You know, he stole Curtis's girlfriend away from him. He filled her head with a bunch of nonsense about how he'd take her to Hollywood and she'd be a movie star. He comes to a small school in southern Indiana, and he acts like he's God's gift to women. Then he gets Glorie pregnant, and she thinks she has to stay with him because of that. He's no good! What kind of a kid kills his own grandfather? You had it in the paper the police say he done it. They been lookin' for him for weeks. They finally got him last evening, thanks to Curtis an' some friends of his. *They* were able to find Kelly Marcott when the whole police force couldn't."

I cut off her rant: "Mrs. Davis, I'll tell you again—I saw Kelly being lynched, and Curtis was doing the lynching."

She screamed at me: "He's still alive! Kelly Marcott didn't get killed. Curtis is the one who got killed."

I said, "Kelly's lucky to be alive after what your son did to him."

"Luck had nothin' to do with it. Curtis wasn't goin' to kill him. If Curtis had wanted to kill him, Kelly Marcott would be dead now. But he's not! That's a fact, and if you'd only just waited another second before shooting my son with a damn shotgun, he would've let Kelly Marcott go. Curtis never killed nobody, but Kelly Marcott sure as hell did. He killed his grandfather. You should be ashamed of yourself for takin' his side."

She stopped to catch her breath, then launched another attack: "Why *are* you on his side? I know why. It's your way of gettin' close to old man Marcott's daughter-in-law. I heard somebody say she's sleepin' with the editor of the *Gleaner*. You're probably after the farm and the money the old man left her. He must've got a pretty penny for that property he sold Walmart. If you can get yourself hitched up with her, you'll be set for life, won't ya?"

I kept my cool. I simply said, "You're barking up the wrong tree, Mrs. Davis."

"Like hell I am," she shouted. "You're just like the old man. I think the only reason that old coot married Marcia Barry was to get his hands on that land on west 50. He prob'ly knew it'd be worth a ton of money someday. He sold it to Walmart after Marcia died." Her voice cracked as she added, "That's what drove us out of business." She sniffled. "I'm sorry," she said. "It hurts to talk about it. She stopped talking for two or three heartbeats, but then the torrent of words resumed: "A fella who was workin' for us quit and got a job at Walmart, and when he came back to pick up his last paycheck, he said my husband and me should sell the hardware store before Walmart puts us out of business. Frank and me should've listened to him. We'd bought the store from Mrs. Barry with money we borrowed from the Meridian County Savings and Loan. After Walmart opened its doors and started takin' our business away, it got harder and harder for us to make our payments. The savings and loan worked with us for a while, but eventually they said they had no choice but to foreclose. That was sixteen years ago, in 1996. We lost everything we had. Two years later I lost my husband too."

She broke down and sobbed. "Poor Frank," she said through her sobs. "He got himself a job at Lowe's over in North Vernon, but he was so down on himself after we went bankrupt that he took to drinkin' again. He had went off the wagon years before, but now he started drinkin' again. It cost him his job. Then he got sick. He had cirrhosis of the liver, and before I knew it, he was dead."

I said, "You've had more than your share of bad luck, Mrs. Davis."

"I don't see it as bad luck," she said. "I see it as a big company beating up on the little guy. I wish a tornado would come and blow Walmart away—not that it would do me any good now. The only thing that would help me now would be if Curtis came back to me."

"I wish he could," I said.

She slammed the receiver down.

The bedroom door opened, and Angela came out. I told her that Curtis had died.

She took my hand and said, "I heard you on the phone. Don't kick yourself, Phil. You kept Kelly from getting killed."

I took a deep breath and said, "I know, but I wish Curtis were still alive too. I'd much rather have seen him go to prison than the cemetery."

• • •

FINALLY I went to work.

The first thing I did was call the hospital to get the official word on the cause of Curtis's death. Doctor Stone had gone off duty in the emergency room, so I called the county coroner's office. When no one answered there or at his home, I caught up with him at his Dairy Queen.

Travis said, "I can't give you any information about it, Phil—not till a pathologist does an autopsy."

"I'm the one who shot him, Travis. I feel bad about it. I wasn't trying to kill him. I shot him in the lower part of his legs to stop him from hanging a seventeen-year-old kid. Why did he die? Did he bleed to death? Did I hit an artery?"

"Uh . . . I didn't know it was you who shot him, Phil. I understand how you must feel. Don't quote me on this, but I suspect it's a case of heart failure brought on by multiple wounds to the forelegs caused by the pellets in a shotgun shell. You probably did hit an artery; however, most people could have survived those wounds, but in this case the victim may have had a congenital heart defect. In other words, he may have had a weak heart. Apparently his condition was never diagnosed, but don't quote me on that. I could be wrong. I'm not a doctor, you know."

"I know, Travis. Thanks for telling me about Curtis. It makes me feel a little bit better."

I updated my online story by adding two sentences: "Curtis Davis died unexpectedly late last night as he was being transported by ambulance to the Meridian County Medical Center. An official who asked not to be identified speculated that Davis may have been born with a weak heart." I wasn't satisfied with the second sentence, but I let it go because just then I got a call from Angela.

"Phil!" she burst out. "Kelly's getting out of jail! Mary Lou Dunn just told me a minute ago. The charges against him have been dropped!"

"How'd that happen?" I said. "Did they hold a hearing without telling you?"

"No. There *was* no hearing. Mary Lou said the prosecuting attorney decided not to prosecute. She said he told her there's not enough evidence against Kelly to get a conviction and he has so many other cases to deal with that he doesn't want to waste time on the ones he can't win. So Kelly's being released, and Mary Lou's coming to pick me up. We're going to the jail to get him."

That's terrific!" I said. "I just wish the prosecutor had reached that decision a few weeks ago. It would have saved you and Kelly a lot of grief."

"No kidding! Oh, there's Mary Lou already. I gotta go." Her voice grew even more excited: "Kelly's free, Phil! It's over! It's all over! Mary Lou said Kelly's in the sheriff's office. I want to get him out of there as soon as I can."

"I'll meet you there." I hung up and went out to my car.

All along I had thought the police would be unable to prove Kelly had murdered Chester, but now that the prosecutor had thrown in the towel I felt a perverse disappointment. It was the same old thing—I was afraid Angela wouldn't need me anymore.

What is it with you, Larrison? She says she loves you. Don't you believe her? Or are you afraid to get married again?

No, I'm not afraid to get married. I'm afraid of another divorce.

You're a jerk, Larrison. She loves you. You love her. So marry her.

I got to the jail before Angela and Mary Lou. I was surprised to see Kelly standing out front by himself. I had expected him to be with Carl. I pulled into one of the parking spaces reserved for cops, and Kelly came running toward me. He got in the car and said, "Let's get outta here."

"Your mom and your lawyer will be here any minute."

"I don't care. I need to find Glorie. Take me to her house, okay?"

When I did not instantly agree, he said, "You don't want to, do you? Okay, I'm outta here." He reached for the door handle.

I grabbed his free arm. He looked as if he wanted to punch me in the face.

"Take it easy," I said.

His chest was heaving.

"What are you so mad about?" I asked him. "You should be happy. The charges against you have been dropped."

"I'll be happy when I know Glorie's all right."

An orange Hummer pulled up next to Kelly's side of the car. I had to bend my head to look up and see who was driving. It was Mary Lou Dunn. She looked like a little girl behind the wheel of the huge SUV. Angela got out and raced around the front of the Hummer to my car.

Kelly's window was closed, so Angela rapped her knuckles on it. Kelly did not look at her. He's still angry with his mom about last night, I said to myself. I turned the key in the ignition two notches and lowered his window from my side of the car. Angela reached inside and wrapped her arms around his neck.

"Let go of me," Kelly grumbled. "I gotta get to Glorie."

"Do you know where she is?" Angela asked.

He leaned across the console between our seats and squirmed out of her stranglehold. "She's at home," he said. "The sheriff said he turned her over to her father this morning."

Angela said, "I wouldn't go to her house if I were you. If her dad's there, there could be trouble. He doesn't like you, Kelly."

"I don't give a shit. I'm worried about Glorie. I have to get her away from him before he does something to her."

Mary Lou said, "Kelly, if you think Glorie's in danger, you should tell the police."

"I told Sheriff Egghead already," he said. "I told him Glorie's father wants her to get rid of our baby. I said he might try to make her get an abortion, or might cause her to have a miscarriage somehow. He might do it himself with a clothes hanger or somethin'." He seemed unsure of himself, then said, "Maybe he's already done it. I gotta get there. I can't sit around like this."

"Phil," Angela said, "would you please take us to Glorie's house so Kelly can make sure she's all right. Mary Lou, I'd appreciate it if you'd tell Sheriff Eggemann where we're going, and why."

"No!" Kelly said. "The cops'll take her father's side. They'll stop me from seeing Glorie."

Mary Lou said, "I'll see if the sheriff will talk to me." She spun around and hurried toward the entrance to the jail.

Kelly hammered the dashboard with the bottom of his fist.

"Hey, easy on the car," I told him.

"Cripes, what are we waiting for? Are you gonna help me save Glorie or not?"

He was seething. He sucked air through his half-open mouth.

Angela put a hand on his shoulder and said, "Calm down, Kelly. We're all just trying to help you."

"Oh yeah? If it wasn't for you, I'd be with Glorie right now."

Angela went rigid. She looked hurt and betrayed. "How can you, Kelly? How can you talk to me like that?"

I wasn't sure how to play this. Kelly was acting like a ticking time bomb. How could he think Glorie's father would let him get anywhere near her? And what was I supposed to do, help him fight his way into the house so he could run away with her again?

Angela said, "Phil, take us to Glorie's house, please. I'd like to talk to her parents."

"Do you think it will do any good?"

"It might be better than if Kelly goes by himself."

"Okay," I said. "Kelly, how about if you sit in the back and let your mother sit up front."

Angela said, "I'll get in the back."

Kelly scooted his seat up and tilted the back of it forward so Angela could climb into the car. He amazed me by apologizing: "I'm sorry, Ma. I shouldn't have blamed you that I'm not with Glorie."

She said, "That's okay, honey. I know you've been under an awful lot of stress."

On our way to Shale Creek Golf Course, I asked Kelly if the prosecuting attorney had talked to him this morning.

"Yeah," he said. "His name is Andy Q. Jackson. The 'Q' sounds good, doesn't it? Maybe I'll change my name to Kelly Q. Marcott."

Angela tapped him on the head and said, "Don't even think about it."

"Just kidding," he said, then resumed answering my question: "Andy Q. wanted to know how my fingerprints got on the bat that killed Grampaw. I told him I fooled around with it a few times hitting hickory nuts in the yard. He took the bat to the forensics guy, and he found some little nicks that were consistent with what I said. So he decided the case against me is weak, and he told the sheriff he should let me go."

"Thank goodness," Angela said. "He sounds like he has a brain in his head."

"I thought so too," Kelly replied, "but he turned out to be another clown. I asked him what's gonna happen to Michael Kovacs and Chad Williams for tryin' to lynch me. He said they told him they were just foolin' around to get even with me for what I wrote in the *Mothermucker*—that the school should drop sports. I told him Michael and Chad didn't do a single thing to stop Curtis from hanging me, but that's not what Andy Q. wanted to hear. I think he wants to drop the whole thing—Grampaw's murder, the attempt to lynch me, the whole deal—like it never happened. What a doofus."

It took fifteen minutes to get to the Shale Creek Golf Course. I felt like an intruder there, just as I did at the Lake of the Woods Club. We wound past the manicured fairways and pricey mansions, most of which were newer and even larger than the ones at the lake.

As we approached the Kovacs house, I noticed that the front lawn now looked scruffy compared with the adjacent ones. The grass was about eight inches high; dandelions were in flower; several crawdad chimneys had popped up on the lawn; and a major eruption of molehills spilled onto both sides of the semicircular driveway.

I parked in front of the front door.

"It doesn't look like anybody's home," Angela said. She didn't sound especially disappointed.

"I'll find out," Kelly said.

He hopped out of the car and ran to the door, where he used the brass knocker. After three knocks, a pause, and three more knocks, he rapped on the door with his knuckles. Then he tried to open the door, but it was locked. He stepped back and yelled at the upstairs windows: "Glorie, can you hear me? Open the door!"

Angela opened the car window and said, "No one's home, Kelly."

"Glorie might be up in her room," Kelly said. "It's on the second floor, and it looks out on the backyard. I'm goin' around back."

The front door opened, and T. Preston Kovacs appeared in a polo shirt with a bright-red collar and thin red-and-white stripes, tan trousers, and red-and-gray running shoes. The trousers fit him perfectly. "You tryin' to break the door down?" he said to Kelly.

"I'd like to talk to Glorie," Kelly said.

"She's not here."

"Where is she?"

"I don't know."

The words sounded dismissive, which I could see made Kelly mad. He shouted past T. Preston into the house: "Glorie! C'mere. I'm outta jail. They dropped the charges against me."

T. Preston tried to shut the door, but Kelly threw his shoulder against it and bulled his way inside.

Angela scrambled out of the car screaming, "Kelly, stop it!"

I went after her, and we raced each other to the foyer, where we interposed ourselves between Kelly and Glorie's father.

Kelly tried to go around us to the stairs, but Angela grabbed one of his wrists with both of her hands and wouldn't let go. In a breathless whisper she said, "Mr. Kovacs, is your wife here?"

T. Preston put his hands on his hips and said, "No."

"Would you tell me where she is, please."

"I don't know where she is."

Kelly said, "That's a crock."

"Be quiet, Kelly," Angela said. She looked at T. Preston again. "When will Mae be back?"

"She didn't say. I imagine she'll come home when she maxes out her credit card." He held his head high. Haughty. Superior.

Kelly said, "Is Glorie with her, or is Glorie here with you?"

"That's none of your business. I don't want her to see you again."

"That's not up to you," Kelly said. "We're engaged to be married, and you're not gonna stop us."

A smug grin played on T. Preston's slightly parted lips. "We'll see about that," he replied.

Kelly raved on: "You better not try to make her get an abortion. And your Neanderthal son better not hit her again to make her have a miscarriage. Only Glorie has the right to end her pregnancy, and she doesn't want to end it."

T. Preston took two steps toward Kelly and got right in his face. "Get out of my house!" he said with a snarl. When Kelly didn't budge, T. Preston opened the drawer in a small table in the foyer and took out a handgun with a long barrel. It looked like a replica of Wyatt Earp's Buntline Special. "I'll tell you one more time," he said to Kelly. "Get out of my house!"

Angela quickly stepped between them and said, "Let's go, Kelly." She spread her arms and tried to back him toward the door.

Kelly said, "I'm not going till I find out where Glorie is."

T. Preston raised his gun and pointed it at Kelly's head. "You're trespassing, young man," he said. "Get out of my house. I'm not going to tell you again."

From behind I put my arms around Kelly's arms and chest and spun him toward the door.

I was surprised at how light he was—he must have been going hungry. When we got outside, I used my excess weight to hold him against the side of my car.

T. Preston began shooting his gun up in the air. I wondered if he had cracked up. I hoped none of his bullets came down on us.

"Come on, Phil," Angela said. "Let's get out of here."

T. Preston emptied his gun. Then he stared at us with contempt and went back inside and locked the door.

I relaxed my grip on Kelly, and he broke free "Glorie!" he shouted at the top of his voice. "Where are you? Make a noise! Break something!"

Angela said, "Let's go, Kelly. Mr. Kovacs might be calling the police. Let's get out of here."

He gritted his teeth and said, "I'm not going without Glorie!" He looked like a wild thing.

I said, "Kelly, if Glorie's in the house, she would have been screaming her head off by now."

"Unless she can't scream!" he said. "Maybe she's tied up and gagged. Maybe she's been drugged."

I picked him up like a sack of potatoes and carried him over my shoulder. I was surprised I could do it. "How much do you weigh?" I asked. "One-thirty? One-forty?"

"How much do *you* weigh?" he countered. "Two-ninety? Three hundred?"

Angela helped me wrestle Kelly into the backseat, where she sat beside him with both arms around his neck so he wouldn't escape.

"Would you please stop choking me, Ma?" he asked.

"Yes," Angela said, "if you promise you won't run away."

"Stop treating me like a kid."

Angela laughed. Then she sniffed two times and said, "Whew, Kelly, you need to do something about your breath."

"You got any mouthwash on you?"

As we went around the first bend in the road, Kelly said, "Something's wrong back there. I *know* it. I can *feel* it! I gotta go back."

Angela said, "You can't, honey. Glorie's father is crazy. He'll kill you."

"I'm afraid he's gonna kill our baby."

I didn't say anything. I kept driving.

Kelly went on: "Maybe Glorie's been hurt. Maybe that's why she didn't scream for help. And there's another garage in the backyard. It's got old cars in it—antiques. She could be tied up in one of them. We wouldn't have heard her if she did scream"

"What's your plan?" I said. "Do you think you can break into the house and the garage in broad daylight? Don't you think Glorie's father will hear you?"

Angela said, "Why don't we tell the police, Kelly. We'll tell them how he threatened you with a gun. Let *them* look for Glorie."

"There's no time!" he said. "He might be doing an abortion on her right now."

He lunged over the console between the two front seats and tried to turn off the engine. I grabbed his wrist, and we swerved in front of an oncoming car. The elderly man at the wheel jerked his car to the right and plowed into a large bed of flowers on someone's picture-perfect lawn. Belatedly he blasted his horn at me, and he and the woman next to him gave us dirty looks as we drove past.

Angela was tearing into Kelly: "Dammit, Kelly, no more! Grow up before you get us all killed!"

I didn't want to stop, but I knew I had to. I had caused property damage. Maybe the couple in the car that I had run off the road could identify me. Or maybe they had the presence of mind to get my license-plate number. The accident would be in the sheriff's log in tomorrow's *Gleaner.*

I drove about fifty feet and stopped. "Get out if you want to, Kelly," I said. "Do what you have to do."

"I'm sorry," he said to us. "Thanks, Phil. Don't worry, Ma. I'll be all right."

Angela was shaking her head. "I love you, Kelly," she murmured. "Why don't we just go to the sheriff?"

"I told you why. There may not be enough time."

"Please be careful, Kelly," she said.

He got out and ran across the damaged lawn toward the fairway behind the houses.

"I'm worried, Phil," Angela said.

"He's taking a risk," I said, "but it's his life. Think how he'd feel if something really bad happened to Glorie, and he hadn't tried to help her."

"I know," she said. "He'd hate me. And you."

I turned my car around and returned to the flower bed. The other car was stuck in black potting soil, and its churning wheels were chewing up the tulips and bedding plants more and more.

I knew my insurance card said that I shouldn't admit responsibility after an accident, but I got out of the car and apologized to the frantic couple in the other car. The owners of the flower bed came out of the house, and I apologized to them too. I gave both couples my name and phone number.

As we drove away, Angela insisted on paying for all the damage that Kelly had caused.

"At least we didn't kill the people in the other car," I said.

"That's looking at the bright side," she said.

CHAPTER 52

AN UNLUCKY LIFE

WHEN I got back to my office, it was the middle of the afternoon, and my boss descended on me like a ton of bricks. "Where have you been?" he shouted as if I had been gone a month.

"Working, Ed. Always working."

"On what?"

"You'd know if you read the online edition of your paper."

"How many online subscribers do we have? We're losing our regular subscribers to it. The damn Internet's gonna put me out of business."

"So tell the advertising department to sell some online ads."

He humphed and retreated to his office.

I wanted to get the latest from Carl, so I phoned the jail and learned he was on break at Mackey's. I needed a cup of coffee, so I ran over there.

Only three customers were in the restaurant, and Carl was one of them. He was not sitting in his "private booth." He was at a table on the opposite side of the jukebox and the kitchen door. His regular spot was occupied by a man and a woman I had never seen before. They leaned toward each other and spoke too softly to be heard.

"Howdy, Phil," he said. "Long time no see."

"Right, it's been about twelve hours now." I sat down across from him at his table and said, "I understand Curtis Davis died last night. The Reverend Mr. Harnish told me. He said he heard it on the radio."

Carl was eating a slice of pumpkin pie with a twirl of whipped cream on top. He swallowed what was in his mouth and said, "Yes, Curtis died on his way to the hospital. He was pronounced dead shortly after the ambulance got him there. The hospital notified the radio stations. They told you too, didn't they?"

"The hospital probably sent me an email," I said. "I was out of the office till a few minutes ago. Then I tracked you down and came over here."

"I see. Well, I'm sorry your competitors beat you." He kept a straight face for a second or two, then cracked a tired smile.

I got even with him by saying, "I'm glad the charges against Kelly have been dropped."

"So that's why you're here. You want to rub my nose in it."

"You know I wouldn't do that, Carl."

"Do I?"

"Yes, or at least you should." I looked around for a waitress. "Is it self-service today?"

"Hold your horses," Carl said. "She must be in the restroom."

"Oh, okay. I guess I've got enough caffeine in my system." *Refocus*, I said to myself. I looked Carl in the eyes and said, "Would you like to make a statement about the decision to drop the charges against Kelly?"

"No," he said.

"How do you feel about it?"

"What part of my last answer did you not understand?"

"I take it you're not too thrilled with the prosecutor's decision not to prosecute."

"I respect the decision. Case closed. Any other questions?"

"Yes. On a different subject. What's going to happen to Michael Kovacs and Chad Williams? When will their initial hearings be held?"

Carl drew himself up and said, "There will be no hearings. Both young men have been released from jail."

"Are you kidding me, Carl? They kidnapped Kelly and tried to lynch him."

"Let me answer your last question: "No. I'm not kidding.""

"When were they released?"

"At 12:15 p.m. today the Kovacs boy was released to his father. At 1:10 p.m. the Williams boy was released to his grandmother."

"Shouldn't there have been a hearing first?"

"I have no comment on that."

"Come on, Carl! Tell me what you think."

"I'm not a judge. I respect Judge Maxwell's decision."

"Did the prosecutor influence that decision?"

"I suggest you ask Judge Maxwell and Prosecuting Attorney Jackson."

"Did either one of them talk to you about it?"

He put his elbows on the table and leaned toward me. "Phil," he said, "I know you want me to cast aspersions on the judge and the prosecuting attorney. I will not do that, so ask me another question or allow me to eat my pie in peace."

I said, "All right, Carl, but it sounds to me like a cover-up— or if not a cover-up, then favoritism for some reason or other. If nothing else, there should have been an initial hearing. Don't you think so?"

I didn't expect an answer to this question, and I didn't get one. Instead Carl said, "Let me ask you something, Phil. I had a call from T. Preston Kovacs a little while ago. Actually it was a complaint. What were you and Kelly Marcott and his mother doing at T. Preston's house today?"

"Kelly was trying to find his girlfriend, Glorie. He wanted to make sure she was okay."

"Was she?"

"I don't know. I didn't get to talk to her."

"Was she there?"

"I can't say for sure. It seemed as though the only person at home was her father, and he said Glorie and her mother were out and he didn't know where they went. Kelly said he thought the guy was lying. Kelly was sure Glorie was there, and he thought she was being prevented from coming to the door."

"Mr. Kovacs said you forced your way in."

"I did not force my way in, Sheriff."

"Did Kelly force *his* way in?"

"No, the door was swinging shut. Kelly stopped it from closing and stepped inside."

"Hmm, who caused the door to start swinging shut?"

"I didn't see who did that, Carl."

"Could it have been Mr. Kovacs?"

"I suppose so, or maybe the wind blew it."

"Mr. Kovacs said the three of you entered his house without permission."

I said, "Kelly was worried about Glorie. He went in and yelled her name. Kelly's mother and I went in to try to keep him out of trouble."

"Where's Kelly now?" Carl asked.

I said, "I don't know," which was true in the sense that I did not know his exact location at that particular moment.

"So Kelly went inside and called Glorie's name. Did she answer him?"

"No. Kelly started to go upstairs to find her, but his mom stopped him. Mr. Kovacs then told him he didn't want Glorie to see him anymore. This led to an argument in which Kelly accused Kovacs of trying to force Glorie to get an abortion because he didn't like it that she was carrying Kelly's child. Kelly also accused Kovacs's son, Michael, of trying to make Glorie have a miscarriage. At that point T. Preston blew up. He told Kelly to get out of his house, and when Kelly didn't leave, Kovacs took a handgun out of a cabinet in the foyer and pointed it at Kelly's head. Angela jumped in front of Kelly. I grabbed Kelly, and Angela helped me get him outside."

Carl said, "Your friend Kelly lives on the edge, doesn't he? Does he have a death wish?"

"Not at all," I said. "He's all about life."

"If you say so."

"There's something else I want to tell you about, Carl. I had a call from Curtis Davis's mother this morning. As you might expect, she was upset with me for shooting her son. I told her I hadn't meant to kill him. Then I listened to her vent. It went on for quite a while."

Carl said, "I know what you mean. I talked to her at the hospital today—or rather, I *listened* to her. She was extremely distraught." He gulped down some coffee, then said, "I feel sorry for Tessie. She's had a hard, unlucky life." His eyes looked like a sad hound dog's. "That was one of the worst things I ever had to do—listen to a mother tell me how she learned her son was dead when the hospital called her in the middle of the night. It was as bad as anything I ever went through in Vietnam."

I said, "It was nice of you to listen to her, Carl."

"Thanks," he said. "I let her talk. She settled down after a while and told me she's going to leave the bedroom just the way it was last night when Curtis 'passed,' as she put it." His eyes met mine. "You're the word expert, Phil. Why don't we say 'passed away' anymore?"

"I still do," I said.

The kitchen door swung open, and a heavyset waitress came out. She was probably in her fifties, and she had perfectly white hair. "What can I get for ya, Phil?" she asked me.

"Hi, Estelle," I said. "I'll have a cup of coffee—if it's fresh."

"It's fresh. I just made it yesterday." She patted me on the back, then stood next to me chewing gum while she scribbled my order on her pad.

Carl propped an elbow on the table and rested his chin on his fist. "Tessie told me something that touched my heart," he said. "She told me she felt bad that Curtis didn't have a room of his own. She said she and Curtis lost their home after her husband died, and since then they'd been sharing a one-bedroom apartment with subsidized rent. She and Curtis slept in the same room. She said, and I quote, 'We've got two single beds. Only they're not really beds. Each of us sleeps on a mattress on the floor.' She took pains to explain that the mattresses are on opposite sides of the room, as far apart as they can be without being right up against the walls. She said it made her feel terrible that she couldn't provide Curtis with a room of his own. She said she offered to sleep in the living room and let him have the bedroom, but he wouldn't let her do that because he knew she didn't want to mess up the sofa with sheets and blankets every night. 'He was a good son,' she said. 'Why did God let him be taken from me?' "

As Carl stood up to leave, he said, "Tessie and Curtis were very close. I hope she can deal with this latest problem." He took a five-dollar bill out of his wallet and said, "Your coffee's on me, Phil."

"Thanks, Sheriff," I said. "The next round is on me."

I began to see Curtis in a better light. I told myself if he went to Chester's house to steal a "treasure," he had not done it for himself. He had done it to help his mother get back on her feet. Perhaps he rationalized that the treasure rightfully belonged to her because Chester had helped put her store out of business by selling land to Walmart. Maybe Curtis killed Chester in self-defense when Chester caught him searching his house.

Okay, say Curtis acted in self-defense. So what? He had no right to be in Chester's house. He had no right to Chester's "treasure." What's more, Chester had every right to sell a piece of property to Walmart. Curtis must have hated Chester. And after Kelly took Glorie away from him and got her pregnant, he must have hated Kelly even more. The Marcotts must have seemed like mortal enemies to the Davises. Perhaps Curtis was out of his mind with hatred.

I was all but convinced that Curtis had killed Chester—he certainly had a motive—but was I right, and if so, how could I prove it?

What if a "treasure" and some documents with Chester's name on them would be found under Curtis's mattress? That would prove Curtis killed Chester, wouldn't it?

Forget it, Larrison. It's not going to happen. Chester's treasure was the horde of gold coins that fell out of the ceiling when the militia shot up the living room.

And does it even matter if Curtis killed Chester? Curtis is dead. You killed him. If you were to prove that he killed Chester, who would suffer? Only his mother. Would that be fair? Hasn't she suffered enough? So give it a rest, Larrison. Quit playing detective.

CHAPTER 53

THE WHIPPOORWILL

I WENT home that evening at six o'clock, and when I stepped into my apartment, I was surprised to see a woman sitting on the sofa next to Angela. It took a second for me to recognize Mae Kovacs.

She had been crying, and she looked tired and drawn. Her hair was disheveled and no longer cinnamon. It was brunette, a better match for the darkish color of her eyes.

"Hi, Mae," I said. "What brings you here?"

"I left my husband," she replied. "Glorie and Kelly brought me here. I told them not to, but they wouldn't listen. I'm sorry to impose on you."

"You're not imposing."

Angela put a hand on hers. "See, I told you Phil wouldn't mind."

"Where are Glorie and Kelly?" I asked.

"They went to get pizza," Angela said.

"That's good. I'm starving."

Mae said, "I should go. This isn't your problem."

"Where will you go?" Angela asked.

"To my parents. They live in Colorado. I can stay at a motel tonight. Then Glorie and I can go to the airport in the morning."

Tears ran down her cheeks and dripped onto her blouse. "I'm a mess," she said. "I got all hot and sweaty today." Gently she rubbed her breastbone up and down. She wasn't wearing a bra, and the upper part of her chest was black and blue.

"That's a nasty bruise you've got," I said. "What happened?"

She covered herself up and said, "My husband hit me. I had told him I want a divorce and I want to take Glorie with me because of the way he's been treating her. This morning he locked her in the attic. It's not really an attic. It's a second-floor room over the garage that's attached to the house. He wouldn't let Glorie eat breakfast. He put a padlock on the door and locked her in there. He told me he was going to starve her unborn child—he called it her 'damn bastard.' He said he was going to starve it to death. I told him he's crazy. He made a fist and hit me with his bare knuckles as hard as he could, right here on my breastbone. It knocked me down. It hurt."

"Is your sternum broken,?" I asked.

"I don't know. I hope not."

Angela said, "Phil, may I borrow your car? I'll take Mae to the emergency room and have it looked at. You stay here and have pizza with Kelly and Glorie, okay?"

Mae shook her head. "No. I'll be all right. It's not the first time he's punched me."

"That's terrible!" Angela said. "You ought to have him arrested."

"I should have left him years ago, but I was always afraid to. I'm still afraid. I'm afraid of him right this minute. If he finds out I'm here, I'm afraid of what he might do to the two of you, too. The kids shouldn't have brought me here." She seemed out of breath. She rubbed her sternum again.

"Would you like a glass of water?" I asked.

"Do you have anything stronger?"

"I've got some Scotch. And a few bottles of beer."

"Scotch sounds good."

"How would you like it?" I asked.

"Straight, please."

While I was in the kitchen, I heard Angela ask her, "How did you and Glorie get away from your husband?"

"Thanks to Kelly," Mae replied. "He was a godsend. He saved us."

I hurried back with her drink, which filled about two-thirds of a juice glass. She downed half of it in one gulp and launched into her story: "After Ted locked up Glorie, somebody called to tell us Michael was being released from the juvenile detention center and we could come and get him. They said no charges were going to be filed. Ted and I already knew Michael was under arrest because they called in the middle of the night to tell us, but they said we couldn't see him till morning. So Ted and his lawyer went to see Michael as soon as they could this morning, and then, this afternoon, when they told us Michael was about to be released, Ted wanted to go and get him right away, but he didn't want me to go with him. I guess he was afraid I'd tell the police how he punched me. And he probably thought if he left me at home I'd find a way to break the padlock and let Glorie out of the attic, so he practically dragged me upstairs and locked me in the attic with her."

Mae finished her drink, and I asked if she'd like another one.

"Yes I would," she said.

Angela glanced at me and rolled her eyes.

This time I fetched my half-empty bottle of Johnny Walker Black Label from the kitchen. I filled her glass two-thirds of the way up and set the bottle on the coffee table. Mae seemed to have forgotten she hadn't finished her story, so I asked her, "How did Kelly rescue you and Glorie?"

She took another swig of Scotch and said, "There's a window in the attic. It's above the doors—the two doors for the cars. We watched Ted drive away, and then we heard Kelly calling Glorie. He was in the backyard. I guess he waited till Ted left. He must've been hiding somewhere—he was prob'ly behind the rose bushes alongside the big garage. I helped Glorie get the attic window open. It's hard to open because we hardly ever open it. We had to push the window up together. Then we started yelling, 'Kelly! Kelly!' He came running around the back of the house and saw us at the window. Glorie told him there was a key to the front door under a big rock. He went and got it and let himself into the house, but first I told him there's a worktable in the basement with lots of tools. Kelly found a screwdriver. He came upstairs and used it to pry off the padlock. He damaged the door doing it. Ted's gonna throw a fit when he sees it, but I don't care. I won't be there to hear him and get beat on again."

She was starting to sound a little woozy, but she kept chattering: "We—Glorie and me—we stuffed some clothes in our suitcases as fast as we could, and we got out of the house. Kelly put the key back under the rock, right where he found it. He said he didn't want Glorie's father to know he knew where it was now in case he ever had to do it again. I told him he wouldn't have to do it again because Glorie and I won't be here anymore. He said he didn't want Glorie to go anywhere without him. I said, 'We're goin' to Colorado,' and he said, 'Then I'm goin' with you.' I told him he had to ask his mother if he could go. He said no, he didn't have to, because you'd understand. But he said he'd have to get some things at home but you probably wouldn't be there because you were staying here with Phil. We got in Glorie's car and came here. Kelly drove. He drove like a wild man. My heart was in my throat all the way. Kelly said he was afraid we'd pass Glorie's father and Michael on their way home from the jail. He said Glorie's car is the only yellow Beetle in Campbellsville, so it sticks out. He said we needed to get off the main highway. He took side streets, and he parked in the alley out back here."

Angela said, "Kelly and I have to talk about this Colorado thing."

"I know," Mae said. "That's what I told him." She finished her drink and set her glass on the very edge of the table. She rubbed the black-and-blue bruise on her chest again and, without realizing it, unfastened the top two buttons of her blouse. "You know what," she went on. "For the first time in years I feel like I'm free. It feels like the sun just came out from behind a big black cloud."

Angela said, "You'd better button up, Mae, or the sun won't be the only thing coming out."

Mae looked down and said, "Oh gosh, I'm coming apart." She made a saucy smile as she refastened the buttons.

Angela said, "If you and Glorie move to Colorado, what about Michael? Won't you miss him?"

"No," she chirped.

"You won't? He's your son. I missed Kelly something awful after I sent him here to live with his grandfather."

"Michael's not my real son," Mae said.

Angela looked puzzled. "I'm sorry," she said. "Are you saying your husband had a previous marriage?"

"No," Mae said. "He had an affair with a woman at work a few years after he married me. Ted told me the pregnancy was an accident. Her contraceptive didn't work. She was going to get an abortion supposedly, but Ted told her he'd take the kid if it was a boy. He wanted a son, and I really didn't want more kids."

She reached for her glass and seemed to realize it was empty. She was beginning to drift off. Her eyes blinked as she turned from Angela to me. "Ted didn't want to wait and take a chance that I might never have a boy," she said. "He had a goofy idea. He thought because our first child was a girl, all the rest of our kids were likely to be girls too. He said he knew several couples who that happened to—they had all girls, no boys. He told his bitch to get a sonogram, and if it turned out to be a boy, he'd raise him. He offered to cover all her expenses. Plus he offered to give her $10,000 for her time and trouble. The tramp said she wanted $25,000, and Ted gave it to her, but guess what—"

The back door opened, and Glorie and Kelly entered the kitchen laughing and chattering.

Mae finished her story in a hasty whisper: "Ted made *me* raise Michael as if he was my kid."

Kelly carried two boxes of pizza into the living room. "Why isn't the TV on?" he said.

Glorie laughed and said, "Why is it so quiet in here?"

"Because we're starving," I said. "We're too weak to talk."

I turned on the TV, but there was nothing good on, so I turned it off.

We ate in the living room. Angela, Mae, and I had a bottle of Chianti; Kelly had a can of beer; and Glorie said she wasn't drinking alcohol since she was pregnant. Mae repeated her plan to go to Colorado, and this generated a debate about whether she and Glorie should go back to the Kovacs house for the rest of their clothes or just take what they had thrown into the car and buy whatever else they needed in Boulder.

Angela said, "If I ever get the money that Kelly's grandfather left me, we can all live together in California. Mae and I can be grandmothers and spoil Glorie and Kelly's baby while they finish high school and go to college."

I thought Angela was joking, but I wasn't sure.

"What about Phil?" Kelly asked. "Does he get to come too?"

"No thanks," I said. "It sounds too much like a commune."

"What's wrong with that?" Kelly cracked.

Glorie said, "I don't want to live in a commune. I'd rather live in Santa Barbara."

Mae said, "Chester Marcott left you a lot of money, didn't he, Angela?"

"So I'm told," Angela admitted, "but I haven't seen much of it yet."

"But you're not his daughter, are you?"

"No, daughter-in-law. I married his only child, Dale, but we got divorced. I was surprised when I learned what was in Chester's will."

"Kelly is Dale's son, isn't he?" Mae asked her.

"That's right."

"And Dale was killed in that . . . that crazy gunfight on Chester's farm."

"Yes," Angela said, "but the strange thing is Chester left me most of his estate while Dale was still alive."

"That's *very* strange, but I say good for you."

"Some of that money is going to put Kelly through college."

"Southern Cal here I come," Kelly said.

"Mrs. Marcott," Glorie said, "why do you think Chester left it to you instead of his own son?"

Angela replied, "Hardly a day goes by that I don't ask myself that question."

When Angela left the question hanging, Kelly said, "So what's the answer?"

She looked at him fondly. "I think Chester wanted to make sure some of his money would be used for your education. I hate to say it, but I don't think he trusted your father to respect his wishes. I think he trusted me more than him. But I don't know. Your granddad never told me what he had in mind, and there were no instructions for me in his will. The only other person he left anything to was Dicey Cockerham. He left her his cabin at the Lake of the Woods Club and a few other things—a shotgun, a couple of fishing rods, and some antiques. The antiques got broken when he was killed."

I chimed in with, "Maybe someday Chester would have told you his final wishes, if he hadn't been murdered."

"Maybe so," Angela said. "Maybe so."

• • •

MAE was sitting on the sofa with her head back and her mouth open, snoring softly. Glorie was sleeping on her side under a blue woolen blanket, with her head on her mother's lap. The TV was still on, but I had turned the sound down a few decibels. Angela, Kelly, and I were in the kitchen discussing the screwed-up Kovacs family. The consensus of opinion was that Glorie was the only normal one in the bunch. The incessant canned laughter on the TV provided a kind of white noise that canceled out our voices and kept Mae and Glorie from waking up.

Angela said, "Do you think Mae's husband will follow them to Colorado? He probably knows that's where her parents live."

"I think he will," I said.

"So do I," said Angela.

"I'll be with Glorie and Mae," Kelly said. "I'll protect them."

He had lost so much weight that he didn't look capable of protecting anyone, including himself. His face was pale. His hair was too long. He looked like a starving artist rather than a bodyguard.

Angela said, "I want you to stay here with me, Kelly. I want you to finish your junior year. I don't want you to have to repeat it."

"What if the principal says I can't go back to school?"

"We'll cross that bridge when we come to it."

I said, "I think they'll take you back. The charges against you have been dropped. They can't keep you out anymore. You're entitled to an education. "

"I'll go to school in Boulder," he said. "I want to be with Glorie."

Glorie appeared in the kitchen archway. "I want to be with you too, Kelly," she said. Her voice was soft, worried, tender. She came to the table and put a hand on his shoulder.

Kelly put an arm around her waist. "What about your mom? What's she gonna say?"

"It doesn't matter," Glorie said. "She's got her life, I've got mine, and I've got yours and our baby's to think about. We belong together."

Angela's eyes gleamed with tears. She dabbed them with a brown napkin from Papa John's and said, "You can stay here, Glorie, if you want to, but I wonder if your father can force you to live with him."

I said, "I doubt it, not when a judge hears he threatened to starve her to kill her baby."

"He can deny it," Kelly said.

"Yes, he can deny it," I said, "but would the judge believe him?"

"I couldn't make up a story like that," Glorie said. "How could I? I can hardly believe my father would do something like that to me."

Sleepy-eyed and yawning, Mae staggered into the kitchen and said, "Don't worry about what your father says, Glorie. I've kept a journal. It's full of things he's done to me and, now, what he wants to do to you."

"Ma," Kelly said, "I want to talk to our lawyer. I want to ask her if she can get a judge to let Glorie and me get married. I know we're still seventeen, but since she's pregnant and we both want to, maybe we'll be allowed to get married."

Mae said, "You can tell the lawyer you have my permission to get married."

"I will," Kelly said.

"You know what," Mae said. "I changed my mind. I'm not going to Colorado. Why should I run away from Ted? I'll stay here and fight him. I'll tell the judge you have my permission to get married."

Glorie ran to her mother, and they wrapped their arms around each other. "I love you, Mom," Glorie said, and they squeezed each other with all their might.

• • •

IN the middle of the night, a noise in the backyard woke me out of a sound sleep. I was in bed with Angela, and the loud, repetitive call of a whippoorwill came through the window, which was open a crack.

Whippoor*will*, whippoor*will*, whippoor*will*. . . .

The bird was close enough to the window for me to hear the sharp click it made after each call.

Angela heard it too. Her head rose, and she stared at the window. Then she went back to sleep. I figured she heard whippoorwills every night at the farm Chester had given her.

Whippoor*will*, whippoor*will*, whippoor*will*. . . .

The bedroom door was closed. Kelly was sleeping on the sofa in the living room. Mae and Glorie had gone to a motel out near I-65. I had offered to let them have the bedroom, but Mae said she didn't want to put us out anymore than she already had.

I was wide awake. Moonlight filtered through the tree in the yard, and I stared at the shadows of leaves on the wall. I happened to remember the story Angela had told me about Dale Marcott's search for something under the stairway in Chester's house. I wondered why it had popped into my head. At first I thought I may have heard a whippoorwill when Angela first told me the story, but then I remembered that just a few hours ago she told Mae that Chester had left her most of his estate instead of passing it on to his son. Neither Angela nor I knew what Dale was looking for in the secret compartment under the stairs. Angela had told me that whatever it was, Dale said it belonged to him rather than Chester. I suspected Dale had been looking for the gold that had been on the militia's airplane. Perhaps Dale had found the gold after the plane crashed and Chester had taken it away from him. Then years later, after Chester was killed, Dale wanted it back.

This possible scenario did not put Chester in the best light. From what I had heard about him, Chester was a good, honest man. He was obviously not greedy. He gave gold coins worth thousands of dollars to Lila Pluckett, who was the widow of Abner Richards and the mother of Andreas Pluckett by her second husband. It seemed to me that the money Chester gave her was most likely intended to make up for, in a small way, the lynching of her first husband. If so, the gift suggested that Chester's father had been involved in the lynching. Furthermore, if Chester was a good, honest man, how could he have kept a fortune in gold that did not belong to him? He should have tried to find out who the rightful owner was so he could return it to him. If he was afraid that some people might wonder how he had acquired the gold, he could have returned it anonymously.

There was an even bigger problem: the two bullet holes in the pilot's head. Who shot him? "Colonel" Bickerstaff, the leader of the militia that invaded Angela's home, blamed the killing on Dale, but Dale blamed it on Chester. I wanted to think Dale was the murderer, but maybe Chester was. Perhaps, as Bickerstaff had said, Chester wasn't as good a man as people thought he was.

No, Larrison. You have no evidence that Chester murdered the pilot. The fact that Dale, years later, came home looking for something under the stairway—something valuable that he still considered his—suggested that *he* was the one who had found the gold and shot the pilot. Perhaps Chester was trying to protect him by burying the plane and the pilot's body. He probably thought he had to bury it to prevent anyone who knew about the flight from finding the plane and discovering that the pilot had been shot in the head and the gold had been stolen.

In keeping the gold, Chester certainly did the wrong thing. True, he gave some of it to Lila Pluckett, which seemed like a good thing to do; however, the gold was not his to give. As far as I knew, the only other thing Chester did with the gold was give a couple of gold pieces to Kelly each year, but those gifts benefited his own grandchild. There wasn't much virtue in that.

Okay, Larrison, maybe Chester wasn't a saint, but you don't have to consign him to hell. True, Chester did not report the murder of the pilot. True, he buried the plane. True, he kept the gold. True, the only punishment he gave Dale was to cut him out of his will. That gesture did not make Chester a great man, but at least it showed he did not condone what Dale had done.

Nor did he condone what the Klan had done.

My brain was buzzing. I couldn't get back to sleep. I got up and went to the bathroom.

Standing over the toilet, I thought of another questionable aspect of Chester's life: his family's connection to the Ku Klux Klan.

Oh hell, did I really want to go there?

Chester's father had been in the Klan. Chester took away the box of Klan photos that Kelly had found in the attic, most likely because he didn't want Kelly to publish them in *Mothermucker*. Later Kelly found another box of photos under the floor of

Chester's bedroom, and one of these showed Chester in a cutesy little Klan robe when he was just a few years old. The first box had not yet resurfaced, which led me to wonder if Chester had destroyed the photos to hide the fact that his father had been in the Klan and may even have helped lynch Abner Richards.

As far as I knew, Chester himself did not join the Klan when he grew up. The gold he gave Lila Richards Pluckett was probably meant to atone for the lynching of her first husband. But Chester was not willing to expose old-time members of the Klan, especially his father. That was understandable—family comes first—but I still considered it a strike against him.

I went back to bed.

The whippoorwill was still calling.

I relaxed into the mattress.

I wished I could tie up everything about Chester and the Klan in a neat little package, but there were some things that I wasn't sure of and some other things that I *was* sure of but couldn't prove.

I remembered a term I had learned in an English class at DePauw: "negative capability," the ability to remain in doubt. That's what I needed, more of that.

Oh well, the bottom line was Chester may have tried to make up for some of the things that his father and Dale had done; however, Chester wasn't perfect. But then who is?

CHAPTER 54

A SPECIAL NIGHT

LATER that morning Mae called up to say she had filed for divorce against her husband. To celebrate she invited Angela, Kelly, and me to have lunch with her and Glorie at Cracker Barrel. The restaurant was near the motel where they were staying.

We found them waiting for us on the front porch. They were the only persons on the white rocking chairs, which stretched the length of the long porch.

Mae said, "Glorie and I are going to look at apartments this afternoon."

Kelly said, "Why don't you stay with us at Grampaw's house? There's tons of room, and we'd all be together."

"Oh, Kelly, we couldn't do that," Mae said. "It would be asking way too much."

"No it wouldn't," he insisted. "It'd be great!"

"Don't bet on it," I said. "That house is a magnet for trouble." I had a second reason for throwing cold water on Kelly's idea: I wouldn't feel right sleeping with Angela if Mae, Glorie, and Kelly were sharing the house with us.

"I'm hungry," Angela said. "Let's eat."

We waited in line in the gift shop until we were seated. Then, as we were looking at our menus, a tall elderly man in a suit walked up to our table and said, "Good afternoon, Mr. Larrison. It's nice to see you again."

He was Henry Barker. I thought about acting as if I didn't recognize him, though I had interviewed him just a few weeks ago, but I figured he would see through the act and I would appear rude.

"Hello, Mr. Barker," I said in as neutral a tone as possible. "How are you?"

"I'm very well, thank you." His voice was strong and confident.

I could see that Kelly recognized Barker's name by the way he stiffened ever so slightly. I wondered how long it would take him to explode, but for now he just sat there tight-lipped, staring at our overly polite visitor.

Barker said, "I've been enjoying reading about your exploits in the *Gleaner*, Mr. Larrison."

"I'm glad to hear that," I replied.

"Very interesting articles."

"Thank you."

Perhaps thinking I sounded curt, Mae joined the conversation by saying, "And what do you do, Mr. Barker?"

He chuckled in a self-effacing way and said, "Oh, these days I do as little as possible. I piddle around the yard mostly. And I like to read. I try to keep my brain active. At my age, it needs all the exercise it can get."

"You make it sound as if you're an old man," Mae said. "You don't look very old to me."

He tossed his head back and laughed. "You just made my day, my dear. I'm old enough to be your great-grandfather," he said. "Maybe great-great."

Mae said, "Really? I find that hard to believe."

Kelly's legs were jiggling up and down. I had a feeling that Barker knew who Kelly was and discerned that he was about to explode. Still chuckling, he turned to me and said, "Well, I won't take up anymore of your time, Mr. Larrison. I just wanted to say hello. Smiling, he scanned our five faces, then drifted away between the crowded tables.

His exaggerated politeness had shamed me, but I didn't care. I did not respect him, and I did not want to act as though I did. Even so, I would have behaved better if Kelly hadn't been sitting next to me. I had been more interested in keeping Kelly's esteem than in being nice to Barker.

Kelly was fuming. I expected a tirade any second. He would jump up and march across the room and shout curses in Barker's face. He'd accuse him of lynching Abner Richards behind the courthouse. He'd say Barker should have been in prison since 1936. I wondered if Barker was carrying a gun. Within the next minute or two, Kelly might be dead.

Angela leaned over the table and whispered to me, "Who is that guy?"

I whispered back, "He's the exalted cyclops of the Meridian County klavern of the Ku Klux Klan."

"Yeah," Kelly said in a louder voice, "and he was the head of the Klan in 1936 when Abner Richards was lynched."

"Oh my God, Kelly," Angela said. "Did you see how he looked at you?"

"Did you see how I looked at him? I'm not afraid of him."

"Maybe you *should* be."

Glorie said, "Did you see that truck out front, Kelly—the one with the two big Confederate flags on poles in the back of it?"

"I saw it," he said. "How could I miss it?"

"Do you think it belongs to him?" Glorie asked.

"He doesn't look like a guy who drives a pickup truck."

Angela said, "Let's get out of here. I've lost my appetite." She started to push her chair back.

"You go if you want to," Kelly said. "I'm staying. I came to have lunch, and no exalted cyclops is gonna scare me away."

Mae said, "You have to think of Glorie, Kelly. She's going to have your baby. You don't want to get in a fight with somebody like him. There may be other Klansmen in here right now having lunch with him. One of them might shoot you."

"I think of Glorie all the time," Kelly said. "She's the only reason I didn't get up and smash his pompous face in."

Several heads at nearby tables turned to see who the hot-head at our table was.

Glorie put a hand on his arm and said, "I love you, Kelly. Don't be mad at my mom. She loves you too."

Kelly's eyes went from Glorie to her mother. "I'm not mad at you, Mae," he said. "Trust me. I'll take care of Glorie, And I won't get myself killed—at least not if I can help it."

I felt proud of him. He had not exploded. He had managed to control himself for once. Maybe he had just grown up.

• • •

AFTER lunch Mae and Glorie went to look at apartments. Kelly wanted to help them look, but Angela said he had to go with her and get back in school, now that he was no longer in trouble with the police. I drove the three of us to the *Gleaner* so I could get some work done, and I let Angela and Kelly use my car.

I was in the middle of a story when, almost three hours later, they walked into my office. They did not look happy. Kelly plopped down on one of the two chairs in front of my desk and put his feet up against the edge of it. Angela sat in the other chair. She had a large purse, which she plopped on the floor. She stared at me for a second, then said, "That was a big waste of time. I'm so mad I could spit!"

I laughed and said, "Not in the office, please. What happened?"

"The principal won't let Kelly back in school."

Kelly said, "How'd he ever get to be a principal? He's a joke. In LA he'd be a janitor."

"He kept us waiting two hours before he would see us," Angela said. "There was no one else in there with him. Except for his secretary once, nobody went in or out of his office in all that time. He just made us wait till he was good and ready to see us. He probably was hoping we'd get tired of waiting and go home."

"That sounds like Jimmy Dobbs," I said.

Kelly piped up: "How can he keep me outta school? What a prick!"

Angela frowned at his language but let it pass. "Can he keep Kelly out of school?" she asked me. "He can't do that, can he?"

"That's a question for Mary Lou Dunn," I said. "But I do know this—in Indiana you can go to any school that will take you."

"I'm taking Kelly back to LA," Angela said. "He can finish high school there."

"I'm not going unless Glorie goes with me," he said.

"I wish she could go with you, but you know her father won't let her. Mae might, but her father won't."

"He can go fuck himself."

Angela said, "I wish you would stop using that word, Kelly!"

He sassed back: "It's just a word."

"Kelly," I said, "I thought you were suspended, not expelled. What reason did Dobbs give for saying you can't go back to school?"

"He called me 'disruptive.' He said I undermined morale by criticizing teachers, coaches, and administrators in the *Motherfucker.*" He turned to his mother and quickly added, "Don't blame me for that, Ma. That's what Dobbs said. *He* used the F word, not me. I put him in his place. I explained to him in words he could understand that the name of the publication is *Mothermucker,* not *Motherfucker.* Then I asked him if he ever heard of freedom of speech." As if to emphasize his next point, Kelly removed his feet from my desk, let them fall on the floor with a smack, and pinned me with his eyes. "Dobbs said, quote, 'You don't have the freedom to criticize people who work in this school.' Guy, I felt like I fell in a black hole and came out in Assholevania."

"It's not that bad," I said. "Don't forget, you met Glorie here."

"Yeah, thanks for reminding me. Without Glorie, by now my brain would be dried up like a piece of dog shit on a beach."

Angela stood up and said, "Let's go, Kelly. Let's leave Phil alone. He has work to do."

"You're the one who wanted to come," Kelly said.

"Where are you going?" I asked Angela.

"I need to talk to Chester's lawyer, Mr. Goen. I want to ask him if I can have some of the money Chester left me."

I said, "I thought you said you were going to get Mary Lou Dunn to handle the estate."

"I talked to her about it, but she recommended that I stay with Mr. Goen. She pointed out that he drew up the will and is probably familiar with Chester's holdings."

"That makes sense," I said.

"Yes, and Mr. Goen told me it would be at least three months before the estate can be settled. That's the law in Indiana. He said we have to put a legal notice in the paper so anybody that Chester owed money to will know they have to submit a bill by a certain date, and if they don't, they won't get paid. He also told me I should open a checking account in the name of the estate so I can pay the bills. I already have some utility bills that came in the mail."

Kelly pretended to snore.

"Okay, we're going," Angela said, reaching for her purse. She took my car keys out of it and laid them on the desk.

I said, "Hang onto the keys so you can drive to the apartment. I'll use a company car."

She waved off the suggestion. "No, we can walk. It's just a few blocks to your apartment."

"You're wearing high heels," I said.

"I have a pair of sandals in my purse."

I looked out my window and watched them cross the street toward the courthouse. Clyde Goen's office was on the opposite side of the square.

I thought about what Angela had told me—she wanted to take Kelly back to Los Angeles so he could go to school. It made me feel as if they were walking out of my life.

• • •

I DIDN'T get home till 6:15 that evening. Angela was watching some old movie on TV, and the apartment was filled with the aroma of spaghetti sauce.

"Guess what," she said. "Chester's lawyer, Mr. Goen, told me I could take $2,000 out of Chester's estate. That'll keep me going for a while."

"That's good." I tried to sound enthusiastic, but her news was like a dark cloud over my head because now she could afford to buy plane tickets back to Los Angeles, and I didn't want her to leave.

Whoa, wait a minute, Larrison. If she had asked you to lend her the money for the tickets, you would have given it to her, wouldn't you? Of course, you would.

Angela went on: "Mr. Goen also told me probate-court proceedings will begin next Monday at 2 p.m. He said, since Chester named me the executor of his estate, I must file two documents: Chester's will and a 'petition for probate.' That means I'm asking the judge to officially appoint me the executor, or personal representative, of the estate."

"Congratulations. Things are beginning to move."

"I hope so. I never did anything like this before, but Clyde told me not to worry. He said it's a very straightforward case. He said if Dale was still alive, he'd be challenging the will and would probably be claiming that Chester wasn't in his right mind when he signed it. That could have dragged probate on for a long time, but since Dale is gone, I have nothing to worry about on that score."

"Excellent," I said. "Maybe you'll get your inheritance in a few months."

"I'll believe it when I see it."

"You can believe it. It'll happen."

"What's going to happen to us?" she asked.

I wasn't expecting the question. It was sort of like a proposal, but I was the one who should have proposed. I reclaimed the initiative by saying, "Will you marry me, Angela?"

Smiling, almost laughing, she said, "I thought you'd never ask. Yes, I'll marry you, Phil."

We gave each other a long, long kiss, and when we came up for air, I said, "I'll sign a prenuptial agreement. You can carry it with you, and whenever you hear someone say I married you for your money, you can show it to them."

"Oh, that's a good idea," she said. Then: "Silly head, I don't give a hoot in hell what people say. And I will *not* have you sign a prenuptial agreement."

"I'll get you a ring first thing in the morning," I promised.

"Good. I don't give a damn about a prenup, but I *do* want a ring."

"Where's Kelly? We have to tell him he's getting a stepfather. Do you think he'll object?"

"No. He likes you, Phil."

"Where is he?"

"With Glorie. They're putting out another issue of the *Mothermucker.*"

"Where are they doing that?"

"At a friend's house."

I took Angela out for dinner to celebrate our engagement. Then I went back to work as usual. I didn't really want to spend the next three hours at the *Gleaner,* but it was a news-heavy evening, and I had plenty to do.

Angela said, "I'm going with you. This is a special night, and I'm not going to spend a minute of it by myself."

CHAPTER 55

ENOUGH IS ENOUGH

THE latest issue of *Mothermucker* came out shortly before dawn the next day, when Kelly and Glorie hammered on my front door to get us out of bed. The paper contained two articles, both under Kelly's byline.

The lead story, which was written in the first person, was an account of the attempt to lynch him, which he accused Curtis Davis, Michael Kovacs, and Chad Williams of carrying out. Kelly went beyond the lynching to say, "In my opinion, the Gang of Three was also responsible for murdering my grandfather, Chester Marcott, in his home in Salt Lick Township."

The second article was an editorial arguing that any of the surviving members of the Ku Klux Klan who took part in the lynching of Abner Richards in 1936 should be arrested and tried for murder. "Justice demands it!" the editorial trumpeted. "If found guilty, as they should be, the murderers must be punished to the full extent of the law, no matter how old they are now."

Angela said, "Unless you can prove it, Kelly, I don't think you should be saying that the 'Gang of Three' murdered Chester."

Glorie said, "I told him the same thing, but he wouldn't listen to me." She looked exhausted. Dark circles had begun to appear around her eyes.

Kelly shot back, "What are they gonna do, sue me? They won't get anything out of me."

"No, but Michael and Chad could try to kill you again," Glorie said.

"Not if I can put them in jail for murdering Grampaw."

Angela said, "And just how do you plan to do that?"

"I'll tell you how," he said. "I think they broke into Grampaw's house to find the photos I wrote about in *Mothermucker*. I'm talking about the issue where we ran the Klansmen's names that were on the back of the photos I found up in the attic—the ones Grampaw took out of my room while I was in school. He never gave them back. The jocks probably found them when they tore the house apart and bashed his head in. My guess is they still have them. All we have to do is get the cops to search where they live. If they find the missing photos there, it'll prove they killed Grampaw, especially if their fingerprints are on them."

Angela said, "Kelly, if they murdered Chester, wouldn't they have destroyed the photos so they couldn't be linked to the murder?"

"Not necessarily," said Kelly. "Maybe their fathers or grandfathers and other relatives were in the Klan. Maybe they still are. Maybe the stupid jocks were proud of the photos and decided to keep them. I wouldn't be surprised if they made copies so they could each have a set."

I said, "Anything's possible, but I think your mom's right. If they killed Chester, they would have destroyed the photos to get rid of the evidence."

Glorie said, "Do you really want the police to find the pictures, Kelly? Your fingerprints might be on them. Mine too. We

both touched them when you were writing about them for the
Mothermucker."

Kelly was getting annoyed. "It doesn't matter if *our* fingerprints are on them," he said. "We don't have to hide the fact
that we touched them. What the freak, I'm the one who found
them in the attic. I never tried to hide that. And we reported
the names in *Mothermucker.* So the photos were obviously in
our possession. But there's no legitimate reason for the jocks'
fingerprints to be on them."

Angela said, "Kelly, you should tell Sheriff Eggemann
about the photos."

Kelly came back with, "I don't think he wants to hear anything I have to say." He turned to Glorie: "Come on, let's get goin'."

"Wait a second," Angela said. "There's something else I
have to tell you about."

"Now what?" Kelly snapped. "We gotta go. It's getting light
outside."

"Hold your horses. This is important too." She began to
smile. "Phil has asked me to marry him, and I said I will."

Glorie's mouth fell open. "Really?" she said. "Wow."

"When's the wedding gonna be?" Kelly asked.

"Phil and I haven't discussed that yet," said Angela. "He
just asked me to marry him last night."

"Hey, you know what?" Glorie said. "We could have a
double wedding. Wouldn't that be cool? But I don't know.
Maybe that wouldn't work for you. I want to get married here
in Campbellsville so my friends can come to the wedding, but
you might want to get married somewhere else."

"My parents live in Martinsville," Angela told her. "My
mother might want me to get married there, but this will be
my second marriage, so she might not care where the wedding
takes place."

Kelly turned to me and said, "Hey, man, you gonna live

here or move to LA?"

"We'll let you know," I said.

"You could get a job with the LA *Times*. I'll give you a pretty good reference."

"Just pretty good? Thanks a lot."

He grinned and said, "Make that *very good*. I won't have to call you Dad, will I?"

"No."

"You and Ma gonna have kids?"

"Why don't you deliver your papers," I said.

• • •

Two hours later I was in my office when Pastor Bob strolled in and bellowed, *"Hey,* Phil! I just heard you and Angela Marcott are getting married."

"Keep it down," I said. "I haven't told anyone here yet. Who told you?"

"Who do you think? Kelly, of course. He and Glorie brought me a copy of the latest *Mothermucker,* and Kelly asked me if I'd rent my little trailer to them. I had to say no. I nearly lost my job because I let him stay there. The elders voted on it, and I kept my job by one vote. Some of them weren't comfortable with two high-school kids living together on church property. I told them I wasn't comfortable with it either, but I didn't know Glorie had moved in with Kelly."

I wanted to believe the last sentence. A clergyman wouldn't lie, would he?

Bob ran on: "This calls for a celebration. Let's go to Mackey's. I'll buy you a cup of coffee for an engagement present. Carl's probably there too right now. You can tell him your big news."

We walked across the square. Small cumulus clouds were spaced out evenly in parallel lines across the entire bright blue sky.

Mackey's was fairly busy this morning, and the sheriff was in his usual booth. Bob slid in beside him, elbowing him into the corner, and I sat across from them.

When Bob told Carl about my engagement to Angela, some nearby customers congratulated me.

Carl said, "I'm glad to hear you're getting hitched again, Phil. Maybe the new Mrs. Larrison can get you to settle down and concentrate on your day job instead of playing detective."

"I don't play detective," I said. "I'm just a newspaper guy who goes where the story takes me, and this morning the story of Chester Marcott's murder took me to Kelly's latest article in *Mothermucker,* the issue that came out this morning. It says the three boys, or rather Curtis Davis and two boys, Michael Kovacs and Chad Williams, may be the ones who killed Chester. Kelly says they may have broken into Chester's house to steal the photos of the Klan that he—Kelly—found in the attic. I'm talking about the first batch of photos, which he wrote about in an earlier issue of *Mothermucker* and which Chester took away from him."

Carl straightened up and said, "Why would they have wanted the photos?"

"Kelly believes the Gang of Three may be related to some of the Klansmen whose names he published in *Mothermucker.* Those names were on the back of the photos he found in the attic. He thinks the gang may have wanted to destroy the photos to keep their ancestors from being charged with the murder of Abner Richards."

Pastor Bob said, "Phil, do you think they found those photos?"

"I think there's a good possibility they did."

"Why?"

"Because the photos haven't turned up again. If they were

in the house, I think Kelly or his mother would have found them by now."

Carl frowned. "That's a far-from-compelling reason," he said. "You're telling us that the three young men wanted the photos so they could destroy them and keep members of their families from being charged with the murder of Abner Richards, and the same young men framed the Klan to make it look like it was trying to lynch Kelly. On the one hand, they're pro-Klan. On the other hand, they're anti-Klan. That's a real contradiction."

I spread my arms and stretched. "Carl," I said, "I didn't mean to suggest that the gang set out to frame the Klan for trying to lynch Kelly. My guess is their Klan costumes were an easy disguise in case someone who just happened to be driving down the road or some raccoon hunters who were running their dogs in the middle of the night would see them lynching Kelly. I think they were just trying to protect themselves by avoiding suspicion of murder. They had their own motives for wanting to get rid of Kelly, not the least of which is that they hate him for putting articles in the *Mothermucker* arguing that the high school should abolish its sports program.

"What's more, Carl, I'm not wedded to the idea that the Gang of Three was looking for that first batch of photos that Kelly wrote about. They may have been looking for something else, namely the so-called treasure that was rumored to be hidden in the house. That could be what they were searching for and what got Chester killed. In any case, I don't think the killing was premeditated."

Carl's eyes looked weary. "Suppose we find the photos, and all three young men's fingerprints are on them," he said. "Would the prints prove they killed Chester? Maybe not. Besides which, Curtis is already dead. You took care of that,

Phil. The other two boys are juveniles, and neither one of them has a police record. This would be their first offense, so I tend to doubt that a jury would convict them of murder. Voluntary manslaughter, maybe. Involuntary manslaughter, could be, if Chester caught them in his house and they got in a fight that led to his death."

He waved at the waitress to bring him his bill. Then he took a deep breath and sat back. "But I'm not sure if fingerprints alone are enough to get a conviction," he said. "Think about it. What if some current member of the Klan killed Chester and found the photographs and showed them to other members of the Klan, past or present? And what if one of those members showed the photos to Chad's or Michael's dad, and then both boys got to see them? That would explain how their fingerprints got on the photos, if in fact they *are* on them."

"What would it take to get a conviction?" I asked him.

"I don't think old photos of Klansmen with hoods over their heads will do it," Carl said. The photos that young Mr. Marcott published a few days ago in that dang 'newspaper' of his don't show any of the Klansmen's faces. Their names are said to be on the reverse side of the photographs, but how do we know the names on the back of each photo actually belong to the men wearing hoods on the front? And most important of all, Kelly Marcott described one photo that he says shows six Klansmen, three on each side of their alleged victim, Abner Richards, but again, how do we know whether the names on the back are correct? I don't think we can be absolutely sure they did the lynching. We don't even know who wrote those names on the photos. It could have been anybody."

"Sheriff," I said, "I think all of them should be held account-able, not just the ones who put the rope around Abner's neck and hoisted him off the ground."

"Even if some of them weren't in favor of the lynching?" Carl asked. "I think the men that Kelly has called cowardly killers based only on names without faces are paying a mighty high price right now. Their names and their family names have been dragged through the mud for weeks. Now, I admit, the men who lynched Mr. Richards should have been punished a long time ago, but not a single one of them has been. I'm not sure it's fair to execute or imprison those who still happen to be alive after all these years. They're too old now. It would be—I don't know what it would be—a perversion of justice, an absurdity."

"I don't agree," I said. "I think Kelly's right. He wants any living Klansmen whose names are on the photos to be put on trial."

"They'd all be acquitted," Carl said. "Nobody in this county is going to send some hundred-year-old men to prison or the electric chair."

Pastor Bob said, "Then maybe the trial should be moved out of the county."

"Maybe so," I said. "Maybe none of them would be convicted. But some effort should be made to enforce the law. Maybe some members of the Klan *would* be convicted. Some of them might confess to taking part in the lynching. Some might incriminate others."

Carl said, "I'm not a supporter of the KKK, but at this point I can't see any good coming from putting hundred-year-old men on trial for murder. I know there's no statute of limitations on murder, but I doubt that we can conclusively prove who lynched him. We know the Klan did it, but did every Klansman play a role in the crime? It's going on seventy-six years since Mr. Richards was lynched. Some of the men who were responsible for it may be too old to stand trial. They may have memory problems, or they may have Alzheimer's. I'm not even sure we could believe some of them if they confessed to the murder. And think about this. Those old men are being punished right now. Their names have been revealed. They've been disgraced. Their families have been dishonored. I say enough is enough."

As he finished his remarks, Carl nudged Bob with his elbow and said, "Excuse me, Reverend, it's time I get back to the jail."

CHAPTER 56

BOWLED OVER

THE following week, at a meeting of the Campbellsville Community School Board, Kelly was readmitted to high school.

He and Glorie had to weather a blizzard of crass comments from certain students, but they had more friends than enemies and managed to get through the insults and name calling. Despite the time Kelly had missed, he went on to complete his junior year with a B average for the final trimester.

"I only got one A," he said. "I would have had two or three more if I hadn't been kicked out of school. Now I might not get accepted by Southern Cal. Dobbs can take credit for that. Thanks a lot."

Both Glorie and Kelly wanted to get married as soon as possible, but because they were still seventeen, Indiana law prevented them from getting a marriage license unless all of their parents would permit them to marry. Glorie's father continued to withhold his consent.

"He hates me," Glorie said with tears running down her face. "I don't ever want to see him again. I mean it. He's not my father anymore. Kelly and I will just have to wait till we're both eighteen. Then we won't need his permission to get married."

Angela put her arms around her and said, "Oh, Glorie, I'm so sorry. Maybe we can get him to change his mind."

"He won't change his mind. He hates me."

Later Mae said, "He's acting like a horse's ass. He'll regret it someday."

• • •

EARLY one evening in June, Dale Marcott's girlfriend, JoElla, showed up at my front door. Her orange hair now had purple streaks running through it, and she had lost some weight. She caught me offguard when she said, "Hi, Mr. Larrison, I'd like to see Dale's ex-wife, if you don't mind."

I wondered how she knew Angela was living with me. "She's not here," I said.

JoElla was chewing gum, which made a smacking sound. I kept waiting for her to blow a bubble. "When will she be back?" she asked.

"I'm not sure. Would you like me to have her call you?"

She frowned and said, "Yes, please. I'll give you my card."

She handed me a business card with the words "Pet Walking and Grooming" on it. Her name and phone number were at the bottom of the card.

She started to walk away, and I began to close the door, but she spun around and said, "Oh shoot, I might as well tell you. Dale, when he was alive, promised me if anything ever happened to him, there was a $5,000 life-insurance policy that his father took out in his name—Dale's name. Dale said he was going to change the name of his beneficiary"—she pronounced it *bene-fishery*—"and he promised to put my name on it instead of his wife's. He said the policy was in his apartment in California and he'd change it as soon as he got back there. Me an' Ginger was gonna go with him, but he never got to change the policy over to me because he got killed. The insurance company probably doesn't even know he's dead. I want to tell his wife what his final wish was and ask her to transfer the policy to me."

Good luck with that, I thought. "All right, JoElla," I said. "I'll tell Angela what you want to talk to her about. She'll give you a call."

"Thank you, Mr. Larrison." She dawdled a bit longer, then said, "It's nice to see you again, Phil. Do you mind if I call you Phil?"

"Of course not. I'll make sure she phones you, JoElla. Now I've really got to go. It's a work night for me."

"Oh, I'm sorry for bothering you."

"It's no bother."

I watched her walk toward her car. I thought she was a tad unsteady.

Angela returned an hour later. I told her about JoElla's visit.

"Dale should have put Kelly's name on that policy," she said. She made a face, then added, "Oh, what the hell, I don't need Dale's money. She can have it."

• • •

THE marriage of T. Preston and Mae Kovacs was dissolved in August, and Mae was awarded fifty percent of their assets, according to the state's equitable-distribution law; however, she accused him of hiding some of his money in foreign banks over the years. Their house at Shale Creek Golf Course was put up for sale, and Mae moved into a nice apartment. She also began taking art courses at Ivy Tech Community College, a statewide system.

Chester's will cleared probate in September, and Angela became a wealthy woman. She let Kelly and Glorie live in Chester's house. Their baby, a boy, was born in October, and they named him Grady because they liked how it sounded with Marcott.

From then on Angela took care of Grady while Kelly and Glorie finished high school. For a while Mae Kovacs competed with Angela to spoil their grandchild, but then she met a good-looking fireman and focused her attention on him.

Kelly went on publishing *Mothermucker*. He also applied for admission to the School of Cinematic Arts at the University of Southern California.

Angela continued spending her nights at my place, unless she was too tired to drive to town. It was an odd arrangement, and sometimes neither of us got to my apartment till after midnight.

• • •

SOMETIME between Christmas and New Year's Day, Tessie Davis died. Her body was found by the manager of the small apartment complex where she lived. Sheriff Eggemann told me about it that afternoon.

"It looks like she overdosed on sleeping pills," he said. "The Campbellsville police found an empty container of them on the bathroom sink."

"Was it suicide?" I asked him.

"Your guess is as good as mine. I know she took it real hard when she lost Curtis, but that was eight months ago." His eyebrows rose as he looked at me over the top of his glasses. "Maybe the holidays got to her. Some people get depressed around Christmas. Here, I've got something to show you," he added.

He swiveled around on his chair and reached for a faded 6x9 manila envelope. Inside were several old photos of the Ku Klux Klan, which Carl placed on the only open spot on his desk. To avoid touching them, he used a letter opener to spread them out face-up.

I glanced at the photos and asked if they were the ones Kelly had found in Chester's attic.

"I believe they are," Carl said. "The names on the back of each one perfectly match the names he had in his underground paper last spring, when he said he found them in the attic."

The names looked like the same skinny, left-leaning handwriting I had seen on the photos Kelly had found in Chester's bedroom. I asked Carl where he had gotten these.

"In Tessie's apartment," he said. "They were inside the hollow pedestal of a big old clawfoot table that nearly takes up the whole kitchen."

"Inside the pedestal? What made you look there? I would have thought the pedestal was solid wood."

He grinned and said, "Call it experience. It was one of the first places I looked. I had to pull the tabletop section apart and then unbolt it from the pedestal. As soon as I got it off, I saw the envelope down inside the pedestal."

"Do you think Curtis put it there?"

"Either he did it or his mother did, I suspect."

"Do you think Curtis killed Chester?"

"His fingerprints were on the envelope and some of the photos."

"What about Michael Kovacs and Chad Williams? Were their prints on them too?"

Carl ran his fingernails up one of his cheeks a few times. Against the grain of day-old whiskers, his nails made a noise like sandpaper. Finally he said, "Michael's fingerprints were on the envelope and two of the photos. Chad's prints weren't on anything. Those two kids are now saying Curtis killed Chester. Michael told me Chester showed up with a shotgun and started yelling at them and waving the gun around like a madman. Chad said Michael ducked into the pantry and Chester started to go after him, but Curtis grabbed the purple baseball bat—Chad said it was standing in a corner of the kitchen—and he hit Chester with it. Chester tried to duck, but the bat hit him on his back, which made him go down on his knees, and then Curtis clubbed him on the head. The two boys said Curtis hit him on the head several more times after that to make sure he was dead. I suspect they coordinated their stories."

"Did they tell you where they found those photos?"

"According to Chad, they were in a locked gun cabinet in the dining room. He said Curtis smashed the glass on the cabinet because he wanted to take some of the guns, but then he found the envelope under several boxes of ammunition, and it took his mind off the guns."

"Carl," I said, "back in April or May, you told me you accepted the prosecuting attorney's decision not to charge Michael and Chad with trying to lynch Kelly. Now that you've found the missing photos and discovered Michael's fingerprints on some of them, are you going to arrest Michael and Chad again?"

"I'm thinkin' on it," he said. "I reckon I'd better, or else I'll get ripped apart in the *Mothermucker* again, and no doubt you'll take some shots at me in the *Gleaner,* right?"

"I'm thinkin' on it," I said. "By the way, I'm still curious why you'd go to the trouble of disassembling a big oak table in the mere hope of finding some old photos of the Ku Klux Klan in the pedestal? Now that you know Michael and Curtis handled the photos, are you going to charge them with Chester's murder, even though Curtis is dead? And what about the attempt to lynch Kelly—will you charge Curtis, Michael, and Chad with attempted murder?"

"Those are good questions, Phil. Thanks."

• • •

Now and then I thought about the photo of little Chester. It made me wonder if he had witnessed the lynching of Abner Richards. Would his father have subjected him to that? Did the experience affect him so deeply that he never wanted to be part of the Klan? Decades later he may have sought to make restitution for the lynching by giving $5,000 in gold to Abner's widow.

At first I had held this against him because I thought the gold didn't belong to him, but later I got to thinking about something Henry Barker had told me—Chester was a coin collector.

I always assumed Barker was mistaken. I told myself that what the exalted cyclops thought was a valuable collection of old coins was probably the gold pieces that Chester had confiscated when the militia's Cessna crashed on his farm. But what if the gold coins that Chester gave Abner's widow, Lisa Pluckett, did not belong to the militia? Maybe Chester had inherited a hoard of gold coins from his father. Maybe Chester Sr. had accumulated the coins before the United States went off the gold standard in 1933. Back then the value of an ounce of gold was set at only $35 an ounce. In 2012 gold was worth about fifty times as much. Maybe Chester Jr. had tapped his gold to keep Mrs. Pluckett in her home.

Wait a minute, Larrison. Before you go canonizing Chester, think about the bank bags the gold coins were in when they were hidden under the floor in Chester's bedroom. The bank that those bags came from was in Murfreesboro, Tennessee. What connection could there have been between Chester Marcott and a bank in Tennessee other than the gold that the militia's plane was carrying when it crashed on his farm?

The gold must have belonged to the militia, and either Chester or Dale must have stolen it.

I preferred to think that Dale had stolen it, that he had shot and killed Captain Murphy, and that Chester had protected him. But maybe I was wrong.

It wouldn't have been the first time.

• • •

In January 2013 Kelly was accepted by the School of Cinematic Arts at the University of Southern California. A handwritten note at the end of the letter from the head of the admissions committee said, "What impressed us the most with your application was the courage and moral thrust of your investigative reporting in *Mothermucker*. Your energetic fight for justice bowled us over. We look forward to welcoming you to the university as a member of the class of 2017."

• • •

ANGELA and I got married on Saturday, March 23, 2013, in Campbellsville Presbyterian Church. The Reverend Mr. Robert Harnish performed the ceremony.

It was a small wedding, nothing showy. After the wedding Angela and I went on a honeymoon to Hawaii.

Why did we get married on March 23?

Because it was the first Saturday in spring and because I had heard that 23 is a mystical number.